Praise for Natasha Rhodes:

"Taut and gripping, Natasha Rhodes's prose is that precious thing: the stuff you just can't put down..."
—Dan Abnett, bestselling author of *Horus Rising*

"*Dante's Girl* breathes some new life into the urban fantasy werewolf/vampire genre, with vivid characters and deliciously evil villains, a fast paced, exciting and enjoyable read. Recommended reading!"
—lovevampires.com

"Rhodes's exceedingly witty and vividly descriptive writing style — not to mention her ability to keep the narrative's pacing consistently pedal-to-the-metal — place this novel a cut above the rest. Smart, sexy, and oh so satisfying."
—*Explorations*

"Natasha Rhodes proves to be a writer who conveys the reality of death and danger in her descriptions to really engage the reader."
—*SF Revu*

"This is a fun, contemporary supernatural action novel."
—*Concatenation*

ALSO BY NATASHA RHODES

NATASHA RHODES

THE LAST ANGEL

A KAYLA STEELE NOVEL

SOLARIS

To Danielle, for being my sister. It's a tough job,
but somebody has to do it.

First published 2008 by Solaris
an imprint of BL Publishing
Games Workshop Ltd, Willow Road
Nottingham, NG7 2WS
UK

www.solarisbooks.com

ISBN-13: 978 1 84416 577 3
ISBN-10: 1 84416 577 9

10 9 8 7 6 5 4 3

A CIP catalogue record for this book is available from the
British Library.

Designed & typeset by BL Publishing
Printed in the US

PROLOGUE

THE ANGEL LAY dying in the gutter on Sunset Boulevard. Blood flowed thickly from the gaping tear in his throat, slowly leaching the life from his body; his first experience of pain, and—he hoped—his last. As the darkness closed in on him like black water over the head of a drowning man, he shut his eyes and wept.

He had failed.

In seven millennia of life, he had never imagined things ending this way—in a stinking, forgotten street corner in Los Angeles, with nobody but disease-ridden hobos and street-whores to witness his death. This, then, would be his final punishment. No liturgies would be written about his final moments on Earth, no sonnets would celebrate his brave fight for life, about the final battle between good and evil that had ended so predictably, with tears and a tragedy.

In the end, he hadn't fought them.

This death had been his choice.

But, as with all choices, there was always room for regret.

Footsteps sounded in the alleyway, moving urgently toward him. The angel's heart fluttered and he opened his eyes a crack as four dark figures approached him.

What was this? Salvation? Or something far worse?

A shadow fell over him, blotting out the stars. The leading figure knelt down beside him, making a noise of concern as he wiped the blood from his throat. The angel felt a cold, calloused finger touch his neck to check for a pulse, and a fierce stab of hope went through him.

Maybe there was still a chance. Maybe he could still save her.

Maybe...

The angel cried out as four sets of hands seized his broken body and greedily tore his expensive black silk jacket from him, revealing the smooth, clean lines of his perfectly sculptured torso. The angel knew that he could put any of this century's male models to shame, but right now the knowledge held no pride for him. He heard four sharp intakes of breath as he half-unfurled his beautiful wings, now shredded and riddled with bullet holes—a reflex action rather than one of defense, for he knew he no longer had the strength to fight.

There was only one thing left to do.

Taking a deep breath, he rallied his fading strength into one last prayer, the words cascading out of him in a soft golden tide of lilting Hebrew that drifted heavenwards toward the sodium-lit skies, born upwards on the fading warmth of the Santa Ana winds. A hush fell over the filthy streets around him, broken only by the far-off wail of a distant siren, too far away to be of any use to him.

A dark shadow fell over him as he prayed.

"Woss'e saying?" said a voice, low and rasping.

"Christ knows. Sounds like German."

"Fuckin' tourists."

A giggle, low and dirty.

"Someone shut 'im up, for Chrissakes. Get 'is boots off, quick."

"Fink we should snuff 'im first?"

"Nah. See what else he's got."

The angel's prayer abruptly choked off as a steel-capped boot pressed down on his throat, cutting off his breath. He felt someone going through his pockets; strong, cold hands running expertly up and down his body. A moment later a voice cried out triumphantly and the pressure on his throat eased. The angel opened his pale blue eyes and watched with a terrible sorrow as his silver Pentangle necklace was torn from his ruined neck and held up for all to see. It spun softly on the end of its hair-thin chain, reflecting the far-off lights of the distant city.

"Looks like we just paid next month's rent, boys."

"No shit, Einstein."

"Hey! Someone take this thing, it's fuckin' burning me!"

"That's cos it's silver, jackass. Here, get 'is jeans off too. Reckon we could get twenny bucks for those down at Ricky's."

The angel's fists clenched as dirty hands tore at his belt, ripping the buttons from his designer jeans. Money had been no object when he'd first come here, but he was starting to regret spending so lavishly on outward appearances. It was a final, unwelcome lesson to cap off what had been a truly shitty week. He felt a flush of cold air as his jeans were yanked off, and a collective gasp went up.

"Jesus! What the fuck—?"

The angel rolled over, his expression a fractured mess of fear and shame.

"What are you, buddy?" said a rough voice.

The angel coughed, feeling blood from his internal injuries starting to seep into his lungs. Fear was another new sensation to him; he regretted that it would probably be his last. With the last of his strength he concentrated hard and touched the mind of his enemy, his savior. He grew cold with disgust at what he found inside.

So the rumors were true, then.

Too bad it was too late to do anything about it.

"Something you'll never be," he replied, and then for good measure, he spat.

Dark eyes regarded him shrewdly. Metal gleamed in the darkness.

"Wrong answer, kid."

Click.

The angel's head rocked back as the bullet tore through his skull, gutting his brain and embedding itself in the concrete beneath. As the echoes of the gunshot died away he felt a great sense of pressure inside his head, rushing outward, dragging his consciousness with it. The last thing he saw before his soul fled was an aerial view of his own ruined body, lying on the sidewalk, his beautiful wings soaked through with blood. He watched in horror as his killers went through his wallet, pulling out the single, hard-won photograph it contained, and reading the address hand-written on the back.

"God, you bastard," the angel whispered.

Then he died.

CHAPTER ONE

THE TROUBLE WITH falling in love with a vampire, Karrel Dante reflected, was that it wasn't over, even when it was over.

He slid his fingers down to touch the reassuring shape of the newly minted A-12 machine pistol strapped to his thigh, and surveyed the terrain around him with a sick kind of dread. He still couldn't believe that she was here, somewhere. Eight years he'd waited for this moment, each year a lifetime of longing, of waiting, of tracking.

Eight years he'd waited to kill her.

Karrel felt something clench nastily in his gut at the thought. He quickly gunned the overheated engine of the Razorback MK1-ZU motorcycle beneath him—once, twice, three times, its roar echoing back off the high-rise urban canyons surrounding him. He felt the warm throb of the chopper's engine flood through his body and hit the gas again, harder, blasting away his nerves with a shot of mechanized bravado before the creeping doubt in his belly got the better of him. The wind raked through his long tangle of black hair as he flicked down the infra-scope on his night vision goggles and scanned the area. The archaic tangle of nighttime Prague sprawled around him in all its moonlit, ancient glory, the silent streets slick with runoff from the peaked slate rooftops. The air was alive with a thousand scents: fresh mud, rain, the peaty smell of the nearby woodlands.

And blood.

A gunshot from a nearby hilltop made Karrel stiffen, his knuckles whitening on the handgrips of his ride. His hyper-keen senses locked down on the sound, his soldier's mind analyzing it even as his gut screamed at him to move, dammit, before it was too late, before someone else made the kill. A 12-gauge shotgun, he decided, probably with a filed-down barrel and some kind of extracurricular ammo judging by the throaty sound of that echo.

One of his guys, he hoped, but there was no way of telling from this distance.

Shit.

The Razorback's powerful engine snarled beneath him as Karrel twisted the throttle hard and nosed his charge in a tight, careful arc down the side of the stony gully, keeping his thumb poised on the brake to guide the monster bike over the worst of the debris. One slip on this hill would mean instant death. The weight of his outsized motor-bike would reduce his leg to a bloody pulp against the razor-sharp flint before the snowballing momentum catapulted him off the hillside.

He should've gone to that career interview, he told himself moodily, as he descended further into the darkness. The one his parents had set up for him before he left high school, hoping to turn his love of phys ed and auto mechanics into a real career.

Just one little interview and his whole life would've been totally different.

Hell, he mused, in some alternate reality he was probably curled up in bed right now, his body draped over the naked softness of a beautiful woman instead of crammed into soaking wet combat leathers with nearly twenty pounds of illegal weaponry strapped to his aching chest. At twenty-six years old, his future should've been bright, filled with fun, normal things like women and cars and drinking and friends.

He shouldn't have this black, howling pit of despair in his gut, slowly devouring him from the inside out.

Nor should he feel like he had an iron clamp around his heart, the screws tightening inch by inch with each passing day.

He shouldn't know all the terrible things he knew, or have seen all the things he'd seen.

Nobody deserved that. Not at his age.

But he hadn't gone to that interview. Fate, bitch that she was, had come to him.

Just his luck.

Sixty heart-stopping seconds later Karrel's bike finally leveled out, its front wheels seizing the lumpy concrete of the sidewalk with a jolt and a shudder. Karrel guided the chopper back onto solid ground and tapped the brakes. He flicked an anxious glance toward the sodium-lit heavens, steeling himself for what was to come. He had never had much faith in God, preferring to trust in what he knew best: cold steel, warm muscle, and good, old-fashioned legwork. But even he had to admit that if he pulled off this mission tonight, he and the Creator might finally make amends.

Hell, he might even go whole hog and attend church every once in a while.

But that was still one heck of a big "if."

In Karrel's head, his alternate-reality girlfriend let out a happy little sigh and draped her deliciously warm legs over him, rolling over in her sleep. In reality, Karrel pulled out a silver hip flask and took a bracing sip of J.D., shivering as an icy squall of rain lashed his face. He stared up the hillside with a hunted expression, trying to pinpoint the source of the gunshot.

It was quiet up there.

Too quiet.

A sudden eruption of noise and light behind him made him jump and spin, putting three rounds through the front tire of the approaching Kawasaki ZJD before he could stop himself. Smoke coiled up from the muzzle of his Colt .45 as he twitched the tip of the muzzle aside, glaring daggers at the dark figures in front of him.

"*Dante?* Oh, great…"

Karrel let his breath out in an explosive rush as seven heavily armed men and women on custom-made motorcycles rolled forward to surround him. The glare of their halogen spotlights pinned him to the spot. He winced and threw up an arm to preserve what was left of his night vision, swearing under his breath. *So much for the element of surprise.* Unit D was the oldest and toughest squad in the Hunters, but they were warriors, not trackers. Sending them out on this mission was about as appropriate as using a hand grenade to clear a wasp's nest. They had saved his ass a million times, but right now they were the last people on the planet he wanted to see.

The squad leader—a woman—snapped up the visor of her helmet and stared unblinkingly into the barrel of Karrel's gun.

"Well," she said, her voice as expressionless as her face, "I guess we'll call off the flowers we ordered for your funeral."

"There's nothing here," Karrel insisted, then stopped, hating himself for the lie. *He knew she was here. He could feel it in his bones, in his blood.* He felt the woman's steely gaze burn into him. He turned away in irritation, gesturing with his gun toward the empty hillside. "See for yourself."

"There were lilies," the woman went on, with infuriating calm. "I particularly liked the lilies. And pansies. Now *they* were just a stroke of genius."

"Did you hear me?" Karrel snapped, his voice rising in frustration. "I said—"

"Yes, Karrel, I heard exactly what you said. And I'm choosing to ignore it." The woman revved her engine, waving on the other riders behind her. They roared past, tooting their horns at Karrel in mocking jest before blazing up the hillside in search of their quarry.

Karrel watched them go helplessly.

"Ninette, please…"

"Don't 'Ninette, please' me. We both know *exactly* what you're doing here."

"We don't know it was her!" Karrel burst out.

Ninette folded her arms and glared down at Karrel. Despite his years of anti-interrogation training, Karrel felt his face grow hot under the heat of her stare. Outrage grew within him. She had no *right* to do this to him. She of all people knew what this particular hunt meant to him, what the kill represented.

"It could've been… I mean… all those deaths, the disappearances… it could've been, uh…"

Ninette sighed, then reached down to adjust the perfectly polished, jet black actuated body armor she wore. "Dante. You know damn well how this one will play out. You will always be a prize pain in my ass, and I will always be waiting for the day when I get to strip your rank and throw you out of this Hunter unit for good for all the boneheaded macho bullshit you pull. I specifically ordered you to stay away from this case and yet here you are, getting in my way again. You wanna go prancing off on your own like that, chasing after whatever supernatural hussy has got your panties in a twist this week, then at least give me a home address so we can mail your body back to your folks when you're done. And don't even get me started on the shit you're gonna be in for stealing that bike."

"But I'm still cute, right?" said Karrel hopefully.

Ninette paused for a second, a dangerous glint in her eye. For a moment Karrel thought he might actually get a reply. Then Ninette sat back on her bike. She removed her helmet and shook her hair out, sending glossy black ringlets tumbling down her back. In the muted starlight, her classic features could have been straight out of a Hollywood movie, if it were not for the faint scar that graced her left temple and the elegant Japanese military tattoo running up the side of her neck.

Ignoring Karrel, she reached into her pocket for a band and started to tie her hair back, her movements brisk and businesslike.

"This mission is top priority, *Dante*. That vampire bitch of yours is Public Enemy Numero Uno right now in twelve different countries, eight of which have a half-million-dollar bounty on her head. And that's not including what her headcase of a boyfriend is worth to us if we bring him in alive. So do me a favor. Don't screw this up for me. From now on we work together, or not at all. You with me?"

"She's not a..." Karrel stopped, listening hard. "Did you hear that?"

"I'm tone deaf to bullshit, Karrel. You know that."

"No. Listen!"

Despite herself, Ninette listened. Then she sighed. "I don't suppose you brought your wing-blades with you?"

"No, 'cause they're illegal and you don't like me carrying them," said Karrel dutifully.

"Good. Get them out then, because I think..."

The wall exploded.

"...you're gonna need them."

Ninette hit the gas and whipped her bike around in a screaming one-eighty as the air split open in a mind-searing blast of heat. Bricks and earth rained

down on their heads, bouncing and clattering off
their bikes and helmets. Karrel slammed down his
visor as a second explosion rocked the street. He
heard Ninette yelling urgently into her radio headset, calling for backup as more debris pattered
down around them. He twisted around in his seat
to see the rest of Unit D pouring back down the
steep alleyway toward him like a herd of spooked
wild bulls, backlit against the rising moon.

Karrel watched in bemusement as the lead
rider—a tough, older guy named Myers—raised his
bike-mounted mini rocket launcher and prepared
to fire a third time at the shadowy figure heading
toward him at an inhuman speed.

The *female* shadowy figure.

Before his eyes had registered what he was seeing, she had flashed past him and vanished into the
darkness. Karrel watched her go, open mouthed,
then threw himself flat on his bike as the streaking,
hissing tail of the missile whizzed over his head. It
slammed into the wall opposite him and detonated
in a spray of flying shrapnel, sending pieces of
razor-sharp rock whizzing in all directions.

"HOLD YOUR FIRE!"

Karrel shoved himself back upright, glaring at
the figure on the green bike. There were reasons he
worked alone, and guys like Myers were one of
them. Turning away in disgust, he reached for his
keys as he stared after the fleeing figure, his heart
pounding a Samba on his ribs.

It couldn't be. Could it…? Gravel flew as he hit
the gas and jammed his foot down into the mud,
using it as a pivot to spin his bike around. Putting
it into gear, he took off at high speed after the

running figure, flinging a rooster-tail of gravel up behind him.

IT WAS HER. *He knew it.* No other vampire he knew of could move like that. Karrel felt a weird surge of pride as he gunned his bike after the fleeing woman. Even on foot she easily stayed on the outer reaches of his Razorback's headlamp, dodging and ducking like a wraith through the winding rubble-strewn streets. He was dimly aware of the rest of Unit D falling in behind him as he leaned his bike into a radical turn at the fast-approaching cross-roads, aiming to keep his body between them and the woman at all times.

If one of them shot her before he could question her, find out the answer to the question that had haunted him all these years...

Karrel shook his head abruptly, cutting off the thought.

No way was he going to let that happen.

Moments later the street abruptly split into a multitude of dirt tracks leading off into the darkness in different directions, hemmed in by high walls. The fleeing figure of the vampire headed at full speed toward the larger central track, and then veered at the last instant down the far passageway in a move that stuck up two fingers at the laws of inertia and one at gravity.

Karrel swore, wrenching his bike sideways down the track after her. He made the turn by bare inches. Darkness enveloped him as he entered the passageway. Seconds later he heard an ear-splitting *CRUMP* of metal on stone from behind him, followed by the rev and leap of engines. His rear-view mirror revealed that one of his team had misjudged the turn and gone down, his smashed bike blocking the alleyway. The rest of the unit used the bike as an impromptu ramp.

Karrel allowed himself a ghost of a smile.

So much for team spirit.

His smile faded and he leaned forward on his bike, closing the gap between himself and the flee-ing vampire. Closer now, he could make out more details. The woman was clad from head to toe in expensive white linen spattered with mud from the chase. Her soaked ebony hair bounced behind her in elegant rat tails. She was unarmed, or appeared to be, although with vampires that meant nothing. In the harsh glare of his halogen headlights he could see flashes of red as she moved, her dress spinning up to reveal the elaborate dragon tattoos on her leg.

Karrel's breathing quickened.

It was her! Cyan X!

Finally, he'd found her!

A large pile of debris loomed. Karrel readied himself to jump it. Ahead of him, Cyan cleared the pile in a single stride. She leaped straight up into the air as though her legs were spring loaded, van-ishing silently into the night. Distracted, Karrel gaped upwards, trying to track her, then swore loudly as his bike smashed through the debris pile in a storm of flying wood fragments. Brakes squealed as the Hunters behind slowed to avoid running into him.

His headset crackled.

"Dante! What the fuck, man!" yelled Myers.

Karrel wrestled his bike back under control, sweating profusely. The stone walls of the passageway seemed to close in on him as he reached for his handgun. His blood suddenly turned to ice. "Fall back, Myers! Did you hear me? Repeat—"

"Yeah Karrel, we all heard you. Now *move!*"

"I said *fall back*, dammit!"

"Why, because you and the lady vampire wanna—"

The radio cut to static.

Karrel braked sharply. "Myers?"

Silence.

The scream blasted through Karrel's headset. He veered sharply and squeezed down hard on his handbrakes. He steadied the bike, then yelped and swerved to avoid the unmanned green motorbike that came flying toward him, one handgrip drawing a hissing line of sparks along the wall. Only its sheer velocity kept it upright.

Myers was gone.

An ear-splitting blast of gunfire rang out overhead, followed by a bloodcurdling shriek. Karrel spun back just in time to see something drop down directly into his path. Instinctively he whipped up his pistol and blasted it away. It exploded messily in midair, chunks flying off in all directions, and Karrel froze as the split-second snapshot of the object burned itself into his brain.

He'd just blown up Myers's decapitated head.

Oh, great.

Karrel yelled and swerved as a sheet of blood and dismembered body parts poured down across him and the rest of his Unit, drenching him and bouncing off his bike. Cries of horror and revulsion came from the troops behind him. A loop of intestines landed on his handlebars like a set of gory Mardi Gras beads.

Yup, they'd found Cyan all right.

As he reached out to gingerly flick the intestines off his bike, an urgent shout sounded in his earpiece. Karrel glanced up sharply through his blood-spattered silver visor. Cyan X stood calmly at the end of the passageway not thirty feet ahead of him, two Hunter-issue TEC-9 pistols aimed dead center at his chest.

Time itself seemed to freeze.

Karrel watched in adrenalin-induced slow motion as the vampiress's dark hair blew out behind her on the cold night breeze, her swirling clothing slowly settling around her stunning figure. The pure white of her dress was a stark contrast to the red flowers carpeting the dirt beneath her elegantly heeled feet, which mirrored the red dragon on her thigh. She looked relaxed, almost amused.

She was Death, and she was the most beautiful thing he had ever seen.

Her guns blossomed with white fire, and Karrel's vision blew out in an explosion of glass and light and noise.

GASPING, KARREL SQUEEZED his brakes with every ounce of strength in his body, swerving violently from side to side before bringing his bike to a shuddering, scraping halt against a side wall. He took a careful breath, heart hammering, as he realized what had happened.

Bitch had shot his front lights out!

An instant later the unmanned green motorcycle tailing behind him hit the bend and went down in a tangle of whirring wheels, bouncing end over end. Karrel heard it coming toward him and spun around in the pitch blackness.

Only one thing left to do.

With a yell he grabbed his handgrips and leapt sideways off his bike, out of the path of the out-of-control motorcycle. He hit the ground in a tight, bruising roll and was almost instantly on his feet, pelting down the alleyway. The crash of the green bike echoed behind him. He put all his energy into running as the tumbling wreckage of the bike came crashing after him. It slammed into a side wall and exploded with a loud *KA-BOOM*. Karrel threw himself flat on the ground as a tidal wave of heat washed over his back, charring the triple-reinforced leather off his riding gear and singeing his exposed face.

Then all was still.

The alleyway flooded with light as the rest of his troops rounded the corner at high speed, homing in on the vampiress. Karrel heard the familiar *snikt-snick* of silenced pistols firing. Tracer rounds zipped over his head, lighting up the night with their hissing orange flares. He glanced up to see Cyan jerk with the multiple impacts, blood flying as she spun half around and slammed into the wall, bathed in the harsh white light of his team's headlights.

Despite himself, Karrel felt his heart constrict with cold fear.

"No!" he cried.

Baring her teeth in defiance, Cyan dropped to one bloodslicked knee and returned their fire, the outsized TEC pistols bucking and jumping in her hands. Karrel watched in horror as one bike after another went down, the riders' helmets erupting inwards as blood sprayed from their visors. Their bikes abruptly veered sideways, smashing into the walls on either side with devastating finality.

Karrel rose to his feet and reached into his jacket for his spare pistol, muttering an oath under his breath. *Fuck this shit.* He wanted to take Cyan alive so badly it made his chest ache, but not at the expense of the lives of his Unit. He heard the ominous *ker-chack* of an armor-piercing rifle being loaded and saw Ninette flash past him on her black motorcycle, effortlessly avoiding the motorized carnage as she aimed her rifle one-handed at Cyan's head.

A mournful howl filled the alleyway, seeming to come from everywhere at once. The wall behind him erupted outward in a storm of rubble. An enormous, hairy black *something* dropped ten feet to the ground, landing as elegantly as a dead bull dropped from the back of a butcher's truck. Its head snapped up and it flew at Ninette's bike in a scrabble of flying claws, baying at her in a shocking blast of noise.

Before Ninette could load a fresh clip it locked its massive jaws on her rear wheel guard and wrenched savagely down. Karrel blinked once and the bike was on the ground. Ninette frantically rolled away from it as the pony-sized creature flew at her, its jaws gaping wide.

A round from Karrel's pistol tore into its haunches and the creature shrieked. It spun around to face him then launched itself in his direction with a bark of rage. Karrel swore and dropped the pistol. He ran back to his own felled bike, wrenched it off the ground, and threw a leg over the soaked saddle in a blur of fear. He fumbled with the ignition with suddenly-numb hands.

The engine wouldn't start.

An instant later the creature hit the rear of his bike full-force. It spun around in a full circle, the rear wheel lifting off the ground in an extreme reverse-wheelie. Karrel yelled and slammed on his booster drive from a cold start, blasting flames a good five feet in the air from the back of the bike. The fiery jets enveloped the monster dog as it passed beneath his bike, torching it. The creature gave a howl and crashed to the ground, rolling and yelping as it tried to put out the flames.

Karrel's rear wheel dropped back down with a tooth-jarring *THUD*. Acting on pure, mindless adrenalin, he jammed his foot down in the dirt and hit the gas, sending his bike blasting back toward the downed creature. Karrel leapt off the bike a moment before impact, sending the Razorback plowing into the monster.

Karrel hit the dirt hard and rolled before coming to a bruising halt. He watched in satisfaction as his unmanned bike tore into the prone creature at full speed, sucking its limbs up into the machinery beneath its whirring wheel arches and flinging it up into the air. Monster and bike flipped end over end before coming to a juddering, sliding halt up against the opposite wall of the alleyway.

Karrel climbed a little unsteadily to his feet. The rest of his troops flashed past him and blazed off after Cyan, who whirled and took off down the alley, vanishing into the darkness. Karrel ignored them, breathing hard as he dusted off his soaked riding leathers. He reached into his side pocket for his wing-shaped throwing knives.

The knives were diamond-edged and cast from solid silver. They made a high-pitched whistling noise as he hurled one after another at the downed form of the creature, which was still heartily and violently alive, kicking and bucking as it tried to free itself from the whirring wreckage of the bike. It jerked as the first blade embedded itself in the crest of hair on the back of its skull, then went limp as the second struck the top of the first with expert precision, driving it deeply into its brain.

Karrel stood stock still, watching the monster dog intently, but there was no need for a third knife. The creature flopped back onto the dirt, twitching and jerking.

Game over.

Karrel slowly pocketed his last knife as Ninette stepped up beside him, limping slightly, watching the creature's death throes with a kind of fascinated horror. She glanced up at him, grudging admiration mingling with her trademark professional detachment.

"You know, you could've just shot it," she said. "Shooting works on werewolves, or so I'm told."

Karrel shrugged indifferently, listening to the echo and roar of engines fade into the distance. "Maybe I did."

"Oh no." Ninette removed her shattered helmet and shook out her hair. She stepped toward him and placed a finger on his chest, shoving him backward a step. "Forget it, Dante. You think I'm going to write this one up as—"

"Gross irresponsibility, endangerment of fellow team members, reckless destruction of Hunter property…"

"We've all seen your rap-sheet, Karrel. No need to flaunt it."

"Oh, but flaunting's what I do best."

Karrel straightened his jacket and flashed his Team Leader his best shit-eating grin. Behind them, the crashed motorbike burst into flames. The smell of burning dog-hair filled the air as he moved toward her, flames dancing in his eyes. "Among other things…"

Ninette's face remained impassive. She reached up to casually adjust her collar, the move exposing seemingly by accident the tarnished gold wedding band she wore on her left hand. "Karrel, the day I feel anything for you that goes beyond the morbid, slightly grossed-out curiosity I feel for cockroaches that are still moving their little cockroachy bits after I've poured napalm over them, set them on fire, and run over them twice with my tank, believe me, you'll be the last to know." She smiled brightly, wiping blood from her forehead. "Cool with you?"

Karrel batted his eyelashes at her, trying not to grin. "Always." He scratched his nose, glancing back up the alleyway. "We just have one problem now."

"Which is?"

"I'm going to need your bike."

There was a click. Karrel's grin grew wider as he felt the cold muzzle of a silver Ruger pistol gently nudge his temple. He cleared his throat and flicked his eyes pointedly down. After a second Ninette followed his gaze to take in the A-12 aimed at her, its snub-nosed barrel a warning shadow inside his army-issue cloth jacket. She sighed as the sound of distant gunfire echoed back down the alleyway.

"Fine. Have it your way."

With her free hand she clipped the safety catch back on her Ruger, then reached into her pocket and pulled out a muddy set of keys

She glanced up at him doubtfully.

"You sure you can drive this thing?"

Karrel moved at the same time as Ninette did. She had her hand on her police-issue stun baton by the time Karrel pulled out his Taser, but she wasn't quite quick enough. The barbed dart of Karrel's Taser buried itself in her thigh and discharged 10,000 volts into her body in a blaze of blue electricity. Ninette crashed to the ground, striking her head on the metal of her own felled bike as she did so.

She rolled over, out cold.

Karrel bent over and took the keys from Ninette's outstretched hand, then pulled the dart from her leg and rolled his team leader over into the recovery position. He checked the pulse at her throat, and then straightened up with a satisfied grunt, fighting the urge to laugh hysterically. There was no turning back now. His fate was sealed. He was out of the Hunters for good. The second Ninette woke up, he knew she would find a way to make him pay dearly for what he'd just done, probably for the rest of his life.

But considering what was at stake, he didn't give a hot damn.

Hauling Ninette's heavy bike upright, he swung his leg over the saddle and checked that the area was secure. Bodies and crashed bikes lay everywhere, blood pooling in black rivers in the mud. The alleyway looked like a scene out of a disaster movie.

By the time backup arrived to contain this mess, he'd be long gone.

As he started to turn the key in the ignition, the sound of pattering footsteps echoed up the alleyway toward him.

Karrel froze.

He spun around as the footsteps darted across behind him, but the street was empty. Karrel sat stock still, listening with every fiber of his being.

A shadow flickered at the end of the alleyway.

Karrel took a deep breath, then resolutely started his engine.

CIRCLING AROUND THE burning remains of the werewolf, Karrel made his way slowly toward the end of the steeply inclined alleyway. There was nowhere to go but up. He deliberately tried not to think about what he was about to do, concentrating instead on keeping the noise from his bike down as low as possible. He had to keep the element of surprise on his side, or all was lost.

Turning a corner at the crest of the hill, he found himself in a small, enclosed area. It was barely more than a courtyard, hemmed by purple night-blooming jasmine. The rich decorations that hung on the walls and from the trees marked it out to be some kind of town square. A strange chill hung in the air like the echoes of a scream, a palpable feeling of dread that stilled Karrel's hand on the gas, making his heart constrict nastily in his chest.

Karrel swallowed hard. He didn't like this.

Not one bit.

He let his bike creep its way over the cobblestones, turning the handlebars this way and that to let its headlights play down the numerous side streets, gravel crunching and popping beneath its fat tires. As he passed the mouth of one alleyway he tapped the brakes and paused for a moment, listening hard, straining his eyes into the inky blackness.

He could've sworn he just heard a faint groan, coming from the darkness.

Karrel swallowed and reached for his Colt, moving as slowly as a cat stalking prey. He switched off the safety with a gentle movement of his thumb and silently brought the gun to bear, scanning the darkness around him, his every sense on overdrive as he moved toward the source of the sound.

He turned a corner and saw her.

She was a slender shape dressed in bloodstained white, one that might be more at home gracing the catwalks of Paris or Rome than crouched in the mud in the middle of nowhere. Her head was bowed as if in prayer, but as the twin beams of Karrel's headlights raked across her, she glanced up sharply and hissed. Karrel's stomach lurched at the sight of the dark, unmoving shape of a younger male Caucasian—one of his scout troops—held firmly in the crook of her arm. A screaming tide of black déjà vu shot through him.

Christ, *no*! He was too late!

Or was he?

Karrel killed the engine, leaving the lights on. His hand crept down toward his hidden rifle as he stared desperately at the man, searching for some sign of life: a twitch of a finger maybe, a movement of his chest. But there was nothing.

Karrel's jaw clenched and an agonized breath hissed from between his teeth. Who was he kidding? Of course the guy was dead.

No one got that close to Cyan X and lived.

As though in a dream, Karrel dismounted and made his way slowly toward the vampiress, feeling the guilty weight of his A-12 thud against his thigh with every step. Cyan made no move to run. She gazed at him with her trademark guarded amusement as he approached her, step by cautious step. She dropped the body she had been feasting on and straightened up, wiping her mouth somewhat self-consciously on her sleeve like a little girl caught snacking in class.

Karrel stopped a short distance away from her, every nerve taut, fighting down an overwhelming sensation of unreality. Every night for eight years he'd imagined this moment, played out every possibility, every scenario.

Now that it was finally here, he wished to God that he had stayed in L.A.

Cyan turned to face him, raising an eyebrow as if in question.

She looked exactly as he had remembered her.

The years had left no mark on her body. Cyan was still as achingly beautiful as ever, perfect in every single imaginable way, plus a few unimaginable ones. Her panther-black hair spilled in a

supine wave over her shoulders, perfectly accentu-
ating her high-cheekboned face with its elfin
features and fiery eyes. The dangerous curve of her
lips framed sharp, pointed teeth; inhuman teeth in
an inhuman mouth. A shocking sight on any other
woman but somehow, with her, it fit. Her white
linen dress was caked in mud and shredded by gunfire, but what was left of it clung seductively to her
powerful, lean body, showing off every incredible
inch of her.

Jesus, she was hot. A powerful shiver of desire ran
through him. Even torn and tattered and looking
like supermodel roadkill, Cyan was still the most
desirable woman he'd ever laid eyes on. His gaze
dipped lower. Her long, supple legs were bare save a
pair of elegant leather boots and the intricate
Chinese dragon tattoo that coiled its way up her
outer thigh. The sight of it unlocked memories that
even now made him shiver, sent his mind flying back
through the years to the moment they'd first met.

SHE'D BEEN HIDING from him when he'd found her,
battered and bruised, weeping outside the jock bar
where he worked double-shifts to pay off his student
loans. He'd taken her in, idiot that he was, cleaned
her wounds, let her stay with him while he coaxed
her back to health. He'd fallen for her long before he
realized what he was doing, but by then it had been
too late.

He'd found out what she was, and who she'd been
running from.

The Hunters eventually found him, three blood-
soaked, terrifying, exhilarating months later, in the

back room of the house he'd shared with his student buddies. It had taken six of them to hold him back, screaming her name as they riddled her naked body with bullets. She'd fought back like a wildcat, killing two of them bare-handed before smashing down the door and vanishing into the night.

And that had been that.

It had been ten long months before he'd finally rid himself of his crack-addict obsession with finding her, eight more before he'd come to terms with his loss and grudgingly called the number the Hunters had given him. Now he worked with them, fighting their fight, ridding the world of vampires and werewolves and whatever else the darkness could throw at them.

But always, in the back of his mind, he'd held onto a picture of Cyan as he'd first seen her, her incredible violet eyes filled with tears, begging him for help. In the short time they'd spent together he'd loved her more than he'd known it was possible to love someone. The fact that she wasn't even human didn't matter to him. He was obsessed with her. That obsession had become almost an end in itself, destroying everything in his life, driving away every woman who loved him or tried to get close to him.

But in all the time they'd spent together, she'd never loved him back. Cyan's heart had a lock on it, a lock engraved with a name carved in torn flesh and outlined in scar tissue.

And that name wasn't his.

It could never be.

Or could it?

It was the question that had haunted him for over a decade. Now, finally, he was about to get an answer...

KARREL DRAGGED HIS eyes upwards, meeting Cyan's gaze. Her eyes were older now, and the intense pain they held stole his breath away. Without thinking he moved forward, his fists clenching at his sides in anger, all thoughts of revenge temporarily driven from his mind. Someone had hurt her, betrayed her, and Karrel knew without asking who that "someone" was. He knew every last inch of her, inside and out, and the years between them seemed to fall away as the realization hit him like a bodyblow to the soul.

He still loved her.

"Cyan," he willed his voice not to shake. "I—"

"Get the hell away from me, Karrel." Cyan's voice was low and chilling. It reminded him of an animal gently growling.

Karrel shook his head, not daring to speak. He fought down a lump in his throat as he gazed at her, memorizing every line, every curve of her body for the long, dark nights alone he knew lay ahead. His hand crept down toward his hidden gun, his Hunter's mind revving in overdrive. *He had two spare clips of silver nitrate bullets for the A-12. Four rounds should release enough silver into her bloodstream to do the job, but he might need more if he missed the heart.*

Cyan's head cocked like a bird, her gaze lingering a little longer than was strictly comfortable. Then she stepped primly over the body of the dead recruit. Even the way she moved was unbearably erotic, the gentle sway of her hips drawing his eyes magnetically. He swallowed quickly and shook himself, his hand flying inside his jacket to his hidden gun.

He knew exactly what Cyan was capable of, if he let her get close.

He'd never make that mistake again.

Cyan paused a few feet away and brazenly dropped her gaze, her eyes raking down his body. "What have you got in there, sailor?" she murmured, eying the budge in his jacket. "Don't tell me you brought me flowers?"

She bared the merest sliver of fang in a smile that didn't quite reach her eyes.

Karrel reached down and slowly opened up his jacket, revealing the A-12. *This was it*. The perfect opportunity to take her out. Cyan—no, *the target vampire*—was cornered at the end of the dead-end alleyway. She was exhausted and injured, whereas he was armed to the teeth, with enough weaponry and explosives on him to lay siege to a large government building.

She could still kill him in a heartbeat.

In one swift move Karrel pulled the gun from its leather shoulder rig and aimed it at Cyan's heart. Cyan's eyes narrowed at the massive pistol.

"And I hoped you were just happy to see me," she said through gritted teeth. "Karrel?"

"What?"

"*Run*."

There was a dripping sound, like water running. It took him a couple of seconds to identify the dark, shining substance pouring down Cyan's arms as blood. Karrel glanced downdown and saw the skin on Cyan's forearms moving as though ants were crawling under her flesh.

"What the—?"

Karrel leaped backward as two bloody, curved blades suddenly burst out of Cyan's forearms, the front ends sluicing from the underside of her wrists beneath her clenched fists, the backs scything out of her elbows in an explosive spray of gore. Cyan doubled over, clutching at her wrists as blood poured from the wounds. A flash of white steel glinted in the moonlight as she bowed her head, cradling her arms protectively. The massive curved blades crossed in front of her pale, bloodied face like the wings of a newly-birthed mechanical butterfly.

"Jesus Christ!"

Cyan turned away from Karrel, grimacing in agony. Blood dripped from her lip where she had bitten through it in pain. She squeezed her eyes tight shut as the metal spikes shoved themselves further out of her wrists. When she opened her eyes again they burned with an almost incandescent light, purple storm clouds whirling in silver depths. "Karrel. I'm not kidding. Get out of here. *GO!*"

Karrel shook his head, unable to tear his eyes away. The ends of the blades were just visible through the translucent skin of her pale forearms, running lengthways within a raised central housing, buried deep within the bone.

An implant, he realized with a sick kind of admiration, *a bio-weapon of some kind.* He'd seen such devices before in gangland L.A., but they were always externally worn—strapped to the wrist rather than implanted inside. He knew of a few wealthy gang members and B-list celebrities who had had metal fixtures screwed to their bones into which a blade or barrel could be inserted, but nothing like this.

This was just—obscene.

And judging by the freaked look on Cyan's face, the surgery hadn't been her choice.

There was only one person he knew of who would do such a thing.

"*Harlequin,*" Karrel breathed.

Cyan flinched at the mention of the name. Karrel let his gun drop and moved closer, being sure to stay out of range of Cyan's blades. The flesh around the edges of the implants was raw and swollen, and there were deep bruises around the sides of the titanium housings that extended all the way up her arms. There was no housing socket, he realized with a wince. Those blades punched their way through her skin afresh each time they were triggered.

But she was a vampire. She'd have no trouble healing those wounds.

Each and every time.

Karrel felt rage spark and build inside him, threatening to sweep away his carefully maintained iron control.

"Oh, my God," he whispered. "What did he do to you, baby?"

Cyan grinned madly. "Doesn't matter now," she said, and then gave a sudden, insane peal of laughter. She put her hand over her mouth like a small child, and mirth danced in her eyes. "They're coming."

"Who's coming?"

Karrel could just make out the sound of motor-cycle engines, heading up the street toward them.

The Hunters' backup squad had found them.

Cyan choked back another fit of laughter, tears welling in her eyes. Faint headlights bounced across them as she steadied herself and glanced down at the obscene metal spikes jutting from her arms. At the body of the young man lying at her feet.

"I didn't mean to end up like this," she whispered.

Karrel dropped the A-12 back into its rig and held out a hand to her, scarcely daring to hope. The sound of motorbike engines was getting closer. "Come home with me," he said. "I can help you. We have medi-labs back at the base. They're pretty good. You could stay with me, I could—"

"You could what?" Cyan stared at him, struggling to stand, dizzy with blood-loss. "Stick me in a cage and feed me ape's blood till your funding runs out and you have to loan me out for medical research?" Her eyes locked on his with a chilling intensity. "Walk away, Karrel. And don't look back. You don't want to know what—"

"Let me finish. I have an idea. There's a cool half-million dollar bounty on Harl—on your loverboy's head. Turn him in, and you'll walk free. I'll make sure of it."

"I can't. He'll kill me."

"If you don't turn him in, *I'll* kill you," Karrel snapped. "*Choose.*"

Cyan stared at him. She slowly reached up and sliced through the clasps of her white dress with the tip of one bio-blade. Karrel's breathing stopped as it fell open, exposing her incredible breasts with their network of intricate tattoos.

"Take your best shot," she said.

Karrel stared at her, his heart turning to lead. He had his answer. Cyan would never love him as long as Harlequin was still alive.

"You have a choice," he repeated. "You *always* have a choice."

Cyan shrugged, a touch of pity in her eyes.

"I'm sorry, Karrel."

Karrel lifted his pistol and sighted on Cyan's heart, a hollow feeling welling up inside his chest. Cyan met his gaze calmly, holding herself unnaturally still as Karrel clicked the safety catch off the mammoth gun. He tensed his finger on the trigger. He'd never get a better shot.

A long moment went past.

Then he lowered the gun.

"Shit."

Cyan laughed. "You haven't changed a bit, Karrel. You never did have the courage to do the right thing."

She moved forward, rattlesnake-fast, closing the space between them in three quick steps. Karrel gave a yelp of alarm as the vampiress ducked under his guard and nuzzled in close to him, twining her arms around his upper body and retracting her blades. He grabbed her by the shoulders, trying to shove her away, but it was like trying to break free from a living vice, a trap made of flesh and bone and sinew and the softest, smoothest skin. Cyan dragged him closer, her deceptively lightweight frame melding to the hard, sculpted lines of his own form. Her cool breath whispered along his neck and Karrel felt the prick of fangs against his throat. Her lips slid upward in a series of deliberately gentle kisses, taunting him with his inability to break free. His muscled arms began to shake with the effort of holding her back.

"What are you doing?" Karrel hissed. The sound of motorcycle engines was getting closer. "Get outta here! I'll stall the Hunters."

"Too late, baby." Cyan's cool eyes met his, and for the first time he saw the madness that danced just below the surface. "It's over. You have any belief in God left, you'd better start praying. For the both of us."

The buzz of engines rounded the hill, perhaps thirty seconds away. If the Hunters saw them like this, they would assume the worst and kill them both. In a blur of fear Karrel swung around and body-slammed Cyan against the wall, trying to break her deadly grip on him. She giggled and clung tighter, burying her face in the crook of his neck as she continued kissing him, still carefully keeping her teeth sheathed. Karrel turned his head away as her kisses reached his jawline and trailed their way unhurriedly across his face, licking and tasting his skin as she went.

This had to stop. Karrel flexed his arms and tried to reach the handgun clipped to the back of his belt. He had to get away from her.

Then her lips met his, and he was lost.

Karrel was vaguely, dimly aware of his A-12 clattering to the ground as Cyan guided him back step by step against the crumbling, ivy-covered wall of the alleyway, her fingers working deftly at the buttons on his leather biker jacket. Karrel shoved her hands away and seized her chin, returning her kiss with a savage intensity that shocked even him.

Eight years' worth of pent up longing and need swept over him, switching his body to autopilot as he ran his hands frantically over her face, her neck, her silken hair, crushing her to his chest as he breathed in the familiar, sickly-sweet scent of her. This was everything he'd ever wanted, everything he'd never dared to need again. Headlights swept over the wall at the end of the alley. Karrel was oblivious to everything but the beautiful vampiress in his arms and the pounding of his heart as she nuzzled his throat, brushing her nose along the pulse point beneath his jaw to locate the vein. Her teeth slid through his skin, sinking deeply into the flesh in the side of his neck. He gasped as she fastened her lips to the wound and began to drink. His grip tightened on her shoulders and he closed his eyes with a shudder, his breathing becoming ragged as a rolling tide of heat flooded through him, stealing his strength, draining away his resolve drop by precious drop.

An unfamiliar sense of stillness filled him as Cyan bent over him. She forced him to his knees with an iron strength as she continued draining his blood, tangling her fingers in his long, dark hair. The roar of the approaching motorcade rang long and loud in his ears; suddenly, getting caught no longer mattered to him. Karrel felt his heartbeat slow. For the first time in over a decade, he felt at peace. *This was where he belonged. This is where things should end.* He was dying in her arms, and there was no place else in the world he'd rather be.

A faint, sad smile stretched its way across his face.

"You know," he whispered. "Funny thing about prayers... they don't mean shit if there's no one listening." Karrel stroked Cyan's hair softly. "And just so you know, when I told you I loved you... I lied."

He jammed the muzzle of his pistol into Cyan's temple, closed his eyes, and pulled the trigger.

HE CAUGHT HER body as it fell. She was feather light, even soaked through from the rain. Blood gushed across him, slicking the tattered remains of his armor. Karrel carefully avoided looking at her as he gently lowered her twitching body to the ground and laid her in the grass beside the pathway.

He knew what damage a bullet would do, fired at close range.

He was still standing there, gun in hand, as the first of the Hunters' bikes reached him. Their engines shut off and he heard them approach, pausing a respectful distance away. Flashlight beams crisscrossed the alleyway, converging on Cyan's body.

There was a long pause, during which he became aware of the gentle chirping of birds all around him. Morning was almost upon them. A set of steel-heeled footsteps came up behind him.

"Did you ask her?" said a familiar female voice.

Karrel gave a slow, wondering shake of his head. "She wouldn't do it," he said without turning around. "She wouldn't turn him in."

"That wasn't what I meant."

Karrel bowed his head. Ninette's armor was dented and she had a smoking hole in the fabric of her flak jacket, but otherwise she appeared to be unharmed. Together, they both stood and gazed silently down as blood ran in sticky fingers beneath their boots.

Ninette shook her head, glancing sidelong at Karrel. "You know... you'll meet someone else. Someone human. Eventually."

"God. I hope not."

Karrel glanced away, at the horizon, where the first slivers of orange light were starting to appear beneath the purplish-black rain clouds. He watched the yellow sun rise, feeling the sunlight warm his face. Beneath him, Cyan's skin started to smoke in the pre-dawn light. Karrel knew she wasn't dead yet. As soon as the sun rose, she would be.

But neither he nor the Hunters would be here to see it.

He owed her that much, at least.

Karrel drew in a deep, shuddering breath and let it out slowly as he turned to go.

It was over...

As the last of the Hunters roared off down the alleyway a few minutes later, empty-handed, a shadow fell over the smoking body of Cyan X. Her eyelids fluttered as she drifted up and down on the waters of consciousness. She could feel the sun's rays on her skin, burning her, but oddly enough she felt no pain. In fact, she couldn't feel anything. Soon she knew she would be dead, but that wasn't all bad.

Finally, she would be free.

She didn't move when footsteps approached her. Nor did she stir when a leather-gloved hand touched her face, rolling her over. The hand felt wet, and oddly sticky. The stench of burned dog hair enveloped her and she frowned, desperately wanting to hold onto the darkness of oblivion, but it was no good.

With a gasp, she opened her eyes.

Five dark shapes loomed over her. A chill went through her as she caught their scent.

Werewolves.

The part of her brain that was still rational kicked in, firing urgent directions through her ruined synapses. She would leap to her feet, take out the first two with two diagonal sweeps of her bio-blades, and then stun the third and forth with a good old-fashioned roundhouse kick to the jaw before disemboweling the fifth with the Japanese Sumari sword she kept in her back-sheath.

An odd sensation stopped her. When you lifted your head, she decided, it shouldn't make a sound like two broken china plates grinding together. Nor should you be able to see pieces of your own brain lying on the ground beside you. That was never good.

She subsided, whimpering very slightly.

The lead figure was a hulking, tattooed body with a shock of spiked black hair. He gazed down at her thoughtfully, cracking his knuckles. Every inch of visible skin on his body was burned and blackened, and he had an odd-shaped throwing knife embedded in the back of his skull. He did not look happy.

"Give me one good reason," he rasped, "why we shouldn't kill you?"

Cyan gave him a reason.

The tattooed werewolf smiled, rubbing his hands together greedily. "Well," he said. "When you put it like *that*..."

As the werewolves dragged Cyan into the safety of the shadows, her blown-open head wrapped in a makeshift splint made of strips of leather and duct tape, only one thought went through what was left of her mind.

Revenge.

CHAPTER TWO

KAYLA STEELE STOOD in the rain, gazing down at the gravestone. The name KARREL DANTE stared back up at her, engraved in large, military-style letters. The name had a border of carved roses that twined around the base of the gravestone beneath an engraving of a small cherub holding a pansy in one chubby fist.

Karrel would have hated it.

Kayla reached down and gently touched the gold engagement ring that lay in her palm. The Chief of Police had returned it to her a week ago, along with the rest of Karrel's somewhat meager personal effects that the LAPD had recovered from the basement of the downtown club where they'd found his body. He'd had the ring in his pocket the night he'd been murdered, torn to pieces in the line of duty as she'd sat oblivious in a bar not half a mile away, waiting for him to show up and propose to her.

On that night, her life as she'd known it had ended, and a new one had been born.

Kayla sighed. It had been several long, eventful days after Karrel's death before she'd found out the truth—that the love of her life did not, as he'd previously claimed, work for the Californian Animal Society, but instead for an underground monster-fighting organization known as The Hunters, a crack squad of highly-trained civilian fighters devoted to protecting humanity from the dark forces of the supernatural.

If that hadn't been hard enough to believe, she'd then discovered that Karrel's killers were in fact werewolves, a notorious L.A.-based gang of hit men under the control of a renegade vampire, Cyan X, a creature who had been terrorizing the state for nearly three decades. She knew his killer's names off by heart: Harlem, Mitzi, Flame and Jackdoor.

And it got worse. The same gang who murdered Karrel was now after her, convinced that she knew some vital piece of information that Karrel had died in order to keep secret. If it hadn't been for the Hunters showing up when they had to protect her, she would be dead already.

Things had pretty much gone downhill from there.

Kayla shivered miserably, drawing her waterproof black cameo jacket a little tighter around her. Thirty short days since Karrel had died and she was still reeling from the emotional whiplash. Finding out that things like vampires and werewolves actually existed in the real world had marked the start of the rapid downward slide of her life into a surreal, supernatural chaos from which there seemed to be no end. Now she didn't only have to deal with the normal trials and tribulations of life—bills, rent, work—she had to deal with the fact that anyone she met could be some kind of supernatural entity sent to kill her. A little under a month ago she'd been a clueless counter girl working at her local mall, scrimping and saving to afford a wedding that had never happened because her fiancé had been murdered by a werewolf hit squad.

Life could be like that, sometimes.

Kayla watched the rain run down the carved letters on the gravestone.

"So," she murmured. "What now?"

"I was thinking dinner and a movie," said a warm male voice beside her. "Or maybe we could just stand in the rain and look gloomy some more."

Despite herself, the corner of Kayla's mouth quirked into a smile. She turned to glance at the tall figure standing behind her. "This is a graveyard," she observed sternly. "We're supposed to look gloomy."

"Spoilsport."

Wylie Thompson transferred the battered umbrella he was juggling to his other hand and gallantly held it over Kayla to shield her from the downpour. His gesture was spoiled by the sudden deluge of drips that chose that moment to pour off the back of the umbrella and cascade down Kayla's back.

He beamed down at her, unfazed.

Kayla slipped the engagement ring into the pocket of her faded jeans and turned to face her best friend, trying to muster a smile despite the icy water now soaking the back of her sweater. Wylie pulled out a tissue and dabbed self-consciously at his kohl eyeliner, which was starting to run in the rain. He wiped his hands on his black jeans and grinned down at her.

Kayla smiled inwardly. Wylie never wore anything but black. Although he claimed not to be a Goth, Kayla was sure that six years working the club circuit as a barman on Sunset Boulevard had definitely influenced his style. But he wasn't about to go changing anytime soon. With his clean-scrubbed good looks and easygoing New York charm, Wylie could have made it big in the fashion or modeling industry if it hadn't been for his healthy distain for anything resembling actual work. Anything that required him to get out of bed before noon or be away from a mirror longer than fifteen minutes he regarded with the kind of convulsive horror most people reserve for boot camp tales of ten mile runs at 4am.

He pretended to cough, peered intently into the tiny compact mirror in his hand, snapped it shut, and looked back at her expectantly.

"So I'm getting that predictable, huh?" she said, poking him in the ribs. She extracted a soggy tissue from her pocket and blew her nose.

"I did take a certain chance on you being here," admitted Wylie. "However, the threat of imminent unemployment was a motivating factor for me to step up my enquiries."

"Meaning?"

"I slipped the cemetery guard a twenty to call me if he saw you here on a work night again."

"Ah. Bribery. That I get."

Wylie nodded. "Makes the world go 'round.'" Concern flickered in his dark brown eyes, then he reached out a ringed hand to brush a stand of hair out of her eyes. It lingered for a moment longer than was strictly necessary. Kayla flashed him a tight smile before pulling away, ducking her face under the furry hood of her jacket.

But Wylie had gotten a good look at her, seen the exhaustion hiding under her heavy-duty makeup and the soaked hair. She'd trowled on enough foundation to cover the damage done by a dozen sleepless nights, but then she couldn't hide her eyes. The annual June Gloom had brought a spell of rain and flash floods to the usually dry Californian streets, so she hadn't bothered to bring her sunglasses with her.

Right now, she wished more than anything in the world that she was wearing them.

"You okay?"

Kayla's gaze flitted around uncomfortably before she reluctantly made eye contact, squirming as she did so. Wylie's barman skills included a freakishly high degree of accuracy when it came to interpreting her moods: a skill which at work earned him the lion's share of tips from the never-ending stream of clients keen for a sympathetic ear as they drowned their woes at the bar. Wylie could spot a torn heart at a hundred feet and keep it at the bar long enough to empty its wallet before sending it spinning gently into a cab via the arms of the nearest bouncer.

She was busted.

"You've been having those dreams again, haven't you?" He folded his arms and leaned back against

Karrel's headstone. Droplets of rain sparkled in his gel-spiked hair. He raised his eyebrows encouragingly, waiting for her to speak.

Kayla glanced around as though they might be overheard. Then she sighed. "Yes."

She stared hard at Karrel's headstone and frowned.

"That's understandable. You've been through a lot in the last month," prompted Wylie.

Kayla nodded thoughtfully. She frowned again.

"Care to elaborate?"

Kayla shook her head. "It's probably nothing," she said. "But the dreams…" She glanced behind her again, lowering her voice. "They've been getting worse. Much worse. And crazy vivid. Last night I had one with Dolby surround sound and special effects by Rick Baker—you know, lots of blood, people's insides coming out in new and interesting ways." She abruptly shivered, rubbing her chilly arms. "Karrel was there. He was on this crazy mission in a foreign land. But he was younger, like it was years ago. And it was so real. It was like I was really there, seeing things through his eyes."

"Who, Rick Baker?" teased Wylie.

"No. You know who." Kayla gazed at the gravestone before her, a faraway look on her pale face. "We'll talk about it later, I guess. Just tell me one thing." She licked her lips and dropped her voice still further. "Would you lie to someone you were about to kill?"

Wylie's eyes widened. He took a quick step back.

"I didn't mean it like that," Kayla said with a little laugh. "I mean, hypothetically."

Wylie stared at her.

"Theoretically?" Kayla tried.

Wylie shrugged, glancing behind him as though waiting for invisible assassins to leap out and rush him.

"That means, 'in theory.' I know it's a long word to use at this time of night." She peered closely at Wylie. "What's got you so spooked?"

"Last night," said Wylie. "In your dream. There were vampires, weren't there? Or rather, just the one vampire. A woman."

Kayla's breathing stopped. "How did you know that?"

"Because I had the exact same dream," he said.

KAYLA PICKED UP another beer glass from the wire rack and began to methodically polish it under the bright blue lights of her new workplace, Club Fury. The glasses above her rattled as bass-heavy music thumped. A forest of undulating bodies swayed on the giant dance floor opposite her, grouped around the low stage that dominated this end of the rock club. Dry ice rose like smoke at a funeral pyre as a female-fronted band clad in leather and rubber belted out girlish pop songs in high-pitched Japanese, their mostly-bare flesh strung with an enticing if unusual combination of jeweled bondage gear and schoolgirl uniforms.

Kayla liked it here. The packed, intimate darkness was as busy as a week-old dead-dog and smelled about half as good, but at least people left her alone. The main clubroom was lit by a wash of smoky red light from the low-slung ceiling lights.

Silver crucifixes were nailed on the walls surrounding the stage, which was ringed by a black metal gantry dotted with smooching couples. A sign reading "CLUB FURY" hung above the stage like a malevolent neon God, dominating the large, semicircular room.

Kayla yawned, trying to wake up before more people arrived for the main band. Judging by the high proportion of young punks with green hair and outfits made of tartan rags and torn black lace, she guessed they were going to be in for a rough night. She eyed the naked kiddy's baby doll that was lashed to the front of the drum-kit with razor wire, its hands and throat painted with fake blood, and shook her head in bemusement. This job was a far cry from her old workplace behind the beauty counter at her local mall, but it was certainly entertaining. Wylie had worked behind the bar in this club for years, so he'd pulled a few strings to get her a job after she'd quit her old one, unable to deal with the looks and the whispers and the sympathetic stares from her co-workers who all knew of Karrel's death.

Club Fury wasn't much of an improvement in terms of the wage, but at least nobody here *knew*. There were times when anonymity was better than all the sympathy in the world. Kayla was grateful for the chance for a fresh start.

Besides, she loved the kids here, the drinkers and clubbers with their wildly-styled, choppy hair, their multicolored, ragged punk clothing held together with safety pins and strips of duct tape. They were beautiful, like motley angels come to Earth, but she felt alienated from them in a way that she knew they would never understand. They smiled at her as they milled past, en-route to the stage or the rest-room.

Kayla smiled back, trying not to cry.

She jumped as Wylie nudged her, gesturing at his Mickey Mouse watch. Kayla plucked another glass from the rack.

"So tell me," she continued, trying to distract herself from her bleak mood. "This dream of yours... did you catch any names? See anyone you recognized?"

"Only, er... you know."

Kayla stopped her polishing and gave Wylie a frank look. "Wylie, it's been a month. You *are* allowed to say his name."

"I know." Wylie eyed up the cavorting Japanese singer with an expression of dubious admiration. "But whenever I do, your face does this sad little thing and you look like someone just ran over your puppy. *Karrel.* See?" Wylie gestured at Kayla's face with his bottle-opener. "Sad little thing. Breaks my heart. But no, I don't remember much. I just remember seeing your man chasing this hot vampire chick through some weird ass foreign country. Like some crazy Anne Rice flick but without the zillion-dollar budget. Then boom! He kills her. I didn't get much more than that."

Kayla shook her head, bemused. "And you heard what he said to her? Before he killed her?"

"He said that when he told her he loved her, he lied."

Kayla paled. The glass she'd been polishing slipped out of her hand and smashed on the bare concrete floor. Wylie reached over and handed her a long-handled dustpan and brush. Kayla took it silently and began sweeping.

"So what does it mean? Us sharing a dream like that?"

Kayla shrugged.

"Maybe we've just been spending too much time together."

"We do share a brain. Or rather, a brain-cell."

Wylie laughed at the old joke. He pulled out a stainless steel chopping block and started to wipe it down. "What's the deal with the vampires? Is this like the time you told me you saw that boy getting killed by a werewolf?" He grinned, nudging her in the ribs. "Remember that?"

Kayla stiffened. She *did* remember that, and in fact had been trying very hard to forget it. A female werewolf had been sent after her to kill her at the same time as the were-gang had been sent to take out Karrel. Only the efforts of one of Karrel's friends had saved her from taking up residence in the graveyard plot next to Karrel's.

One of Karrel's *werewolf* friends...

Kayla quickly stifled all thoughts of Mutt, hardening her heart. Wylie was asking her too many questions that she didn't want to answer, and she was fast running out of excuses.

"I remember," she said with a weak laugh. "Pretty crazy, huh?"

"Comin' from you, I wouldn't expect anything less."

Wylie ruffled Kayla's hair affectionately and stepped back behind the bar, whistling a Motley Crüe song off-key under his breath.

Kayla watched him pick up a giant cleaver and start slicing olives and limes, working in a calm, practiced fashion as he prepared for the evening's first drinks-rush. She leaned back on the bar, feeling some of the tense lines in her face relax. There was something very comforting about Wylie. He was a cool, calm oasis of sanity in the middle of her own drowning pool of chaos. She *liked* the fact that she could still be "normal" around him, as though everything was still fine and Karrel was still alive and that the world was a calm, predictable place where people you loved didn't get murdered by monsters.

Wylie was normal, or at least semi-normal, she thought, as she watched him attempt to balance an olive on the end of his nose, trying to impress a nearby Hollywood starlet who watched him with a faint expression of alarm on her face. Kayla shook her head. Wylie had never had much luck with women. She knew him better than anyone and took a huge amount of comfort in his simple, unquestioning friendship.

But then, said a nasty little voice in the back of her head, *you thought you knew Karrel, and look what had happened there.*

The thought bothered her.

"Wylie?" she murmured, leaning in close so he could hear her above the hot thump of the club music.

"Hmm?"

"Do you ever wonder how much you can really know a person?"

"Keeps me awake most nights," agreed Wylie, popping the olive into his mouth and pulling a face.

"That, and the guy next door who insists on having sex with what sounds like a mongoose at ungodly hours of the morning."

"Exactly," said Kayla, completely ignoring most of what Wylie had just said. "That's what scares me. You can know someone for years and you think you know everything about them, but you don't."

She paused, biting her lip as Karrel's face loomed painfully in her mind. She struggled to shut it out. "I wonder if that would even be possible?"

"To truly know someone? Doubtful," said Wylie, chewing on his olive. "But that may not be such a bad thing. I mean, think about it. How many secrets do *you* have that you'd want to keep that way?"

Kayla opened her mouth to reply and then shut it again, her mind suddenly full of werewolves and blood and black-clad Hunter troopers shouting incomprehensible things at her. "I have enough," she said, picking up her bar tray. There was a Celtic cross inscribed on it in blood-red ink. The sight of it sent a shiver down her spine. "And I never said anything about secrets. I'm talking about *really* knowing someone. Inside and out."

Wylie's eyes flickered and he closed his mouth firmly, pressing his lips together as though he'd said too much. "We all have secrets," he said, his tone carefully light. "And you don't want to know most people's insides. That's why they're, you know, inside."

"Is that why God hates us?" said Kayla, staring down at the cross on the bar tray. "Because He can see inside us?"

Wylie put down his knife and turned toward Kayla, his eyebrows raised in consternation. "Now where did *that* come from?" he admonished. "Kayla. Tell me the truth. Have you been eating the cocktail cherries again?"

Kayla shook her head, a sudden wave of misery sweeping through her. "I don't know. All I can say is that if there is a God, every single member of the human race is screwed."

"Why on earth would you say that?"

Kayla glanced up helplessly at the wall-mounted plasma-screen TV, currently blaring out the local news. The vampire dream had awakened her own insecurities again, and she was fighting to get them back under control. She remembered her reaction to the news of Karrel's death—shock, denial, and then the worst feeling of all, the creeping, burning, sickly feeling in the pit of her stomach that somehow his death had been *her fault*. Perhaps there was something she could have done to keep him alive, to stop him from going out the night he'd been killed. She could have been a better girlfriend, a better lover, anything to make him want to give up his demon-fighting career and settle down with her instead.

The feelings had only grown stronger in the last month since his death, her every waking moment devoted to thoughts of their relationship and the myriad of things she could have done to prevent him from getting himself killed. She wished she could tell Wylie everything, pour out her heart to him, tell him about the dream and the deadly cross she silently bore.

But she couldn't.

Not unless she wanted to put his life in danger, too.

Kayla pulled herself out of the endless, pointless loop of self-condemnation. "I've just been thinking a lot, lately," she said. "Since Karrel died. Questioning things I shouldn't."

"Like why he died?"

Kayla glanced up at the TV so Wylie wouldn't see the look on her face. She tried to keep the anger out of her voice as she replied, conscious of the clubbers around them waiting to be served. "Like why people die. In general. Why bad things happen to good people."

She twisted a napkin between her fingers as she stared down at the unswept floor.

"Kayla," Wylie quickly put down his knife and lifted the service hatch that separated them. He stepped through and leaned on the bar next to her, close enough that she could feel the comforting warmth of his body through the cloth of his work shirt. He reached out and gently rubbed her shoulders, kneading some of the tension out of her. "You know as well as I do that there's no 'should' or 'shouldn't,' he murmured. "There's just 'is' and 'isn't.'"

Kayla relaxed against him cautiously, balling the shredded napkin up in her fist with a tiny, grudging smile. "Don't go all existentialist on me, Goth Boy. That's not a proper answer."

"'Tis for me, kiddo. You know my deal."

Kayla wrinkled her nose at him in grumpy affection. "What, that you're a no-good two-bit heathen?"

That made Wylie grin. "Call me what you will. I was raised to believe in God, same as you. I just started asking questions earlier than most."

"Such as?"

"Such as why two people would have the same dream on the same night, a month after someone they both knew was killed. Coincidence?" He tapped her lightly on the nose with his bottle opener. "Or something more sinister?"

This was a regular argument of theirs, and there was something oddly comforting in that. "Christ knows," she said, then gave a small smile, realizing what she'd just said. "But he won't tell you, because you don't believe in him."

"And you do, I suppose?"

"I believe in… something." Kayla shifted uneasily. She started fiddling with the bandana she wore around one wrist. "I don't believe everything the Bible says, word-for-word. But I do think that there's a power out there greater than ourselves, watching over us. Surely that's better than not believing anything at all, like you do?"

Wylie inclined his head magnanimously and pulled her into an awkward bear hug, resting his chin on the top of her head. "I dunno, kitten. I believe in a lot of things. I believe in people, and I believe in myself." He paused, staring up at the stage. The Japanese singer had now pulled out a plastic snake and was doing something obscene with it, to the general amusement of the mostly male crowd. Wylie shook his head, squeezing Kayla tightly as though to ward off the weirdness of the world. "But I don't believe in God. I don't see why I should put all of my faith in some mythical father figure who lets His own children suffer the way we do." Kayla felt a muscle in his jaw twitch. "Like you suffered for Karrel. It's just not right."

A lump rose in Kayla's throat at the mention of Karrel. She quickly swallowed it and tried to change the subject. "Perhaps it's all a test. Perhaps God wanted to see how I handle adversity."

"Bullshit." Wylie released her and turned away, gazing out of the darkened window at the waiting crowds outside. He was getting mad. "What about Karrel?" he asked. "Why sacrifice him, just to test you? Was your life worth more to your God than his?"

"Who knows," Kayla said, hating the words that were coming out of her mouth but unable to drag herself out of this uncomfortable conversation. "They say God knows everything that's going to happen. Perhaps He knew how Karrel was going to turn out, and decided that I was worth more for some reason."

"That's totally logical. And total horseshit." Kayla recoiled slightly as she saw the look on Wylie's face. His usually calm brown eyes were lit by a spark of red from the moody club lighting, and for a moment she didn't recognize him. Wylie was very rarely angry, but when he was it usually had to do with injustice of some kind.

Knowing his background, she understood why.

"They *also* say that God is supposed to love all His children equally," said Wylie. "That we all get the same chance in life. That not a sparrow falls without Him seeing it fall."

He stepped closer and fixed Kayla with a hard look. "But it's up to people like me to ask the *real* question: 'Who shot it?'"

That did it. Kayla's eyes filled with tears as an image slammed into her head of the crime scene photograph she'd seen of Karrel's body. He'd faced six full-grown werewolves on his own, with only one bullet left in his rifle. He'd used the bullet to take out the biggest wolf before being torn apart by the other five.

At least, that's what the Hunters had told her.

The cops had told her he'd been killed by a wild dog.

Kayla reached into her pocket for a tissue and blew her nose, only half aware of Wylie's arms going around her again.

"Oh shit, girl. I'm sorry."

Wylie squeezed Kayla to his chest, gently smoothing her hair down. "I guess both of us are a little sleep deprived today. Here, don't cry, your eyeliner will run and you'll wind up looking like me." He glanced quickly around, searching for something to distract her. His gaze fell on the muted bar TV above them. He grabbed the remote off the bartop, rapidly flicking through the channels. "Here, check this out. Might cheer you up. Talking about religion, what do you think 'bout that dead angel they found up on Sunset?"

"The dead *what?*"

"Haven't you heard?" Wylie blinked at her in amazement. "It's been all over the news. Should be right up your alley. Weirdo." He gave Kayla a peck on the forehead as she took a half-hearted swipe at him. Then he released her and hit the volume button on the remote control. The strident voice of a TV newscaster filled the bar.

"*Courtroom officials say that the body of the victim has not yet been identified, although evidence suggests that his internal injuries point to a fall from a high building before the shot to the head that killed him. Meanwhile, a crowd has gathered outside the police station where the so-called angel body is currently being held. Rumors of the deceased having wings are unfounded, although a leaked LAPD crime scene video is currently the number one download on YouTube.*"

Kayla peered in fascination as dozens of people holding "*HEAVEN FORGIVE US*" placards flashed up on the screen. The image faded into a second shot taken from a grainy computerized video. It showed a naked male body being covered and loaded into the back of an ambulance.

The video was blurred and indistinct, but seen from a certain angle, it really did look like the dead guy had wings.

Kayla gripped the edge of the bar. A sudden surge of excitement raced through her, blowing away her tiredness and her grief. It could be a hoax of course, some guy on his way home from a costume party or a movie set who ended up in the wrong place at the wrong time. This was L.A., after all. Things like that happened every day. It could be some kind of setup, some religious nut trying to pull a fast one and push his cause, whatever that might be. People always saw what they wanted to see, particularly where their own faith was concerned.

But there was a third option. In the last thirty days working for the Hunters, she'd seen things that ordinary people would never see outside of their nightmares, an alarming number of which seemed to want her dead.

Kayla reached for her cell phone, still staring up at the TV.

As much as she hated to admit it, there was a very good chance that this angel might be real.

CHAPTER THREE

IN THE BASEMENT of a squalid brick warehouse, the sounds of cheering filled the dusty air. A hulking brute hit the dirt in the roughly constructed ring, blood pouring from his broken jaw. Three short electronic tones sounded and the crowd erupted into a mixture of cheering and catcalls. They stabbed their fists into the air in gestures of triumph and threat, depending on how much money they'd just won or lost.

On this fight, most of them were losers.

Moonlight poured in through the dozen slatted windows as the lone male figure stopped in the middle of the ring and half-turned to throw a look of contempt at the baying crowds. Dust clung in a powdery film to his lean, toned physique, and steam rose from the sweat that slicked his bare and muscular upper body. His skin was marred by a dozen cuts and bruises. Blood seeped in dark lines down his chest, slicking the slim metal collar around his neck and soaking through his torn black jeans

As the crowd started chanting "*Off! Off! Off!*" a beer bottle flew toward the back of the man's head, thrown with malicious accuracy. Without even seeming to notice what he was doing, the man snapped up a hand and caught the bottle an inch from his head. He flipped it over in the air, then tensed his arm and crushed it with one sharp squeeze. He tossed the handful of glass away in a parody of the handful of salt thrown by the Japanese sumo wrestlers who usually frequented this ring. It increased the volume of the crowd's chanting tenfold. He turned away with a grunt of disgust, his eyes flashing silver in his darkened face.

If he'd been human, he would have been dead before the end of the first round.

But he wasn't human.

Right now, it was the only thing he had left in his favor.

Mutt wiped the blood from his hands and scraped back his long, unruly locks. He took a few careful breaths, planning his next move. The crowd was about to get ugly, but there was not much he could do about that. This whole damned sport was ugly, but there was nothing he could do about that, either. His participation here wasn't voluntary. One glance down at the rusty steel ring he wore around his ankle reminded him of that. It was connected by a chain to a brass ring set in the dirty concrete, limiting his range of movement and effectively hobbling him. Each step caused it to cut further into his already torn and bleeding ankle. But that hadn't stopped him from taking down his last three opponents barehanded in the last ten minutes of this twelve-minute round.

Under the current rules that meant he should be freed, but he knew how little rules meant in a place like this.

Besides which, he'd just decked the crowd favorite, a giant of a man known only as Razor. That made him dead already.

What else did he have to lose?

Mutt wiped his bloodied lips and gave a ghost of a smile, then threw a wary glance up at the wooden booth that sat at the top of the splintery plank-based seating. Thirty rows of noisy humanity filled the room: shouting men and women in rumpled shirts and ties, stern-looking businessmen in suits, the silent row of black-clad figures at the back who attended every fight and made the occasional purchase.

Mutt's fists clenched as his gaze sought out one individual in particular, a red-headed man in a red baseball cap. The man was sitting on the planks and watching him smugly as he sipped his Starbucks coffee. Mutt felt every hair on his body stand on end as he tensed, weighing his chances of getting to the hated man and ripping his throat out before Security caught him.

A sudden chilling growl came from the prone body at his feet. Beneath him, the big man's eyes snapped open and locked on his, his face contorting into a rictus of outrage.

Damn vampires.

Mutt lunged for the side of the ring just as Razor lurched upright and flew at him, his enormous hands reaching for his throat. Mutt managed to throw himself out of reach before being brought up short by his ankle chain. Impossibly, Razor changed direction in mid air and came at him again almost instantly, but Mutt anticipated this. He sidestepped and brought up a booted foot to kick the man in the backside as he passed by, sending him crashing into the crowd barriers.

It wasn't an elegant move, but it was an effective one. It drew a chorus of hoots from the still largely hostile audience, who were now starting to settle back into their seats at the promise of some unauthorized entertainment. Out of the corner of his eye Mutt saw two huge security guards make their way down the center isle toward him, armed with police batons and Tasers. He knew he had to move fast.

Encouraged by the crowd's response, Mutt reached out and grabbed the man by the hair before he could recover. He yanked him backward and down with all his strength. The man was almost twice his size, but Mutt knew a thing or two about leverage, and a whole lot more about showmanship.

Razor made a satisfying crash as he hit the ground a second time, throwing up an almost comically large cloud of dust. Mutt drew back a booted foot to kick him in the face, then pulled the kick at the last moment and jumped over him with an exaggeratedly balletic pirouette, spreading his arms to invite applause. Razor threw up his arms to guard his face from Mutt's kick, then froze and peered idiotically out from behind his hands, frowning in confusion at the sight of the suddenly empty ring before him.

A ripple of laughter went through the crowd as Mutt gave a campy little bow. He tapped a finger to the side of his head and jerked his thumb down at the fallen giant, kicking him hard in the backside again. The crowd roared.

That did it.

Razor snapped out his arms and spun around in the dirt, his piggy eyes narrowing to wrathful slits at the sight of the grinning Mutt above him. *Nobody* laughed at Razor. At least, nobody who wanted to go home with all their body parts attached.

With a murderous growl he lumbered to his feet and charged. Mutt danced back out of reach and spun around, still hamming it up to the crowd. He waited until the very last instant before sidestepping, waving his arms like a matador. He kicked out with his other foot, wrapping his ankle chain around the man's neck as he ploughed past him. Mutt threw himself flat on the ground and seized the big metal ring on the end of his chain, feeding it quickly back through itself in a slipknot to take the strain.

Razor jerked to a halt with a sudden strangled grunt. Mutt cried out in pain as the chain sprung taut and snapped his leg back before he could brace himself, badly wrenching his knee. He watched through a haze of pain as the big man whirled, grabbed the chain, and tried to drag him backward. But now, every yank he gave on the line tightened the chain around his own throat. It took the big man a second or two to work out what had happened, his tiny black eyes almost popping out of his head as he once again tried to haul Mutt closer.

Stalemate.

Mutt grabbed the other side of the chain and started slowly pulling it through the ring embedded in the concrete, link by link, forcing the giant to stumble forward, cursing him every step of the way. His eyes scanned the man's swarthy, sweaty face with its latticework of tribal scarrings, searching for any shred of hope that he could communicate with him. Razor opened his mouth and roared in defiance as the chain cinched tighter, baring sharp teeth. Mutt noted that the vampire's front canines were missing, bloody sockets gaping in their place. A stab of anger went through him.

It looked like he wasn't the only one here against his will.

"Don't make me do this," Mutt grit his teeth as his wrenched knee screamed at him. "Work with me, big guy. We could both get out of here, free the others."

"Screw you, shit-for-brains," growled the giant, his face a grimace of hatred. "Ain't nobody gettin' free tonight but me. Go to hell, you an' the rest of yer stinkin' kind."

"I'm guessing that's a 'No.'"

Mutt glanced up at the audience, who were starting to rise to their feet to see what was going on. The giant abruptly let Mutt go, his hands flying to his own neck to rip the chain off.

Too late.

Before he could free himself, Mutt grabbed the top of the slip-knot and pulled with all his strength, dragging the giant to his knees. He braced his good leg and gave a second gargantuan heave. The force of Mutt's tug dragged Razor face-down into the dirt, hauling his neck up to the ring embedded in the concrete where it stuck with a clink. Razor floundered around for a second, trying in vain to pry the chain loose from his throat, but his fingers were too thick to get a good grip on it.

"Last chance, bud," said Mutt in a monotone.

"Fuck... you!" gasped the giant, then yelled in fury as Mutt yanked on the chain again, this time putting his entire bodyweight behind it. Razor's yell turned into a shriek as the sharp, rusty chain sliced through the soft flesh of his neck. A second, violent pull severed his spinal column, forcefully decapitating him.

Razor's head flew off his body and bounced away across the ring. The freed chain finally pulled through the loop with a sad little clinking sound. The giant's headless body thrashed around for a horrible second before an orange light erupted from the stump of his neck and belched fire. For an instant, every bone in his body was visible, glowing blue-hot as the flesh that surrounded them crystallized like melting sugar. Then his body exploded, spattering the crowd barriers with hot, smoking goo.

In the ensuing silence, Mutt rolled over, sweating, and scanned the faces of the crowd with exhausted trepidation.

If he was lucky, they'd kill him for what he'd just done.

The room came back to life with an uneasy rumble. It grew louder as the security guards thundered down the steps toward the ring, blue lightening crackling from their primed Tasers. Mutt tried to stand, staggering as his wounded knee gave out on him.

"Anyone wanna see a magic trick?" he said with a weak grin, glancing toward the exits. The guard's only response was a growl as they closed in on him. Mutt stepped back with a put-upon sigh, letting his limbs fall into a defensive position as the adrenalin from his fight coursed through his system. He'd been in deep shit so many times in his short life that it was almost a natural state for him.

Mutt tensed, preparing to fight for his life.

The guards were almost upon Mutt when a voice rang out, cutting through the babble of voices that filled the makeshift arena.

"Leave him!"

The crowd turned as one to face the back of the room. A tall, elegant man stood outside the opened door of the wooden booth. He was wearing a black two-piece suit and a silver mask covered half of his face. What Mutt could see of the other side of his face sent a chill down his spine, but he had seen such things before. He wasn't as shocked as some of the newer members of the crowd.

Mutt's hackles rose at the sight of him.

The silver-masked man lifted a taloned fingernail and daintily brushed back his long, perfectly combed white hair, which spilled out from behind the mask and flowed down his shoulders before vanishing under his theater jacket. He regarded Mutt for a moment, one corner of his deformed mouth lifting into a sneer of recognition. As a buzz of conversation rose around him he turned and made a sharp hand-gesture. Down in the ring, the larger and uglier of the two guards raised his radio to his lips and spoke quickly into it.

The main door to the ring crashed open and a third guard came out, dragging the struggling shape of a young girl with him. The girl was soaked through and barefoot, clad only in a thin cotton dress that barely covered her thighs. She fought every inch of the way as they hauled her into the makeshift arena, clawing at their arms and swearing at them in what sounded very much like Italian.

Mutt frowned, sniffing quickly at the air. The girl was human. Why were they bringing her in here? There was no way in hell he was fighting a girl, particularly not an unarmed and terrified one like this. The fight would be over in about two seconds flat.

What kind of entertainment would that be?

Unless...

Mutt watched in sudden and rising dread as the guards secured the girl to the empty second anklet ring in the middle of the room. They backed off, glancing up past him smugly. The silver-masked man raised his right hand, holding up what looked like a remote control with a flashing green light.

At the sight of the device, the crowd leaped up and erupted into cheering, stamping their feet and chanting.

Mutt backed away, shaking his head in horror. With a cry he grabbed the chain that tethered him to the center of the ring, leaning his entire body-weight on it as he strove in vain to free himself.

He wasn't quick enough.

The metal collar around his neck gave a sharp buzz as the man pressed the green button on the remote control. The collar lit up with an answering green light. Mutt yelped as a dozen steel needles punched out of the hollow collar and stabbed into his neck, discharging their icy chemical contents into his bloodstream with a hiss. His vision blacked out and a terrible sense of pressure filled his head, racing down to fill his entire body.

"Son of a bitch!" he gasped.

His legs buckled and he crashed to the ground, clawing helplessly at his neck. The crowd roared gleefully and Mutt grit his teeth, feeling his insides twist and turn like a sack of deadly snakes. A murderous rage filled him as he stared up at the man in the red baseball cap, gasping in pain as his muscles convulsed with the effects of the chemicals.

If it was the last thing he did, he'd make him *pay* for this.

But right now, there were more urgent things to consider.

With a desperate lunge, Mutt grabbed his ankle chain with suddenly numb fingers, trying to loop it through his own collar and create a leash for himself. But his hands changed shape before his eyes, his fingers retracting into his palm as glossy ebony claws punched bloodlessly through his fingertips. Mutt howled in frustration as the chain slipped through his mutating fingers and clattered to the ground. He tasted the metallic tang of blood in his mouth as his canines elongated. His face stretched into a long, black muzzle in a series of horrendously gristly pops.

He heard the girl scream in horror before his consciousness was obliterated in a roaring red rush.

MUTT OPENED HIS eyes and rolled over. An overlapping confusion of sounds and smells assaulted him. He sniffed the air briefly before rising to his feet on powerfully clawed hind legs, stretching his new, sinewy muscles until his joints popped. He felt good—strong and alive—the ache of his twisted knee already faded to a dull throb. He snorted at the stench of the humans who surrounded him on all sides. His belly rumbled and his mouth watered at the smell of blood that permeated the air of the ring.

He sensed a presence, close behind him.

Slowly, Mutt faced the cowering young girl, the pupils in his green eyes dilating sharply in hunger. The chained girl backed away from him in terror. Mutt stepped out of his suddenly-loose ankle cuff, every hair on his newly-furred back bristling, the longer hair around his neck standing out in a ferocious lion's mane. He could hear the blood pulsing hypnotically in the girl's veins, smell the delicious, salty sweat on her skin as she shrank away from him. An uncontrollable growl of hunger rose in his throat as he focused on her, his entire body tense with anticipation.

The crowd held its breath.

The girl made a break for the side of the ring with an ear-piercing shriek. She had almost reached the door before the chain around her ankle halted her mad dash.

The crowd roared for blood and she turned to face him, screaming.

With a snarl, Mutt attacked.

CHAPTER FOUR

MOONLIGHT FILTERED IN through the giant, Spanish alabaster windows of the Cathedral of Our Lady of the Angels, reflecting its famous white light off the polished floors. Candles flared in tall, condemning legions around the edges of the sandy walls, illuminating the orderly rows of wooden pews and the imposing cherry-wood pipe organ, which rose a full eighty feet above the congregation. When it was full, the huge cathedral could seat some three thousand worshippers. Tonight, the vast chapel was empty.

There were three dark figures beside the altar, facing the absent congregation in a frozen tableau of pain. One figure was on its knees, staring down at the body of a second man sprawled beneath him. The third figure stood over them both, in an almost mocking caricature of the Cathedral's famous Annunciation window above them, depicting the

Angel Gabriel standing over the kneeling Virgin Mary.

Unlike Mary, however, the bowed figure held not a psalm book in his hands, but a bleeding, freshly-torn-out human heart.

Sage Griffiths tried to breathe around two broken ribs and didn't enjoy the experience one bit. He gazed numbly down at the fist-sized heart that lay in his cupped palms. Faint tendrils of heat-mist rose off it, spiraling upwards before vanishing into the chill chapel air. Given mankind's eternal preoccupation with Hell and Heaven, he thought, it was funny how no-one ever pointed out that heat naturally rose. It was a theological screw-up that he was sure explained a lot about the world these days.

The strangest thoughts went through your head when you were minutes from death, but Sage knew better than to question the workings of his own brain.

Particularly bearing in mind the attitude of his present company.

"Wrong answer," came a rich, baroque voice from above him, making him jump and almost drop the heart. "Would you like to guess again?"

Sage shook his head *no*, slowly at first and then with increasing vigor as his mind played through the various consequences of such a decision. He ran his tongue over his cracked lips and stared down at the body of the dead priest before him. The poor man was sprawled on the edge of one of the square tiled patterns in the limestone floor. There was a bloody hole in the center of his chest and another in his lower abdomen. His head had been split open like a ripe melon, the two empty halves of his skull stacked neatly on one side of his body. His brain lay in dozens of thinly carved slices on the nearby pulpit, as if in preparation for a lecture on anatomy. Blood covered the vestry floor in ragged splashes, pooling around the priest's decimated body.

Sage felt bile rise in his throat.

The figure above him sighed at his silence, a sepulchral sound in such an atmosphere.

"Arise. The lesson is ended."

"Wait!" Sage cleared his throat, coughing as his lungs filled with a trickle of blood. His broken ribs creaked as he drew a wheezing breath. "I have a fourth answer."

"Which is...?"

"You're not going to like it."

The figure made a sound of impatience and dismissal. "Then it is of no interest to me. You are just like the others." Metal clinked ominously as the figure reached inside the heavy cloak he wore, fishing around within. "There is no magic in you, old man. I had been led to believe that you were the oldest and bravest of your kind. A great warrior, one who could finally answer my question, end my torment. And yet I find out now that you cannot."

Sage gazed down, studiously avoiding the other's gaze. "One cannot teach a man what he does not wish to know."

"And half a lie engenders a new truth." A beam of stray light found its way under the hooded mask the standing figure wore, revealing a flash of the horrors that lay beneath. Sage shuddered and looked away as the voice went on.

"I was told that you have forbidden knowledge of the Dark Arts, that you are immortal, unkill-able. Tell me. Is this a lie also?"

"We both have our secrets, but the answer..." Sage paused, breathing deeply to calm himself. He glanced down and pulled an apologetic face. "May I?"

The figure inclined its head in a ghastly mockery of graciousness.

"You may."

Sage dropped the heart down onto the floor with a shudder and began compulsively wiping his bloodied hands on his starched coattails. He had worn his very best suit to this meeting, anticipating that this might well be his last chance to wear it. Besides, he didn't trust the fools at home to find it when they needed something decent to bury him in.

Grabbing hold of the pulpit, Sage Griffiths arose to his full height a little stiffly, bringing his face up into the light. He wiped the blood from his lips with care, glancing at his reflection in the silvered reading stand. His worn face was clean-shaven, his graying hair recently cut.

He wiped the blood off his well-defined cheek-bones with a tissue. He removed his expensive spectacles with their gold-tinted glass and began cleaning them, revealing intelligent gray eyes, currently creased in an expression of deep regret. In his day Sage had been a handsome man. Even now, in his twilight years, he still had a certain charm that was hard to resist.

Right now, he was giving that charm its final airing.

Sage replaced his glasses and met the eye of his captor unflinchingly, something that no human would be able to do with any measure of comfort. He briskly straightened his suit, glancing once again at his image in the reading stand, trying not to think about the fact that the man facing him had no reflection.

"Right, then," he said with the air of one reading out his own death sentence to a pitchfork-waving crowd. "The answer you seek is not obtainable to mortal men. To find it, you must first pass over to the Other Side, or"—he held up a hand as the vampire bared his teeth in outrage—"you must find one to act as a missionary for you. To boldly go where no man... you know the rest. Only then will you be able to recover that which has been lost to you. That is all I know. I give you my word."

There was a deep, reflective silence that seemed to last a lifetime as the other considered this.

At last, his captor nodded.

"It is agreed, then," he said. "You will go, on my behalf. After all, it is only fitting."

Sage paled, although inside he felt a secret flood of relief. It was the verdict he knew would be delivered, with the certainty of a cat chasing a mouse. The only difference, he knew, was that *this* mouse was running to take shelter in the kennel of a very large, very hungry dog. He held up his hands in a gesture of horror that was only partially an act.

"But you gave me your word!"

"My word? What is a word but a breath in the air?" The dark figure licked his thin, inhuman lips and leaned closer, his golden eyes burning with the fire of a zealot. "Man's time on earth is short, and his actions fade 'neath the black curtain of night. But a soul... now, a soul lasts forever. Help return mine to me, and I will spare the rest of your miserable, wretched race."

"Harlequin, you need to end this!" Sage reached up to touch his face, then held up his trembling, blood-smeared hand in accusation. "Give up this ridiculous quest of yours! How many more will give their blood, their lives to your self-indulgent fancy? It hasn't even been proven that the soul exists!"

"I need no proof!" spat Harlequin, rounding on him in anger. "The soul is real! I have spent eternity trying to find it, and I will succeed!"

"And if you don't?" Sage looked down at the sad shape of the dead priest, and waved an ironic hand at the body. "You've looked everywhere, after all."

"The human body is flawed," snapped Harlequin. "I have long suspected it does not house the soul at all. Look here."

He lifted his enormous broadsword off the pulpit and touched the tip to the neatly sliced brain resting on the reading stand.

"The soul is not in the mind, a mere puppeteer in the gantry pulling strings from on high. Nor is it in the heart, stoking the body's poor embers with its eternal fire." He moved the sword to nudge the priest's torn-open belly. "It lies not in the gut, immune to reason as a drill chief herding his men toward a despotic war. And if it is in the blood," a drop of crimson glinted on the razor edge of the broadsword, "then God help us if we should ever bleed."

"Very poetic." Sage sniffed and pushed his glasses back up the bridge of his nose. "Are all vampires as deluded as you?"

"You're a Hunter, old man. You should know." Harlequin drew himself up to his full, seven-foot height and hefted his acid-etched broadsword, staring down at Sage.

Then he smiled.

Despite his resolve, Sage found himself wavering at the sight of the grinning master vampire. Teeth as long and as sharp as a dentist's needle gleamed in the light as Harlequin stepped up to him, his hind claws clicking on the limestone flagstones. In a burst of uncharacteristic panic the old Hunter's powerful mind reached outward, searching the chapel for unbarred exits.

He found none.

"Come now," he wheedled, flicking his gaze toward the giant bronzed doors that stood at the rear of the Cathedral. "We don't need to do this. Men since the age of the gods have searched for the soul, to no avail. It's an impossible quest, even without the Prophecy. What makes you think you have a shot at finding it?"

To his surprise, Harlequin laughed.

"Because, my dear little man," the vampire said, drawing out each word in his rich, purring voice. "They *knew* it was an impossible quest. Have you not heard the tale of the boy who arrived at his classroom late to find a mathematical equation on the board?"

"No, but I presume you're going to tell me."

"It is an old fable. The boy copied it down, and by morning he had solved it. His teacher told him that, far from being homework, the boy had just completed one of the seven great unsolved mathematical equations of his time."

"And your point is…?"

"If you think a problem's impossible, you have no chance of solving it."

"I don't think it's impossible to find the soul, you fool!" Sage shouted. "I *know* it's impossible!"

Harlequin's grin grew broader, seeming to expand until it filled the room. Drawing his sword, he gave it an extravagant flourish. "No knowledge comes without sacrifice, my friend. How would you explain our famous winged visitor, for instance, with regards to the soul?" He cocked his monstrous head, watching Sage's reaction closely. "Would he argue against man's celestial immortality, or does his presence here on Earth by definition confirm it?"

For a moment, Sage was speechless. Then he paled, the breath leaving him in a rush. "He is here?" he whispered. "Already?"

Harlequin's eyes glittered in the dim light. "Come, now," he purred. "Have you not heard the news? The church has already denied it, so it must be true. You know what will happen next."

Sage stiffened, his eyes widening in horror. "The Bateaux Prophecy," he whispered. "Surely, it can't be?"

Harlequin inclined his head smugly.

"One who has died, and yet lives…" Sage stared blindly at nothing. "It makes sense, if taken literally. But one such as yourself… it would be a blasphemy!"

Harlequin spun his sword, advancing on Sage. "They say that demons creep in where angels fear to tread—I'm guessing angels will be staying well clear of L.A. from this point on. Don't you think?"

He gave a short, barking laugh, baring his inhuman teeth for emphasis.

"And what do you know of angels?" Sage said, with as much hauteur as he could manage. *If only he could make a break for the exit...*

"Enough to know that I must have that body. According to the Prophecy, one drop of angelic blood will restore my soul, set me free from this immortal prison." Harlequin's eyes burned with a feverish fire. "And in these technological times... just think what I could do with two drops!"

"But the Prophecy was intended to be fulfilled by a human, not a vampire!"

"I'm not speaking of the Prophecy. I am speaking of genetic manipulation, the creation of embryos combining two different species."

"I know what genetic manipulation is, *vampire*. But I am not a fool. The cost alone..."

"The cost is of no consequence. You forget my peerage." Harlequin licked his lips, gazing hungrily at Sage. "Just imagine—a melding of the vampiric and angelic bloodline, a race of superior beings who would combine the best of both of our races, with none of the defects. They would be perfect creatures—beautiful, powerful, impossible to kill. Best of all, they wouldn't need to drink blood in order to live." He shuddered. "Filthy creatures, vampires."

"But you're a vampire!"

"Exactly." Harlequin pulled back his hood with contempt, gesturing at his self-inflicted scarring. "I never said I liked it." He lifted the hood back into place, rubbing his hands together obsessively. "Soon I will be reborn, and I will live among my new children in a state of grace. If my calculations are correct, my new race would quickly replace Man as the dominant species on this Earth."

"*Pffft*. It'll never work."

"But if it does... all bets are off. And I'm guessing that my people will need a leader... the original progenitor of the new master race."

Harlequin struck a heroic pose, laying his sword over his shoulder.

Sage shook his head, wondering whether he should applaud such a speech or just run for his life. He eventually settled on, "You're quite mad, you know that?"

"Implicitly." Harlequin bowed his head. "But all genius comes at a price. I bear my cross of my own free will, just as you do. And the price will be the same for both of us—as a man in Galilee once said, our blood shall set our children free."

He raised his sword to strike, towering over the Hunter.

"There are no vampires in the Bible, you fool!" cried Sage. His eyes blazed with incandescent rage. As Harlequin's broadsword whizzed down toward his head, his hand shot out and caught the razor-sharp metal of the blade in his bare hand. He gave it a sharp, violent tug, wrenching it from the powerful vampire's grasp.

He flung the sword across the cathedral and then turned to Harlequin, his face set in an expression of savage intensity. "If you complete the Prophecy and you're wrong, you are condemning millions to a terrible and wrongful death, including the entirety of your own kind."

"And if I'm right?"

Sage held up his hand, completely unmarked from the sword. Green fire flickered in his eyes as he advanced on the master vampire.

"Then may God be with you."

The echo of his words seemed to linger in the air before dying away. Harlequin stiffened. A roar ran through the church, extinguishing every candle in its wake. Door after door slammed shut all around the vestry in a cacophony of noise. An instant later every cross in the Cathedral sparked to life, heating up and burning with a dull orange glow. Harlequin hissed as his giant broadsword began to melt in his hand. He dropped it quickly and glared at Sage.

Beneath them, the body of the dead priest ignited with a muted rush of imploding air and began burning with a greasy flame.

"Parlor tricks," Harlequin spat dismissively. He glanced up sharply as the golden cross on the front of the altar started glowing red hot, then white hot. The cross melted with a scream of super-heated air, dripping down the front of the altar. There was a series of scritching sounds as intricately carved symbols began to extract themselves from the smooth stone walls of the Cathedral, writhing like insects. A flame flickered among the drapes, casting shadows over his demonic visage.

"Just so you know, I gave up on God when he did *this* to me." Harlequin reached up a clawed hand to touch his own face. "The way I see it, he *owes* me an angel."

"But that's just it! Angels don't exist anymore!"

"Oh, but they *do* exist." Harlequin gave a ghastly little grin. "If enough people believe in them, they do."

"But—"

"Enough!"

Harlequin gave a contemptuous flick of his arm, knocking the older Hunter sprawling. Sage hit his head on the pulpit, sending his glasses flying. He staggered, clutching at the lectern as silence fell over the cathedral. The molten gold puddle on the altar began to cool.

Harlequin pulled himself up to his full height and reached out toward Sage, who shrank away from him.

"Tell me, Hunter. Are you a God-fearing man?"

Sage slowly pulled himself back to his feet. He turned to face the grinning master vampire, carefully straightening his tie as he took what he was sure would be one of his final breaths.

"It is human nature to fear what one does not understand," he said stiffly. "In that sense, I could be considered God-fearing."

Harlequin gazed at him, the light from the Annunciation window staining his demonic face a garish patchwork of color.

"Then allow me to rid you of your fear."

Before Sage could respond, Harlequin snapped out his hand. His razor-taloned fist punched through Sage's solar plexus and emerged from his back in a spray of torn flesh. The old Hunter jerked, blood spurting from his lips. He hung there a moment, impaled on Harlequin's spiny arm. With an inhumanly powerful yank, the vampire ripped his hand back out of the old Hunter's body.

The remains of Sage Griffiths' collapsed face down on the floor.

Harlequin nudged the body gently with his clawed foot. A two-foot-long section of the man's spine dangled from his fist, gleaming in the alabaster light. Clear spinal fluid dripped onto the floor, mingling with the oily blood of the burning priest.

Harlequin sighed, turning to gaze up at a nearby golden statue of Christ on the cross.

"So much for immortality," he said.

CHAPTER FIVE

It was close to midnight when Kayla finally emerged from the thumping, noisy depths of Club Fury, holding a small bag of ice to her bruised forehead and limping slightly. She stormed down the darkened back corridor and opened her steel work locker with a violent yank. She started stripping, muttering under her breath all the while.

Contrary to her expectations, the club had been fairly quiet tonight, the term "quiet" in this sense meaning slightly less noisy and seismically disruptive compared to, say, an earthquake. But to her relief she had escaped her shift relatively unscathed. Unlike last night, nobody had thrown ice at her, tried to molest her while she was carrying a fully-laden drinks tray through the tightly packed crowd, or—a particular favorite of the Club Fury patrons—poured a sticky glass of Jagermeister on her head from the safety of the second-level gantry. However, the Punk-Ska head-liner had chosen to break into an AC/DC cover for their second encore, and the resultant mosh pit had swallowed her whole for the best part of two verses. If it hadn't been for Larry the bouncer spotting the flashing lights on her tray and hauling her bodily out, she would have had more than a bump on the forehead to show for it.

Kayla began undressing, glancing sideways into the scratched and tarnished mirror on the concrete wall. She gave a deep sigh.

She didn't *deserve* to get treated like that, she thought, gazing at the tired, harassed stranger in the glass. The daily nine-hour stint behind the bar was doing wonders for her legs, but not much for the rest of her. The smoky atmosphere was starting to dull her long, chestnut hair, which hung in sad spirals down her back, and her usually tanned and rosy complexion was turning pale from the lack of sleep and light. If the werewolves didn't kill her, this double-shifting would probably do the job just as well.

So be it, then. At least she had her independence back.

She'd undressed down to her bra and jeans when a sharp buzzing from inside her locker drew her attention. Muttering darkly to herself, Kayla reached into a small black leather bag hanging inside her locker and pulled out a two-way CB radio.

She switched it on. "Hello?"

"Kayla?"

Kayla put a finger in her ear and turned away from the main door behind her, making sure she couldn't be overheard. "No, this is Domino's Pizza. Can I take your order?" She paused as the radio crackled ominously. "Course it's me. What's up?"

"What's *up*," said a clipped female voice, "is that I've been out here waiting on you for twenty minutes, which is nineteen minutes longer than you said you'd be. Would you like me to wait any longer, or should I send in an extraction team?"

"Hey, not my fault, okay?" Kayla grabbed her bag and began stuffing clothes into it. "There were two encores tonight and some jackass celebrity threw a bottle at me when I yelled at him for doing a naked backflip off the stage. And don't even get me started on what the third band did to the dressing rooms after their set. Took us twenty minutes to scrub all the raw meat out of the light fixtures, and I think their merchandise girl's gonna need therapy when she wakes up. *If* she wakes up. Believe me, I got out as quick as I could."

There was a dangerous pause.

The radio crackled. "I thought we agreed that if you were going to carry on this ridiculous charade of a job, you'd make an effort to be more punctual."

"Tell you what, next time I'll bleed more quickly, okay?"

As a comeback, it lacked a certain finesse, but by this time of night Kayla was too tired to care. She touched a finger to her forehead with a wince, then swapped the radio to her other hand as she hunted through her locker for her shoes, hopping on one foot as she pulled off the high-heeled monstrosities the club made her wear for her shift. "Gimme a break, boss. I'll be out in five."

"That's what you said last—"

Kayla clicked the radio off and hurled it into her bag with more violence than was strictly necessary. "And so my day begins," she muttered.

She stowed away her waitressing uniform, then pulled out a bag containing her *other* uniform—a jet-black cotton suit with buckle-up arm guards and bulletproof Kevlar panels across the chest and back. It had been tailor-made for her, and looked like a cross between a keikogi and a SWAT uniform. She hated it already. The collar was itchy and the nickel plating on the Kevlar vest gave her a rash, not to mention the whole thing was heavy as hell. But she pulled it on quickly, grumbling quietly to herself, then drew her jacket on over the top and slipped out into the night.

It was dark on Sunset Boulevard. Neon lights crackled and flashed spasmodically from the strip joint opposite, dimly illuminating a main road jammed with cars double- and triple-parked outside the clubs. The streets were alive with singing and laughter and shouting as an eclectic mix of clubbers, tourists, street performers, hookers, and cops wound their way home at the end—or for some, the beginning—of their night.

Kayla shivered as she hurried down the sidewalk, her eyes scanning the cars parked in the overflowing parking lot behind the club. The stench of dumpsters enveloped her as she cut quickly across the lot and made her way toward the main parking bay. The litter-strewn curbs were spray painted with band logo stencils and clogged with gangs of young girls and guys in their late teens and early twenties. They were all decked out in the latest of the latest Hollywood fashions of lace and leather and Nu-Grunge-style chains. They eyed each other from across the street as they waited for their rides, hurling abuse and the occasional beer bottle at passing cars.

Kayla jumped as a young teen crashed drunkenly across her path; his spiked, bleached hair and punk leather outfit made him look like the result of a strange breeding experiment between Billy Idol and Edward Scissorhands. He was filthy and unshaven in contrast to the sleek, well-scrubbed creatures of the night around him, and he had a bewildered, lost air about him, as though he'd just been dropped out of a spaceship and hadn't a clue what to do next.

He paused in his raucous carousing and gave Kayla a lecherous, if slightly confused, look before grabbing her hand and pressing it to his lips like an old lover.

"It's you," he said in wonder.

"Er, yeah. I was the last time I looked. Do I know you?"

Kayla tried to pull her hand away, but the boy held on tightly and leaned in close, pressing something cold and metallic into her palm.

"Be here on the seventh day, when the darkness comes. Or they'll take you too," he whispered, his breath a hot gust of marijuana smoke on her neck. He pulled away and blinked, giving her a look of total surprise and disgust before stumbling off into the darkness. Seconds later, she heard the sounds of him throwing up noisily in a corner.

Kayla stared after him in bemusement.

"Weirdo," she muttered, then opened her hand. A silver pentangle necklace glinted in her palm, strung on a hair-thin chain. It was warm to the touch, and seemed to glow slightly in the cool blue neon light from one of the neighboring clubs.

Kayla raised her eyebrows and turned the trinket over, tilting it into the light so she could see it more clearly.

There was an inscription on the back, written in elaborate flowing script.

"*Fiat Justitia, Ruat Coelum,*" Kayla read. "Huh."

Probably stolen, she thought. She should probably get rid of it immediately, but the thought of tossing such a beautiful necklace away was abhorrent to her. Perhaps she could flog it on eBay if she was short on spending money next month.

Whatever. She'd deal with it later.

She pocketed the trinket with a shrug, then jumped as a loud horn blasted behind her.

A big black SUV detached itself from the surging metal river of traffic behind her and pulled forward, its eight front-mounted chrome headlights blasting away the shadows of the night. It did a flashy turn and stopped a short distance from her, caught in the line of cars waiting to leave the parking lot. The driver's door swung open to reveal a striking woman in her early thirties, tall and athletic, with razor cut blonde-and-black streaked hair. She was dressed casually in a black wifebeater and dusty tan jeans, such as might be worn by any young woman heading out on the town for the night. But her commanding presence betrayed a wisdom and authority well beyond her years.

"Kayla!" she yelled.

A group of passing teenagers turned to stare at Kayla, then broke into giggles. Kayla shot a withering look at them before turning to make her way over to the SUV. Tossing her bag through the open back window, she popped the lock on the passenger side and climbed in.

"Ninette. Do you *want* me to have no life?" she demanded.

Ninette shushed her, listening intently to her radio headset. "Close that door."

Kayla did as she was instructed, feeling faintly foolish, and sat back in the cool leather of the front seat. Around her, the familiar interior of the Hunter's vehicle flashed and beeped with more lights and control panels than most passenger jets had in their cockpits. Jury-rigged wires snaked their way across the ceiling, connecting the boot-legged military satellite guidance system to the high-tech tracking console before vanishing behind the neatly welded bulletproof cladding that lined the seating compartment.

Kayla noticed a dog-eared handbook lying open across the futuristic dashboard, entitled *SAS Core Survival Training Tactics*. A newer one beneath it was *The Blind Watchmaker* by Richard Dawkins.

Kayla picked the book up in curiosity and began flicking through it as three teenage girls passed in front of the vehicle, banging on the hood in a derisory fashion and trying to peer in through the mirrored glass. She saw Ninette's hand unconsciously go to the hunting knife clipped to her belt. Kayla shook her head in amusement and her eyes fell back to the book. She read the same sentence three times before giving up and dropping it back onto the seat, thinking longingly of her warm bed back at the Hunter base. She hoped that whatever this mission was, it would be over quickly so she could be home and tucked up under the blankets before the sun rose.

"So where's the fire?" she asked, rubbing her eyes. She still didn't see why she had to come along on these training missions, but the rules were the rules. It helped having an evening job so she could sleep through the morning, but already, the punishing schedule was wearing on her.

In reply, Ninette handed her a clear plastic earpiece with tiny blue lights that winked and flashed in the darkness. Her hazel eyes sparkled with mischief.

"Listen," she said, pressing a finger to the headset in her own ear.

Kayla was confused. She'd expected anger, perhaps even a reprimand for her surly behavior, but her team leader's excitement was contagious. She quickly clipped the earpiece on and listened, scowling up at Ninette in suspicion.

A man's voice crackled up from the headset, his Canadian accent apparent even through the tinny radio speakers. His words as clipped and concise as Ninette's but with a richly sardonic undertone, as though he were reading from a script that he didn't quite believe and found rather amusing.

"...said he paid him to dispose of it, not to think about it. The price was set at sixty-eight million dollars, half delivered on word of retrieval, half upon delivery. Guess they don't trust the good old U.S. Postal Service anymore." There was a snort of laughter, quickly smothered. "Anyways, I'm guessing they don't have a full lockdown on the main hospital yet, so me and the guys are heading over there to secure the body before Crawley and his boys in blue start tearing up the place. Kind of money that's involved, I'm thinking we better move fast. Whaddaya think, Ni?"

"I think you should get your ass in there before the Feds beat you to it, Phil," replied Ninette. "We don't want a repeat of last July. If our friend Feathers reanimates anywhere in public and chows down on some civvies 'fore we get to him, it could be bad. As in, Biblical bad. Know what I'm sayin'?"

"Oh shoot, girl, you know I'm on it. Have I ever let you down before?"

There was a long pause.

"Just be careful. You hear me?" said Ninette quietly.

Phil laughed heartily. "I'll bring an extra bullet, if that makes you happy. Oh shit, here come the cops."

The radio emitted a high-pitched squeal and clattered around before cutting to static. Ninette glared at it. "Dammit, Phil!"

Removing her earpiece, she turned to Kayla, sweeping her with an appraising look. "So," she said, the word more a challenge than a question. "You ready for this?"

"For what?"

Ninette put the big car in gear and headed for the exit. "Watch the news today?"

Kayla stared at Ninette. She shook her head, firmly folding her arms across her chest. "Nu-uh. No way. You don't expect me to believe..."

"I don't expect you to believe anything. You're a civilian. I expect you to load this while I drive." Ninette pulled a .44 semiautomatic out from between the seats and tossed it into Kayla's lap along with a box of ammo.

"Oh, and Kayla?"

"Yes?"

Ninette allowed herself one of her rare grins. "You're not allergic to religion by any chance, are you?"

TWELVE BLOCKS AWAY, Deputy Sheriff John Timmerman lay back on the cheap, musty bedspread of the Sunset Motel and gazed up with rapt attention, a look of wonder on his scarred, forty-something face. Across the room, a svelte young woman with pure white hair lifted her red satin club top over her head and let it drop to the carpet, taking her time about it.

Her name was Dana, and she was on a mission.

Turning to face the off-duty cop, she gave him a coy Mona Lisa smile, watching his bloodshot eyes rove greedily over her petite, naked body. She fought down a shudder of disgust, trying to concentrate on the job at hand. She knew she looked incredible, and one glance in the cracked mirror above the sink only confirmed it. She was clad only in a black lace thong with her stockings and garter belt. A diamond ring sparkled on a slender steel belly-chain. Her smooth, pristine skin was white as bone save the pink-and-black tattoos that flowed in graceful waves across her flanks and down her well-toned legs. She would have been beautiful had it not been for the look in her ice-blue eyes, the cold, calculating stare that drained her youthful warmth and could freeze a would-be suitor at ten paces.

But the cop wasn't looking at her face, so to hell with him.

Dana had left her strappy high heels on as an afterthought. They clicked lightly as she made her way coyly over the kitchen tiles to the tiny mini-bar. There was a crucifix on the wall above it. She glowered at it for a moment before grabbing a stained washcloth and dropping it unceremoniously over the figurine's head. She opened the fridge and searched through the bottles inside.

"Beer or wine, baby?"

"Beer," said Doll promptly, lifting her head from the cop's lap for a moment to wink at Dana. The two girls exchanged a knowing look, then Doll stretched lazily and slipped off the edge of the bed, leaving the cop lying among the coverlets. She padded over to the window to gaze out at the moonlit urban sprawl of L.A., a pensive look on her ruined face, completely unashamed of her nakedness.

Dana watched her out of the corner of her eye, and then looked away with a shudder. Doll's body was a polar opposite of Dana's, a study in tormented femininity. The once-graceful curves of her body had now thinned to the point of emaciation, not from some fancy Hollywood diet, but from old-fashioned hunger. She'd been working this job much longer than Dana, and it showed. Her left forearm was bruised and crisscrossed with track marks. A row of piercings ran up the side of one ear, and a silver ring gleamed in her right nipple. A curtain of dark hair hid the worst of her facial scarring and for once Dana was glad of it, although she knew the cop was the kind of guy who didn't care much about appearances. The dramatic scars that ruined one side of Doll's angelic face extended down her neck, slashes of white standing out against her lightly-tanned skin with an almost terrible beauty. The sight of it made Dana shiver.

She still couldn't believe that Doll had done all that to herself, but then, she hadn't survived this long in the City of Angels by asking questions.

Dana counted to five, waiting for the deputy to snap out of his post-coital stupor and raise his head to watch them. She stepped up behind Doll, ran her hand up her bare ribcage and over the full swell of her breasts, lingering.

She heard the cop grunt in approval and grinned to herself as Doll turned to face her, taking her hands as she gazed raptly into her eyes, biting her lip in an unspoken question. Doll winked at her, a hint of mischief spicing her pierced lips. She took the beer from Dana and took a swig, then leaned forward and brushed her mouth softly over Dana's, kissing her full, plump lower lip before taking it gently between her teeth and nipping it lightly. Then she deepened the kiss. Doll tasted of beer and sex and cigarette smoke. Dana chuckled to herself as she felt Doll's long-nailed hand run over her own naked shoulders before grasping the back of her neck and pulling her closer, returning her kiss with an enthusiasm that brought a soft groan to her throat.

Dana heard a gasp from the cop, and broke the kiss for a moment to allow herself a tiny, mocking smile. This was almost too easy. Getting the information they needed out of this guy would take about—she glanced at her tiny gold watch—four minutes, call it five if they actually got round to drinking the champagne he'd ordered for them both, and then they would be out of here. Job well done, so to speak.

She leaned back and gazed into Doll's eyes, nodding slightly. Stepping away from her, she turned around to direct a soulful gaze back at the cop, one hand on the open door of the fridge.

"Beer good for you too, kitten?"

The cop nodded wordlessly, staring at the two of them as though still unable to believe his luck. Dana shook her head in disgust before turning back to the minibar. Opening the door, she removed a freezer bag from the lower shelf, unzipped it, and pulled an ugly black Russian pistol out of the bag.

Flipping off the safety, she turned around and leveled the gun at the cop's head with a sweet smile. She heard a neighboring click behind her as Doll primed her own gun to back her up.

The cop froze, his face paling in sudden sick horror as he stared at the two naked, beautiful women pointing guns at him.

However he'd seen this night turning out, it certainly hadn't been like this.

"The body," said Dana crisply, dropping her bedside manner like a hot coal. "Where is it?"

"The what? I don't know what you're—hey, whoa, whoa, lady!" The cop cringed away as Dana pulled back the hammer on the modified gang pistol.

"You were on the search and recovery team that *reacquired* the body from its original finders," said Dana, her manner brisk and professional. Contempt curled her lip as she stepped toward the bed, pinning the cop in her sights. "And I use that word very loosely. You've got one chance to stop the worms from *reacquiring* your body. I suggest you take it."

"And if I don't?"

Dana jerked her chin back at Doll. "Show him."

There was a rustle from behind her. A small, dripping cloth bag sailed past her and landed on the bed. There was a strangely shaped lump inside the bag, about the size of a football. The cop stared down at the blood soaking onto the mattress, and suddenly grew very still.

"Say hello to the last cop who preferred not to help with my inquiries."

The cop swallowed a couple of times, his eyes flitting nervously over her shoulder.

Then he started to laugh.

Dana tightened her grip on her gun, glancing quickly at Doll as the deputy pushed himself up on the pillows, hooting like a madman. Merriment danced in his eyes as he winked at Dana.

"Round of applause, precious."

Dana blinked a bead of sweat out of her eyes. "For what?"

"For makin' me a very rich man."

Dana stared at him, then jumped as something sharp embedded itself in the back of her neck. She yelped in pain and surprise, convulsively pulling the trigger.

Nothing happened. The gun was empty.

Growling, Dana slapped a hand on her neck. Her questing fingers closed on the shape of a twin-tailed glass dart. She pulled it out with a wince, squinting at it fiercely as her vision started to blur. She could just make out a drop of green liquid sparkling on its needle tip.

She spun back to Doll, accusation flaring in her eyes.

"What the hell have you—?"

Dana broke off with a gasp. Her vision flared red and the ground spun sideways before coming up to smack her in the head.

Hard.

Dana was dimly aware of Doll stepping over her prone body to free the cop. She lost all awareness of her surroundings as the world around her erupted in a burst of mind-splittingly bright colors and light. And then all she could feel was pain.

Dana clapped her hands to her head and curled into a tight ball, shrieking in horror as she felt her skull elongate, the plates in her head slipping over one another with a tectonic relentlessness that she knew she was powerless to stop. Her spine bowed and cracked and she felt her body change, power thrumming through her as her muscles expanded, wrapping themselves around her bones in a series of agonizing pops before settling into a new configuration.

She threw back her head and howled as hooked claws burst out of her fingertips and her naked body coated itself in a fine white fur. Her belly chain snapped and flew off as her ribs expanded. Something cold and sharp closed around her ankles and she spun around mindlessly, snapping jaws that suddenly held a set of inhumanly pointed teeth. She heard a voice cry out in alarm, then a club connected solidly with the back of her head.

She flopped to the floor, yowling in stunned fury.

Deputy Timmerman slid off the bed, tottering slightly. He reached for his pants as he stared down at the bizarre tableau in front of him. He watched Doll heft her baseball bat and move to stand over the kicking, struggling white wolf that just a moment ago had been a very attractive young lady.

He shook his head, stretching a shaking hand toward the bedside table for his pack of smokes. He'd headed this investigation for so long that even he had started to doubt the veracity of the reports.

But finally, he had his proof: he'd just caught himself a real live werewolf.

"Well," he said, lighting a cigarette and inhaling deeply. "*There's* something you don't see every day."

CHAPTER SIX

KAYLA WATCHED NINETTE carefully as her team leader guided the big Hunter SUV out of the parking lot of Club Fury and headed off down Sunset Boulevard, weaving effortlessly in and out of the traffic. She'd been the butt of numerous jokes during her single, short month working with the Hunters, but just because she was new didn't mean that she was stupid.

Or so she hoped.

"So run that whole thing by me again," she said, checking the newly-loaded clip in the semiautomatic. "The angel..."

"Is real, yes," said Ninette. She glanced in her rearview mirror and watched the cars behind her intently for a couple of seconds, as though they might be somehow listening.

Kayla stared blankly at Ninette, waiting for the knowing smile, the roll of the eyes that would indicate she was pulling her leg. But her team leader remained impassive, flicking restlessly through the channels on her dash-mounted CB radio.

Kayla sighed, idly drawing a smiley face on the foggy window. "Are you going to elaborate, or should I just go mad right now? I have pencils and everything."

Ninette gave her a blank look.

"*Blackadder*? British TV show from Comedy Central? The bit where he tried to avoid being sent to the front line in the war by sticking pencils up his nose and pretending to be mad?"

No reply.

Kayla pursed her lips, drumming her fingers on the dashboard. "You know, it wouldn't hurt for you to turn on the TV once in a while. Then we could have, you know, a conversation."

"We're having a conversation. You're talking, and I'm waiting for you to stop talking so I can tell you something important."

"What's more important than TV?"

"And that's precisely why I said you shouldn't be enrolled in the Hunters in the first place!" Ninette burst out, obviously continuing some kind of argument she'd recently been having with someone else.

Ignoring Kayla's strange look, she swung round in her seat to close the windows, then whipped off her sunglasses. "You think this is all a game? Some kind of imposition you have to put up with till we all go away and stop being silly and let you get back to your real life? Hate to burst your happy little bubble, Kayla, but life as you knew it is over. *This* is your life now, so you'd better get used to it.

Unless you want to wind up as an entrée for a werewolf, that is."

"What if I don't want it to be my life?" said Kayla quietly, turning over the loaded gun in her hands.

"Do you *want* to live to see your twenty-fifth birthday?"

Kayla shrugged indifferently.

"I know you don't mean that," said Ninette softly. "I swear, you and Karrel both…" She shook her head as if to dislodge an unpleasant memory. "Listen to me. I don't *like* having to play nanny and drag a civilian around with me, just because the guys at HQ think you might just be trainable. But you're the only lead we got on the Harlequin case, so for now, we'll both have to put up with it."

Kayla started to speak, but Ninette shushed her with a hand. "However, this work thing… you being late all the time, wandering around by yourself… those creeps who killed your boyfriend… do you have any concept of what they could do to you if they caught you? It would make what they did to Karrel look like a picnic."

Kayla slammed the box of ammo shut in frustration. "That's what I keep saying! Why don't we go out and find them right now, 'stead of messing around with all this angel crap?"

"Because this angel crap could get a lot more people dead, Kayla. As in hundreds, maybe thousands. And don't look at me like that. I know what I'm talking about. We need to contain it right away, which means we move tonight."

"Great." Kayla stifled a yawn. "What do we have to do?"

"Firstly, we need to find out who killed that angel. Then, we'll recover the body and destroy it before the Seekers come looking for it."

"Oh, so another easy mission, then," Kayla said, frowning. "What are Seekers?"

"Avenging angels. They haven't been seen since Biblical times, but we know they still exist. Seekers are from the seventh order of angels, one down from the Hierarchy of the Militants. They're the rarest kind of angel, and they have a very specific job to do."

"Which is?" asked Kayla, writing the words "Crazy Lady!" beneath her smiley-face doodle on the window and drawing an arrow pointing toward her team leader.

She rubbed it out quickly.

"Every seventh day, all the angels are counted. It's traditional. If one is missing, the Seekers are sent to Earth to find it. And believe me, we really, really don't want that to happen. They're nasty motherfuckers, worse than angels. They don't have souls, unlike us humans, and no sense of compassion, or pity, or conscience—hey, get outta the road, asshole!" Ninette cut the wheel to the left, swerving to avoid a homeless man who had gotten one side of his wheelchair stuck in a drain in the middle of the road. "Jeeze. Can you believe some people?"

"So what's the deal with this dead angel?" said Kayla, trying to change the subject.

Ninette turned back to Kayla, fixing her with an appraising stare.

"You'll be briefed properly when we get back to base, but for now, all you need to know is that you don't want to know. Forget the fluffy-winged, blue-eyed pictures you've seen of angels. They're all wrong. If you had any idea of what a true angel was, you'd be out of this car so quick we wouldn't see you for smoke."

Kayla laughed heartily, shaking her head in amusement. Her laughter faded somewhat as she saw the look on her team leader's face.

"You're really taking this all seriously," she said.

"More than you could ever imagine."

Ninette turned across a red light, ignoring the honking of horns all around her. She flashed Kayla a dark look. "You think you know the world, Kayla, but you don't. What you've seen so far is nothing, the PG trailers before the Tarrantino film. And if you don't learn to follow procedure, you'll wind up getting us both killed."

Kayla gave a snort of derision, but something inside her grew cold at Ninette's words. Her voice was flat and hard and it held the unmistakable ring of truth, even to her skeptical ears. She didn't like being talked to in this way, like she was a child.

But she also wasn't stupid.

"So what happens if we don't find the body?"

Ninette gave her a chilling look as she flicked on her turn signal and headed downtown.

"Does the word 'Armageddon' mean anything to you?" she replied.

BACK IN THE motel room, Doll flashed the cop a meaningful look as she fished in her bag for a second set of restraints. Despite the ever-changing

daily challenges of her profession, it wasn't every
day she had to tie up a werewolf, and the job was
already proving to be a little more difficult that
she'd thought it would be. The wasted muscles in
her arms shook as she hauled the heavy creature
around and began securing its front paws to the
iron bedstead. She'd had to go to three different
zoo sites on eBay before she'd found manacles that
were thick enough. These were lion chains, used in
the veterinary treatment of large cats. She only
hoped they'd be strong enough.

Finishing the job, she stepped back and regarded the fallen figure of Dana with a certain
amount of regret. Since they'd met three months
ago she'd found she had a lot of affection for her
new work partner, even though their meeting had
been a setup, a ruse to blow her cover and reveal
her true werewolf nature.

But on some level, she couldn't help feeling
sorry for the girl. She knew what it was like to
have people think you were a monster.

She jumped back as Dana snarled up at her.
The white werewolf jerked sharply on her chains,
a disturbingly human look of accusation in her
blue wolfeyes.

"You sure you wanna go through with this?"

"What, and lose all that lovely money? You
crazy?"

The deputy reached into his bag and pulled out
a fistful of crumpled documents, printed on
LAPD paper. His dark eyes gleamed with greed as
he scanned through them. "Says here the force
will pay twenty grand for conclusive proof of the
existence of werewolves. This shit's top secret.

Only the top Ops get to play. I signed twelve different bits of paper before I even got to read this."

"Great." Doll moved back as the leg of the iron bedstead started to bend alarmingly. She glanced back at the deputy with a shiver.

"Those chains won't hold her long. You bring the tranq darts?"

"Of course."

"And you'll give me…?"

"Fifteen percent. As promised."

"Make it fifty."

"Or what?"

Doll calmly lifted her gun and aimed it at the deputy's chest.

"And I thought you were helping me out of the goodness of yer heart." The deputy shook his head slowly, looking Doll up and down with undisguised contempt. "Whatcha gonna do, lady—shoot a cop, then walk to the nearest police station carrying a two-hundred-pound dog and tell them you've come to prove the existence of werewolves?" He gave a laugh that was as short and nasty as he was. "Don't waste my time, precious. Let's bag this bitch and make a move."

Doll didn't lower her pistol. "I've told you my terms."

"And I've told you mine."

The deputy's stubble-roughened face creased into a leer. He reached down to unbuckle his pants. He let them drop to the floor with a clink, and looked up to check Doll's reaction. "How 'bout we strike a deal here, princess," he said, smirking. "I've done my job… now you do yours.

Then I'll up your cut to twenty percent." He folded his arms triumphantly. "It's my final offer,
take it or leave it. An' that's cheap, for spoiled
goods like you."

Doll stared at the cop in disgust, her hand
unconsciously creeping up to touch the scarring on
her face. Her jaw clenched and her knuckles
whitened on the trigger.

The deputy dove to the side with a yell as Doll's
gun went off, horrifically loud in the tiny room.
Timmerman watched in horror as Doll squeezed
off two more fast shots to sever the links in Dana's
restraints. They flew apart with a tinkle of
rebounding metal. Doll grabbed her leather jacket
and stormed out before the echoes of the gunshots
had faded, slamming the door behind her.

The deputy's expression froze as the deadlocks
clunked into place, sealing him in the motel room
with the werewolf. He slowly turned in the
suddenly-claustrophobic atmosphere, his heart
hammering in his throat.

The huge, snow-white creature was already on
its feet, staring up at him in terrifying silence. Its
lips curved back, exposing inch-long teeth.

Twenty years of boozed-out police service
flashed before his eyes. He didn't think about his
friends, his family, or his two young children currently being raised by his third ex-wife on a
low-budget housing estate somewhere south of
Kansas.

Instead, he wondered briefly if there was an
afterlife, and if so, whether it contained beer of
any kind.

"Um... good doggy?" he tried.

As last words, the hotel room had heard far worse.

His scream pierced the night as Dana launched herself at him, teeth bared, claws extended. The deputy might have made it all the way around the bed to grab his service revolver if his pants hadn't been caught around his ankles, effectively hobbling him.

There was a brief struggle, a sudden wet crunch, then a ringing silence.

Ten seconds later, Dana's head jerked up from the deputy's twitching carcass, her bloodstained white muzzle a bright, crimson red. She stared hard at the door, her furry brow wrinkling with the unaccustomed effort of thought. Her eyes narrowed and she sniffed sharply, once, a wrathful growl rising in her throat as she caught the scent of the one who had betrayed her.

Her claws scrabbled on the floor and she leaped through the window, crashing through it in a spray of glass, hot on the trail of Doll.

Dana disappeared into the night, leaving the body of the dead cop—and the LAPD papers—in the room behind her.

CHAPTER SEVEN

"Psst... wanna see something really freaky?"

Doctor Mia Bexley glanced up in irritation as her assistant burst into the clinically-sealed examining room of St James's Medical Center, his face glowing with excitement. Mia's scalpel paused over the left heart ventricle of the dead teenager beneath her and she let out a long-suffering sigh. It was only two o'clock in the afternoon and she was already up to her elbows in it, quite literally.

Working as a forensic pathologist in the greater Los Angeles area, there was *always* something freaky to see. If it wasn't Beverly Hills kids offing themselves with their parents' badly-hidden coke stashes, it was bondage couples mistakenly strangling their partners, weird-ass religious suicide pacts covered up with faked automobile accidents, or gang-versus-cop shootouts that had her pulling slugs out of civilians for days in a vain attempt to

ID the bullets and work out which police department to sue. She was just an intern, but already the hospital was heaping work on her in abundance, assigning her the shifts of her fellow interns as the less patient and strong-of-stomach dropped out by the dozen.

At the rate things were going, it would be at least midnight before she wrapped up her last autopsy of the day. But something in her assistant's manner made her pause. She regarded him shrewdly over the top of her rimless glasses.

"John. I already told you," she sighed, putting down her scalpel and wiping her gloved hands on a paper towel. "Yes, it *is* normal and it *does* happen to most men. You don't need a forensic pathologist to tell you that."

"How would you know?" said John. "You never leave this lab."

"I do too!"

"So when was the last time?"

"Monday. I went out for a sandwich."

"A whole sandwich?" John pretended to stagger in amazement. "What kind was it?"

"Veggie. Or so I thought." Mia picked at the hem of her hospital gown. "But then I found turkey in it too. I threw it out."

"God, not turkey!" John clutched his heart. "Honestly, Mi. I don't know how you stand such excitement."

"I don't," said Mia firmly, turning back to her work. "I leave the excitement for other people. My job is in here, which is where I'm staying."

John pushed his glasses back up his nose, regarding his co-worker with impatience. Mia's short blonde hair was tied up in a neat bob covered with a light blue hairnet, revealing a pretty, pixie face with soft features and kind brown eyes. Her white surgical gown was a painful contrast to the blood-ied, battered form of the dead teenager on the table before her, his ribs held open with giant metal clips and half his innards in steel bowls beside him. It was a tribute to Mia's almost pathological neatness that she didn't have a drop of blood on her. Her pristine gown seemed to glow in the clinically clean room, and for some reason, John found that a huge turn on.

But then, he was twenty-four. He found *linoleum* a huge turn on.

"C'mon, Mi," he wheedled, dropping his gaze to the long, tanned legs that emerged from beneath Mia's mid-length hospital skirt. "Five minutes. You won't regret it."

"You know I always do, with you."

That made John smile. He glanced behind him again, checking that they weren't being watched. Then he stepped up behind Mia and began gently tugging open the strings on her hospital apron. He heard her intake of breath as he ghosted his lips over her smooth, tanned shoulder, and then cheek-ily ran his tongue up the back of her neck.

"Knock it off, John." Mia swatted ineffectually at him with the roll of paper towels. "You know what'll happen if someone catches us."

"Yeah, your daddy's lawyer will beat the crap out of my lawyer. Same old. Big deal."

Ignoring her half-hearted protests, John buried his face in Mia's hair. He breathed in deeply as he slid his arms around her waist, pulling her tightly against him. He'd been working under Dr. Bexley for almost five months now, but not in the way he'd anticipated. Mia's hardworking, pure-as-the-driven-snow attitude had been a turn on at first, but now it was beginning to get on his nerves.

It wasn't what she did that bothered him so much, it was her *attitude*. Mia was the kind of girl who you knew just by looking at her that she had at least one shelf full of stuffed animals in her bedroom, and that they all had names. In all the time John had known her, he'd never once heard her swear, preferring to say things like "Dang!" and "Jeeze Louise!" when she lost her temper. Which she very rarely did.

If he hadn't known her better, he could have sworn she wasn't human.

"Spare us the high-and-mighty, sugar pie," he whispered, kissing her ear as he reached up to try and cup her breasts. "If God had meant us to be monogamous, he would've given the dicks to the women."

"And the brains to the men," Mia finished, shaking her head at their well-worn exchange. She awkwardly patted his arm before breaking his hold on her with a remarkably powerful snap of her wrists. She turned around and quickly folded her arms, holding him at bay with a warning flash of her brown eyes. "And speaking of brains, I'm curious. Do the words 'bomb threat' mean anything to you?"

"About as much as it does to you, apparently."

John held her gaze, fighting down his howling libido, then winked at her and strolled across the room in a display of calculated indifference. Lifting the blind, he glanced out the window.

Down below, dozens of police cars were parked haphazardly on the manicured hospital lawns. Uniformed officers swarmed around the ambulance parking bays like ants, redirecting traffic and sealing the exits.

John looked back at Mia, his boyish good looks lifting in an expression of curiosity. "And you're still here because...?"

"I've got work to do," said Mia, a trifle defensively. "If I ran out of the building screaming every time some idiot phoned in a bomb threat, I'd never get anything done. You?"

"I was having a nap in the CAT-scanner when they evacuated the hospital. Forty-two hour shift'll do that to you." John let the shutter go with a snap and yawned heartily, stretching his burly arms over his head. "Bomb threat, fire drill, attack of the Flying Spaghetti Monster... it's all the same. Just another way to get us all out of the building so the cops can raid our lockers for dope."

"So why are you still here?"

There was the slightest hesitation before John replied. "Raiding people's lockers for dope." He grinned disarmingly. "And you'll never believe what I found."

He winked at her and nodded toward the door.

Mia rolled her eyes, counting to ten.

She threw a cloth over the dead teen on the slab and pulled off her hairnet, shaking out her hair. "Okay, fine. You've got five minutes, O'Connell. This had better be good."

* * *

IT WAS EERILY quiet upstairs without the constant background noise of patients and nurses scurrying back and forth across the hallway. Mia fought down the urge to glance constantly over her shoulder as she followed John toward the Medi-Bay, where unusual cases were sometimes brought for study, depending on how much budget the hospital had left to run the machines that month.

Usually, the door was locked and the lights were off. Today, it was brightly lit.

"Wait," said John, as Mia put her hand on the door handle. "Take this."

He handed her a clipboard.

Mia took it and peered down at it with intense curiosity. She glanced up at John. "There's nothing on it. These charts are empty."

"I know," said John, with an impish grin. "But *they* don't know that." He nodded through the checkered glass window. Mia followed his gaze and saw three police officers standing outside the door to the main lab. One of them was drinking a Styrofoam cup of coffee. Another—a woman— had her ear pressed up against the door.

Mia nodded, getting his meaning instantly.

"Gotcha."

Every intern knew about the Clipboard Ruse. There were three kinds of invisible people in this city: homeless people, environmental street-team fundraisers, and people carrying clipboards. People very deliberately did not see the first two kinds, and the third kind was only there because they had been called in to fix or check something.

Fighting down her professional misgivings, Mia tucked the clipboard under her arm, jacked up her best professional smile, and followed John through the door.

IT WAS COLD inside the big lab. The air was tinged with the smell of antiseptic and cleaning fluid.

Mia let out the breath she hadn't been aware that she'd been holding, and turned to John, trying to hide the fact that she was impressed. "You bullshit artist, you. We're not even supposed to be in the building. How do you do it?"

"Years of practice," John breezed, running his lips over her shoulder. "Besides, if they really thought there was a bomb, why would they leave three cops in the building?"

"You have a point."

"I tell you. 'Bomb-threat' my ass. It's all about the dope. Here, hold this."

Shrugging off his lab coat, John removed an aerosol can of sanitizer from his pocket. He stood on tiptoe to mist the lens of the security camera above the door.

"What?" he said, catching Mia's look. "Don't tell me you've never gone out of bounds before?"

"Only with you," said Mia, but she was smiling as she said it. "Come on, Trouble. Show me whatever it is you want to show me, and then let's split."

"I'll show ya something, all right." John grinned and brushed his hand suggestively across Mia's belt buckle. He licked his lips and fixed his fellow intern with a boldly appreciative stare. "But first..."

He waved at her to follow him across the lab. He stopped in front of a large, covered slab at the back of the room. With a flourish, he slipped off the green plastic cloth, revealing a large, steel freezer case. The case was the size of four coffins stacked two abreast, and had a complicated series of inter-locking clasps on the joined lid.

John ran his hands over it, melting patterns in the thin coating of ice with his warm fingertips before popping the locks at the top and sides.

"Ready for this?"

"Just get on with it."

Mia tapped her fingers impatiently as John care-fully rolled the two sides of the casket down. It was already coming up to quarter-after four, which meant that her lunch break would be down the tubes unless she got those plasma samples from the Sepulveda hit-and-run case off to the UCLA pro-cessing lab before five. The shipping depot was just a short walk from her lab, which meant that even if it was unmanned from the bomb threat, she could still have the samples in the mail and be back to start on the League Club poisoning case before...

Mia's brain froze, her hand still on her watch as the two sides of the case hit the ground.

"Oh, sweet Jesus!" she said.

CHAPTER EIGHT

"SO... THESE ANGELS," said Kayla, feigning interest as she tried to keep the sarcasm out of her voice. "Where did they come from, then?"

Ninette changed gears, smoothly overtaking a white pickup truck as they cruised down Melrose Avenue. "How much do you know about angels?" she asked.

"Nothing. Because they don't exist."

"Like you used to think werewolves and vampires didn't exist?"

"That's different!"

"How is it different?"

"Because they..." Kayla floundered. "They're *in* the world. They're real things you can touch, with genes and bones and teeth and everything. They evolved, alongside humanity. They're just evolutionary dead ends, freaks of nature. Vampirism is caused by a virus, so I'm told, and werewolves... I still don't know how that shit works. And yes, I *know* you explained it to me three times, but I can't even pronounce lupo... magnobiology, let alone understand it. But I know there's nothing *outside* the world, outside physics. Nothing supernatural. It can't be. Or else..."

"Or else what?"

"Or else everything I've been brought up to believe about the world isn't true."

There was the slightest pause before Ninette spoke. "So when you said you saw Karrel's ghost, that wasn't true either?"

Kayla hesitated, glaring at her team leader.

As she opened her mouth to reply, an almighty crunch came from the white Toyota pickup truck in front of them. Ninette reacted immediately, twisting the wheel and hitting the gas to hop the big SUV up onto the sidewalk. She slammed on her brakes to bring their car to a shuddering, controlled halt. The Toyota ahead fared less well, slewing wildly to the side before noisily embedding itself into the side of a car in the next lane. Kayla had no time to prepare as a pale, barefoot young woman clad only in a long suede jacket darted out from in front of the truck. She fled desperately across into the opposite lane, making cars skid and veer to avoid her as she headed for the safety of the opposite sidewalk.

A speeding yellow taxicab swerved around the stopped cars and screamed at full speed toward the woman as she started to cross the empty fourth lane of the boulevard. By the time the driver saw the woman, it was too late for him to stop. Kayla's heart leaped into her mouth as she realized the cab was going to hit her.

But at the very last instant…

Kayla blinked. She reached up to rub her eyes. She could have sworn the front of the taxicab *melted* as it hit the woman. It couldn't have done that, though, because it was impossible. Nor could a line of bubbling blue fire have streaked down its center, parting the cab like the Red Sea around her. That was impossible too. Kayla watched as the two sides of the taxi passed safely on either side of the mysterious woman before rejoining with a snap and a sizzle on the other end, leaving behind a faint cloud of blue smoke.

The cab swerved sharply before vanishing into the night. Horns honked as the woman hopped onto the opposite sidewalk, completely unharmed, knocking over a loaded trash can before disappearing down a darkened alley.

Kayla stared at the spot where the woman had vanished, then obediently turned to look up at Ninette. Her team leader said nothing for a moment. She hit a button to lower her window, and sniffed delicately at the air.

"Ozone," she muttered, and sniffed again. "Sulfur… definite trace of plasma… oh, that's not good."

"Not good?" Kayla gripped the dash in front of her. "Of course it's not good! I just saw a half-naked woman run straight through a taxicab! What the *hell* was that all about?"

"I mentioned the whole 'Armageddon' thing, didn't I?" murmured Ninette, staring fixedly up at the sky.

"Okay, that does it." Kayla turned around, hunting around in her bag. "Where are my pencils? I'm sure they're—*HEY!*"

Their SUV rocked suddenly to the side as something large and heavy smacked into it at high speed. Kayla screamed and ducked down in her seat as the passenger window thumped inwards, dissolving into a maze of cracks and showering her with glass. She thought they'd been hit by another car, until she heard the shriek of claws on metal. She saw an enormous furry *something* scrabble its way onto the hood of their stopped vehicle, leaving in its wake a trail of dark blood. Kayla ducked down in her seat as the creature used the hood as a springboard to launch itself onto the roof of the crashed Toyota next to them, then leaped down the other side and barreled straight across the road toward the alley, chasing after the woman.

Kayla's jaw dropped. It was a werewolf.

"Shoot it!" yelled Ninette.

"What?"

Ninette grabbed the loaded gun out of Kayla's hands with a growl of her own and fired three shots across the road at the back of the retreating wolf. Kayla saw the first shot strike the creature square in the back of the head, but the impact merely slowed it down for a second before it picked up speed again.

"Shit! Right out in the fucking open!

Ninette tore off her seatbelt and wrenched her door open. "*Stay*," she commanded. Handing Kayla the gun, she leaped out of the cab and pelted off across the three lanes of stopped traffic after the creature.

Kayla slowly slid back upright in her seat as the sound of Ninette's footsteps died away, every nerve screwed tight as a bowstring. Her pride smarted at being left behind. She poised her thumb over her own seatbelt release button, staring after her team leader in an agony of indecision. Ninette hadn't even stopped to pick up her own gun before going after the werewolf.

What was she thinking? She was going to get herself killed!

Kayla ripped her seatbelt off and frantically twisted around in her seat. She opened the armored lockup beneath the dashboard and hunted through it, trying to remember which box the silver bullets were kept in.

A scream rang out, then suddenly choked off.

Grabbing her half-loaded pistol, Kayla jumped out of the SUV and dodged her way across the road as horns honked and braked all around her.

She was half a block down the alley before the foolishness of her decision hit her. She skidded to a halt, blinking frantically as she tried to see in the darkness. Her heart started pounding, and a sick feeling of dread settled in her throat. If the werewolf had killed Ninette, the oldest and strongest member of their team, what chance did she stand? She was all alone in a dark alley with a werewolf and a half-loaded gun, and she hadn't even thought to bring a flashlight.

What had Ninette said about her getting them both killed?

Nice one, Kayla, she thought.

She froze as a growl sounded in the blackness, making the hairs stand up on the back of her neck. Kayla gasped as two reflective eyes snapped open and locked on hers.

CHAPTER NINE

KAYLA FUMBLED BACK the safety as the werewolf advanced on her, its eyes glowing blue in the darkness. The werewolf's growling increased in volume with every step it took. Kayla tried to stop her hands trembling as she aimed the muzzle square between the eyes of the big creature.

"Kayla! *Freeze!*"

Kayla hesitated, her finger on the trigger. Her eyes flicked to the right and saw a human shape hidden amongst the moonlit street clutter and brickwork. Highlights of the wall became muscled female limbs padded with black armor. The air seemed to blur as Ninette stepped soundlessly out into the alley, moving with all the stealth and grace of a lioness stalking jungle prey.

"If you move, you'll provoke it," she said in a bare whisper, her eyes never once leaving the giant beast.

"My gun..."

"Wrong caliber," replied Ninette, without moving her lips or even looking at the pistol. "That's the .22. You need at least a .45."

"Which means?"

"You're fucked."

Kayla closed her eyes, willing herself out of this nightmare predicament. When she opened them again Ninette was edging around behind the werewolf. The giant creature had fully emerged from the shadow, its white coat a beacon of light in the darkness. It either did not see or did not care about Ninette; its entire body was pointed at Kayla like a quivering canine arrow.

Kayla stared at it, transfixed. She'd only seen werewolves a couple of times before, and each time she'd been running at full speed in the opposite direction. She fought the overwhelming urge to flee. This one was small, as far as werewolves went, probably a female. Its head was blunt and wedge-shaped, its features a curious blend of canine and human, with intelligent eyes, a snub nose and over-long canine teeth on both top and bottom, which protruded from between its lips in either direction. The werewolf's scrubby white coat gave way to a thick ruff around its throat, which tapered on either side to form an S-shaped ridge of longer hair that ran down the center of its spine and peaked at the top of its head like a crest.

Long, wispy tufts of fur fringed its huge paws and feathered its ears, but any thoughts Kayla might have had about the creature being in any way cute or cuddly ended at that point. The werewolf's hind limbs possessed an extra joint and were larger and more developed than the forelimbs; both ended in a set of fearsome curved black claws that would put a velociraptor to shame. Blood was caked up the creature's front and around its muzzle. Human blood.

The werewolf gave a sharp bark and attacked. Kayla jerked up her gun and managed to fire two shots before the creature hit her, knocking her off her feet with the force of a speeding truck. Before she hit the ground she felt its teeth clamp down with appalling force on her armored throat, right at the hinged joint where it met the collar plate that protected her right shoulder.

It bit down hard and started to shake her.

Kayla, who had grown up watching action movies where the heroine was always saved in the nick of time, was extremely surprised by the fact that no one was coming to save her. She slammed her fist into the werewolf's furry flank several times, then gave up and tried to bring her gun to bear, but her gun arm was pinned beneath her. Kayla gasped in pain as the wolf whipped its head back and forth with immense strength, scraping her body over the filthy concrete. She felt the plates of her body armor buckle and bend under the intense pressure of the creature's bite.

Where the hell was Ninette?

As she felt her shoulder dislocate she prayed with everything that she had that someone, anyone, would come to save her. The stars above her spun in a mocking dance as she was jerked around, and she wondered dizzily why they were getting brighter, flooding the alley with a wash of yellow light.

A big, black vehicle rocketed up the alleyway in a blaze of headlights and hit the werewolf at full speed, sending it flying through the air. Kayla screamed as the creature's teeth were ripped from her shoulder. She rolled frantically to the side and curled up into a tight ball, screaming, expecting at any minute to feel the crushing pain of a tire running over her. Instead there was a loud whooshing noise, then a wet thud followed by a screech of brakes.

Kayla uncurled and rolled over, moving very, very carefully, in case any bits of her fell off. After making sure everything was still attached, she pulled herself up into a sitting position, her head buzzing with shock. She watched as the SUV rolled to a halt and the door flew open.

Ninette jumped out, drew a tranquilizer gun from the dark recesses of the cab, and aimed it at the prone werewolf. Even now, it was still struggling to rise. She approached it cautiously, a disgusted look on her face.

"I can't believe you just did that!" gasped Kayla.

"Did what?" said Ninette, giving the dazed creature a poke with the end of her gun, with complete disregard to her own personal safety. It snapped at her and she backed up a step, firing a dart into its neck at close quarters, then reloading. The creature lunged to its feet with a snarl, then yelped as one of its forelimbs buckled.

Kayla got to her feet on her second attempt and walked up behind Ninette, staring down at the felled werewolf. The creature seemed more shocked than hurt, but Ninette was taking no chances. She shook her head in disbelief. "You hit it with the car."

"So I did."

For the first time in her life, Kayla was completely speechless. She turned angry eyes on her team leader, who had pulled a handful of thick plastic ties from her pocket and was now clipping its feet together. "You could have killed me!"

"I could have just left you. In fact, I was going to, till I remembered you still had my gun. So I came back for it." She held out her hand for the gun.

"Jesus." Kayla's legs gave out, dumping her into the dust. She pulled gently at the mess of torn material at her throat. She could already feel the bruises burning with a slow heat beneath her collar.

Ninette straightened up and brushed herself off. "I'm sorry, Kayla. This can't go on. I'm going to have to suspend you from training."

"What!" Kayla gaped at her. "Why?"

"Why didn't you fight it?"

A dozen answers went through Kayla's head, not all of them polite. "Because," she said in the calmest voice she could muster, "it was trying to eat me. It's hard to do all those cool kung-fu moves when you've got a three hundred pound monster trying to chew your head off." She snorted and wiped at her bloody lip.

"You don't need fancy moves," said Ninette with infuriating calm. "You just need the right attitude. If something's trying to kill you, you have to kill it first. No excuses."

"With no weapons?"

"The only weapon you need is in here." Ninette tapped a finger to her head. "You stop using this, you're dead. Or worse." Ignoring Kayla's protests, she reached out and removed her neck plate. She held it up to the SUV's headlights. Kayla's armor had a neat ring of teeth marks in it, through which light was faintly visible.

"What about, you know, my powers?" said Kayla, feeling faintly foolish. "The ones Karrel gave me?"

Ninette snorted dismissively. "What powers? I haven't seen you do a thing out of the ordinary since the day we rescued you. You said that Karrel's ghost appeared to you, said he'd given you his strength? Well, missy, you better find some kind of instruction manual for that shit, and soon. It's been a month, in case you haven't noticed. If you don't figure out how to hold your own in a fight, you're out of the Hunters for good."

"But—"

"I'm serious, Kayla. I have no other choice. You disobey direct orders, you're clueless about weaponry, you fight like a marshmallow…"

"Hey, now wait a minute—!"

"Where's your fire, your anger? Why don't you hate them?"

"I *do* hate them," said Kayla fiercely. "They killed the man I love. I'll kill them all if I have to."

"Bullshit," said Ninette. "You don't hate them. You're afraid of them. And that makes you a victim. If you were a true Hunter, you'd give up everything—including your own life—just to kill a single one of them. Without that hatred, that drive, you're nothing more than prey. Now get your ass up and help me with this werewolf before I run the car over you too."

Kayla stood up without a word, seething inwardly. Ninette checked the creature's bindings before reaching into her pocket for another tranquilizer dart. The dart deployed with a dull hiss. The were-wolf gave a little muzzy yip and kicked a couple of times, its movements jerky and uncoordinated, hampered by the serrated plastic ties that bound its four saucer-sized paws together and tied its muzzle shut.

"So where's the girl, then?" Kayla asked grumpily, as the silence stretched between them. "The one that was running?"

"Gone. There's a dead-end back there. Very odd."

"Do you think she walked through the wall, like she did with that cab?" Kayla obstinately nudged the sedated werewolf with a toe, and was rewarded with a muzzy growl. "That would qualify as 'odd' to me."

"Anything's possible. Want to go turn the car around for me?"

"Not really." Kayla folded her arms and jerked her chin at the weakly struggling creature. "What are you going to do with it?"

"Ask it a few questions and kill it," said Ninette brightly. "Wanna watch?"

"I'll get the car," said Kayla quickly. Then her eyes met those of the werewolf.

She stopped short, frowning down at the creature.

"What?" asked Ninette.

"That wolf—it looks familiar."

"Kayla, this is a *werewolf*."

Ignoring her, Kayla gave the creature a long, hard stare. A memory blossomed, and not a pleasant one. There was only one werewolf she'd ever met with eyes that blue, and that angry.

"*Dana?*" she said in astonishment.

The creature reacted to the name, its white eyebrows drawing together in frustration as it lifted its head and tried to focus on her, its bloodied mouth gaping in a snake-like hiss. It was Ninette's turn to stare as Kayla moved around the werewolf, studying it.

"I think… I'm not sure," Kayla murmured, feeling her heart race. "This wolf… she's one of Harlem's pack. I've seen them together a bunch of times." She glanced up at Ninette, her eyes shining. "If this is Dana, then we've got ourselves a new lead on Harlequin."

"We'll see about that one, Twinkie."

"Don't call me that."

Ninette reached into her utility belt and pulled out one of a dozen capped mini-syringes filled with bright green liquid. The liquid was one of the Hunter's main weapons against the werewolves—a bio-engineered, highly magnetic compound known at ADHT. When injected into the bloodstream of a werewolf, ADHT produced the same chemical reactions that occur during the rising of a full moon. It enabled the Hunters to induce a rapid and immediate transformation in a werewolf, turning it from human to wolf. The antidote compound produced a reverse reaction, turning a full-form wolf back to a human, for questioning or identification.

The werewolf growled as Ninette held up the syringe. Its ears flattened back against its skull and it lunged forward, knocking the syringe from Ninette's hand with a surge of frantic energy, trying to snap at the ties that bound it.

Too late.

The chemicals hissed into its bloodstream. Thirty eventful seconds later, Dana lay naked on the sidewalk in front of them. Ninette hadn't given her a full dose so her body was still partially covered in short, white fur. As Ninette fussed around her, cinching the bindings on her slim wrists and ankles tighter, Dana stared up at Kayla with contempt.

"Not you again," she sighed.

CHAPTER TEN

KAYLA STEPPED CAUTIOUSLY around Dana, aiming her pistol at the naked young woman's head. Dana glanced briefly at the gun then yawned.

"Safety's on," she commented.

Kayla clicked the catch off and tried again, leveling the pistol between Dana's eyes. "You're Dana, yes?"

"Depends who's asking." Dana flicked the tip of her vestigial tail, her eyes darting between the two women standing over her. "So you're the Huntress everyone's afraid of."

"They are? Really?"

"Not you." Dana jerked her chin at Ninette. "Her."

"That sounds like me," said Ninette, ignoring Kayla's miffed look. She put her hands on her hips and peered down at Dana in disgusted curiosity. "Have we met?"

"Once. At a party. You killed my date."

Ninette shrugged offhandedly. "I go to lots of parties."

"It *was* you. I remember. You were wearing an unbelievably short red dress and silver stiletto heels. You stabbed Enrique through the heart with one after they brought out the appetizers."

"Right. Human hearts on sticks. Served on little golden trays," said Ninette.

"We were out of puff pastry," replied Dana, not batting an eyelid. "Besides, it was a werewolf party. You weren't supposed to be there."

Kayla looked between the two women in bemusement. "Werewolf party?"

Ninette nodded, not taking her eyes off Dana. "Initiation thing. They have them once a month down at the Meat Market, or used to, before we busted them. Newly-turned werewolves show up with a human date, who finds out that the only thing on the menu is them. Ghastly practice."

"Who are you to judge us?"

"I'm the one with the gun," said Ninette. Her eyes sparkled. "Or rather, I'm the one with the hopelessly inept sidekick clutching a gun she hasn't a clue how to use. Could take her quite a few shots before she hits your heart."

"*Sidekick?*" protested Kayla.

"Dana," said Ninette. "You have thirty seconds to tell me where Harlequin is, and I promise I'll take that gun off her and shoot you myself. I promise. If you don't feel like talking then I'll go get Kayla some extra clips." She smiled for the first time that evening. "God knows the girl could use the target practice."

"Harlequin?" Dana smiled cruelly. "Harlequin is a myth. An urban legend. A scary vampire story made up by old werewolves to scare their pups into line. Don't waste my time."

"He ate my great-great-grandmother," snapped Ninette. "Back in the seventeen hundreds, if I recall correctly. As well as killing everyone else in the town and setting light to all the cattle. Or possibly it was the other way around. Are you telling me that an urban legend did all that?"

"Any vampire could have done it."

"'Any vampire' doesn't go around carving the letter 'H' into people's throats when they turn them." Ninette drew herself up to her full height. She wasn't particularly tall, but most people who talked to her for any length of time pictured her being about eight feet tall, and would swear so at gunpoint. Ninette didn't just stand; she loomed. Her personality was much too big to be contained by her mere physical presence.

Particularly when she was pissed off, like she was right now.

Kayla felt the air sizzle between the two women and stepped into the firing range against her better judgment. "Look, how about we just start with the basics. We know you hang out with Harlem's pack. What happened to Magnus, their leader? Did Harlequin kill him too?"

"He's gone," Dana sniffed. She rolled over and sat up, eyeing Kayla with a scowl. Her startlingly blue eyes were an incredible contrast to the whiteness of her fur. Kayla saw with amazement that they brimmed with angry tears. "They took him."

"Who took him?"

"The cops."

"Figures."

"The LAPD arrested a werewolf ?" asked Kayla. "Why?"

"Because they're run by the vampires," said Ninette distractedly, rubbing her chin. "Where did they take him?"

"Away from me." Dana pulled a face, reaching up with her bound hands to furiously wipe her eyes. "He cheated on me, the sonofabitch! With a *vampire*, no less!" She sniffed again, scowling. "Harlem wanted him dead anyway. So I pulled a few strings and had him sent to the Ring."

"The Ring?"

"It's a new vamp thing. Any werewolves the cops catch are sold to the Ring, for cash. They put on daily fights, pit the wolves against each other, bet on the outcome. A fun time for the whole family, right?"

Ninette stared at her, her expression turning glacial. "And you approve of this? You're a werewolf too."

"I do whatever it takes to survive." said Dana smugly. "Why should I care about a bunch of criminals tearing each other apart? Best idea the vampires ever had, if you ask me. They're doing you Hunters a favor, really."

"You sound like a vampire," said Ninette. She grabbed Dana by the scruff of her furred neck and hauled her effortlessly off the ground. "And you smell like a rat. You betrayed your own kind—for what? How long has this been going on?"

"Long enough," said Dana. She struggled weakly, still feeling the effects of the tranquilizer dart, all injured innocence. "But I thought you Hunters already knew about it." She looked up at Ninette, recognition sparking in her eyes. "Didn't you once—"

"Do any humans ever get sent there?" Ninette interrupted. "Captured Hunters, perhaps?"

Dana shrugged indifferently, heeding the warning tone in Ninette's voice. Her gaze flicked back to the gun in Kayla's hand and the fur began to rise on her back. "Maybe the odd one or two. Who knows? Who cares? I thought we were talking about Harlequin."

"Ah, yes. The vampire who doesn't exist." Ninette dropped Dana abruptly and straightened up, wiping her hands on her combat jeans. She glanced up at the moon, just visible through the dark clouds above them. "Kayla, how's your apprenticeship with the hydraulic hunting bow coming along?"

"Absolutely abysmal," said Kayla cheerfully. "I nearly shot Dan in the ass last week."

"Brilliant. I have one in the trunk."

"Hey! I told you what I know!" Dana protested.

"Then you obviously have no clue who you're dealing with," snapped Ninette, her face darkening. "If Harlequin is back, then I am going to be *very* unhappy indeed. Kayla, tell her what happens to people when I'm unhappy."

"Things you don't want to happen," replied Kayla dutifully.

"This 'Ring' thing has Harlequin's name written all over it" said Ninette. "Tell us where it is, and we'll free you. I mean kill you." She waved a hand vaguely. "One of those."

"Why should I?" said Dana. Her mouth twisted in a mischievous grin as she turned to look at Kayla. "And shouldn't *she* be the one doing the asking? What with her being 'in training' and all."

"I'm not in training," said Kayla. "I just quit."

"You mean I just suspended you," replied Ninette.

"Shame," said Dana. "So you won't be sticking around to help your Hunter buddies free all the poor little wolfies from the Ring?"

Kayla shrugged. "Why should I?"

"You *do* know they have your little boyfriend in there, yes?"

"Karrel's dead."

"Not him. Your other boyfriend. The werewolf who calls himself Mutt."

Kayla froze, feeling her throat instantly tighten. A conflicting rush of emotions went through her, a sickly mixture of embarrassment and hope. "Mutt's alive?"

Dana didn't reply, her eyes flickering impishly back to Ninette. "Quite the crack squad you've got here, I must say. New recruits running around shacking up with werewolves," a sly look crossed her face, "who would do such a treacherous and tactically dangerous thing? Last time I heard of that happening, it was—"

Dana's body suddenly jerked. She broke off with a gasp. Her hands flew to her throat before she pitched over backward, sprawling onto the moonlit asphalt.

Kayla turned to face Ninette, who was thoughtfully adjusting the spring on her dart gun.

"Woman talks too much," Ninette said calmly, loading a fresh dart.

"But she knows where Mutt is! And possibly Harlequin!"

Ninette shrugged indifferently. She slipped the dart gun back in its holster on her belt and held out her hand for Kayla's gun.

Kayla pulled back, shaking her head. "We need to go find him first."

"Who? Harlequin? Or your boyfriend?"

"Mutt's *not* my boyfriend. I don't even like him."

"Good. If you did, you'd be off this team so fast it'd make your head spin," said Ninette promptly. "C'mon, Kay. Gimme the gun. We've got the info we need."

"She didn't tell us where the Ring is."

"We can find that out. We'll send a team. Our top priority is finding that angel, in case you'd forgotten."

"But—"

"Harlequin has been around for centuries. He'll still be around in two days."

Kayla floundered, her eyes going desperately to Dana and back. She folded her arms and stood over the unconscious form of the werewolf. "No. You can't shoot her. We need her alive."

"The only good werewolf is a dead werewolf. You know that as well as I do."

"You sound like you're quoting the Bible."

"I'm quoting the Hunter Code. It's as good as."

"I've read it," said Kayla. "It's crap. Not to mention outdated. It's all 'trust thine instincts' and 'cavort not with thine enemy.'" She snorted. "The guy on the cover looks like the guy on the KFC bucket, for Christ's sake! Why should we make our decisions based on what some little man with glasses and a deeply unfashionable beard said hundreds of years ago?"

"His name was Sage Griffiths, Kayla. He founded this organization. You'd do well to listen to him." The stern look on her face softened somewhat. "If you want to be a real Hunter, you must *never* let your feelings get in the way of your judgment or you'll wind up dead. Remember what happened last time you let yourself get mixed up with that Mutt guy?"

Kayla hung her head. "I nearly got us all killed."

"Right. And what did we find out about him?"

"He said that Karrel died because of him."

"And you still want to save him?"

"I need to talk to him," said Kayla, not quite meeting Ninette's eye. "He knows things... like why everyone wanted Karrel dead. And he wasn't to blame for Karrel's death. Cyan said that Karrel was protecting him, that Mutt died *for* him, not *because* of him."

"That damn mercenary bitch will say anything to get her own neck off the line. You know that."

"But why would she lie to me? She was about to kill me when she told me." Kayla took a deep breath, playing her last, desperate card. "Please, Ninette. This could be my last chance to find out what really happened to Karrel. I need to know. For my own sake."

"Kayla..."

"Imagine how you'd feel if something happened to *your* guy." Kayla removed her jacket and bent down, draping it over Dana's unconscious, naked form. "What if Phil found out something bad, like

Karrel did, but then the next thing you know he was dead? Wouldn't you want to know why the man you loved had been murdered?"

Ninette glared down at her, her hand on the hilt of her dart gun. She sighed, shaking her head.

"Fine, then," she said. "We'll take Dana back to HQ for questioning. But she will be *your* responsibility, and any drama she causes will be on your own head. You'll have to wait til the weekend before we can spare a team to track down this 'Ring' thing. The angel mission is too important to wait, even for the chance of finding Harlequin."

"But..."

"We've been after Harlequin for years. A few more days isn't going to hurt. You get me?"

Kayla nodded in relief, bending down to stroke Dana's furry ears.

Beneath her hand, Dana opened one eye a crack and smiled. She kicked her leg slightly, trying to ignore the itching tingle of the implanted tracking beacon lurking deep beneath the muscle of her inner thigh. She curled up tighter beneath the soft warmth of Kayla's jacket.

Her day was finally looking up.

CHAPTER ELEVEN

MUTT WOKE UP with a groan and a shudder, the fading echoes of a scream ringing in his head. He licked his lips, smacking them once or twice as his brow creased in a frown.

Blood. Why could he taste blood?

He ran his swollen tongue around the inside of his mouth, then coughed and rolled over, shifting groggily on the hard stone floor in a vain attempt to get comfortable. His limbs were numb from sleep, and he was grimy and sore all over. A wash of pins and needles flooded his hands as he curled his naked body up into a tighter ball, shivering involuntarily from the cold. His wrists and ankles ached like crazy. He felt like he had recently and repeatedly been beaten around the head by a gang of drug-crazed loonies wielding steel baseball bats.

Mutt groaned low in his throat and reached up to cradle his aching skull. Considering what his life had been like over the last few years, there were times when he actually prayed to see drug-crazed loonies with baseball bats upon awakening. In fact, already a tiny part of his mind was jumping up and down and pointing gleefully at a new and terrible scar in his memory, thankfully still fogged by sleep, which he knew would make itself horribly real the moment he woke up properly.

Only one thing to do, then: put that moment off as long as possible.

Mutt curled up into a tighter ball and squeezed his eyes shut, baring his teeth against the pain that throbbed in his skull. Sleep. He needed to sleep. Everything else could fuck off. When he woke up, everything would be fine and his headache would be gone and the floor wouldn't be so hard and he wouldn't be chained up and naked and...

Mutt's mind backtracked a couple of steps. He tried to lift his arms. A metallic clinking rang out and a sharp pain stabbed him in the wrists.

Ah, shit.

With a grimace, he opened his eyes.

Dirt coated every inch of the tiny cell he was lying in. The room was no more than ten feet square, made up of moldering brick and corroded iron paneling. The corners of the room were shrouded in darkness. Muted red light poured from a small slit set halfway up the opposite wall, where the dim outline of a door was just visible in the gloom. There was more dirt on the crude wooden bench, which had been scored and carved into by dozens of different hands. Judging by the smell, it had last been slept on by some kind of incontinent wildebeest. The place reminded him of a jail cell he'd once spent a night in during a drunken bender in Mexico City. Unlike Mexico, the air in this cell was freezing and wet with a damp chill that suggested he was somewhere deep underground. Steel rings studded the walls and ceiling. The metal floor beneath him was pitted with age and wet with condensation and years of accumulated grime.

He'd slept in worse places, but not many.

His inspection of the room finished, Mutt turned his attention to himself. He was naked, which was not in itself an unusual thing. What was unusual was that there was no similarly naked girl lying beside him. To add insult to injury, he had been tied up and chained to a wall. That was either really bad or really good. The fact that one of his eyes was swollen shut gave him some clue, as did the flashing, beeping radio collar that was cutting into his throat. Blood was caked on his arms up to the elbow and spattered across what he could see of his naked chest. The blood had dried, so he must have been lying here for some time. His legs were almost completely numb.

And hot *damn,* his wrists hurt.

Things clicked and crunched in Mutt's back as he rolled over, bringing his throbbing wrists up to his face for inspection. In the half-light, he saw that the thick steel manacles that bound his wrists were lined with metal barbs, angled upwards to embed themselves in his skin should he try to break the chain or pull the cuffs off. Two similar manacles encircled his ankles, the steel barbs already half-embedded in his flesh on one side from where he had lain on them in his sleep.

Mutt kicked at them reflexively, trying to knock the barbs from his skin. He only succeeded in driving the spikes further and his half-healed wounds started to bleed. Mutt forced himself to relax, staring up at the wet stone ceiling above him. His mind started to remember how the hell he had gotten into this sorry state.

"Karrel, you bastard," he muttered. "This is all your fault."

"Karrel is dead, my friend," said a smooth voice.

Mutt's body was moving before his mind kicked in. He lunged to his feet in a blur of motion, then yelped and crashed sideways into the wall as the steel barbs slashed open his already torn and tender skin. He hit the stone wall with a bruising thump and spun around in a low crouch.

A peal of female laughter rang out, echoing in the tiny stone cell.

Mutt dragged in a slow breath and held it. He was on firmer ground now. He cautiously relaxed, casting back and forth in the darkness as he peered blindly around the room, sniffing groggily at the air. He *knew* there'd be a girl involved in this somehow. There always was. This was probably just another training mission, a stunt pulled by—

He froze as a memory slammed into him.

A girl.

The scar in Mutt's mind suddenly blossomed like a rent wound, and his subconscious finally came back online. Memory flooded his brain with a rapid-fire succession of bloody images. Mutt stared down at his hands, at the manacles that bound him.

"The girl," he started.

"Is dead," finished the voice. "You killed her. Want to see the video? It came out *great*."

Mutt clutched at his stomach as it convulsed inside him. He pressed a clenched fist to his lips and fought a sudden and violent urge to throw up. He was barely aware of the unseen woman as she circled around him, watching as he bent over, panting hard in distress. The scent of her sickened him.

She was a vampire.

And a familiar vampire at that.

"I'll kill the lot of you," he managed between heaves.

"Go for it, champ," said Cyan X, stepping out of the shadows. "But for now, I have a more realistic offer to discuss."

She slipped a cool, soft hand down over Mutt's bare shoulder and caressed his chin like a lover, gently wiping away a smudge of dirt. Mutt growled and lunged at her, snapping jaws at her that he was sorry were still human. His chains snapped taut, bringing him up short, his face just inches from hers. Cyan pulled her hand back quickly, her eyes sparkling with amusement, but she didn't move away.

Mutt spat blood on the floor in disgust. He rose slowly and deliberately to his feet, not for one moment taking his eyes off her. The pumped muscles in his biceps and forearms stood out as he put his full weight against the manacles that held him, straining against the chains, scarcely feeling the raindrops of blood that slipped from his wrists as a result.

"So tell me, Mathias," said Cyan, looking him up and down with undisguised approval. "Were you planning on killing Karrel's girl in such an entertaining fashion?"

"Come a little closer and I'll show you," hissed Mutt. Blood dripped from his elbow and he jerked in pain.

"No, really," said Cyan. "I need to know. If you are, we'll book you into the nine o'clock slot in the Ring. Prime-time. Always good for business to have the odd public fatality."

"I'd rather die, thanks all the same."

"That could be arranged." Cyan's eyes sparkled as she stepped around the chained werewolf. Her eyes slipped down Mutt's well-muscled chest, examining with interest the intricate tribal tattoos that slashed their way over his flat belly and curved up across his powerful back, barely visible under the light coating of dust and blood and bruising that covered his flanks. Mutt's body was a sculpture of youthful pride and confidence, the arrogant jut of his jaw complementing the coiled-spring tension that filled the rest of his body.

"Like what you see?" murmured Mutt.

Cyan ran a gentle hand across his flanks. Mutt's strong, well-shaped limbs were tanned and corded from years of fighting to stay alive on the streets of L.A., providing a delectable canvas for the minor works of art that graced his flesh, almost as numerous as the interesting assortment of burns and scrapes that marred his skin. When she glanced lower, she was reminded of why she'd found herself falling for him in the first place.

Cyan reached out a curious finger to touch one tattoo, a band of flowing Arabic writing that formed a broken ring around Mutt's hips before dropping tantalizingly close to his groin. "What does this one say?" she asked.

"It says 'If you can read this, you're about two seconds away from getting your face chewed off by a *very* pissed werewolf.'"

That made Cyan smile. Her hand lingered, her eyes shamelessly raking down Mutt's naked body as she moved closer, ignoring the growl of warning that rose in his throat. "I don't see a werewolf," she murmured, leaning up against him as she brushed a lock of his dark, tousled hair out of his eyes. Steam rose between them as her silver rings burned his cheek. Mutt didn't so much as flinch. "I see an opportunity."

"For what? Some extremely painful oral sex?" Mutt glanced at her small, sharp fangs with a shudder.

Cyan chuckled. Slinking closer, she cupped Mutt's chin and planted a soft kiss on his forehead, ignoring the furious tension in his body as he continued to lean all his weight on his chains, trying to snap them. She was playing a dangerous game, taunting a werewolf like this, but hell, she was bored and he was naked. What other excuse did she need?

Her eyes glinted as she ran the tip of her pierced fingernail down, across his chest, before tracing a circle around the ugly, cross-shaped scar that marred the skin over his heart.

"Where'd you get this, Mutt?" she asked, all innocence.

Mutt's eyes burned a defiant green in the darkness.

"I heard some *very* interesting things about you. Some very interesting things indeed. The others wanted you killed on arrival, but I requested that you be spared. I would be very disappointed if you died before I found out your secret." She tilted her head, regarding him coyly. "You *do* have a secret, don't you Mutt?"

"I thought you let me live because of my devastating good looks and my incredibly beautiful yet masculine body," Mutt said through his teeth.

Cyan smiled thinly, but there was no trace of humor on her face. "I must confess. You're something of an enigma, *werewolf*. Your involvement with Karrel and his accursed band of Hunters was of particular interest to me."

"Yeah yeah, blah blah. Spare us the bad guy monolog, darlin'. You want to talk about Karrel, run along upstairs like a good girl and grab me a six-pack of Corona and a *South Park* DVD. At least then I won't start snoring before you get to the second chorus of 'betray everyone and everything you've ever known and loved and I might just pretend to promise to let you live.' Jeeze." Mutt sneezed explosively, then rubbed his nose with a manacled wrist. "Isn't that what you were about to say?"

The vampiress smiled thinly. "You're brave, werewolf. I'll give you that. But don't even begin to think that you know me." She stepped closer to him and ran her manicured hand down the inside of his bare leg, a dangerous smile on her red lips. "*Yet.*"

Cyan straightened up and winked at someone over his shoulder. Mutt turned to see the tall, gangling figure of the silver-masked man from the Ring standing behind him.

Not *him*. Not here!

The figure regarded him for a long moment before pointing a pierced, painted fingernail at Cyan, who reached into her pocket for a key.

"This one due for transfer?" she asked sweetly.

"Transfer?" Mutt stared at her. "What transfer?"

The masked man nodded ominously and clapped his hands together. Five burly vampire guards burst into the cell and grabbed Mutt's arms and legs, pinning him down.

"I'm not doing any stinking transfer!" yelled Mutt, as they started removing his chains. With a wild sweep of his leg he managed to catch one of the guards on the kneecap. The man howled and spun away, slamming into the masked man, knocking his mask off. A gasp went up from the assembled guards as the mask clattered to the ground. As one, they all turned to stare at the man's exposed face.

Mutt froze, staring in disbelief. "What the hell is that!?" he shrieked.

CHAPTER TWELVE

So THIS WAS Hell.

Karrel slowly rose to his feet, staring around him in horror.

He was dead. He knew that much.

He'd given his life so that another might live, and had been sent to Hell for his efforts.

He'd tried to warn them all, to warn Kayla, but he had failed.

So here it was, finally.

The afterlife.

Karrel inhaled hesitantly, the foul-tasting air catching in his throat. The anguished cries of tormented lost souls filled the air, echoing through the dank, disease-ridden atmosphere. His non-existent heart pounded in his spectral chest.

Karrel's jaw dropped and he pressed a hand to his mouth, sickened.

In his wildest imaginings, he'd never imagined that Hell would be this bad.

He heard someone behind him clear their throat.

Karrel turned to see the tall, dark shape of Death standing over him. Death was a nightmarish skeletal entity over seven feet high, made up of raw wet muscle and interlocking, rotting bones: Dali's vision of Death. The creature's front limbs were a pair of joined, organic scythes gleaming in the darkness, held at the ready to harvest souls. It had a triangular, eyeless head covered in flayed human skin. Its lipless hole of a mouth was filled with needle-sharp teeth set in a perpetual grin.

The creature moved toward him with a spider-like clack and skitter of limbs, and stopped a few feet away.

"Well?" it said in a breathy hiss. "What do you think?"

Karrel shook his head, nausea filling his chest like hot lava. He breathed in the stench of rotting meat and the poisonous sulfuric fumes, and the terrible, ceaseless noise of...

"West Hollywood?"

The thing inclined its head with a shudder.

"I know," it said miserably. "Horrid, isn't it?"

Karrel jumped back as bus 666 blasted past him, scattering trash in all directions and almost mowing down a middle-aged homeless guy who wandered dazedly across the road. The man swore and rattled his bag of cans at the receding tail lights of the bus before lurching off down the sidewalk, screaming abuse at the filthy walls. Karrel tottered mindlessly away from him, backing up until his back hit a grimy, graffiti-covered wall. He glanced down, and a shock of unreality went through him. A golden name glinted up at him from the grimy sidewalk, set into a red marble star.

His name.

He was on Hollywood Boulevard, standing on the Walk of Fame.

Death clicked his way over the sidewalk to join him, watching him intently with his horrible eyeless face. All around them, traffic honked and screeched as tourists in brash neon shirts brushed past, chatting loudly on their cell phones. In a back alley nearby, a ragged bunch of street people stood hunched around a blazing fire set in a steel trash can. One of them, a haggard-looking woman wearing horseshoe earrings, raised a hand and waved at the nightmare entity at Karrel's side, earning herself a weird look from her buddies.

"Hi, Skippy," she called cheerfully.

To Karrel's surprise, Death raised a claw and waved back, looking faintly embarrassed. "Hey, Lucy," he said.

"Skippy?" spat Karrel.

The bubble burst. Karrel swung round and glared up at the creature, the fear inside him suddenly and unexpectedly turning to fury. "I thought you said you were Death? Or 'a' Death?"

The thing shrugged, a complicated gesture involving much popping and clicking of slime-covered joints. "I *am* Death," it said, somewhat pompously. "Everyone sees me differently. That lady, for example—she sees me as a small, flea-bitten dog of the mongrel variety. Helps her deal with the fact that she's dead. The human psyche is a fascinating thing." The creature swiveled around on its legs and cocked its head, regarding Karrel with curiosity. "How do *you* see me?"

"Oh, I see a dog too." Karrel stared fixedly up at the creature's dripping mandibles. "Definitely a dog."

He licked his lips, his anger growing inside him like a cancer. Whatever he had expected to happen to him after he died, it certainly wasn't this.

"Wasn't Skippy a cartoon kangaroo?"

"I have many names."

"Oh, come on. Don't give me that bull. *Skippy*, indeed." Karrel clenched his fists, glaring up at the nightmarish creature. "Fine. You want to be like that, that's what I'll call you." He spun around to gesture at the streets around him. "And why the fuck am I still in Hollywood? I thought you were sending me to Hell?"

"No need. You're already there."

Karrel glanced around him in dismay, trying out this new concept. He shook his head. "Sorry, buddy. I don't buy that. Hollywood isn't Hell, it's just a bit run down, that's all. In need of some urban renewal. If it's the whole 'Hell-on-Earth' concept you're after, why not send me to some war zone or famine-ridden third-world village? Then you'd really be cooking."

"You don't get it, do you?"

Karrel clenched his jaw. "If you give me the whole 'Hell is a state of mind' speech, you know I'll slap you."

"You're too short to reach," said Skippy mildly. "But you're half right."

Death leaned back against a fire-blackened lamppost, being careful not to touch anything. He started methodically cleaning his hide with his serrated forelimbs. "For Satan's sake," he grumbled, "this place is disgusting. I don't know how you can stand it."

Karrel snorted, pacing back and forth impatiently. "So is that the deal? I'm stuck in Los Angeles forever? Is that my punishment?"

Skippy straightened up and fixed Karrel with a baleful look. "You'll find out," he said ominously. "Have fun."

He raised a claw in a brief gesture of farewell, then stalked off down the street.

Karrel ran after him.

"Wait! Where are you going? You can't just leave me here! I have to get back to Kayla! She's in danger. She needs me!"

There was no reply.

"At least tell me what I should do next!"

Skippy paused, peering back at him doubtfully. "You will shortly be consigned to Limbo, a swirling, gray void filled with lost souls. Limbo is where the murders, the suicides, the general cosmic fuck-ups go. It is a place between Heaven and Hell where the boundaries are blurred, where souls go who are awaiting judgment, or who still have work to do in the world."

Karrel perked up. "Work to do? Like avenging their deaths?"

"Indeed."

"Tell me more. I need to know everything!"

Skippy sighed petulantly, tapping his claws on a lamppost. Then he turned and clicked his way back across the sidewalk, raw flesh glistening in the dim orange light. He squatted down next to Karrel, who to his credit recoiled only slightly. He gestured up with a serrated claw.

"The deal you made with the Other Side still stands. But you're in our world now, so you must play by our rules. You sacrificed your own life to save an innocent, then rejected your reward by spurning Heaven. Very few do, which makes you an anomaly."

"Great." Karrel rubbed his hands together, trying to warm them. "That makes me feel a whole lot better."

"Regardless. The fact remains that you screwed up, bigtime. You had a chance to go to Heaven and you threw it away. Now it's a whole different ballgame. You must go to Limbo to await judgment. We will consider your case, and see what can be done. You'll either be sent back to Heaven or, if you're found guilty of being a suicide, you'll be sent to Hell. My boss will be along shortly to collect you."

"Your boss? You mean the Devil?"

"No. Devils are common demons. They have no place in this world. I refer of course to Lucifer, the Shining Prince. It is he who will judge you."

"Can I call my lawyer first? I'm not so sure I should trust shining princes."

Skippy looked at him oddly.

"Forget it." Karrel shook his head, gathering his wits. "This is bullshit. No way am I going through all this 'Limbo' judgment crap. Kayla's wide open right now. She needs me to protect her." He folded his arms, glaring up at Skippy. "Your boss can go take a flying leap. I'm staying right here."

"There will be no arguing!" Skippy slammed his scythe-arm against a nearby lamppost, slicing off the metal "*No Littering* sign". It fell to the ground with a loud clatter, startling several nearby passersby.

Karrel stared down at the sign and turned back to Skippy.

"How did you do that?" he asked. "You're like me, right? You're dead. You can't touch anything?"

"It is irrelevant." Skippy's ruffled feathers settled, and he gingerly sat back down on the sidewalk, taking care to avoid the worst of the urine stains on the concrete. "Look, here's the breaks, guy. I don't have the power to help you out of your little metaphysical screw-up, but," a sly look came over his blind face, "if you're *really* desperate..."

"I'll do anything," said Karrel fiercely.

Skippy grinned and rubbed his forelimbs together like a cockroach, looking Karrel over gleefully. "I can't promise you any kind of absolution, but I could probably bend some rules, delay your judgment. Keep you out of Limbo long enough to buy you some time to wrap up your affairs here on Earth."

"Great."

"But there will be a price."

"There always is."

"You've already made a bargain with Heaven. Want one with Hell instead?"

"Sorry, Skip, no-can-do. I'm in enough trouble as it is. Plus I'm fresh out of firstborn babies."

"Don't need babies. Just souls."

"Whose soul?"

Skippy licked his lips greedily. "The soul of one we have been tracking for many centuries: a vampire. A creature who is responsible for many thousands of innocent deaths, and who is currently making a plan that, if it succeeds, may result in the deaths of millions more."

"Who is this vampire?" Karrel reached for the ghostly shape of his Hunter's CB radio, but his hand went right through it. Some habits died hard. "We've been hearing about this 'master plan' thing for years. Just tell me who the sonofabitch is and I'll send my guys out to nail him. No problem."

"The creature concerned currently goes by the name of Harlequin."

"*The* Harlequin?" He whistled. "Jeez. You want the president's head on a spike while I'm at it?"

Skippy grinned hideously. "We're working on that one. But in the meantime, do we have a deal?"

"No! No way! I can't ask Kayla to help me kill that monster!"

"Hate to break it to you, monkey boy, but you already have."

"What?"

Skippy smugly inspected one of his long claws. "As part of your bargain with Heaven. To avenge your death by…"

"…killing all those responsible for murdering me." Karrel stared at the wall for a moment and his eyes filled with terror. "No!"

"Afraid so, short stuff. The vampire Harlequin was involved in the chain of events that lead to your death. Near the top of it, from what I hear."

"Then I'm screwed." Karrel sagged against a lamppost. "My soul will only be returned to me if I kill everyone on the list. But Kayla can't take down Harlequin. He'll kill her. She's not strong enough to fight him on her own."

"Not necessarily."

Karrel looked up to see Skippy practically dancing with glee.

"Go on," he said tiredly. "Out with it."

"You ready for this?"

"Just make it quick."

Skippy leaned forward and whispered something in Karrel's ear.

"Uh-uh. No way. I'm not bargaining *that*."

"Suit yourself," Skippy sniffed. "Go to Limbo, wait for your true love to die. Next!"

"She won't die. She's smart."

"She's clueless. That makes her dead." Skippy leaned in closer to Karrel, so close that he could feel the heat emanating from the rotting patchwork of flesh that made up the entity's flanks. Death spoke clearly and distinctly, every word revealing his glinting, razor-sharp teeth. "Save Kayla, or she will die and you will face eternal damnation. You've got one shot at this, little guy. I advise you to take it."

Karrel shoved his hands into his pockets, staring at the ground.

He was quiet a long time.

Then he cleared his throat, flicking a glance up at Skippy.

"Just tell me what I have to do," he said quietly.

CHAPTER THIRTEEN

KAYLA WOKE TO the sound of screaming, as she did most mornings. She groaned and pulled her pillow over her head, wriggling around irritably in her warm, comfy bed, but the screaming didn't stop.

So much for sleeping in.

Kayla stared at the ceiling for a long moment, then flung her pillow across the room and swung her legs out of bed. She padded across her cold, dark cubical to the metal washbasin. The living cubical had been her home for the last month since the Hunters had "rescued" her. Already, she hated it. Living in the triple-reinforced underground bunker that was the Hunter's headquarters was one thing, but getting a decent night's sleep was another, particularly when some of the more "interesting" cases were brought in.

The screaming got louder. Kayla splashed water in her face and clicked on a light, somberly studying her tousled reflection in the mirror. The left side of her face ached where she had lain on her rock-hard army-issue pillow, and her hair looked like she had slept in a wind-tunnel. She found a few spots of dried blood on her cheek she must have missed the previous night, and took a moment to wash them off.

She peered into the mirror again and groaned.

She was also getting a pimple. Great.

By the time she had finished brushing her teeth the screaming had reached ear-splitting levels. She dressed quickly and made her way into the next room. A group of young Hunter recruits stood in the darkened hallway in various stages of undress, peering through the porthole in the door to the training room.

"What's all the fuss?" she asked Dan, a young recruit who stood at the back of the group and peered down at the floor with a look of intense concentration. "Someone steal the Sarge's breakfast bagel again?"

"Worse," replied Dan, still studying the floor. Dan had uncontrollably curly brown hair and an expression of perpetual bemusement. He was the only person she knew at the base who was actually younger than her. Kayla couldn't resist grinning as he glanced up at her briefly, a conspiratorial expression on his young, earnest face. "They got a Primal in there," he said.

"A who's-a-what?"

"A Primal," repeated Dan. He reached into his pocket for a stick of gum. "It's a kind of spirity… thing. They use them in exorcisms. It's all smoke and mirrors but it looks good." He popped the

gum into his mouth and began chewing thoughtfully, nodding down at the carpet. "Does that look
like blood to you?"

"Exorcisms?"

"Yeah. People getting all, you know, possessed.
By spirits and stuff. Always good for a laugh."

"Doesn't sound very funny to me," said Kayla.
"Who've they got in there?"

"Dunno. Some chick they brought in last night."
Dan folded his arms, looking glum. "And you
know what else isn't funny? People getting blood
on the carpet. I'm up next on the cleaning roster,
you know."

"Who is she? The girl?"

"No idea. I think she's some kind of hooker or
something. Which brings us full circle back to the
Sarge." Dan grinned and nudged Kayla, nodding
at the door of the sleeping quarters beside them.
"I'm surprised he's not out here too. Noise like
this'd wake the dead."

"Last night?" Kayla's eyes widened. "That's
Dana they've got in there!"

"Uh, Kayla... I wouldn't go... oh."

Kayla shoved past Dan and elbowed her way
through the other new recruits. She peered through
the reinforced porthole window. The training
room on the other side was mostly shrouded in
darkness, but she could just make out the faint
glow of a spinning blue light, confined inside the
glass sparring box at the end of the training room.

A dark figure was inside, surrounded by the
light.

Muttering a dark oath, Kayla pushed through
the swing door.

If anything happened to Dana, they would lose the only real lead they had on Harlequin, and she would never find out what had happened to Mutt.

She only prayed that she wasn't too late.

Kayla stopped outside the pen and stared upwards, her heart speeding up.

The Box, as it was called, was thirty feet square and resembled a giant, transparent die made out of thickly cut glass. It was two feet thick on all sides and reinforced with sturdy iron girders. It was used mainly as a sparring ring by the older recruits, but it sometimes served as a makeshift holding pen for some of the more aggressive nasties the Hunters brought in, until more suitable accommodation could be found for them.

If Dana was in there she couldn't see her, and the idea of going into the Box while it contained 'spirity things'—as Dan had called them—was not a fun thought.

She moved closer and cupped her hands to the cold glass, trying to see through it. It was dark inside now that the blue light had gone out, but she could just make out two indistinct humanoid shapes moving around at the back of the pen. She raised an eyebrow as one shape rose up one wall, defying gravity. There was a flash of light and the figure fell to the ground with a muffled explosion. A wall of smoke billowed outward, clouding the interior of the Box. Kayla jumped back as the smoke seeped through the cracks around the keyhole.

When the smoke had subsided a little, Kayla stretched out a cautious hand toward the door. She leaped back as it suddenly flew open.

Phil stepped out, rubbing his hands together.

"Ah, good morning Kayla," he said, zipping up his tailored biker's jacket as though he had just stepped in from a walk on the town. "You're up bright and early."

"I saw, er…" said Kayla. She stopped when Phil fractionally raised a pierced eyebrow. She knew that look by now, and what would happen if she pressed the subject. Phil shut the door firmly behind him and turned the key in the lock. "What exactly did I see?"

"Moonlight reflected off cabbage leaves," said Phil promptly, with a grin.

"Huh?"

"Standard explanation offered by the government for UFOs. Back in the Sixties. In other words, ask a stupid question."

"Gotcha."

Kayla backed off, her eyes still firmly fixed on the Box. There was definitely something moving inside it, just visible through the dissipating smoke. If it was Dana, at least she was still alive.

"Is Dana in there?"

"No."

"Ah. That makes me feel better," said Kayla, not feeling better at all. "So where is she? You didn't kill her, did you?"

"Kill her? Oh, no." Phil swept a hand through his lion's mane of thick dark hair. It reached almost halfway down his back, in direct defiance of the Hunters' official dress codes. He chewed on a black-painted fingernail. "I think," he added, looking distracted. "We took her up to the Blue Room. Some of the boys from Unit Z wanted to talk to her. About you-know-who."

"Who? Harlequin?"

"Shhhhh!"

"Ah, whatever. No one's listening," said Kayla. She stepped slightly to the side to block Phil's view of the recruits peering through the porthole door. "So you took her to the Blue Room? Isn't that place restricted access?"

Phil shushed her again hurriedly, glancing over his shoulder as though they might be overheard. He ducked his head and waggled his eyebrows at her. "Of course it's restricted access," he said, in a monotone. "I'd never invite you to come and check it out."

"Well, that's—"

"And it's definitely not cold in there, so you shouldn't go and grab a jacket first."

"I don't think that I—"

"And it's absolutely not on Level Three behind a secret door you activate by flushing the fourth toilet in the men's room while pulling the security cord and turning the third tap on the left. I'd get in deep shit if I told you that, so I won't."

Phil paused, his eyes creasing in an expression of rich amusement. "Just so you know."

He grinned down at her, his intelligent, friendly face set in an expression of wicked innocence beneath its customary three-day stubble. Phil was Unit D's other team leader and, like Ninette, Phil took a great deal of pleasure in systematically undermining anything the Hunters had in the way of rules.

Kayla noticed a smoking hole in the side of Phil's armor-plated flak jacket, and felt a pang of worry. If he'd been messing with the Dark Arts again...

"You know, I'm just a trainee," she started, glancing behind her unhappily. "I'm not allowed… to… er, to *not* see the Blue Room."

"Says who?"

"Says the rules."

"Oh, right. Gotta obey the rules." Phil held up a newly-minted set of keys, brandishing them like they were the Holy Grail. "Want to come obey the rules in The Blue Room?"

KAYLA'S MOUTH WORKED soundlessly as she stared around her in awe, one hand still on the open door. Phil stood beside her, hands on his hips proudly.

"Well?" he said. "What do you think?"

Kayla slowly shook her head. "It's…"

"Big?" suggested Phil.

"Yeah. And very, er…"

"Blue."

"Right. That's why it's called the Blue Room. Come on, we're going to be late."

"For what?"

"You'll see," said Phil ominously.

Kayla jogged after Phil as he strode through the enormous room, his steel-tipped army boots ringing on the ribbed metal flooring. The Blue Room was as tall as an aircraft hangar and twice as wide. Its enormous, domed ceiling was crisscrossed with a myriad of silver-plated wires, from which hung hundreds upon hundreds of cross-shaped lights made of fluorescent UV tubes. Every light was attached by a long, silvered wire to a central glass cube that sat in the center of everything like the center of a busy spiderweb. The curved outer walls were plated with black silver, forming a mirrorlike surface and giving the rather alarming illusion that each wall disappeared into infinity. This gave the room its ghostly blue light, although nothing in the room was actually blue.

Kayla looked around in fascination as she made her way down the walled path that bisected the cavernous room. The place was filled with out-landish training equipment, interlocking fighting pits, enormous barbells, hanging punching bags, and a series of strange machines that pulsed with white light and emitted the occasional puff of smoke to the accompaniment of loud swearing from whoever was inside. A swarm of older Hunters populated the room, all dressed in identical black cotton jumpsuits padded with steel plates at elbows and across their chests. Their arms were bedecked with cloth patches denoting rank and Unit. They spun and fought on padded crash mats. Kayla passed between them, their swords and wooden training batons whistling through the air at dizzying speeds.

Kayla had heard tales of the Blue Room ever since she'd started training, but had been assured time and again that there was no such place. She felt the curious eyes of the older Hunters turn on her as she'd walked past them, heard the hushed conversation that arose in her wake, as they eyed her plain black uniform that marked her a new recruit. She couldn't have felt more out of place if she'd been wearing a pink tutu and a ski mask.

Kayla reached up to touch the bronze coin she wore on a loop of black leather around her neck. The coin had a Chinese fighting dragon on it, with its tail curled around the square hole in the center. The talisman had been a gift to her from Karrel, which he'd won for her on a fairground stall on their first date.

She hadn't taken it off since the day he'd died.

It seemed to grow warm under her fingertips as she looked around the room, seeing Karrel in all the things there. She tried to imagine him in the room, working out on those mats, sparring with other Hunters, doing bench presses with those barbells till his forehead dripped with sweat. A flood of longing filled her and she quickly clamped down on it, trying to drive all thoughts of Karrel from her mind.

There would be time enough for questions later.

Kayla peered over the top of one of the fighting pits as she passed by, trying to distract herself. She jumped back as a set of horned fangs chomped shut just a few feet from her face, then a pair of suspicious gray eyes slammed into the reinforced viewing window that topped the pit. The eyes bore hungrily into hers with a strange silver light like the strobing of a camera flash. Kayla felt a lurching sensation in her gut, as though the light had captured something in her. Her jaw fell open as the creature's nondescript scaled face sloughed away like a melting candle, revealing a perfect copy of her own face beneath.

A hand touched her shoulder and she spun around in alarm. "Entropy daemon," Phil explained with an apologetic shrug. "Look into its eyes for another two seconds and it'll get your soul, too. I hear they're very popular in Vegas."

"Vegas?" Kayla couldn't tear her eyes from the duplicate of her own face. As she stared, the creature unfurled a long black tongue and wiped the remains of its scales from "her" face with a hearty burp. "What for?"

"That's what we want to find out," said Phil, beckoning her back onto the path. "We think it has something to do with Elvis."

"Elvis?"

"Uh-huh-huh." Phil mocked. Kayla rolled her eyes. "What? I'm deadly serious. I mean, think about it. How many Elvis impersonators is it possible to have in one city without there being some kind of supernatural explanation behind it all?"

"Riiiiighht," said Kayla. "That explains Siegfried and Roy, too."

"Nope. They defy all rational explanation. But we've got a team working on it. Come on. We'll be late for the meeting."

"Meeting?" Kayla stopped dead. "I thought Ninette said that I was suspended."

"You are. This is a different kind of meeting."

"Does it involve people hitting me in the head with one of those?" Kayla pointed to one of the giant barbells that littered the room. Phil shook his head.

"That belongs to Monster. You don't want to touch that."

"Which monster?"

Phil smiled enigmatically. "I'm just going to say 'Don't ask' this once. Then, every time you ask me a question in here, I won't need to reply. I think that about covers everything."

He led her down the rows of equipment to the center of the room, where a huge glass cube stood.

It looked similar to the training cube in the recruits' training room, only ten times larger.

Phil rapped on the side, making it ring like a gong.

Over by the main entrance, Kayla noticed a very old Hunter with a scarred face and a broad-brimmed hat putting an intricate harness on an enormous, bull-sized creature. The animal looked like a tank with legs. It had a flattened, pug-like face, large hands and muscles the size of melons. Five or six younger Hunters held the creature in place with a dozen thick ropes tied to its legs and neck. They all looked absolutely terrified.

Kayla turned back to Phil, nodding at the giant, freakish creature.

"What the hell is *that* thing?"

Phil raised his eyebrows pointedly.

"Right. Don't ask," said Kayla mechanically. "Got it."

After a few more moments the main door was jerked open a crack by a man dressed in chainmail. He had a shaved head and a proud, regal bearing. His strong, wiry arms were covered in swirling, ocean-themed tattoos, and he was wearing a pair of seventies-style mirrored sunglasses.

"Password?" he asked, aiming a stubby black gun at Phil.

"Nachos," said Phil quickly, holding up a packet.

"Pass, friend," said Tony, taking the bag and winking at Kayla. "You're just in time. Come on in. We're about to get started."

CHAPTER FOURTEEN

IT WAS HOT inside the cube. Kayla stiffened as she accompanied Phil over to the other side, everyone's eyes on her before turning back to the fight on the other half of the room.

Ninette stood waiting for them. She was freshly showered and dressed in a skin-tight wifebeater with camouflage pants and a studded silver belt. The other occupants of the room were clad in black hunting uniforms positively dripping with rank patches and stripes. Behind Ninette stood a small crowd of about a dozen Hunters, watching two armed and masked combatants duel on the far side of the cube behind toughened safety glass.

Kayla heard a loud sizzling sound, like sausages frying on a hotplate. She looked up just in time to see the first combatant, a young female Hunter with blue hair, turn and direct a bolt of shining black plasma at her masked male opponent. The

man retaliated with a flamboyant sweep of his own
arm, sending a wave of orange light spilling toward
her. The light engulfed the black plasma ball in a
splutter of greenish sparks. A burst of heat hit the
glass safety shield with an audible hiss.

The two combatants circled, watching one
another warily as they searched for an opening.

Kayla nudged Phil urgently in the ribs. "They're
using the Dark Arts," she hissed, trying not to
move her mouth in case that caused a fireball to be
directed her way.

"Are they?" Phil's face was curiously blank.

"But—" Kayla's own face went through six different emotions as she tried to process this. She
ducked as a fierce beam of light melted a pit almost
a foot deep in the reinforced safety glass. The liquid glass hissed and bubbled. Kayla eyed the
charred hole with a certain feeling of inevitability.
"I take it Sarge doesn't know about this," she said.

"About what?" Phil asked again, nodding his
head slightly to emphasize his deliberately blank
expression.

"Oh, my God." Kayla pressed the heels of her
hands over her eyes, making little blue explosions
dance around inside her head. "What was the
German for 'We're all going to die', again?"

"*Wir werde alle sterben,*" said Phil. "You
remember the Spanish version?"

"*Somos todos que van a moror,*" said Kayla.

"*Morir,*" corrected Phil, slapping her heartily on
the back. "You'll get there in the end. World dom-
ination awaits."

"I don't want to take over the world. I want to
go home and sleep in it." Kayla folded her arms.

"Either give me a good reason why I'm here, or bring me a cup of coffee."

"I wanted you to see the possibilities." said Ninette, handing her a steaming cup.

"What possibilities?" Kayla took the coffee and stared down at it warily. It smelled good, so she took a sip. It wasn't bad.

"Of what you could become, if you tried." Ninette looped an arm around Phil's waist and pecked him on the cheek.

Kayla shook her head unhappily. "But you're doing the Dark Arts! Illegally! What if someone told the bosses about this?"

"We'd deal with them," said Phil calmly. "They'd be out of the base."

"But what if they tried to get back in and kill you using the Dark Arts you just taught them?"

"The base is sealed, Kayla," said Ninette calmly. She turned and idly adjusted Phil's amour. "Even if they fought off all the guards and broke all the locks, they'd need a very expensive negatively-charged looping device to get through the security seal without setting off the alarm."

"Or a Coke-can," Phil grinned. "See, the metal of a Pepsi can is made of a mixed alloy, which doesn't conduct electricity, right, but a Coke can is made from pure aluminum, which would fool the circuit into thinking that—"

"What Phil is *trying* to say," Ninette cut in quickly, giving Phil a stern look and ruffling his hair good-naturedly, "is that we're safe. We live in an underground bunker for a reason. Nobody's breached security in the eighty-plus years the Hunters have been based here, and if they did, we'd be ready for them. The Dark Arts are simply one more weapon in our armory against the forces of Darkness. If the big bosses don't get that, that's their problem."

She straightened up and nodded at the assembled group behind her. "But first, we've got a meeting to finish. Listen and learn, Twinkie."

"Don't call me that," Kayla called after her.

Behind her, Phil laughed.

They both watched as Ninette pushed her way through the crowd. Reaching the front, she hit a button to slide back the safety wall and stepped boldly between the two fighters before they could pull any punches.

Kayla gave a cry of alarm as she saw a black plasma bolt scream toward Ninette's head. But instead of turning her boss's face into a ball of charred flesh, the bolt imploded loudly about two feet away, bursting into a cloud of dust that scattered over the floor, coating the boots of the crowd. Ninette waved a hand and the blue-haired girl's opponent bent double and collapsed on the floor. For an instant a flickering white wall of energy was visible around her, protecting her like a case of curved ice. Then it vanished, leaving behind nothing but a faint glow in the air.

Ninette turned to face the crowd as both fighters stood down respectfully. Silence settled over the room.

"Now, kids, where did we leave off?" she asked, folding her arms. The small crowd drew in closer, one or two of them glancing toward the door.

"Rains of blood," said Tony.

"The seas boiling," piped up a younger Hunter.

"Armageddon," volunteered Kayla, feeling a certain inevitability about where this meeting was going.

Ninette nodded. "Then you all know why I've summoned you and what we're dealing with. These are grave times, indeed."

"Is it true that Harlequin's back?" asked a guy in a black vest with red-streaked hair. Like the rest of them, he was eyeing Kayla suspiciously.

Ninette held up her hands. "All in good time, J-Bo. We have more important issues to deal with here."

"What's more important than Harlequin?"

"The Bateaux Prophecy is what's more important. It could kill more people than Harlequin could in a thousand years, unless we prevent it from taking place. What I need to know from all of you, now, is how far you're prepared to go to stop this thing."

"All the way, baby!" called out the masked Hunter, from his prone position on the ground. A couple of his buddies cheered and whistled.

Ninette narrowed her eyes at him. "Calm down, Marius. Take a few deep breaths, the pharmacy will still be open in the morning. Now tell me. Who knows anything about angels?"

"I know they won the World Cup in 1967," said Marius, winking at Kayla. He clambered to his feet and pulled his fencing hood off with a flourish, shaking out his mop of smoking, dirty blond hair. He was actually quite attractive, in a lean, hungry kind of way. She saw the way his eyes caressed the curves of Ninette's athletic body. Phil folded his muscular arms and stared at the young Hunter, cocking his head in interest.

Kayla grinned wryly to herself. She'd known the pair of them long enough to know that Phil never worried about any of their team making a pass at their stunning team leader. He knew full well—as they all did—that Ninette could more than take care of herself if need be, as she'd just amply demonstrated.

This Marius guy was either new, or extremely slow on the uptake.

Marius pretended not to notice Phil's attention, his eyes creasing in mirth as he pulled a cigarette out of the rumpled folds of his uniform and lit up. He blew smoke at the ceiling as Ninette went on.

"Here's what we know, my lovelies. The term 'angel' is derived from the Greek word '*Angelos*', meaning 'messenger.' Traditionally, an angel is an aspect of God's will, given human form, but... yes, Marius?"

Marius put his hand down. "Can New Girl be my guardian angel?" he asked, nodding at Kayla. "I'll need one, after what you just did to me."

"In which religion?" Ninette asked, her smile as sweet as honey.

"Religion?"

Ninette pulled a stack of leatherbound books out from the depths of her battered army bag and brandished them like weapons. "We can't understand what an angel is without knowing something about religion first," she began. "The average person's idea of what an angel is varies from culture to culture, from religion to religion, but we almost always get it wrong. The key to cracking this case lays solely in separating fact from fiction. Which is where you come in."

She began tossing the heavy books at Hunters at random. Kayla saw one clip Marius on the side of the head and suppressed a giggle, sharing a knowing glance with Phil.

Ninette turned around and opened one book at a marker. "There are so many different conceptions of what an angel is, of why they exist and what they are here for, that it's very easy to get confused."

She ran her finger down the page, then held up a picture of a winged man dressed in bronze Roman armor, carrying a bloodied spear. "In Zoroastrianism, for example, each person has a guardian angel. In other regions, angels are merely metaphorical. In some sacred texts angels have six wings, but in the Greek and Hebrew texts they're never described as having wings at all. To make things even more complicated, popular art and literature through the ages have drastically changed the public's conception of them. Most people have a wildly inaccurate picture of what an angel really is. For instance, if I say the word 'cherubim,' what do you think of?"

"Little fat children with wings," said the blue-haired girl, scratching a tattoo.

Ninette shook her head. "Not before the Renaissance, Giselle." She wagged a cautionary finger. "Some Italian guy with a paint brush confused cherubim with putti—innocent souls who look liked winged kiddies and fly around singing God's praises. But hell, it looked good in the pictures and the commoners didn't know the difference, so who cares?"

"So who's Cupid?" asked Marius.

"Cupid was one deeply scary individual," said Ninette, without batting an eyelid. "I think you two would get on well. But more on him another time." She slammed the book shut and wheeled around, making one or two of the more nervous Hunters jump. "You see what I'm getting at, kids. Even in these modern times, people still have no idea of what they're really dealing with, and they've got good reason to be confused. Look up the term 'angel' on Wikipedia and you'll find so many conflicting definitions, histories and descriptions that you'll be there all day." She paused for a breath. "You'll end up on a porn site before you get to the bottom of it all, if you're lucky."

"Which goes back to what I was saying earlier about the Internet being evil," said Tony.

"You think the Internet is evil?" asked Kayla, surprised.

"All that free information floating around in the sky? Definitely evil," said Tony, with a shudder. "I mean, where exactly *is* the Internet?"

"It's in servers. Thousands of them. Owned by lots of different companies," said Phil. "I keep trying to tell you, man."

"Yeah, but has anyone ever actually *seen* one of these 'servers?'" said Tony, tapping the side of his nose. "Or does everyone just take everyone else's word for it that they exist?"

"Getting back to my point," Ninette went on, giving him an odd look. "A person these days can pretty much pick and choose what they want an angel to be, depending on their personal or religious preference. Ask ten people at random and you'll get ten different angels. Everything from your traditional, Biblical angels riding around in the Heavens and dispensing God's fiery judgment for picking our noses in church on the wrong day, right up to your garden variety New Age angel, watching over us and conveniently saving us when our car breaks down in a snowdrift. Some people think that angels might be extraterrestrials or visitors from the future, with their 'flying chariots' being spaceships and their space helmets seen as shining halos. But then, some people will believe anything so long as they've seen a documentary about it on TV."

Ninette paused, glancing pointedly at Kayla, who scowled at her. "Myself, I prefer to stick to more traditional sources."

She tapped the front of her Bible meaningfully.

"All religions seem to agree on one thing. Whatever they look like, and whatever you call them, angels are beautiful, powerful, and deadly creatures, endowed with all God's wisdom and knowledge of Earthly events, created purely to carry out His will, whatever that may be. Whether you believe they're real or not, they *do* have power over people who believe in them, which includes over thirty-nine percent of the American population. That many people and that much belief could be a very powerful force if mobilized."

"Do you think the 'dead angel' thing's a hoax?" asked Kayla.

Ninette shifted uncomfortably, glancing at Phil. "It's too early to tell," she said. "But if someone's deliberately set this whole thing up to mislead people, we need to know who they are and what they want. Things could get real bad, real fast. We need to recover this body and analyze it, so we can narrow down our search."

"No big easy, given that it's plastered all over the news," cut in Phil, turning to face the group. "The US government will almost certainly have the body by now. Last night, we intercepted police communication that led us to believe the body is being held temporarily in an evacuated hospital just south of Downtown—St. Gabriel's, to be precise."

"A hospital?"

Phil blew the foam off the top of his coffee. "They've got some state-of-the-art scanning equipment up there. They're probably checking this 'angel' out for themselves before they bring the Feds in and cost the taxpayers millions of dollars trying to cover it all up and bribing the media to kill the story. I did a drive-by around midnight, but the place is crawling with more cops than a Dunkin' Donuts on giveaway day. It's going to be a bitch getting in there, but slightly easier than getting an actual doctor's appointment in this day and age."

He gave his metal leg brace a hearty slap for emphasis.

"What if it turns out to be a fake, after all that?" asked Giselle. "Seems like a lot of trouble to go through if no one's even sure these things exist."

"Oh, they exist," said Ninette reassuringly. "Or at least, they used to. Trouble is, nobody's seen one for generations now. The last reported sighting was over a thousand years ago, too long to be scientifically verified. There's no real *evidence* for any of this, which is unfortunately what we need to get any kind of funding."

She stood up straighter, her clear, confident gaze unflinchingly meeting the eyes of every man and woman in the room.

"That's why I called you all in here. The uniforms upstairs want to wait 'til their reports are verified before blowing this month's budget, but by then it'll be too late. They say it's not our deal, that we're only paid to cover up proof of the existence of the Supernaturals: the werewolves, the vampires, the demons and so on. But if this thing is real, I reckon its ass is ours. I say we mobilize Unit D ASAP to get the evidence ourselves. That means moving tonight."

"Wait," said Kayla, as a hubbub of excited voices rose in the big glass room. "If angels are just aspects of God's will, how *can* there be evidence?"

The older Hunters turned to face her, their voices dying away one by one. "Surely religion relies on faith to keep it going," said Kayla, holding up a copy of the Koran like a shield. Her unadorned trainee uniform seemed to glow like a beacon under the harsh cube lights, but she pressed on regardless. "If we had actual evidence of God's existence, then that would deny faith. And without faith, God is nothing."

"Not so sure I'm following you," said Ninette.

"I'm just repeating what I've heard on TV, obviously," said Kayla, tossing her head slightly. "But it's an argument I hear over and over again. If anyone dares to question God's existence, people just jump in and say hey, *of course* we can't show you any concrete evidence of his existence. He's God. He works in Mysterious Ways, He's Unoffable—"

"Ineffable," Phil snorted into his coffee cup.

"Ineffable, right. He's all-seeing and all-knowing. He can do whatever He likes. If He chooses not to show up in Times Square in a big golden chariot pulled by fiery horses, that's His choice, right? He hasn't shown or manifested Himself to mankind in over two thousand years, so why should He suddenly start now?"

Kayla turned back to face Ninette, rocking thoughtfully back on her heels. "But if a dead angel turned up—say in L.A., the media capital of the world—that would be the biggest thing ever, surely? Conclusive proof of God's existence… just think about it, guys! The press would go crazy. The press *has* gone crazy. But no one really believes it. Because if it were true…"

"Carry on," said Ninette.

"If it were true," said Kayla slowly, "then it would mean the end of religion as we know it."

CHAPTER FIFTEEN

KAYLA STOOD IN the middle of the giant glass room, surrounded by a circle of older Hunters. None of them looked particularly pleased at her interruption, but she stood her ground, feeling Ninette's eyes bore into the back of her head as the group processed what she had just said.

Giselle was the first to break the silence.

"You're wrong, girlfriend," she said, snorting derisively. "You've got it backwards. If we had concrete proof of God's existence, that would mean that religion would finally be proven *right*. It would be the end of Atheism and Agnosticism, instead."

"Agnosto-what?" asked Marius. "Sounds painful."

"It means sitting on the fence," said Kayla. "Just in case."

"A real fence or a religious fence?"

"A religious fence, Marius," said Kayla, rolling her eyes at Ninette. "My point is, no self-respecting God would directly and obviously reveal His existence to His followers if He wanted to retain any credibility. Especially not in L.A. So the angel *can't* be real."

"Because…?"

"Because," said Kayla, getting into her stride now. "If we had final, conclusive proof that God exists, we wouldn't need to have faith in Him, any more so than we feel the need to have faith in the fact that the sun will rise tomorrow. That's why we don't have sun gods anymore. Science has explained the rising of the sun due to planet rotation, rather than a big War God heaving it into the sky each morning on the end of a long chain… a chain that might snap if you didn't put eight percent of your weekly earnings in the bucket at the back of the church every week."

"I rather liked the War God theory," said Tony, brushing an imaginary speck of dust off his chainmail. "Always know where you are with War Gods."

"But *personal* faith is what drives religion," Kayla went on, flipping thoughtfully through the Koran, which was bound in soft white leather. "Without it, a lot of people are suddenly going to be asking a lot of very sticky questions, which I think the Church would rather like to avoid." She snapped the book shut and put it down on the table. "The point I'm making is, a great general doesn't need to toot his own horn. He has men to do that for him."

"Or women," added Giselle loudly.

"Exactly. So… if the existence of God were finally proven, say, by scientifically analyzing the body of one of his messengers, His angels, then people would no longer *need* to have faith in God, because they'd *know* for a fact he existed. Religions the world over would just fall apart. And that would be bad for a lot of people."

"You sound like you've got it all worked out," said Marius. "Maybe *you* planted this angel."

"Why would I?" asked Kayla. "I have nothing to gain from it. But someone in power might. They say that religion is the opiate of the masses, and if this angel turns out to be real… let's just say a lot of masses are going to go through detox." She glanced up at Ninette for reassurance. "What we need to work out now is who would stand to gain from the public suddenly thinking that God is real, and the resultant crisis of human faith that this would create?"

Kayla took a deep breath, glancing down at the drink in her hand. "*Wow* that's good coffee," she added.

Ninette slowly applauded her. "Well done, Kayla," she said, standing up. "I'd just like to make one very minor point."

"Which is…?"

Ninette stepped forward and put an arm around Kayla's shoulders. "You're not thinking like a Hunter. You're thinking like a civilian. It's a good argument, but all this armchair philosophizing is worth diddlysquat in terms of actually helping us to crack this case."

She turned her back on Kayla to address the room. "Use your brains, children. Let's work with what we've got before we start agonizing over the theoretical ramifications."

She glanced down at her own coffee cup with a frown, and quickly put it down, then settled back on the table.

"The facts are these: a supposedly mythological creature has just turned up dead, in Los Angeles of all places. And Harlequin is back, which may or may not have something to do with this. If it turns out it's a real angel, then humanity will face the wrath of the Seekers. In a little under three days, in fact." She paused. "I explained about Seekers, right?"

"Avenging angels," said Tony, cracking his knuckles with gusto. "I like them already."

Ninette rolled her eyes.

"Where does the Bateaux Prophecy come into all this?" piped up Giselle.

"Very good, Giselle," said Ninette, proud of her for making the connection. "The Bateaux Prophecy states that the blood of an angel will restore 'one who is dead and yet lives' to Heaven. I'm guessing that Harlequin plans to use the obvious loophole in the Prophecy to restore his own soul and ascend to Heaven. He is a vampire, so he's dead. And yet he lives. But the Prophecy is supposed to help a human."

"A human?" Kayla's heart started to thud.

"Wait," Giselle interrupted. "Let me get this straight. Harlequin grabs a drop of this angel's blood, does some kind of hocuspocus with it, and bingo! Mister Mass-murdering Psycho's got his soul back and can go to Heaven? That's so messed up!"

"Correct. Unless Lucifer gets there first. In which case things could get really bad, if you know what I'm saying."

"Whoa, whoa!" Kayla stared around at the group in alarm. "Did I miss a meeting?"

"About twelve," said Marius smugly. "Try to keep up, newbie." He extended a gloved hand in mock-graciousness to Ninette. "Go on."

Kayla glared at him.

"This is about as serious as it gets, children," sighed Ninette. "If Harlequin gets into Heaven, there's no telling what would happen. Maybe nothing. But it could be the end of everything. There's a rumor that Harlequin made a deal with the Devil a couple hundred years back, and I'm guessing that the two of them still have coffee from time to time." She leaned forward on the table, her eyes glinting as she looked at every single Hunter in turn. "We have to get that angel's body back before Harlequin gets his grubby little claws on it. If we're going to do that, we need to work together. No exceptions." She flicked a glance at Kayla. "So I'm asking you all now, as Hunters—what's the first question we need to ask ourselves about angels before we go around pointing fingers?"

Marius cautiously raised his hand. Ninette glared at him, and he quickly raised the other in supplication.

"Just one question. I'll make it quick," he said.

"Please do."

Marius took a long, slow drag on his cigarette, his amber eyes sparkling. "How do we kill one?" he asked.

Ninette beamed at him. "Now we're *really* getting somewhere," she said. "It's almost impossible for a human to kill an angel, which leads me to believe that some other race did it."

She swung around to face the group, excitement crackling in her warm hazel eyes. "Which is a nice segway into the highlight of our meeting. We have a very special guest here to see us today, who should be here soon." She glanced at her watch again. "Our guest is the only person we know of in modern history who has had direct contact with an angel, and he's the only man who knows how to defeat them."

"Defeat them?" asked Kayla, glancing unhappily round the room. "But I thought you said..."

"I know what I said," Ninette cut in, a little too quickly. "And I'm sure our guest will be happy to answer all your questions."

On cue, there was a knock on the door.

"Ladies and gentlemen," she announced. A dark shape loomèd on the other side of the foot-thick glass, and she flung out a hand toward it dramatically. "I'd like to introduce you to a very special man. He is the founder of the Hunters, and one of the few surviving experts on angels. He's come a very long way today to talk to us. May I present to you..."

She stopped as the door burst open and a short, red-headed Hunter practically fell into the room. He was white as a ghost, and looked utterly panic-stricken.

"Drew. What is it?" Ninette asked urgently. "Is everything okay?"

It took the young Hunter several attempts to speak. "Not really," he said, giving an awkward bow to the assembled Hunters. "It's Sage."

"What?" Ninette asked. Drew stared down at the ground.

"He's dead," he said.

CHAPTER SIXTEEN

THE NOTORIOUS BAR known as The Viper Pit sat between two upperclass dining establishments like a canker sore on Sunset Strip. As the Town Hall clock struck two in the morning, Karrel led Skippy cautiously down the trash-strewn path that led down beside the square, black building, negotiating his way past, and in some instances over, the black-clad teenagers. None of the young hipsters crowding the street outside saw them, much to Karrel's relief. People seemed to magically drift out of the way as he reached them. One or two of the younger kids glanced in his direction as he passed by, but their expressions quickly glazed over and their eyes slid off him, frowning vaguely as though trying to remember what had caught their attention.

People only saw what they wanted to see, Karrel figured. It was impossible that a dead man had just walked past them on Sunset Strip with a seven-foot-tall skeletal praying mantis trotting at his heels like an obedient puppy, so people simply didn't see them.

That suited Karrel just fine.

He edged past two hulking security guards, who shivered and glanced around with uneasy looks on their faces, and arrived at a dark red door. It was lined with grimy red velvet, worn from years of heavy usage and inset with a solid silver plaque bearing a foreboding Latin inscription. The lights were out inside. The place appeared to be closed.

Karrel glanced up at Skippy, feeling excitement collide headlong with fear in his stomach.

"You're not shitting me? He's really in here?"

Skippy nodded.

"Can I run home and grab my camera?"

Skippy shook his head.

"Spoilsport." Karrel started forward and then paused, an apologetic look creeping across his face. "Uh, I don't know if they'll let you in here. Club rules and all that."

"Rules?"

"No, er, pets." Karrel pointed to a notice on the door.

There was a hissing, bubbling sound, and then all the paint melted off the sign, leaving it blank.

Skippy bared his teeth in a hideous grin.

"Right." Karrel quickly backed away as the molten paint began to eat into the brickwork. "Good call. Now, how do we, uh…"

Skippy clicked past him with an arrogant swish of his spiny tail and vanished through the door, ducking his head to pass under the low doorframe.

Karrel winced. He wished that Skippy had actually opened the door instead of walking through it.

Plucking up his nerve, he strode purposefully toward the closed, barred door, picking up speed as he neared it. He'd seen people walk through walls in a million ghost flicks; he'd always wondered what it would be like. Now, he was about to experience it for himself.

He reached the closed door and braced himself. He could do this!

This was going to be...

"Ow!"

Karrel picked himself up off the ground, rubbing his head. He stared up at the closed door in confusion and disappointment. Skippy's hissing, scratchy laughter was audible even through the foot-thick oak door.

"All right, fine. Very funny. You're a regular hoot. They should put you on *Oprah*." Karrel brushed himself off and took a step back, glaring up at the building. A faint red glow emanated from an open window near the top.

Karrel muttered an oath under his breath, then rolled up his sleeves and started to climb.

To KARREL'S SURPRISE, the club was packed. He jumped down from the open window and looked around in guarded interest. The polished dark wood floors reflected a sea of yellow candlelight, and the muted overhead lights gleamed in an expensive but tasteful way off the mahogany grand piano, which sat atop a low riser above the thronged dance-floor.

Karrel stopped at the bottom of the staircase, peering around him. The place had certainly gotten an upgrade in the four-plus years since he'd last been here, when it had been a dive bar owned by some drummer from a famous seventies rock band. The place had since been completely remodeled by someone with a fetish for red velvet and polished mahogany.

The five-piece band was between sets, and the air was filled with the soft chatter of polite voices mingled with the delicate tinkling of canned piano music. A pair of jazz trumpeters sat at the side of the stage, swinging their heels and having an earnest conversation with a young lady in a bleached yellow sundress. A tall, elegant black woman made her way slowly through the crowd, plying them with drinks from the exquisite multicolored crystal tumblers on her silver tray.

Not at all what Karrel was expecting, considering who they were here to see.

Karrel caught up with Skippy over by the bar.

"I gotta say, Skippy old boy. You keep some good company."

Skippy leaned back, revealing the crumbling skull of the barman, who grinned at him amiably. Not that he had much choice in the matter, on account of his having no lips.

Karrel tensed up, glancing at Skippy in distaste and surprise. He knew a zombie when he saw one, but this guy was getting no reaction whatsoever from any of the assembled patrons. Nor did he seem particularly bothered about eating anyone's brains, which was Karrel's usual experience with the species.

The barman turned to pull a steaming green pitcher of some ungodly liquid off the top shelf. He served a thimbleful to a well-dressed young woman in a white slip dress. She took a sip and hiccupped, two tiny gold flames puffing gently out of her nose.

"Excuse me," she giggled, turning away to hide her blush.

Karrel shook his head in bewilderment and impatience. He turned away and tugged on Skippy's slime-covered forelimb, then looked down at his hand in disgust. "Come on, man. Don't hold out on me," he said, wiping his hand surreptitiously on the leg of his jeans. "Is he here or not?"

"Relax. He's on his way," mumbled a weary businessman perched next to him on a sticky barstool, nursing a tumbler of whisky.

"And you are?"

The guy's whole attitude changed immediately. He tossed back the whisky with a gulp and stood up, dusting off his caramel suit before offering Karrel his hand with a bright smile.

"Peter Jones, at your service."

"I didn't ask for your service."

"Tough. You're going to get it." The man cocked his head, looking at Karrel knowingly through a drunken haze of exhaustion. His eyes were completely colorless, and they gleamed like two diamonds in his gray, sleep-deprived face. "You're here to meet someone, yes?" he said, with a hint of a smile. "A very *special* someone."

"How did you—"

Karrel froze, looking the man up and down appraisingly. "You're *him*, aren't you?" he asked. "You're Lucifer."

At the sound of the name, every head in the plush club turned in his direction. A couple of women gasped. Somebody in the next room dropped a plate with a loud crash. The barman stopped wiping his glass and gave Karrel a look of profound distaste.

The man stared coolly at Karrel, his diamond-hard gaze unflinching. "Most of our patrons would prefer if you don't use *that name* in here," he said. "In the interest of safety, of course."

"Your safety or mine?" said Karrel. He was beginning to see how this meeting was going to go.

The man laughed heartily, clapping Karrel on the shoulder.

"I like you," he said. The conversation around them restarted, obstinately a little louder than before. "And I never like anybody, so that's a big deal. You've got spirit, kid."

"See, that's the problem. I don't." Karrel shrugged the man's hand off his shoulder and turned worried eyes up to Skippy, who was sniffing the air thoughtfully. "It's kind of why I'm here."

"Karrel, my boy," said Peter expansively, straightening his suit and winking at him. "That's why we're all here. Right, people?"

There was a general murmur of assent from the bar.

"Let me guess," he said. "Murder victim? Big strapping young lad like you, I'm guessing you didn't die of a heart attack. Somebody got you good, and you want to find a way to make them pay." Peter peered closer, leaning right into Karrel's face. "I'm guessing there's a girl involved somewhere, too. Am I right or am I right?"

Karrel's defenses slammed down like iron shutters. Something was very wrong here. He felt the hairs stand up on the back of his neck.

Someone was watching him.

He glanced surreptitiously around the room, his mind clicking over into surveillance mode. At the top of the second-level gantry, a black velvet curtain behind a small sound booth window twitched back into place.

Ah-ha.

"Well?"

"What does it matter how I died?" said Karrel absently, eyeing the window. He didn't like this one bit.

"It's *everything*," breathed the man. The humor left his face completely. His unnatural eyes shone as he looked Karrel over. "Let me make this real simple for you, pal. You tell me what you've got to lose, and I'll tell you what we can do for you." He glanced at Skippy. "And tell your *friend* to stop licking the ceiling."

"Be glad to," said Karrel, not taking his eyes off the window. "Just do me one favor."

"Which is?"

Karrel swiveled around on his barstool. His eyes narrowed until they were as hard as the businessman's diamond eyes.

"Don't call me 'pal'."

Peter casually reached through Karrel's spectral chest to pick his beer up off the bar.

He took a sip, then raised it in a toast to the outraged Karrel.

"As you wish. *Sir*."

CHAPTER SEVENTEEN

As DAWN BROKE, Kayla lay on her bunk in her room, staring at the gunmetal-gray ceiling. She knew that she should probably get some sleep before the daily Roll Call at eight, but she was too wired. The base had erupted into chaos since Drew's little announcement, with Hunter teams sent out right, left, and center to look into Sage's death.

Kayla knew from her scant few weeks at the base that the Hunters lost team members on a fairly regular basis, but this Sage guy seemed something of a big deal. Kayla didn't get it. Ninette had told Kayla that the Hunters had been founded over seven hundred years ago in Europe, so how could this Sage be their founder?

It didn't make any sense.

Kayla rolled over in bed, sighing deeply. Angels and werewolves and conspiracy theories paraded through her exhausted mind, morphing back and forth and laughing at her as she tried in vain to put all this into context, to meld it with what she knew.

First fact: Harlequin was back. She was never really sure where he'd gone in the first place, having been told only that he'd vanished decades ago on some evil mission "to find himself," like some weird-ass vampire road trip. But nobody would tell her any more than that.

What were they hiding from her?

Second fact: Someone wanted the public to believe that angels existed, so they'd planted a fake angel body. Kayla knew this implicitly. If it had been a real angel, she reasoned, there was no way this thing would be receiving the media coverage it was currently getting. She'd checked both the TV and the Internet in Ops before returning to her room. This thing was all over the place. The media was in a feeding frenzy; the public was going nuts, their faith shattered by the daily overdose of wars and bombings and political misery. They needed something miraculous to believe in, to distract them from reality. And this cute little angel story was giving them just that.

Third fact: this Prophecy thing existed, and Harlequin was trying to use it to restore his own soul. But if a drop of angel's blood could restore someone's soul... Couldn't it work on Karrel?

There was a connection between all these things. Kayla just didn't know what. There was a piece of the puzzle missing. And she knew exactly where to start looking.

She groaned and rolled over, wrapping the thin blue coverlet around her bare legs in an attempt to stay warm in the cold, metal-walled room. She was exhausted, mentally and physically, and her eyes burned with the need for sleep.

But her mind wouldn't stop spinning. The knowledge that Mutt was still alive and somewhere nearby was driving her crazy. Mutt was her last link to Karrel, and before his capture by the LAPD, he had claimed to be Karrel's best friend.

Mutt knew why Karrel had been killed, what he had died to cover up. Kayla flung her coverlet aside and abruptly sat up, giving up on sleep.

It was no good. She had to find out more.

And right now, there was only one person who could help her.

"SORRY, LOVER. I'M busy," said Dana.

She folded her arms the best she could around her reinforced handcuffs, gazing smugly out at Kayla from between the thick square bars of her holding pen. She was naked save her tiny jeweled collar, and didn't look too pleased about it. Someone had found her an old leather trench-coat, which hung on her skinny figure like it had cost a thousand bucks. Kayla straightened her own rumpled clothing self-consciously.

"You're busy? Doing what?"

"Talking to all your friends," said Dana, with a malicious grin. She indicated the empty cell around her with a sweep of her hand.

"Yeah. You're funny. In fact, this room is full of people who think you're funny." Kayla rubbed her eyes with both hands. "Just give me a straight answer. Can you do that?"

"What's it worth?" asked Dana, her ice-blue eyes glinting.

"Everything," Kayla said, keeping her voice down. She moved closer and gazed at Dana through the bars. "You and I both want something here. You want out of here, I want into wherever they're holding that friend of mine. I need to ask him some questions. He could save the world, if he knows what I think he knows. So let's strike a bargain and save ourselves some time."

"Your friend? You mean the werewolf boy?" Dana smirked, enjoying Kayla's discomfort. She slouched down in her chair in the middle of the small square cell, swinging her dirty bare feet childishly.

"Listen. If you don't talk, they're going to kill you."

"They said they were going to kill me anyway," drawled Dana. "Remember? Your female drill sergeant of a boss kept reminding me of that when she was chaining me up." She flexed her bound wrists with a wince. "I swear she drew blood a couple times. What's her problem?"

Kayla shrugged. "There's no problem. She just hates werewolves. Hence her job as a werewolf Hunter."

"No kidding."

"She means well," said Kayla, almost to herself. "She's just very... practical. Very *decisive*. She does her job, and makes sure everyone else does theirs. She's saved my life about three times in the last four weeks. I owe her a lot."

Dana sniggered. "How 'bout you pay her back by having a word with her about her issues?"

Kayla shook her head. "No can do. She doesn't talk much about her past in the Hunters. I get a feeling that she'd prefer to leave it that way. But I've heard things—" She broke off. "I probably shouldn't talk about it. Not to you, at least."

"I can feel my heart bleeding already."

"I mean," Kayla went on, ignoring her. "Everyone here's had something bad happen to them. It's how we get new Hunters. Everyone here's had some family member or loved one killed by something nasty, eaten by a werewolf or a zombie or whatever. We save people; they come work for us. They help save others. That's the deal. That's how Ninette joined. That's how I joined."

"So she's training you to be just like her?" Dana snorted. She gave a delicate little yawn, exposing unnervingly pointed teeth. "*That* should be entertaining."

"Oh no. I couldn't be like her. Ninette... she's a cool cat, but she's too black-and-white about things. She's all 'Kill or be killed! Good or bad! Right or wrong!'" Kayla sighed, a wistful look on her face. "She just doesn't get that sometimes, there are shades of gray that aren't in that stupid Hunter handbook..."

"Are we talking about your little werewolf friend here?"

"Hey, screw you, okay?"

"I'll take that as a yes." Dana folded her arms in satisfaction. "Am I right?"

Kayla felt the blush start somewhere in the region of her feet and work its way up her body. She cleared her throat, once again glancing sheepishly toward the door. She had come down here to interrogate a suspect, and here she was, spilling her guts to a woman who had just tried to kill her. Great.

"So she doesn't get it?" Dana rose to her feet and moved over to the bars, gazing out at Kayla with a curious look on her face. "How a Hunter can be friends with a werewolf?"

Kayla shook her head, not daring to look up. She picked at a flake of rust on one of the bars, feeling like an idiot. "It's stupid, right?" she said quietly. "You guys are all evil. You kill people."

"People kill people, too," purred Dana, her voice as smooth as brushed silk. "That doesn't make them *all* evil."

"But still," said Kayla. "This guy—werewolf—whatever. He helped me. Even when it meant putting his own neck on the line. He stayed behind... he had a bomb strapped to his chest in a burning building, and he told us all to go, to save ourselves rather than save him. Then the police got him."

"So you want to go galloping off on your white horse to save him, like he saved you," said Dana, not sounding at all sympathetic. "How romantic."

She stepped up to Kayla, running her fingers seductively up the bars before gripping them tightly and baring her teeth. "Listen up, Sweetpea. Let me make one thing very clear. I don't like you. I don't like any of your gung-ho Hunter buddies. But I'll be honest with you. Right now, I like Harlem and his gang of meatheaded freaks even less. My life has gone to shit ever since Harlem took over leadership of the pack from Magnus. Times have been... difficult. I couldn't even begin to tell you what he…" Dana's voice began to shake and she broke off with a growl. "So here's the breaks, little girl. I tell you where to find your friend, and you put me into protective custody and sign something legal saying you won't kill me. Then you let me make a phone call. If you can do that for me, I might just consider telling you where to find Harlequin. Deal?"

"Why should I trust you? What if you're sending me straight to him?"

"Why would I do that?"

"Because you're a werewolf. You're evil."

Dana closed her eyes and banged her head against the bars. "Tell you what. Forget it. Just kill me. Then I won't have to talk to you anymore. Jesus…"

"I know the Dark Arts," said Kayla, with as much hauteur as she could muster. "I could do a Truth spell on you."

"*You?* You know the Dark Arts?" Dana let out an unladylike hoot of laughter. "Pull the other one, kid. There's no way you could handle forces like that!"

"So you won't mind if I run that spell on you?"

"Be my guest. I could use a good giggle."

"Fine." Kayla cleared her throat, feeling slightly foolish. She closed her eyes and cleared her mind, letting the words come back to her in a rush. "*Ignus… crescentum. Parlez-vous mon chat…*"

"Is that French for "Do you speak my cat?"

"Shut up," snapped Kayla. "I'm just warming up."

She rolled up her sleeves and focused hard, with what she hoped was a suitably mystical look on her face.

She wasn't lying about the Truth spell. At least, not completely. She'd had a lot of free time since she'd been moved into protective custody with the Hunters. One afternoon, she'd discovered a gap in the wall in the women's restrooms, which were located right next to one of the training rooms for the older Hunters. Since then she'd spent many very informative hours perched on the toilet, squinting through the gap with a notepad balanced on her knee. Ninette held very informal, extremely hush-hush meetings for the senior Hunters every Thursday. One day Kayla had been lucky enough to catch her teaching a colleague a minor Dark Arts spell.

From what she could gather before she'd left the Blue Room, Ninette and Phil were the only Hunters who openly practiced the forbidden Dark Arts. Only the most trustworthy older Hunters were selected by the pair to secretly learn minor spells, and even these were kept hidden from the big Hunter bosses, who constantly and publicly threatened anyone caught practicing the Dark Arts with expulsion.

The Dark Arts were the tools of the Necromancers, she'd been told. They had no place in the Hunter's armory.

Yeah, right.

Kayla took a big breath, wishing she'd brought her notebook with her. She tried to recall Ninette's words, muffled through the thick oak paneling.

"Empty your mind. Focus on your breathing, your pulse. Now... remember the last time you felt a strong emotion. Any emotion will do, so long as it affected you deeply. Focus on that feeling; let it

grow inside you. Perhaps someone hurt you, insult-ed you. Let yourself feel your anger. Feel it grow like a burning storm in your blood... connecting you to the elements outside. Visualize a target for your anger outside, you are a lightning bolt waiting to strike. Have you got it fixed in your mind? Good. Now repeat these words, and let it rip."

Kayla closed her eyes.

It was harder that she thought to focus, with Dana standing there staring at her like she was a loon. She concentrated until the sounds from out-side faded away, leaving behind a ringing buzz in her ears.

She remembered a month's worth of frustration at the Hunters, at being passed around from one Unit to the next like a disobedient and unwanted child, a child who nobody had the time or the incli-nation to take care of. She recalled being stared at yet overlooked, kept in the dark and ignored by a group of supernatural freedom fighters too intent at getting their own revenge on the underworld to care much about her personal tragedy. Of putting rounds in the concrete wall four feet from the tar-get while every other Hunter her age blew the center out with every slug, clip after clip. Of feeling like everyone else apart from her had superpowers, or at the very least were trained well enough to make it seem like they did.

About being treated like she was a nobody.

Kayla heard Dana snigger. She ignored the sound, drifting deeper into her own subconscious. She listened, focused on her breathing, on the tiny sounds around her, until a huge yawning space opened up inside her head, stretching off into the distance all around her. She heard two faint clinks as Dana took hold of the bars in her ringed hands to watch her intently, her breathing becoming slightly accelerated. Kayla knew right away what that meant.

Dana was worried.

Good.

Kayla began to chant the syllables she'd memorized softly under her breath, felt her own inner frustration flow out of her and join with the palpable feeling of distress that lingered in the air around her, down here in the cells, where a handful of captive vampires slumbered fitfully around her, awaiting questioning and their inevitable demise.

She drifted down further, letting the acoustics of the room form three-dimensional shapes inside her head.

Cells. Cages. Chains. A barred door.

The taste of ancient fear lingering in the air.

She felt a sensation of misery. It was coming from Dana like an invisible wet blanket, a tangible force in the air surrounding her. Dana knew she was going to die, and soon, if not at the hands of the Hunters then at the hands of Harlem's pack. She felt the sharp stabbing fear that went through her at the sound of Harlem's name, felt her hopelessness at ever escaping from him. She knew she wasn't strong enough to kill him, and couldn't run fast or far enough to get away from him. She knew that her days were numbered, that only her usefulness to the pack kept her alive. A succession of red-tinged images flashed through her mind, none of them pleasant. Kayla shuddered, quickly closing her mind to them.

That wasn't what she was looking for.
She went deeper.
Kayla's eyes flew open.
"You *have* got to be kidding me," she gasped.

CHAPTER EIGHTEEN

IN THE MAIN lab of the Downtown hospital, Mia stood frozen to the spot, her eyes riveted on the contents of the case. It was a good ten seconds before she could move again. She felt the cold metal of the lower part of the case nudge her thighs and realized that this was her cue to stop walking.

She stared, dumbfounded.

"Who did this?" she whispered when her voice started working again.

"They found him like that," said John, practically vibrating with excitement. "I heard them talking earlier, when I woke up from my little nap in the scanner. The police are trying to keep a lid on it in case people go nuts, but some guy leaked a cop-cam video to CNN and now it's all over the news. Only wish I'd found him myself. Just think of the money we could make! For the hospital, of course."

He stood opposite Mia, on the other side of the opened case. "Well?" he prompted, as the silence between them thickened. "What do you think?"

"I *think*, whoever did this should be horse-whipped," snapped Mia.

She spun around to face him, her eyes alight with anger. "What kind of fool do you think I am, John?"

"What do you mean?"

"Playing a joke is one thing. But messing with a body like this, *deliberately*... I want names, records, department numbers, and don't you dare hold out on me. If there are relatives involved, I want a plastic surgeon team in here, stat."

"Whoa, whoa, hold your horses, girl! This is how the guy came in!"

"Bullshit!"

"This is real, Mia! Look at it! Look!"

Mia glared at John, her lips set in a tight line of fury. Unwillingly, she turned her gaze back to the body. She didn't want to look, didn't want to see what had been done to the poor young man. She had to fight the urge the pull the cover back over the body, to hide it from unsympathetic, prying eyes. No wonder there were cops outside. If this was an inside hatchet job, and someone found out... oh, God, the lawsuits were going to close them down!

But to evacuate the whole building, patients and all...

Something felt wrong here.

Sucking in a calming breath, Mia reached into her pocket where she kept a spare pair of surgical gloves, eyeballing John sternly the whole time.

Pulling them on, she turned away from him and gave the body her full attention.

The corpse was a young man in his late twenties. He lay on his side, twisted over amid dozens of bags of surgical ice. He had been stripped almost naked but for his shoes and shirt. Aside from the terrible injuries that had caused his death, the man seemed to be in excellent physical condition. He was tall and graceful in build, and had one of the most perfectly symmetrical bodies Mia had ever seen in her life. His shoulders were broad as an ox, and his strong biceps bulged proudly in the cold blue light, leading down to powerfully corded forearms with gracefully slender wrists and hands. His long, impossibly fine, white-blond hair wrapped around him like a cocoon almost to his waist. The face beneath it was strangely androgynous, a wide, gently curving mouth offsetting his finely-chiseled cheekbones, almond-shaped eyes and thick black eyelashes. His creamy skin was lightly flushed, even in death.

He could have been handsome if it wasn't for the fact that part of his head was missing.

Mia cupped her hand to her mouth in sorrow. It was heartbreaking just to look at him, at what had been done to him. The man's chest was caved inwards in a gory mess of black blood and bone splinters. The wound extended down his stomach, the skin scraped away as though the man had been dragged over asphalt. Mia winced as she saw that his genitalia was completely missing, his thighs and groin caked in dried blood.

She reached a gloved hand out to cautiously touch the twisted, broken remains of some kind of

fake wings, probably bought from a movie collect-
ables store somewhere on Hollywood Boulevard.
The wings were huge, stretching down the dead
guy's back almost to his feet, and must have cost
whoever did this to him a fortune. The wings'
feathers were so fine they were almost translucent,
the majority being smoke-gray, arranged in sweeping zigzag arcs that bore only a passing
resemblance to the feathers on the wings of birds.
The shafts of the larger flight feathers were tinted a
pale, eggshell blue and marbled with silver. Every
feather shone with a rainbow oil-slick gleam, as
though each had been individually polished on a
daily basis.

Mia carefully stroked back the gray feathers to
see what the wings were made out of, but they were
so tightly packed she couldn't see through them.
She started idly stroking the wing, her mind a blur
of fury and fear. Whoever had done this to the poor
young man was just evil. There was no other word
for it. Her gloved hand continued to stroke the
wing of its own accord.

She stopped, frowning.

Carefully, she stroked the wing again, then again,
paying particular attention to the base of the wing
and the body. The wings had been implanted into
the young man's back. The sight made her shiver.
The neat slabs of muscle that covered the man's
shoulders had been parted and lifted up to surround the base of the wings, then somehow
stitched back into place. The base-posts of the
wings were just visible under the flesh, a graduated
whiteness of animal bone or possibly enamel making an organic-looking joint where the wings met

the body. Tiny feathers had even been implanted into the skin around the wings. A sweep of pin-sized feathers lightly furred his shoulder blades, then increased in size until they met the larger feathers and tawny down of the wing.

Mia peered closer and traced the joint with a cautious fingertip, hoping that the whole thing wasn't about to fall apart and make an even unholier mess of the man than he already was. If this was a big stitch job, it would have taken a very skilled surgeon to reposition the muscle like that and reattach it to the bone without subcutaneous bleeding or bruising. She mentally went through the list of people she knew who were qualified to do such a job. On a live patient, the bruising and swelling that occurred after even minor surgery often took weeks or months to go down. As it were, she couldn't see any scarring, or even the marks where the stitches had been taken out. This couldn't have been done to the guy after his death, as all the stitches had healed.

Mia jumped as John stepped up beside her, reaching out to touch the bloodstained wing. She'd completely forgotten that he was in the room.

"Any thoughts?" he asked, his young, arrogant face alight with self-importance.

Mia cleared her throat and knocked his hand away, her manner at once becoming professional and businesslike. Her voice sounded like it was coming from a long way away as she reached out to touch the gaping wound in the man's chest. "Gunshot wound to the right auxiliary muscle... severe head and spinal trauma. Second gunshot wound to the upper cranium, exiting at the base of the spine." She stiffly moved around the body, ignoring the wings. "Genitalia absent; complete removal of both penis and scrotum from the body possibly caused by impact of a large speeding object. Crush wounds to the chest and lower pelvic region."

"Mia. The guy's got wings. Would you stop being forensic for a moment and tell me what the hell is going on?"

"I'll tell you what we're going to do," Mia said quietly, without looking up. "We're going to get our asses out of this room and call the department head. Nobody goes in or out of this room until I've found out who's responsible for this."

"For killing him?"

"No, for stitching wings onto a dead body."

"But what if they're real?"

"Then we've got the world's first winged human on a slab, right here in L.A." Mia rubbed her eyes, feeling a wave of exhaustion pass through her. "The tabloids are going to love this one."

"But what if he's not human?" John's face brightened, his denim-blue eyes lighting up with wonder. He could already see his name on the cover of *Medical Science*, hear the dollar bills cascading into his bank account as his agent sold his interview to Oprah. "You've seen the news reports. You know what people think he is?"

Mia gave John a withering look.

"John," she said. "I'm a woman of science. I'll be the first to admit we don't know everything, nor do I truly believe a day will come when we do. Right now I'm sticking with what I do know, however misguided and feeble-minded that makes me."

"But think about it, Mi! A real live angel! And we've got him!"

"You mean a real *dead* angel," said Mia primly, pulling off her gloves with a snap. "And we haven't got him. Whoever brought him in here's got him. And that someone is plainly a fool."

"Because?"

"Because, if *I* found this guy and believed even for a second that he was a real angel, I wouldn't just leave him lying around unguarded. I'd seal off the place, surround it with police, call in the army, and kill anyone who caught even the *tiniest* glimpse of…"

Her voice tailed off as she became uncomfortably aware of John's eyes on her.

"What?" John cleared his throat. "Um," he said. He lifted an arm and pointed weakly to the big bay window at the end of the room.

Mia followed his gaze. Her eyes widened.

Three black-bellied army helicopters were approaching the hospital at high speed, their long rotors casting spidery shadows over the urban plains. Even a half-mile away, the enormous black gunpods were clearly visible.

The blare of sirens from outside suddenly sounded very loud to her indeed.

"John," Mia said softly. "I think we've just been very, very stupid."

The sound of the lab's deadbolt shooting back rang out like a gunshot.

The two interns stared at each other in horror as the sound of dozens of booted footsteps filled the corridor, coming their way.

The lab was bare apart from the freezer chest. There was nowhere for them to hide.

CHAPTER NINETEEN

Kayla's heart raced as she walked quickly through the underground maze of darkened corridors of the Hunter's base, heading toward her sleeping quarters, lost in thought. It was now coming up to five-thirty in the morning, but she was wide awake. Ideas and plans spun like fiery constellations through her head. A hastily-packed leather bag dangled from one hand, clanking softly as she walked.

Kayla was so preoccupied with her own thoughts that she didn't notice the figure tailing her until she was outside her own door. As she fumbled with her key in the lock, a gloved hand fell on her shoulder, making her jump.

Kayla spun around. Marius was standing behind her.

"Oh," she said flatly. "It's you."

"It was the last time I checked," said Marius, grinning down at her. He straightened his Upper

Division combat jacket meaningfully, opening his Sergeant-Pepper-style studded collar to reveal several dozen combat award patches.

Kayla relaxed slightly. She'd been convinced it would be the Sarge, descending on her like a gleeful vulture to grill her at length about the secret meeting she'd just had.

Or rather, to use Phil's logic, the meeting she *hadn't* just had.

Marius gestured toward her bedroom door.

"Can I come in? I'd like a word."

"How 'bout no?" said Kayla. "That's a good word. I use it a lot. I'm sure you're used to hearing it."

Marius's grin widened. "You always this jumpy?"

"Depends. You always this nosy?"

"Always. It helps me get what I want."

"Which is?"

Marius gave an infuriating smile in reply, straightening his decorated jacket as though this was the only answer she needed.

Kayla scowled up at him, feeling her temper rise. The coffee Ninette had given her had woken her up a little, but what she was really craving now was a quick nap, preferably with a pillow over her head and a chair under the door handle, before she put her plan into action. Her head was buzzing and she needed some time alone to process. Now this overdecorated idiot was standing between her and her warm, comfy bed.

She tried to suppress a growl as Marius smirked at her and moved casually between her and the door. He settled back against it, folding his arms.

"Come on. Admit it. You're curious, aren't you?"

"About what?"

"About what you saw back there. The fireballs and stuff."

Kayla shrugged. "Couldn't care less," she lied. "Besides, I already know about the Dark Arts. Ninette said she'd teach me when she got around to it."

"Bullshit." Marius brushed a lock of Kayla's hair off her shoulder. "But points for trying though, cutie. I'd been here three years before she even mentioned it to me. It's all, you know, classified."

"You want to tell me what you're doing here, or should I beat it out of you?"

"Feel free." Marius leaned back against the door, eying her bag. "After you tell me why you're leaving the base."

"I'm not leaving the base! I was just... tidying."

"Yeah, tidying your wallet and the keys to Phil's truck and about half a dozen maps of the city into your bag," scoffed Marius. "I saw you stop at the Recon room on the way back here, right after you came out of the werewolf pens. I know you've been talking to that crazy werewolf chick. Don't try and jack me around."

"Wouldn't dream of doing any kind of jacking around you, believe me," said Kayla, through her teeth. "Now scram. I'm busy."

"I bet you are."

"Marius, I'm only going to tell you once..."

"There was no way in hell you should have been in that meeting, let alone in the Blue Room. It's why I followed you back here, to see what your deal was. You got me intrigued. I think you and I might have a lot in common."

"Think what you want." Kayla prodded him in the chest. "I'm going to bed. *Goodnight.*"

"Suits me," said Marius with a dirty chuckle. He caught Kayla's finger and pressed it gently to his lips, regarding her shrewdly with caramel-colored eyes. "Just tell me one thing." He glanced back down the corridor, then moved in closer to her, lowering his voice to a whisper. "You're Karrel's girl, aren't you?"

Kayla hesitated, the humor leaving her face in a rush. She jerked her finger back and lowered her head so he couldn't see the look on her face. "Maybe. So what?"

"I *knew* it!" Marius punched the air triumphantly. "I knew there had to be a reason for a newbie like you to be in the Blue Room!"

Kayla shushed him quickly, glancing down the corridor in the direction of the shower room. "Yeah, well," she said impatiently, jangling her keys. "I'm not supposed to be here at all, so what do I care? I'll be leaving soon, then you guys won't have to worry about me anymore."

"Leaving? But Ninette said…" Marius studied her for a moment and his mouth fell open in wonder. "She hasn't told you, has she?"

"Told me what?"

"Oh, my God." Marius's face lit up with an astonished grin. "And you're just wandering around, out there in the world—ha!" He bent over and slapped his knee. "Absolutely priceless! Wait till I tell the boys about this!" Marius took a step back and put a hand on Kayla's shoulder to turn her into the light, regarding her with eyes that sparkled with mischief and amusement.

"Come on, cutie. Open that door. I promise you, I'll make it *well* worth your while."

"That's quite a claim." Kayla folded her arms, staring up at Marius. "And you can move that hand of yours. The next part of you that touches me you're not getting back."

"You promise?" Marius's grin was positively wolfish.

"I promise. Now either tell me why you're here, or go away. I need to sleep."

"How 'bout I tell you why Karrel died?"

Kayla was stunned. Her mouth fell open and she floundered around for a couple of seconds, staring up at Marius in amazement.

He *couldn't* know. Could he?

But wait. Her situation with Karrel was common knowledge amongst the Hunters. Nobody believed that she had really seen his ghost, or that he had appeared to her from beyond the grave. This guy was just using her tragedy to get what he wanted, whatever that might be.

By now, she had a pretty good idea.

"Not funny," Kayla said, her eyes flooding with hostility and suspicion. Abruptly, she shouldered Marius aside and jammed the key into the door lock. "You want to discuss dead people, do it on your own time. I'm going to my bed, and you can go back to yours."

She turned the door handle and pushed it in hard, but to her surprise the door didn't open. Kayla shoved it a couple more times, then frowned as a strange sensation filled her arm. She glanced down to her hand on the doorknob.

A wash of black static hovered around her hand, shooting out fuzzy white sparks that landed painlessly on her arm, tickling her skin like spider's feet.

Kayla gave a yip and snatched her hand back, then gasped as the black cloud followed it, trailing behind her hand like a swarm of tiny black bees. It spun around before reforming in a perfect ball of black plasma, orbiting her hand in a small vortex.

She shook her hand quickly and the plasma ball dissipated in a bright flash of light, shooting up her arm with a bang.

Kayla blinked as a strange wash of unearthly light filled the corridor. The Chinese dragon coin around her neck glowed with an unearthly white light, throbbing in tempo with her pulse like a disembodied heartbeat.

She looked up at Marius with dark, accusing eyes.

"Whatever you're doing, stop it," she said, in a hard, cold voice.

Marius shook his head, his face somber as he stared at the coin around her neck. "I'm not doing anything. Just running a couple of little tests on you. What's that coin thing you're wearing?"

"Lucky charm. Karrel gave it to me. On our first date." Kayla's hand closed defensively around the talisman. It was cool to the touch. "You can't have it."

"I don't want it. I want that other thing you're wearing. What is it?"

"This?" Kayla looked down at the inscribed silver pentangle necklace she was wearing on top of Karrel's coin. "Something else you can't have."

"What does it say?"

"I dunno. It's in Latin or Italian or something."

"May I?"

Kayla stood awkwardly as Marius touched the pentangle, turning it over in his hands. "*Fiat Justitia, Ruat Coelum,*" he read. "Interesting."

"What's it mean?"

"It means '*Let justice be done, though the heavens fall.*'" He looked up at her, his face serious. "Where did you get this?"

"None of your business." Marius caught her by the shoulders and held her still, raising a cautionary finger. He lifted his hand and placed it over her own on top of the dragon necklace. He jerked slightly as a golden white light shot up through his fingers and slipped down his arm. Kayla watched as the light vanished beneath his skin like oil seeping down a drain, making him glow from the inside out.

"Watch," he said with a grin.

Marius tightened his fingers on hers. The light blazed a blood-red trail through his veins, spreading up his arm and chest and into his face. It reached his eyes and shone out through his pupils, burning so brightly Kayla had to look away.

Then the light faded. Marius gasped. He released her and staggered away from her, visibly shaken.

"Now check your shoulder," he wheezed, after a moment.

Kayla glared at him, let go of her coin, and reached up to her shoulder. Her fingers traced the outline of the white gauze pad that lay beneath her uniform. She'd worn the bandage ever since Cyan had stabbed her through the shoulder a month ago.

The wound was partially healed due to Ninette's expert ministrations, but it still hurt like hell.

Kayla slid a hand under the cotton of her suit, then her eyes widened in astonishment. She ripped the pad off and stared down at her shoulder.

The skin beneath was smooth, unbroken. Her wound had disappeared.

"How the hell did you do that?" she burst out, her cynicism forgotten.

"Magic," smirked Marius.

"No such thing."

"Sure there is. If you really want to believe in it."

"Does that logic work on grownups, too? Ones who don't go to Disneyland alone at Christmas and believe that fairies hide their car keys?"

"Fairies don't take car keys. It's the elves who do that."

"That's it. I'm off to talk to the normal people."

"Kayla! This is important... just *wait!*"

Marius grabbed Kayla's arm, spinning her around. In a fit of annoyance Kayla yanked free, shoving Marius away from her. There was a bright flash of light from her necklace and a sound like electricity snapping. Marius yelled as he was flung bodily through the air, landing twenty feet down the corridor in an ungainly heap.

Kayla froze, staring at Marius.

The dragon coin on the necklace around her throat glowed red, awash with bright sparkles of energy that buzzed and zipped around its edges like a miniature firestorm on a string.

Marius raised his head with an oath.

"Oh yeah. That's *real* normal," he said.

CHAPTER TWENTY

KAYLA STRODE AT high speed down the service corridor, tailed at a short distance by Marius, who bounded after her like a small, excited terrier.

"Remind me again why you have to come with me," she muttered, turning a corner and stabbing the call button on a chrome elevator.

"Because I can help you."

"I don't need your help!"

"Fine. I won't help you." Marius caught up with her and leaned against the wall next to the call button pad, pushing a strand of hair out of his eyes. "The basement's on floor G, by the way. Not floor B."

"Why are you still here?" Kayla burst out.

"Because!" Marius checked his volume and regarded her with bright, impish eyes. "Because," he amended, "I want to see how this all ends."

"It'll end with you in a body bag if you don't move your Hot Topic Wannabe ass out of my way."

Marius smiled an infuriating little smile and scampered after her, hopping into the elevator as the doors slid closed behind them. Lights blinked inside and they dropped rapidly with an unhealthy grating sound. Kayla guessed that this particular elevator wasn't used much.

"You said you knew why Karrel died," snapped Kayla, peering down at the hastily scrawled address she held in one hand. "Talk."

"Not here."

"Why?"

"Because they'll kill me if I tell you."

"Who'll kill you?"

"The Hunters. This thing could be bugged."

Kayla slammed her hand down on the Emergency Stop button. The elevator groaned and lurched to a halt, jolting them. As Marius yelped and clutched the walls for support she stabbed a finger on the Door Open button. "Out."

"Wait! Gimme a chance!"

"You had your chance. Now scram. And don't tell anyone about this."

"For a price."

"What?"

Marius dipped his head and pressed his lips against hers, quick as a flash. Kayla was so surprised that it was a second or two before she responded, shoving him away from her.

"What the hell did you do that for?" she yelled. She wiped her lips and raised a hand as if to slap him, then thought better of it. She doubted this ancient elevator could take the strain if she shoved him through a wall.

Marius shrugged. "Because I felt like it."

"And what's that supposed to mean?"

"It means that if we all did whatever we felt like, the world would be a pretty senseless place. Like you, little missy. Running off and leaving us just three days before humanity is due to be destroyed because someone killed an angel, just because you feel like it."

"But I'm not leaving!"

"'She lied,'" Marius finished for her. "Listen up, New Girl. You're cute, but I'm not buying your bullshit. I've got plenty of my own. But I'm not gonna let you screw this up for us."

"Who says I'll screw it up?"

"I do. I knew Karrel, by the way. He was a good man. It sucked that he died. I get why you're so obsessed with finding out who killed him."

"Get to the point," growled Kayla.

"My point is, Karrel was impulsive. Just like you. And in the end, that's what got him killed. If he had done what he was told to rather than running off and sticking his nose in everyone else's business, he'd be here right now." Marius paused, grinning. "And I just got to kiss you to make that point. If Karrel was here right now, he'd totally kick my ass."

"That could still be arranged." Kayla rubbed her eyes, glaring at Marius. The only person who had kissed her since Karrel's death had been Mutt, and only because she'd made the huge mistake of being semi-naked around him while he was drunk and half-delirious from a gunshot wound.

It would never happen again.

She should really beat the crap out of this guy just for existing, but right now, she had more urgent matters to take care of. She put a hand on the Door Close button.

"Any parting words?" she said with ill grace.

"Don't get killed. That would make me sad."

Kayla glared up at Marius, but for once, he appeared to be genuine.

She hesitated, then flashed him a quick, tight smile.

"No promises. Now *move*."

THE DOORS SLID aside a half minute later, revealing the darkened clutter of the basement. Nobody came down here often, that much was obvious. Dust lay in a thick layer over a damp jumble of cooling pipes, water storage tanks, and moldy storage boxes filled with an assortment of decades-old rusted armor.

Kayla clicked on her flashlight and made her way swiftly toward the back of the room. Reaching the wall, she ran her hand across a series of hatches, keeping an eye out for spiders or anything nasty that might bite her. In a place like this, they would probably be flesh-eating vampire spiders, knowing her luck. Kayla shook her head with a sigh, thinking wistfully of her old, uncomplicated life. She never knew what she'd had until she lost it. If her little plan succeeded, it would be a start at getting it back.

She put the flashlight between her teeth and pulled a crumpled blueprint map out of her bag. It was amazing what you could download off the Internet for a small fee. If the location of the Hunter's base hadn't been such a closely-guarded secret, she wondered if their L.A. headquarters would've lasted this long.

Tracing her finger across the glowing page, Kayla turned the diagram upside down, then glanced up at the vent above her head. It looked fairly solidly sealed, but after a couple of minutes' work with a screwdriver the cover popped off, sending a blast of cold, fresh outside air into the musty basement.

Taking a deep breath, Kayla muttered a brief prayer, then swung herself up into the vent and vanished into the square of darkness.

Ten minutes later, the earth in a long-disused parking lot bulged and split as an overgrown drainage hatch was flung open to the accompaniment of muffled swearing. Kayla's head popped out into the dim blue morning light in a shower of dust with a gasp of relief, like a diver breaking the surface of the water. Dropping her borrowed bolt-cutters back into her bag, she stayed down, listening carefully to the sounds around her. She was sure that she would hear alarms, see the huge Hunter security guards pounding toward her, their faces set in masks of thunderous rage, their Doberman charges baying at her as they slipped their choke-chains and flew for her throat, jaws gaping.

Somewhere, a cat yowled.

Reassured by this, Kayla waited a further minute, then threw her bag out of the vent and scrambled out after it. The dark shapes of the disused warehouse that sheltered the entrance to the Hunters' base lurked through the scrubby palm trees to her left, about five hundred yards away. To her relief, they seemed to be deserted. There was only one entrance to the Hunters' base, for obvious reasons. What with all the hubbub surrounding Sage's death the guards were concentrating their attentions on guarding that entrance, marching around it and whistling at each other in Hunter code.

They never thought that someone might want to break *out* of the base.

Once she was sure the area was clear, Kayla shone her flashlight back down the vent. She ran her hand guiltily over her improvised circuit-looper device, making sure it was firmly stuck in place. The piece of Coke can laid across the security circuit, fooling it into thinking that the circuit was unbroken. Kayla taped it in place with some duct tape she'd stolen from the club. Phil's unwitting advice had worked.

She was a genius.

Kayla carefully closed the hatch and covered it as best she could with earth and the stringy grass that grew nearby, hardly able to believe that her plan had succeeded. She felt on fire; she felt alive. For the first time since Karrel's death, she was out on her own, and nobody was keeping track of where she was. For a whole month she'd been under constant surveillance with a Hunter agent tailing her everywhere she went.

Now, she was free. She would go out, rescue Mutt, find out what he knew about Harlequin, and be back in her cubical before Ninette came to pick her up for her night shift at the club. Perhaps she could even find out some info about where this angel's body was, and save them all the effort of tracking it down in order to save the world by Sunday.

She would be a hero.

Kayla sucked in a quick, delicious breath, relishing the freedom, then headed as quickly as she could toward the main road.

KAYLA WAS SO intent on her own top secret mission that she didn't notice the silently flashing lights of the dozen or so cop cars flooding down the dirt track a half mile behind her.

Nor did she spot the four repainted LASD choppers moving in quickly from the south, their searchlights blazing.

By the time she reached the main road, eight minutes later, the two dozen hired men in policemen's uniforms had arrived at their destination, and their canines were making short work of the fresh trail she'd left to the rear service hatch.

The *unlocked* rear service hatch.

As Kayla vanished into the darkness, heading for civilization, Harlem hit the brakes on his requisitioned police motorcycle and pushed up the visor on his gold-plated helmet. He sat back in his saddle, surveying the scene before him with deep satisfaction. His stolen cop uniform bulged obscenely over his wrestler-sized muscles as he slowly cracked his leather-clad knuckles, one by one. A gleeful look settled over his scarred, vicious face. Engines buzzed as a dozen other werewolves on stolen motorcycles rolled forward on either side of him, converging on the disturbed spot where an

Alsatian was excitedly baying and digging at the earth.

There was a hollow scrape of metal, followed by a triumphant shout from the dog's handler.

The wind ruffled Harlem's spiked black hair as he pulled out a handheld tracking device. He peered down at it in the dim, unearthly early morning light, its flashing L.E.D.'s glinting off his various facial piercings and the pornographic tattoos scrawled across his heavily built upper body.

A tiny red beacon lit up on the tracking device, under a digital caption that read simply, "*DANA.*"

Harlem grinned, exposing pointed, gold-capped teeth.

He reached for his shovel and started digging.

CHAPTER TWENTY-ONE

DOCTOR PIERCE MORGAN was having a good day. There were three things he liked best in this world, at this particular moment. Two of them were currently standing in the hospital's main lab beside him, having an animated conversation about how wonderful he was.

Which led to the third thing he liked best in the world: beautiful, talented women saying nice things about him.

He tried to suppress a beam of satisfaction as they turned to him, their coy smiles of admiration hidden behind their clipboards. They giggled at each other as he smoothed down his graying hair and treated them both to a short, curt nod of what they took to be professional recognition. It was actually intended for the benefit of the surgeon standing beside them. Dirk. Dirk knew all about Piece's failing marriage, his two ungrateful, sickly kids, and his newly-acquired Beverly Hills condo. Dirk knew that the only thing Pierce was interested in was himself, hence the hastily-scribbled note to invite his two head female interns to this momentous, world-changing meeting.

If all went well, changing the world wouldn't be the only thing on Pierce's agenda tonight.

Pierce grinned to himself at the thought. Behind him the lab door swung open, disgorging a pair of hulking paparazzi photographers into the already-packed lab: a slender black man wearing an immaculate suit and dark glasses, and a scrawny, rat-faced man with tattooed knuckles and stringy hair, also in a suit. People shuffled out of the way, making room for them. Pierce's smile faded slightly; he wondered who had invited them. He had been told that only the winning bidder from today's meeting would have exclusive rights to any pictures of the body, or rather The Body, as it was now being called, which he thought was a touch pretentious.

Pierce didn't like people being pretentious. It reminded him of his evil schoolmistress Mrs. Morris, who would go through his painfully hand-written essays with her red pen, gleefully circling every error. Each and every stroke of her pen would earn him an extra beating from his jackass of a father, who tried to teach him spelling with his leather belt, or whatever else he could lay his uneducated, filthy hands on. The now-elderly Mrs. Morris had been admitted to the County General hospital several months earlier with a mild case of pneumonia, which had mysteriously turned into a major case of pneumonia under his expert personal care. They'd buried her in the Hollywood cemetery three weeks later. Pierce had personally gone on record saying that the Lord worked in mysterious ways, before taking the thousand dollars she'd generously bequeathed to him and blowing it on booze.

Mysterious ways, indeed.

Pierce winked at the two fawning interns and worked his way through the group to the front of the room, smiling and shaking hands en-route. He flashed a particularly warm smile to the archbishop, who stood somewhat nervously beside two representatives from the Vatican, who had flown in last night after hearing the news of the angel. Their tailored purple suits stood out from the ranks of gray government officials. The room around them was packed. Police chiefs rubbed shoulders with a number of mean little men with clipboards from some obscure CIA branch, to whom everybody gave a wide berth. Uniformed LAPD officers were dotted randomly throughout the large room, wearing identical looks of bored suspicion. They hefted their police-issue machine guns and scanned the room from time to time, ready to club people to death should any of the assembled clergymen or priests get too excitable.

Enough.

Pierce cleared his throat loudly, placing one hand on the large freezer cabinet beside him. One of the latches had popped up somehow, and he idly clicked it closed with his thumb as an expectant hush fell over the room.

"Ladies and gentlemen," he began, his melodious, charismatic voice ringing clearly through the lab. "What you are about to see here today is quite possibly the most startling thing you will ever see in your lives." He shifted, scanning the room. "What lies inside this freezer is no secret. You may have already seen its contents on the news, thanks to a certain, untrustworthy member of the force, who is regrettably no longer with us."

Beside Pierce, a pair of cops sniggered.

Pierce held out his hands to the assemble crowd.

"Today, I stand before you not as a doctor, but as a fellow member of the human race, in awe of this incredible turn of events which has gifted us with the key to unlocking the greatest mystery of this world: Why are we here?"

"Why are any of us here?" the bored voice from the back of the room said. "Make it quick, Morgy. My parking meter's about to run out."

Pierce shot the man an irked look, cringing at the sound of his unfortunate nickname. Detective Ned Crawley had been a thorn in his professional side ever since the man's recent and highly suspicious promotion. Crawley had risen to head detective a month ago after his boss, the charming Detective Jake Collins, had committed suicide while investigating a suspicious homicide case concerning a young man who had reportedly been killed by a wild dog.

Pierce even remembered the murdered man's name—Karrel Dante—because he'd been reading *Dante's Inferno* at the time, an ironic choice of reading material given his occupation and the city where he lived.

Pierce himself had conducted the autopsy on the late Detective Collins, and he had become intensely curious about how Collins had managed to shoot himself in the stomach from five feet away with his own gun. Before he could file a report and voice his doubts about the cause of the man's death, he had received a large check from an unknown branch of the police department for conducting the autopsy in such a professional and *discrete* manner. He had promptly and conveniently forgotten all about his curiosity.

Pierce put his hands on his hips and treated the diminutive Crawley to a long, blank look. Crawley's expensive suit looked about two sizes too small, and his trendy pink-tinted shades utterly failed to match his tightly curled red hair and sunburnt, pasty complexion.

"Patience, Ned," he said loudly, trying to hide his irritation. "This is a momentous occasion. It is not to be rushed."

"If I get another parking ticket from this rat-infested joke you call a hospital, it's coming out of your monthly budget," griped Ned. But he settled down, contenting himself with staring at the female intern's legs until she covered them with a swish of her hospital scrubs.

Ned winked at one of the photographers.

Pierce mentally counted to five, then flashed the assembled ranks of dignitaries his biggest, warmest smile. In the back row, a prominent cardinal folded his swarthy arms and frowned at him. Pierce felt beads of sweat break out on his brow. He spread his arms in the universal gesture of goodwill before launching back into his prepared speech,

"It is no joke that in these times we are at the brink of a crisis in faith," he began. "We've got wars going on, people killing each other because of what they do or don't believe. The world over, people are at each other's throats, dying by the hundreds of thousands in the name of their faith, all because they are convinced that theirs is the only true religion. What I am about to show you today could end all of that."

He looked from face to face. "Imagine a world without religious conflict, a world united by the love of a one, true God. A God who loves His children so much that he finally sent them a sign: real proof of His existence. A heavenly being who has made the ultimate sacrifice to restore human faith in his Creator."

"Yeah, right," sniffed Ned. He pulled out a tissue and noisily blew his nose. "Get on with it. Show us this fake angel of yours so I can get to Mao's Kitchen before closing time. They do a wicked coconut curry, and I'm starved."

"You mean that place in Venice?" piped up one of the photographers, the scary man in the dark glasses. He hefted his camera and glanced at his short, greasy friend. "We just ate there. We liked it. Good food. Big portions."

"The waitresses were pretty tasty too," added his friend with an odd smile. The larger man elbowed him hard in the ribs.

"Hell yeah," grinned Ned, warming to his game. "It's all good. That plum sauce dip they give you, with the free crispy wantons... it's like crack, I swear. I could just drink that stuff."

"*Thank you,* Mr. Crawley," Pierce said loudly, with a worried glance up at the security camera. It was recording his every move, beaming the meeting back to his boss, who he knew would not be amused at all these interruptions. If that arrogant little prick opened his mouth one more time, he would have Security remove him from the room. "Now, unless anyone else has something of equal relevance to add to the discussion, I propose that we open the bidding at five million dollars."

"Five million dollars!" Ned's eyebrows shot up. "We haven't even seen the body yet! Come on, Morgy. Give us a peek. What did you guys use to hold the wings on, superglue?"

"Enough!" shouted Pierce.

His voice echoed loudly around the room. A couple of the more timorous priests shrank away from him, glancing worriedly at one another. Whatever they had expected from this meeting, it certainly wasn't this. Pierce felt the sweat run down his forehead and wiped it away with his sleeve.

Fixing his gaze somewhere above Ned's head, he bared his teeth in an ingratiating smile. "Five million dollars," he repeated, sticking to what he knew. "I assure you, my friends, it pains me to put a price on the contents of this freezer, but you'll have to have faith in me when I tell you that the body of an angel—a real, flesh-and-blood angel—is beyond priceless."

He paused for a calculated beat as he recovered his lost composure. "You do all have faith, right?"

"OH, GOD. Is he still talking?"

Inside the thick, insulated walls of the freezer chest, Mia rolled over fractionally, shifting her weight off her left hip. It was in the process of freezing to the ice bags packed around the mutilated corpse beside her. The smell of the thing was appalling. She wriggled around in the dull, cold darkness until her left eye was level with the small metal vent grill in the side of the chest. A crack of blurry yellow light came into view, a triangular portion of the lab containing a large number of feet wearing worryingly shiny shoes.

They weren't going anywhere anytime soon.

Mia sucked in a huge, slow breath of warm outside air, trying to shake the feeling that she was suffocating in the confined space. There was the strong smell of antiseptic inside the freezer, mixed with something very much like chloroform.

She tried not to breathe too deeply.

"*Yes*, John, he's still talking," she whispered, fighting to keep her voice down. "And *yes*, I'm blaming you for this mess. My pants are stuck to a dead man! He's leaking all over my shirt! And if that smarmy doctor with the big hair opens this box up, there are at least fifteen cops with guns out there who I'm sure would like a word with us about what we're doing eavesdropping on this super-secret meeting. *Jeeze Louise!*"

She flopped back onto the plastic floor of the insulated chest, hyperventilating.

"Keep your pantyhose on, woman." John shuffled his legs to put the maximum amount of distance between his knees and the naked corpse's blood-smeared groin. "They aren't going to shoot us. Not in front of all those people. We'll just tell them what happened, then sign something that says we'll keep this guy a secret." He swallowed, his face sickly pale. We'll be fine."

"They're going to kill us." Mia lifted her head to glare at John, trying not to look into the frozen face of the still, white body beside her. There had been barely enough room for them to dive on either side of the angel's corpse and hit the *close* button on the freezer's keypad before the lab door had finished unlocking, but they had managed it.

Just.

The lab door had burst open just as the hydraulic locks on the freezer snapped closed, the sound muffling Mia's cry of disgust as she found herself lying in a half-melted pool of body fluid.

It wasn't, in retrospect, a particularly intelligent move, but it was all she could think of at the time.

Now, they had ample time to regret it.

John held up an irked hand to silence her, listening as the voice of the older doctor droned on outside. He tried to think of a way to get himself out of this mess. He had always wanted to get horizontal with Mia. Just not with the frozen body of a dead angel lying between them.

Considering the way his life was going at the moment, it figured.

He felt the heat of Mia's furious glare burning into the side of his face. If the cops didn't kill him for this, he mused, there was a very good chance that Mia just might.

THE BIDDING REACHED ten million, then stopped. All eyes in the room were fixed on the freezer chest. Pierce could practically hear the air sizzle with the tension in the room. If a troop of zombie clowns tap danced past the freezer, not a single person would notice them.

But orders were orders, and he had a job to do.

He had been told not to reveal the body before the bidding reached at least twenty-five million, to keep the suspense at its peak. However, Ned's childish banter seemed to have destroyed the carefully cultivated air of trust that he had built up in each prospective buyer in the hours preceding this meeting.

It was a shame, really. He'd been in on some scams in his time, but this one blew every shady deal he'd ever done in his life out of the water.

In the twenty-four hours since its discovery, every church, every government branch, every home security office in the country had been on fire with the news about this body. Especially since he'd leaked an internal hospital memo stating that it was real, and then paid a half dozen hospital staff to go on TV and deny it. He'd drafted over a hundred temps into the regional medical headquarters, just to answer the phones. Everyone had been told it was a hoax. If they had money, they'd been told to make a small 'donation' of five thousand bucks to St. Gabriel's to show good faith. In return, they had been put into a lottery, the winners of which were sent a single email containing a place, a room number, and a time.

That time, it seemed, was now.

As mutters of suspicion rose around him, Pierce surreptitiously crossed himself as he reached for the keypad on the freezer chest.

CHAPTER TWENTY-TWO

MIA AND JOHN stared at each other in mute, wide-eyed horror as four loud *clunks* rang out. A quiet beeping sound filled the air as Pierce disengaged the locks that held the case closed. The hydraulic jacks began to move smoothly upwards, spilling a hiss of refrigerated air out into the room. There was a gasp of anticipation from the watching crowd of dignitaries outside.

Mia tensed herself as the lid began to open, preparing to leap out and make a run for it.

Then...

A miracle.

The freezer lid stopped with a jerk, barely four inches up. The jacks shuddered with a drawn-out whining sound before retracting themselves, oil pattering out of a leak in one of the tubes. The lid closed partway, resting at an angle with a low crackle of fried electrics.

Inside the chest, Mia let out a breath of relief. They had been given a respite, for a few seconds, at least.

C'mon, girl. Think! Mia's frantic gaze raked urgently around the inside of the freezer. There had to be something in here she could use as a weapon.

A treacherous thought shot through her mind, and she willed it quickly away. Hell, no. There was no way she was going to do *that*. If she did that they would definitely shoot her, then she wouldn't be able to save John.

Not that he deserved saving right now...

Mia squeezed her eyes shut and let out a painful, long-repressed sigh. Not only was she going to die less than five miles from the town she was born in, the town she'd grown up in and sworn that she'd someday leave, at the age of twenty-five, she was going to die a virgin.

"Oh... *frickin' Hell!*" she whispered crossly.

Adrenalin raced through her system, making every sense hyperalert. She ignored John, who was waving frantically at her, and stared hard at the cold dead face of the poor man beside her. Her mind ran in frantic circles like a cat after a mouse, trying to think of a way out of this ridiculous situation. The angel's closed eyes were rimmed with ice-encrusted black eyelashes, his face still and twisted with death. As she stared at him through her haze of panic, something struck her as strange about his face.

He looked *different,* somehow.

She peered closer, gazing at the man's eyes.

Which suddenly and impossibly opened.

* * *

PIERCE JUMPED BACK as a loud female scream tore through the air of the lab, shredding his already-tattered nerves. He gave an echoing yell of fright and snatched his hand back from the stuck keypad as though it had bitten him, nervous sweat pouring off him in buckets. Every face in the room turned to stare at him. If he hadn't have known better, he would have sworn that the scream had come from the chest.

He ducked instinctively as the freezer suddenly thumped to the side as though possessed, sliding two inches across the metal work surface. He reached out for it without thinking to push it back onto the table, which was already creaking under the strain. Before he could reach it the five hundred pound chest jolted again, leaping upwards before crashing back onto the aluminum table, as though whatever was inside was fighting to get out.

But what was inside was dead.

Wasn't it?

MIA SCREAMED AGAIN, her brown eyes wide with fear as she stared at the impossible sight before her. The dead man had come back to life. He had seized John's throat in a death grip, a look of insane fear on his handsome, face.

He began shaking John back and forth with remarkable energy for someone who, just a few seconds ago, had been dead and frozen.

She saw John's face come into view beneath a blur of the dead man's flailing limbs and fluttering wings. His mouth was open in a soundless scream, his pupils dilated in a look of pure terror.

The angel rolled over him with a cry of fright and opened his mouth in a flash of blue, revealing teeth that appeared to be made out of pure pointed light. His blond head flashed down and John's body jerked. Blood sprayed out from beneath him and splashed in a wave across Mia.

John's body flopped back onto the metal floor, twitching and jerking, blood gushing from his torn throat.

Spinning around with a screech, the angel flexed its wings, bracing one on either side of the roof of the box. There was a loud, bass-heavy thrumming sound that Mia felt rather than heard. The metal of the freezer chest began to creak and tear as wet, hungry sounds came from beneath them.

Mia's throat closed in a paroxysm of panic. She drew back her stocking-clad knees and kicked as hard as she could, aiming blow after blow at the inch-wide crack of light above her between the two broken doors. There was hardly room to get any leverage. As a quiet, sickly bubbling noise came from John, she redoubled her efforts, putting every ounce of strength in her petite, five-foot-two frame into trying to free herself from this giant metal coffin.

She screamed as hands suddenly grabbed her by the shoulders. Mia whipped up an elbow and knocked them away but a second set replaced them, taking her arms and wrists in a firm grip and pulling her out. Light spilled over her. The freezer chest was open. She gave a yell of fear as the angel suddenly released its hold on John and spun around to face her, its wings clattering on the inside of the metallic box, its maddened blue eyes locking in on hers. And then everything went still.

Mia stared into the angel's eyes. She felt herself start to fall forward without moving, drawn inexorably into their whirling blue depths. A burst of painfully white light went off in her head and she felt the world fade away from her. A blurry blackness crept in around the edges of her vision, a blackness thronged with tiny white sparks of light.

As she looked into the eyes of the angel, Mia felt a truly sickening sense of aloneness. It was as though the entire gut-wrenching, mind-boggling blackness of true infinity was suddenly there in the freezer chest with her, crushing her into oblivion, surrounding her on all sides while she shrank to total nothingness, a pinprick on a dot on a crumb in the trillion-mile-wide universe, spinning away her pointless and empty existence in the ice-cold blackness of infinity with nothing but more blackness to look forward to at the end of it all.

A red star filled her vision, followed by a sharp splintering sound. Mia gasped as infinity shattered into a million pieces like safety glass, leaving behind nothing but confusion.

The world came flooding back. Her thoughts snapped off as adrenalin sluiced through her like cold water. Mia felt her body stretching and changing. She was buffeted around in a series of sharp, painless blows, as if in a giant tumble-dryer. There was a loud clanging noise, a series of screams and gasps, and suddenly she was free of the chest, tumbling in slow-motion through the air. Lights and people spun around her as she rolled and caught herself on her front paws, flipping over before righting herself and rocketing off in the direction of safety.

Mia was vaguely aware of panicked people fleeing all around her, but she kept blindly running,
batting aside legs and snapping at feet until her
head struck something metal and unyielding that
halted her panicked dash.

And then the world went away.

PIERCE MORGAN SHELTERED under the crushed
remains of a metal gurney and let out a long,
world-weary sigh. The lab which, moments ago
had been full of calm, important and above all *rich*
people, was now a confusion of running dignitaries, expensive equipment being smashed in a
series of drawn-out clatters, and the sound of gen-
eralized pandemonium. People who, moments ago
were about to give him lots of lovely money were
now shouting at each other and fleeing en-mass
through the air-locked doors.

The sound of multiple gunshots ripped through
the sterile air, further adding to the excitement.

Well, there went his early-retirement plans. Pierce
drew in his legs and curled up tighter under the
gurney, absent-mindedly wiping the blood off his
hands onto his five hundred dollar gray jeans as he
cursed feverishly under his breath. His mysterious
benefactor had promised him a cut of the profits
from this auction, which would've enabled him to
finally pay off his accursed mortgage and leave this
deathtrap of a hospital for good, but his dreams
had evaporated like water on the hood of a hot
Lamborghini the moment that cursed angel had
come back to life. His boss had sworn that the
industrial-strength chloroform they'd poured into

its nostrils should've kept it down and out for at least another twelve hours, but those things apparently had the constitution of a whole heard of oxen, and at least twelve times the strength, judging by the mess it was making of the freezer cabinet. Now look what had happened.

They should've just cut off its head and been done with it, but he hadn't wanted to get blood on his new jacket.

And Heaven alone knew how or why those two Pathology interns had got into this room, let alone what they were doing inside the freezer with his precious angel body. The first one they'd pulled out had been dead, with a hole the size of a football in its chest where his heart should've been. The second one had jumped out of the chest and then quite unexpectedly turned into a giant blonde dog. The dog was now hiding under the CAT scanner in the corner, refusing to come out.

Pierce sighed.

As far as days went at St Gabriel's, this was pretty typical.

Pierce watched in numb terror as the angel finally rid itself of the remains of the chest, punching through the shattered remains of the lid and hauling itself upright with a panicked cry. It spread its bloodied wings with a snap and turned to face the shocked onlookers, most of whom were determinedly trying to get as far away from it as possible in the confined space of the lab. A strange sound filled the room as it stretched its huge wings out on either side of it to shake the last of the icicles from them, the feathers vibrating with a low roaring sound that rattled the crystal beakers in the lab and sent beakers and bottles tumbling and exploding off the shelves on all sides.

Pierce saw the nearest cop raise his gun with trembling fingers and sight on the angel's head. Before Pierce could cry out a warning, the man had opened fire. Priests dived for cover as the other cops reverted to their training in the face of the impossible and mindlessly joined in, laying down a volley of covering fire. The angel turned and stared at them as bullets peppered his naked, ice-slicked torso. Pierce watched as the slugs sunk into his skin and vanished without leaving a mark, like pebbles thrown into a pond.

Pandemonium reigned.

As the crowds parted, his investors fleeing in all directions, Pierce saw the short, suited figure of Detective Ned Crawley making a beeline for the other side of the room, keeping himself pressed firmly against the wall as he ran in a low, urgent crouch toward the CAT scanner. Pierce watched in growing bemusement as Ned drew a strange-looking gun and fired four shots at the dazed creature beneath it. There was a yelp and the big blonde dog came barreling out from under the scanner, knocking Ned over like a nine-pin in its haste to get away.

It was a funny-looking dog, Pierce thought, with that surreal, all-accepting glow that came with shock and mild hysteria. Its hind legs seemed too long for it, and it had a short, scrubby mane of blonde hair, almost like the hair of the young intern it had been two minutes ago. They said that people came to look like their dogs, or perhaps it was the other way around, but still, *goddamn*...

He watched in bemusement as Ned picked himself up and chased after the dog, firing shot after shot at its retreating furry back. Pierce could've sworn it glanced in his direction and gave him an extremely dirty look, as though he was somehow responsible for all this mess.

Well, responsibility was a problem that he very soon would no longer have to face. Mainly because he wouldn't be here.

Hey-ho. It was time to go.

He surprised himself by letting out a sudden high-pitched giggle.

Pierce Morgan stood up carefully and deliberately, then tottered through the melee toward the door. Working in his profession, he'd never really had much of a grasp on reality, but after the intense pressure of the last day or so, he felt his ever-tenuous grip on sanity starting to slip. His boss would surely kill him now, if not for failing to get the cash for the angel, then for creating this unholy and very public mess. He'd thought the cops would've been enough of a safeguard, but he'd obviously failed to get the memo about bullets not working on angels. He hoped that the L.A.P.D. had enough cash left in its banks to cover all this up, and if not, that they wouldn't use his medical incinerators to dispose of the bodies again.

Those things were a pain in the ass to clean.

As the last of the imported dignitaries shoved past him and fled through the door, Pierce turned and cast a last, ironic look back at the lab, muffling another inappropriate wave of laughter. Everyone was gone now except for the police, who even now were falling back as they saw that their bullets were having no effect on the angel, and the two photographers, who were astonishingly walking *through* the fusitile of bullets toward the angel. They appeared to be completely unaware of the blood pouring from their bodies as they pulled out a set of block cuffs and a reel of thick rope, seemingly intent on capturing the crazed angel.

Pierce shook his head and gave another little gibber of laughter.

The world had quite clearly gone mad, and was now taking him with it.

The angel itself was crouched over the body of the dead male intern amid the ruins of the freezer, staring stupidly down at it as it reached down to touch the butchered man's throat, as though checking for a pulse. It made a soft noise of distress in the back of its throat, then bowed its head, apparently in prayer.

As Pierce stared, the angel froze, and then raised its head, staring past the police, through the hail of bullets, until its weird blue eyes met with his.

Pierce's hand fell from the doorknob as a sudden feeling of mindless, infinite terror slammed into him. He felt the world dropping away from him and stumbled, gasping for breath. Looking into the angel's eyes was like looking into the eyes of an alien in a far-off star-system, whirling endlessly in space where no light or life ever went, utterly alone, with no hope or reason or anything approaching meaningfulness to cling to. Pierce gasped as a vast, incomprehensible sense of distance hit him, and clutched at the doorframe for support. The angel wasn't human—he knew that at gut-level—but also, somehow, this non-human thing was *judging* him, deciding his fate based on what he was, what he had done, things he hadn't even thought of doing yet.

But it wasn't the one doing the judging. The angel's eyes were like that damned security camera, taking everything in whilst giving nothing out, relaying everything back to Head Office where his eventual fate would be decided by forces outside of his control.

In both cases, he knew he'd screwed up, big-time.

For the first time in his short, self-involved little life, Pierce experienced a horrifying moment of existential doubt. Everything he'd seen and done in his life was laid bare before his own eyes, stripped of all pretense and ego.

When Pierce came to, a moment later, he was ashamed to find himself sobbing mindlessly for his father.

And the angel had gone.

ALARM BELLS RANG as Mitzi and Jackdoor hurried down the long sea-green corridor of the hospital ten minutes later, their fake cameras slung forgotten over their shoulders. The hospital was deserted, but here or there they ran into a cowering government official, or the occasional lost and panicked-looking priest, all of whom fled with muffled shrieks when they saw what they were carrying.

Mitzi turned his head, tilting his expressionless dark glasses toward Jackdoor. One lens was smashed, the other coated in blood. "So?" he said in his characteristic monotone. "What'd it say?"

"What?"

"Your fortune cookie? From Mao's Kitchen. You never told me."

Jackdoor grunted non-committally, adjusting his own sunglasses and wiping blood off his chin. He hefted the struggling form of the hogtied angel a little higher up on his left shoulder, looping his fingers into the magically-charged steel rings that bound him to get a better grip. Harlequin had been very precise when it had come to the instructions on how to deal with this little guy. The trick in capturing an angel was to never, ever look into its eyes under any circumstances, he'd told them, hence the dark glasses.

However, it hadn't been as simple as that.

It never was, in their line of work.

Being werewolves, they'd had no problem in subduing the strange winged man, but the guy had put up an astonishing amount of resistance for someone whose body was still half-frozen, mortally wounded and had his entire body cavity packed with ice. Mitzi's favorite Japanese Samurai sword had melted when he'd tried to pin the man to the wall before cuffing him, and Jackdoor had lost two of his front teeth when he'd tried to bite out the winged guy's throat, only realizing his mistake a couple of seconds later when he'd felt his saliva start to boil. The teeth would grow back in a couple of days, but still, that wasn't the *point*...

"Well?"

"It said nuthin', alright?" snarled Jackdoor. "It was a dumb fortune cookie. Quit askin'!"

Mitzi smiled the scalpel-thin, patient smile of a man who knew without a shadow of a doubt that he was the most intelligent person in the room, or in this case, the corridor.

"You got *that* one again. Didn't you?" he asked.

"I said forget it!"

Mitzi shook his head in amusement. He reached back to pull the red silken band out of his hair, letting his waist-length black locks spill sinuously across his shoulders.

He picked up his pace, glancing sidelong at Jackdoor.

You didn't live long in L.A. as a hired assassin without learning a few tricks about people. Right now, those tricks were coming in damned handy, from a financial point of view. Jackdoor wasn't strictly a person, but he was as easy to read as one of those kiddies books with big fluffy pop-up animals in them, and about half as bright. Last night, Mitzi had overheard Harlem telling Flame how much they were getting paid to take care of this little job. He'd had to go and have a long lie-down to get his head around all those lovely zeros. That was the one good thing about being blind. It did wonders for your hearing.

Now, if he could just get Jackdoor off the job, he'd be set for life.

The two werewolves eyed each other as they hurried along the corridor.

"Not feelin' *superstitious* today, are we?" Mitzi prodded, trying to suppress a grin.

"'Superstition is for idiots what can't be trusted to think for themselves,'" Jackdoor snapped. "Least, that's what Harlem said."

"*Sure*, man. Whatever you say. But if you think you can't handle this job…"

"Look—" Jackdoor broke off and flashed a dirty grin at a fleeing female nurse, who took one look at the pair and very wisely ran for her life. "Mitzi, bro." he continued. "You know what I think about all o' this. I don't *like* workin' for that snotty vampire Harlequin, runnin' around wearin' out me new shoes—"

"You stole those shoes," Mitzi pointed out.

"*Point* I'm makin' is, right, that when a fortune cookie tells me I've got four days to live, I don't *wanna* be out here, doing Harlequin's dirty work! I wanna be snuggled up inside in me bed, safe an' sound, stayin' away from sharp pointy things and things that could fall on me and things what go bang when you stick your head in 'em. You get my drift?"

"The last cookie said you had eight days left."

"Yeah, an' that was four days ago!" wailed Jackdoor. "That's two in a row! It *can't* be a coincidence! Face it, man. I'm doomed!"

"No such thing as 'doomed,' said Mitzi calmly. "It's just a bit of paper in a cracker. How can it know your fate?"

"Because it's a *fortune cookie,* dumb-ass!"

Jackdoor hung his head, staring furiously down at the floor as they stopped outside an elevator. He was going to die, and he'd never really begun to live. The last woman he'd tried to date had dumped him as soon as she'd found out he was a werewolf, and he'd eaten her out of spite. She'd given him bellyache for days...

The elevator arrived with a *ding* and they stepped inside. He miserably punched the button for the basement, where an unmarked delivery truck was waiting to pick them up.

"It's not fair," he whined, as they dropped down with a smooth hum of hidden machinery. "Why can't I ever get one of them nice fortunes? Huh? One what says, "Be nice to chil'ren an' small furry animals and then good things'll happen to you?" It's a conspiracy, I tell you…"

"You're a werewolf, Jack. You're never nice."

"Yer, but I got the *potential* to be nice. I jus' never actually use it."

"Jackdoor." Mitzi peered out at his friend from beneath a bloodstained gray wing, a look of mock-amazement on his pale, hard face. "Are we having a theological debate here?"

"Shit, yeah!" Jackdoor giggled loudly. "P'raps it's because we're carrying an angel."

"It's not a real angel, dumb-ass."

"I know, but—"

"Do you think *he* knows that?"

Jackdoor glanced upwards. "Fuck knows." He shivered, licking his pierced lips. "C'mon. Let's get this guy locked and loaded so we can get outta here. I'm parched."

"Wanna hit Mao's again? I'm sure that this time it'll be—"

"I said *no!*"

CHAPTER TWENTY-THREE

HARLEQUIN SAT IN the darkness, brooding.

He liked to brood. It was one of his favorite pastimes, next to killing people and enslaving the odd civilization. Right now, he was brooding in a richly decorated antechamber at the top of a tall glass high-rise, drumming his clawed fingers on the pewter ballroom table that sat before a giant hooded window, looking out on the nighttime sprawl of Los Angeles. The room was cold and silent, decorated with the finest high-tech baubles money could buy, with HD plasma screen TVs and leather massage sofas. A silver mask hung on the door beside a fireproof black cape. AI waiter robots bearing trays of gold-rimmed glasses full of black absinthe cut with blood stood unmoving by the door, still sparking where he had torn their circuitry out with his bare hands. The werewolves had spared no expense in decorating his cage, and he'd repaid them early on by smashing it to pieces.

For that was all it was.

A cage.

The room was built of silver alloy walls eight foot thick, ringed with a high-tech array of motion sensors. It was built to trigger the accursed UV collar he wore around his throat, which would burn him bone-deep with its unholy radiation should he set one foot out of bounds.

Harlequin sighed. He lifted a clawed hand and fiddled with the steel-barred mask that was clamped over his mouth, Hannibal Lecter-style. Here he was, the oldest and greatest of the vampires, killer of kings, tyrant and despot, once worshipped by thousands, muzzled like a blood-crazed dog.

For he belonged to the werewolves now. He had been betrayed by his own people and sold into slavery for an obscene amount of money and drugs in a deal so shady it was said that the Devil himself had taken an interest. The werewolves let him out from time to time under heavily armed guard to do their high-profile hit work, before returning him to his prison to brood some more. And plot his revenge.

He was, he felt, in something of a post-homicidal depression. He hadn't killed anyone in at least ten minutes.

Already, this enforced captivity bored him.

He gazed out at the rich, sprawling view of L.A., a pensive expression on his monstrous face. Spotlights wheeled through the air outside and the occasional siren sounded, but aside from that the night was still. There were many memories here, in this young county.

Too many.

But soon, he would be free.

A quiet buzzing drew his attention. Harlequin looked down to see a large bluebottle fly buzzing in slow circles against the window. It hummed against the glass in a disconsolate fashion, then bounced off the pane and began whirring up toward him, drawn by the scent of the fresh patches of blood that were scattered up his chest and forearms.

Harlequin watched it for a moment, then snapped up his scaly fist and caught the fly. It buzzed hollowly inside his fist, its wings tickling his skin as it sought a way out. Then it was quiet.

The master vampire slowly opened his hand. The fly was sitting quietly on his palm, cocking its cone-shaped head this way and that in insect curiosity. Harlequin's enhanced vision brought it into sharp focus in the low light. The sprawling neon vista of the city was reflected a thousand times over in the tiny hexagonal crystals that made up the fly's multifaceted, rainbow-hued eyes. To him, the fly was beautiful.

"Tell me, little one," Harlequin said. "How goes it?

The fly buzzed excitedly, then revolved in a quick circle and began cleaning one of its wings with a black clawed hind leg.

"I would like very much to understand you, friend." Harlequin tilted his head to one side and brought the fly up to his face, inspecting the insect as though it were a fine diamond. "Yet I know that I cannot. Are you alive? Or do you merely look like you are alive? It is a mystery that could drive man mad."

He gave an odd smile.

A female scream erupted from next door, quickly dying away to a gurgle. Harlequin sighed and refocused on the fly, which was busily rubbing its forelimbs together and using them to clean its goggle-like eyes.

"You are but an insect, yet you have it all," Harlequin went on. "You have a body and a mind, a dozen fine senses, a will of your own. But for what purpose?" He gazed moodily around his prison. "I have to say, I envy you. You are but a tiny scrap of life, yet you bow to no one. You fly with the wind, and you go where you wish. The laws of mankind do not bind you, and they with all their wiles and brains cannot replicate you."

He settled back in his chair carefully, so as not to disturb the fly.

"Aye, they try, mind you. I'll give them that. But they are forever doomed to fail, the greatest human minds in existence outdone by a mere insect." He raised a hand to gesture toward the window. "The humans build immense flying machines that traverse the skies, but which cannot choose to fly on their own. They build artificial brains in their labs that cannot think for themselves, and fake hands that cannot clap to applaud their Creator. They make artificial bodies from mined ore and tamed lightening, superhuman bodies that cannot choose to go for a walk, or climb a railing to woo a lover. Man thinks himself superior because of this, his technological genius. Yet the lowliest worm that crawls in the dirt can make another worm, with not a brain cell or a flicker of intelligence to show for it."

The fly finished its bath and crawled to the edge of the vampire's hand. Beyond, the sky outside began to flush a rosy pink with the first light of dawn.

It buzzed its wings speculatively.

"Perhaps they are jealous of you," mused Harlequin. "They can create others like themselves, but even the highest-paid scientists amongst them can never create one such as you. Only the Creator has that pleasure, if one could call it that."

A doorbell tinkled on a spring above his head. Harlequin glanced up at it, but didn't stir from his chair.

"So what say you, little fly?" he asked the insect. "Where will you go now, and what will you do? The choice is yours alone to make. No jealous God can sway you to act against your will, so once again you top the humans. Your Lord demands no sacrifice, no offering from you, just that you eat and drink and spawn and die. You have no rules, nor are you made to feel shame for your actions. If you feast upon the rotting flesh of a king's corpse, you go unpunished. If you have ten thousand children on the Sabbath, you are simply doing God's will by being fruitful. If you kill a newborn babe with disease, they don't hunt you down as a murderer, but simply kill your kinsman in your place, in your image, and say that justice is done."

Harlequin's face darkened behind his barred mask.

"Where is the sense in that?"

The fly crawled to the end of the vampire's finger. It flicked its wings once, and then leaped into the air with a hum.

Harlequin snapped his hand shut, quick as a rattlesnake.

The buzzing ceased.

Harlequin closed his eyes, feeling the mysteries of the universe weigh heavily upon him. He slowly uncurled his hand and gazed down at the sticky remains of the fly.

"Where are you now, friend?" The vampire reached out and mournfully prodded a twitching leg with the tip of his talon. "Are you still here? Or did you go somewhere else?" He gave a strained laugh. "Perhaps you were never here in the first place."

The bell above his head rang again, impatiently.

Harlequin pulled out an enormous Magnum pistol and unloaded three rounds into the bell.

The ringing stopped.

Harlequin stowed the pistol beneath his leather chair and began painstakingly washing the fly's blood off his hands in the already bloody bowl of water that sat on the end of the table.

"This morning I asked a priest the same question," he continued, in the same pleasant, conversational tone of voice. "Like you, he did not answer me. He told me I was insane, that I was wasting my time with these riddles. Yet I know I am not. I know I can solve them, given enough time. For I am a vampire, after all. Time is my friend, though the world is not."

He let out a deep sigh, staring down at his reflection in the cloudy bowl of water. "Between you and me, I'm beginning to grow impatient."

"Talking to yourself again?"

Harlequin stiffened. He shifted his focus in the glass of the window so that the view of nighttime L.A. became a reflection of his antechamber.

A svelte female figure was silhouetted in the doorway, watching him. Moonlight poured across the table, picking out highlights of the trashed room in blue as he sat back with a creak and resumed his brooding.

A silence filled the room, heavy as lead, cold as the stars.

After what seemed like an eternity, Cyan X spoke again, her voice filled with a brittle brightness. "They brought the angel in a minute ago. Just so you know."

Harlequin inclined his head magnanimously and steepled his fingers, gazing quietly out of the window.

Cyan hesitated, clicking her polished fingernails against the doorframe. She paused and then backed up a step, her red heels clacking on the marble flooring. She could sense that the older vampire wanted to be left alone, but she couldn't bring herself to leave after such a brief exchange. She'd spent a good half hour in the restroom before this meeting, enduring Mitzi and Jackdoor's lewd catcalls from the next stall as she fixed up her silky black hair and touched up her makeup. She was wearing a rich red dress with diamond earrings, despite the early hour. She looked stunning.

Harlequin hadn't so much as glanced at her.

Cyan took a deep breath.

God, she was pathetic. Why did she keep putting herself through this?

It had to be love. Nothing else would make her act this crazy.

Cyan worked up a winning smile and cast around desperately for a topic of conversation, anything so that she wouldn't have to leave the room containing the only man—vampire—whatever—she had ever loved.

She had been obsessed with Harlequin since she'd first met him, now close to over sixty years ago, by her reckoning. Even now he held the same unspoken thrall over her. He was her sire, the one who had taken her plain, ordinary, boring life all those years ago and made her into something more, something better: an immortal vampire. It was he who had singled her out of the crowd of fawning she-vamps begging for his favors. He had gifted her with impossibly expensive bio-cybernetic enhancements, making her more deadly than any other vampire in the kingdom... except possibly himself.

At least, that was the way he saw it.

Every minute of every day her thoughts were filled with him, of what she could do to win his love, of what they would do together once he was hers. They would rule the world, and she would finally be happy.

It was just a pity that he couldn't stand her.

Other than that, they were perfect for each other.

Cyan bit her lip, her eyes tracking around the room as a clock ticked loudly above her. A flash of inspiration struck and she briskly straightened, rubbing her hands together.

"Have you seen Rosita?" she asked, peering around the edge of the door into the room. "We've been looking for her everywhere. She tends to wander off. Probably stealing the silverware, you know what those filthy werewolves are like…"

She broke off as Harlequin pushed back his chair slightly, revealing a dark shape on the floor before him.

Cyan glanced down and paled, her hand flying to her mouth.

"Oh," she said, trying not to gag. "There she is."

She swallowed hard, feeling bile rise in her throat. "Bits of her, at least."

A hand clapped her heavily on the shoulder and she spun around with a yip of fright, glaring at Harlem. The big serial-killer werewolf stood in the doorway behind her. His clothes were charred and he had a leaking bullet hole in the side of his neck, but he didn't seem to notice his injuries.

He nodded amiably at Harlequin, then turned his knife-sharp gaze back to Cyan.

"You look nice today, Cyan," he said, somehow making those few bland words sound like a mortal threat.

"I look nice every day," replied Cyan, distracted, still gazing at Harlequin. "Not that anyone else around here seems to notice."

"I *always* notice, darlin'." Harlem sounded offended. He frowned at her, shrugged his charred weapons harness off his shoulders, and dumped it down on a tabletop. Brushing past Cyan with a sly caress, he moved into the room.

"Is that an eyeball?" he asked.

Harlequin didn't reply.

Harlem reached down and picked the object up, inspecting it closely. "You gonna eat that?" he asked. "That's the best bit, you know."

The big werewolf popped the eyeball into his mouth and bit down on it with apparent gusto.

"Not bad," he said, sucking his fingers. "Could use some ketchup, though."

"Is there something you wish to discuss with me?" snapped Harlequin, speaking for the first time. He didn't rise from his chair, but his tone of voice made both Cyan and Harlem take a quick step back.

Harlem shrugged nonchalantly, turning to study Cyan, his amber eyes narrowing. "So what's been going on up here? Huh? You two havin' a little vampire meeting? Plotting against me behind my back, perhaps?"

His tone was light, even as his fingers crept down to his six trademark throwing knives which he kept in a sheath strapped over his shoulder.

"I told him about the angel. That's all, baby."

"You'd better *bet* that's all," growled Harlem. He moved back and protectively looped a tattooed arm around Cyan's waist. "I catch you touchin' what don't belong to you, things could get bad. A man could lose his head over somthin' like that." He tapped the beeping UV remote unit in his pocket meaningfully. "You get me, creature features?"

Harlequin didn't even bother to look up. Even if he killed Harlem to get the remote, he knew there were at least eight werewolf guards watching him on the closed-circuit camera mounted in the ceiling. Their leader had a copy of the remote. He would be dead before he got to the door, his two-thousand-year-old life cut short before he could put his ultimate master plan into action.

That would suck, to put it mildly.

"Wouldn't dream of it," he smiled.

"You wouldn't?"

The words were out of Cyan's mouth before she could stop herself. She felt Harlem silently lift his arm from her shoulders. She'd screwed up, maybe fatally. Harlem kept her around because she was useful and because he was obsessed with her, like every man that ever met her was. He hoped that one day she would return his feelings, but knew she never would. Already she was living on borrowed time—a vampiress working in a werewolf den— and any wrong word from her could end that.

She reached for her gun and Harlem backed off a pace or two, a look of hurt flashing in his burnt amber eyes. Before she could open her mouth to fix what she had just said the big werewolf backhanded her with all his strength, sending her flying across the room.

The vampiress hit a glass cabinet and fell to the ground in a blaze of flying glass. There was a familiar stabbing pain in her arms as her four bio-blades automatically deployed, ready to defend herself, a blade shooting out from beneath each wrist and one down from each elbow. Cyan twisted in midair and landed on all fours like a cat, her blades striking white sparks as they embedded themselves point-down on the marble flooring. Her head whipped up and she stared at Harlem in disgust, her eyes burning violet in the semi-darkness.

"Do that again, asshole, and I'll—"

"And you'll *what*, exactly?"

Harlem cracked his knuckles and folded his wrestler-sized arms, glancing back at Harlequin with violent mirth in his eyes. "Gee, I dunno.

Whatcha think, big guy? Should we just kill her now and get it over with?"

"What, and ruin my appetite for dinner?"

The master vampire waved a claw at the mutilated body of Rosita and grinned, revealing inch-long teeth.

Harlem grinned back at him. "Touché," he said.

CYAN LICKED A drop of blood off her lips and rose to her feet with as much dignity as she could muster. The only thing that had been hurt was her pride, but still, she was livid. She felt hot, bloody anger boiling within her as she smoothed her hair back and primly straightened her red velvet dress, now torn. She stared daggers at the two smirking men, one vampire, one werewolf. It wasn't bad enough that Harlem had burst in here like this and spoiled her one chance so far at getting Harlequin alone; now he was embarrassing her by belittling her, just like he always did.

Well, she'd show him. She'd show *both* of them.

As Harlem snaked toward her she clenched her fists, her bio-blades hanging down at her sides. Looking deeply into Harlem's eyes, she shifted, locking her wrist-blades with her elbow blades and transforming her arms into two deadly white swords. Moonlight glinted off them as she turned back to Harlem, brandishing her organic weaponry, ready to kill them both if need be.

She almost sliced her own leg off with surprise when Harlequin broke into a deep, throaty laugh. She glanced up in time to see him wink at

Harlem, then unfold himself from his chair and make his way in a leisurely fashion toward her.

Harlequin stopped three feet from Cyan and turned his mocking eyes on her, inspecting her like livestock. She cowered back from him, afraid of the ancient vampire's wrath.

"They say there are none so blind as those who will not see," he tilted his head in curiosity. His steel mask muffled his voice slightly, and the slatted bars over his fangs threw creepy shadows over his face. "Tell me, child. Is this true?"

"Sure. Especially if you eat their eyeballs," said Harlem gleefully, sucking on his fingers.

Harlequin ignored him. He gently put a ringed hand on Cyan's forearm, stroking the top of her bio-blade as he searched her face.

Cyan shook her head, not daring to speak. The master vampire's touch sent a rush of feelings through her so powerful that she could barely draw breath to reply.

"I think you're full of shit," she eventually managed, staring down at his hand on her arm. "You have no idea what you're talking about. Do you?"

"Your implanted weaponry," Harlequin said mildly. "I have given you a great gift. Do you not see it as such?"

Cyan bit back the torrent of resentful words that were forming on her tongue. The master vampire couldn't possibly know what he had put her through with his unwanted and irreversible surgery. "The pain is not so bad now. The new blade-sockets helped a great deal. But I still can't control—"

"You will learn," interrupted Harlequin, with satisfaction. "Time heals all things. Broken bones knit, broken hearts mend. The worms deal with all else."

Cyan drew her arm back sharply, glaring up at him. His tone was genuine. Was this some kind of apology? Maybe there was hope after all. Harlem's grin widened as he saw Cyan's confused look.

"I told you, sweetheart," he said. "This guy's got no time for women. Typical Hollywood dude." He gave a dirty chuckle and wiped his bloody nose on a sleeve. "And you say *I'm* a lousy date."

"What the hell would *you* know about women, freak?" Cyan whispered.

Harlem glanced at Cyan, looking her dismissively up and down. Then he folded his arms, turning his back on Harlequin.

"Last Tuesday," he said brusquely. "You tried out a new lipstick. It wasn't a big thing, but I noticed. I love that red one you wear normally, but that new orange one, with the bits of sparkly stuff in it that looks like bone chips on a smashed-up brain?" He nodded approvingly. "Suits you better. Goes with those little slinky dresses you likes to wear to kill people in. More, y'know. *Coordinated.*" He gave a small grin, revealing his sharpened canines. "Man like me's gotta appreciate that, cos I can't dress for shit. Although they say blood goes with everything... but I digress."

He tossed his head and stepped closer to her, his punk black hair casting strange spiky shadows over his scarred face. "Yesterday afternoon, you broke your shoes after kicking that doorman's head in down at The Kitty Club. They musta been pricy, 'cause when you got back from the can you looked like you'd been cryin'. The boys said you weren't upset about the shoes, but I fixed 'em anyway, when you were asleep."

He paused, looking hurt. "You didn't even say *nuthin'* about that. Cost me ten dollars to fix 'em, too. Sometimes I dunno why I even bother."

"I have no idea either," said Cyan. Harlequin had gone back to staring out of the window again. She wished that Harlem would just leave and quit spouting his usual pseudo-romantic crap, trying to get back on her good side so she would sleep with him again.

Harlem stepped up to her, reaching out to awkwardly touch her jaw with a sausage-sized finger.

"I'm a good man, Cyan," he said, straightening up proudly. "If you could just see that."

"Good man?" Cyan stared at him. "You kill people for a living!"

"So do you! Bein' a vampire and all that." Harlem stared at her defiantly. "I told you. We're *perfect* for each other!"

Yeah. Apart from the fact that I can't stand you, thought Cyan acidly.

Harlem froze, staring at her with his mouth open as if he had just read her thoughts.

Oh, shit.

Cyan swore to herself, flashing him a tight little smile. Harlem *could* read her thoughts, thanks to Harlequin's damned bio-technology experiments. He'd genetically altered hundreds of werewolves and vampires back in the Nineties as part of some botched master plan. Harlequin *always* had a master plan. That was the whole point of being a master vampire. Unfortunately, for both parties involved, most of his experiments had died.

But some of them—including Cyan and Harlem's pack—had lived.

Judging by the look on Harlem's face, that might not be the case for much longer.

"Look…" Cyan raised her bio-swords fractionally, getting ready to fight for her life.

She was spared the effort when the door to the room flew open, rebounding off the wall with a painfully loud *crack*. A short, scrawny vampire ran into the room, his eyes glowing a dim yellow in the darkness.

He skidded to a halt beside Harlem and saluted sharply. "Sir! Can we borrow you for a moment? We have a small problem."

"A problem?" Harlequin wheeled around to face him.

The young vampire strained his eyes into the shadows. He saw Harlequin and froze.

"Guh," he managed, staring in shock.

"Breathe, Spider," said Harlem, striding up to him. "What's up?"

"I… it… There's a… er," said Spider, unable to tear his eyes from the fabled King of Vampires. Legend said that he was dead, sent to Hell to pay for his crimes. Yet here he was, very much alive. He flinched as Harlequin turned toward him in interest. Spider quickly crossed himself, his face a gray mask of terror.

"English, man!" snapped Harlem.

"The angel… It kind of… set itself on fire," blurted out Spider in a panicked rush of words. "And now we can't put it out. We were wondering if you could, er, I mean, if you're not too busy right now to, um... We'd really appreciate it."

He clenched his fists and lapsed into a sweating, panicky silence.

Harlem rubbed a hand over his eyes. "I had to choose management, didn't I?" He sighed deeply. "Just deal with it, okay? There's a fire extinguisher on Level—"

WHAM!

"...two," Harlem finished. He stared, disbelieving, at the giant six-foot iron sword protruding from the top of Spider's head.

Harlem stared at the impaled vampire in shock. The sword had gone cleanly and vertically down through the unfortunate man's body, parallel to his spine. It emerged through the bottom of his pelvis between his legs, pinning him to the floor like a bug on a spike.

There was a moment of intense silence as Spider swayed unsurely on his feet. As one, Harlem and Cyan swiveled to look at Harlequin. The master vampire was watching the young vampire's twitching body with great interest. He chewed a fingernail thoughtfully for a moment, then pulled out a small pad and made a short note.

The *drip... drip... drip* of blood was clearly audible in the silence.

"Okay, I'll bite," said Harlem, in a quiet, careful voice. "Why did you do that?"

Harlequin watched closely as the young vampire jerked up his arms in a sudden burst of panic and groped around on top of his own head. His white, shaking fingers closed on the sword hilt.

He tried in vain to pull out the sword, his eyes rolling back in shock as he did so.

"Hmm?" said Harlequin, chewing on his pen.

"Do you have any *idea* how hard it is to find good staff these days?"

Harlequin's shrug indicated that not only did he not know, he didn't care.

An instant later a bright orange light spewed out of Spider's slackly dangling jaw. It rushed up to engulf his head in a blaze of supernaturally hot flame. His hair caught fire and began to burn with pyrotechnical gusto, a giant vampire match.

"Twelve seconds," said Harlequin with satisfaction. He clicked the top of his pen and wrote the figure with a flourish in his notebook, then snapped the book shut and stowed it away in the recesses of his clothing. There was a crackling sound as the fire spread down Spider's torso, white sparks flying as he burned the inside out.

"You never had any friends in high school, did you?" asked Harlem pleasantly, the heat of the flames washing over his face.

Harlequin ignored him. He moved forward and peered into the flames. Spider's bones were now visible through the glowing ruin of his flesh, hanging limply off the giant sword like a broken puppet dangling on a string.

"Vampires are such fascinating creatures," he said, in a dreamy voice. "It is their *resilience* that interests me. I have done many experiments. Cut a single limb off a human and it will usually die. A werewolf will regenerate its limbs if removed one by one, but not its head or heart. A vampire, on the other hand," he reached calmly into the blazing inferno, fished around for a moment, and then pulled out a sticky black lump of goo. It steamed lightly in his palm. "You can destroy the head or the heart of a vampire and it may regrow, after a fashion. But stake it with silver or wood and its regenerative properties instantly cease. I wonder: why is that?"

"You're a big freak. You know that, right?" said Harlem.

Harlequin touched the tip of his tongue to the heart, then smacked his lips a couple of times, looking speculative. "I'm not the one wearing leather pants," he said, glancing at Harlem's attire and winking at Cyan.

"The sword is silver?" asked Cyan.

"It is coated in silver dust." Harlequin eagerly turned toward her, dropping the remains of the heart. "You see, the iron alone won't kill it, but when the silver particles are absorbed into its bloodstream, they combine with the binucleated red blood cells that are the trademark of the vampire physiology, and—"

Harlem cleared his throat loudly. "Much as I hate to interrupt this fucked-up little vampire science experiment, we have business to discuss."

"Business?" Harlequin's face went curiously blank before he snapped back into awareness. "Ah, yes, business. The angel. Of course."

"That's one tough little motherfucker you got there, lemmie tell you." Harlem held up one hand, which had a hole bitten clean through it. "It kept trying to eat us so we knocked it out and tossed it in a pen. Bit clean through my hand when I was tying it up, the little shit. Now apparently it's on fire."

"The angel is still alive?" Harlequin sounded surprised.

"You don't want it alive?"

"No. Kill it."

"But—"

"It is no use to me alive. It is a liability. The fire cloak is a defense mechanism, nothing more. Dispatch it however you wish, and extract its blood for me. A drop will do, but better safe than sorry. Then we must begin the second phase of our plan."

Harlem scratched his head, looking doubtfully between the two vampires. "Ain't it bad luck to kill an angel?"

"Only for the angel."

"Gotcha."

Harlem turned to go then paused, glancing over his shoulder. Cyan was gazing up at Harlequin again, hero worship shining in her beautiful violet eyes. Blood began to well in Harlem's fists as he dug his curved nails into his palms.

"By the way," he added without turning around. "We killed the Hunters."

"Excellent," said Harlequin, still staring thoughtfully at the blazing skeleton. "How many?"

Harlem shrugged casually. "All of them, I think."

The master vampire slowly turned to face him, raising his eyebrows in an expression of genuine amazement. A heartbeat later his usual look of malignant boredom returned. Harlem realized with a jolt of satisfaction that the older vampire was trying not to be impressed.

"We found the base and torched it," he went on, trying not to sound smug. He saw Cyan turn to stare at him in admiration, and his black heart swelled with pride and satisfaction. "Wiped them all out like vermin."

"Any survivors?" Cyan asked.

"Nope." Harlem inspected his nails, delicately licking the blood off them. "Left Flame and a cleanup crew behind to blitz any survivors. Job done." He flicked a triumphant glance up at Harlequin. "Any other requests?"

"No." Harlequin sounded distracted. His eyes flashed with a brief pinpoint of red fire. He studied Harlem unblinkingly, as though calculating the exact level of Hell he would send him to for showing him up like this.

"No," he said, smiling suddenly. "That will be all. For today."

CHAPTER TWENTY-FOUR

THE TROUBLE WITH Hollywood audiences, thought Detective Ned Crawley, was they were so *jaded*. They had seen it all, done it all, and, in some cases, it had done them. Nothing surprised them; nothing moved them.

When he was a teenager, he'd been in a little garage band, like most kids growing up in L.A. He'd always hated playing L.A. shows. It was like playing to a house full of zombies, for all the audience response his band got. Nobody sang along, nobody danced. They just stood and stared, as though waiting for something better to come along. Occasionally, someone would take a picture.

Well, Ned thought smugly, this was one gig that was guaranteed to get a reaction.

Reaching the end of the corridor, he wiped the blood off his hands and punched a passcode into a keypad set in the black-painted wall. He gave a heave and pushed the heavy steel door open, letting a blast of noise out into the hall.

Inside the room, there was chaos. Dozens of off-duty cops sat on makeshift wooden benches, chattering excitedly. Above them were cleaner, newer stands padded with seat cushions and dotted with officers and sharply dressed businessmen in untucked shirts and ties. The ceiling and walls of the room were low and close, their metal corroded and smelling strongly of damp.

The air of low-tech disuse was largely an illusion. It was all about show in this town, and they had one hell of a show on their hands here.

In the middle of the room was a giant, brightly-lit fighting ring, twenty feet long by about ten feet high. Its thick plexiglass was reinforced by two-inch-wide metal bars. Steel rings had been hammered into the girders shoring up the walls. Thick chains the size of ship-mooring tethers snaked down from the rings and joined to ten heavy brass collars.

Nine of the collars were empty. The tenth was locked securely around the neck of a short-haired, tan werewolf. In the corner opposite the creature, a hulking, uniformed guard was in the process of removing the shackles from a scraggly teenage boy with wild eyes and dirty hair.

Ned watched, sipping his coffee. The guard got one shackle off the boy, then was forced to duck as the teen tore free and took a fear-crazed swing at him, revealing inhumanly pointed teeth as he snarled and spat at his captor. His silver eyes were locked on the werewolf, which was going almost insane with rage. It was practically strangling itself in its efforts to get to the boy.

There was a steel door set into the far end of the cage. On the other side of it Ned could see a terrified middle-aged man warming up, bouncing on his toes and stretching half-heartedly. His trainer stood by his side, one hand on the man's shoulder, no doubt going over defensive strategies.

Ned's eyes went back to the werewolf. He adjusted his red baseball cap and took another sip from his paper cup, swishing the warm, bitter liquid over his teeth reflectively. They were really scraping the bottom of the barrel today, by the looks of things. Thursdays were always slow, and he could tell that this new guy was in for a tough time. The werewolf they'd picked to go in the Ring with the paper-pusher looked half-starved, judging by its emaciated appearance, and the vampire didn't appear to be much better off. Werewolves and vampires traditionally hated one another, but they hated humans more. That combination of hate and hunger could easily drive both species over the edge.

Ned sniggered, looking the guy over critically. He was toast. The dude looked like some kind of home gym bodybuilder who worked out for four hours straight six nights a week to make up for the fact that he'd signed what little life he had away to his company years ago. All those muscles wouldn't do the guy any good if he didn't know how to fight. The man probably paid a small fortune and signed a hundred different liability waivers for this experience: the chance to fight a real live werewolf or vampire. Or both at once, in this case.

It was the ultimate ego trip.

A small knot of drunken men in rumpled shirts waved beer cans above their heads and cheered the man on. He responded with a small, sick smile before he resumed looking terrified.

It was going to be a massacre.

Cool.

Ned drained the dregs of his coffee and tossed his empty cup into the trash. He turned and made his way behind the stands toward the back door. Behind him, the cheering increased in volume. The guard strode across the cage to unchain the werewolf, but Ned had already lost interest. He'd seen it all before.

He had important business to attend to.

Passing through the door at the other end, he walked down a long, echoing steel tunnel before slipping quietly into a ventilation access door marked with large warning symbols. After descending a set of stairs into the semi-darkness of the lower levels, Ned glanced behind him once more before inserting a skeleton key into a small lock at the bottom of a bolted metal door.

Twisting it, he opened the hatch.

A pair of orange eyes gleamed in the darkness.

"You took your fuckin' time, mate," snapped Jackdoor, as he clambered through into the room. He straightened up, stretching his greasy muscles with a variety of stomach-churning crunching noises. "Where's this dude, then?"

"We put him in the pens. Level 3."

"Wanna draw me a fuckin' map?"

"I thought Harlequin gave you the details of this place." Ned paused, frowning at the werewolf. "You're one of his boys, right? You're sort of hairy for a vampire."

"Sure. Whatever." Jackdoor smiled evilly. Ned stepped back in disgust at the foul stench of decay on his breath. Jackdoor licked his lips and glanced around him with interest. "Cool place you got here. The gloom, the cobwebs, the stench of blood and death in the air..."

"Just do the guy. No other casualties. Got that?" Ned turned to pull the hatch closed, then paused, staring into the darkness.

The twitching body of a vampire lay dumped at the back of it, its head at an unnatural angle. It was too dark for details, but Ned could just make out the letter H branded in black tattoo ink on the skin of its torn-open chest.

"H" for Harlequin.

Ned's heart gave a nasty thump.

The other vampire—if he had been a vampire— had gone. The door to the stairs gaped.

Cursing under his breath, Ned pulled out his radio and dialed the emergency code. "Code nine," he said tensely. "We have a breach."

CHAPTER TWENTY-FIVE

THE COMPACT, MIDNIGHT-BLACK truck rolled to a halt in the weed-strewn parking lot behind the Los Angeles City Police Station. Inside the truck, Kayla killed the headlights and sat back on the warm leather. She gazed out the window, getting up her nerve as the sky around her steadily lightened from dark blue to a pale, delicate turquoise.

The station was deserted this time of the morning, or appeared to be. Two empty police cruisers sat forlornly next to the back door, the rest of the force apparently still out taking night calls. The main door was locked, the windows barred. It was coming up to six-thirty a.m., and crickets buzzed in the trees. The pale sun crept slowly up into the sky, as though afraid of what it might find after the horrors of the nighttime.

She really wasn't doing anything illegal, Kayla told herself as she jumped out of the truck and fished around in the back. Just a little breaking-and-entering. Nothing she hadn't already done a hundred times over as a kid. Growing up on the streets of New York, she'd had many opportunities to pull one over the eyes of the law, a little childish revenge on the people who had screwed her life up, following the events of...

Her brain stalled. She shouldn't be thinking about that now, of all times. She was a fine one to criticize people who didn't like talking about their past. She couldn't even think about her own, about the events that had led her to leave New York last year and move to Los Angeles.

And a fine time she'd had here so far.

So much for her "fresh start."

Kayla shut out all thoughts of her childhood and pulled her canvas bag out of the back.

Matches. Wire cutters. Pliers. A coat hanger. Her notebook.

Kayla was generally a law-abiding person when she didn't have a good reason not to be. She had a very philosophical attitude to the law: if she was breaking it for a good cause, or if nobody was watching her, then it didn't count. Since she'd moved to L.A., that "good cause" had been nothing more serious than her growing collection of novelty mugs and glasses, which she'd "borrowed indefinitely" from her various places of work. And the street sign, which had been permanently relocated to her bedroom in the middle of the night with a little help from Wylie and his ever-handy Swiss Army knife. It helped kill the boredom, and cheered her up in the process.

But now... Now, all the bets were off. The cops had taken something of hers, and she was going to get it back. Whatever it cost her.

Kayla locked the truck and marched determinedly toward the back door of the Police Station.

In the bushes beside her truck, a dark female figure watched her go.

GETTING INTO THE police station had proven easy enough. Kayla had simply walked right through the front door. The waiting room had been packed with the usual nightly refuse scraped up from the streets of L.A., everything from scowling Beverly Hills young bloods bitching to anyone who would listen about their "unfair" DUIs, to drug-addled ex-rock stars who had forgotten which street, and in some cases which city, they'd parked their fifty-thousand-dollar Hummer in. Addicts nodded and moaned in their metal chairs, the handcuffs that chained them to the benches clanking as they tried to roll over in their sleep. Sunburnt homeless people sat opposite them, ranting to each other or to the nearest potted plant, as they counted out sock-loads of quarters to pay off their Sleeping Violation tickets.

There was one cop in attendance, slowly processing people at the swing counter at the far end of the room. Judging by the look on his haggard, unshaven face, that figure was about one fistfight away from going down to zero.

Kayla hunkered down in her cheap plastic seat, silently scanning the room. There was only one door. She quickly made a plan.

She knew how this place worked. People were booked in over there, at the main desk. Then they were led, one at a time, to separate interview rooms for questioning or to pay street-offense fines. The burley security guard standing by the main door ensured that nobody caused trouble, or left without being seen to. A security camera relayed the events of the room to a video center in the back, which was probably being watched by some equally exhausted security chief who glanced up at the monitors from time to time while thumbing through a dog-eared copy of *Penthouse*.

Nobody would be looking for a young girl who wanted to get into the basement.

Kayla felt a quick flash of guilt for what she had done, which she quickly quashed. She was thrumming with nervous excitement, at the thrill of doing something daring by herself, without the Hunters to back her up. She still couldn't believe that Mutt was here, not twenty blocks from her old apartment. Screw what the Hunters said. She didn't need them to protect her.

She didn't need anybody.

Kayla glanced at the young homeless boy beside her, sizing him up. He was small and stocky and seemed to have at least a few of his marbles left. Unlike the wizened rastafarian in the seat opposite him, who raved at length about the end of the world to a nearby radiator.

"Hey," she said, smiling reassuringly at the homeless boy. "Want some gum?"

"They watch you from the trees, you know," he replied, nodding over at the cop. "You can't trust 'em. You can't trust any of 'em."

"I'll take that as a yes," said Kayla, handing him the gum. "I'm Kayla, by the way."

"Niko," said the boy, shaking her hand without taking his eyes off the cop. "Have you met The Lady?"

He shyly opened up the blanket on his lap, revealing a piece of polished driftwood dressed in a bonnet.

"Er, hi," said Kayla. "How's it going?" For want of anything better to do, she reached out and awkwardly shook hands with a twig sprouting out of the piece of driftwood. There was a knot in the wood at one end, which, seen in profile, did indeed look a little like a lady's face.

Niko nodded to himself in satisfaction, covering the piece of wood back up as though she'd passed some kind of test.

"I think she likes you," he said, then giggled. He turned and treated Kayla to a sudden, radiant smile, like a child given a bag of candy. "Welcome to the City of Angels. Have you come to save us?"

"In a manner of speaking, yes," said Kayla.

She reached down and gently plucked the Littering Offense ticket from Niko's unresisting hand. She couldn't help noticing how painfully thin he was, how his ribs showed under his skin beneath his dirty white T-shirt. He was scarcely older than she was. His pale arms were covered in cigarette burns and homemade tattoos. She wondered what stroke of ill fortune had brought him here, to this Godforsaken place, at the ass-end of the night.

She shook herself, trying to stay focused. There would be time to save the rest of the world later.

If the world lasted that long.

She stood as the night-duty cop waved a hand at Niko, gesturing him to come over. She put a hand on the young boy's shoulder, helping him to his feet. "Let's go sort you out, little bro," she said loudly, surreptitiously pressing a twenty-dollar bill into his hand.

"Sure thing, big sis," replied Niko, quick as a flash.

Kayla grinned to herself. This was going to be a piece of cake.

GETTING INTO THE basement, however, was not a piece of cake. Kayla hunkered down in the shadows, swearing to herself softly as running footsteps passed her on the metal ceiling above. Some plan this was turning out to be. She'd must have doubled back on herself at least twice since she'd slipped down here, and now she wasn't even sure which door she'd come in. If anyone caught her, her cover would be blown. The basement of the police station was a maze of interlocking backrooms and offices, and she couldn't even find the restroom she'd excused herself to use, let alone find her way out of here.

But she knew it was here. It *had* to be.

When she'd gone into Dana's mind, Kayla had seen this place from the inside out. She'd recognized it immediately. This was the station they'd brought her into after Karrel had been found murdered. She'd spent almost twelve hours here. In her surreal, shell-shocked state, every tiny detail of the place had been etched into her memory.

Or so she'd thought. Maybe they'd remodeled since she'd last been here. Either that or they'd just had a very organized earthquake.

She tried the handle to a random door.

Locked.

She moved on and tried the next one.

Locked.

Six doors on, she found a door that opened. She slipped inside.

DETECTIVE NED CRAWLEY pounded up an iron staircase at the station, barking orders into a walkie-talkie.

"Yes," he snapped. "A werewolf. In here. No, I don't know how it got in." He paused for breath, listening as the radio crackled irritably in his ear. "I think it was heading up to Level Three. Yes, the holding pens. No, sir. I have no idea. Maybe we bagged his girlfriend and he's come to rescue her. If he's male, that is. I wouldn't know about these things." He gave a brittle little laugh then subsided into silence, listening intently. A muscle twitched in his jaw. "Very good, sir. I'm on my way."

He clicked his walkie-talkie off and paused, frowning at the door in front of him. It was slightly ajar. He could've sworn he had closed it when he'd come down these steps, just a few minutes ago.

Which meant that someone had come down after him.

The detective backed up a step, then turned around on the stairwell and peered back down the stairs into the gloom of the next level.

A faint clatter sounded from below, followed by a muffled curse in a young female voice.

Ned reached silently down to his belt and drew his Glock.

He crept soundlessly back down the steps.

CHAPTER TWENTY-SIX

IN THE BASEMENT of the police station Cyan X lightly ran her hands over the captive Mutt's flanks, caressing each tattoo as though reading it with her fingertips. He had been moved to the main holding pens. Eight chains bound him, two on each arm and leg, to avoid any possibility of escape. She heard him suck in a suspicious breath as her expensive perfume washed over him. It was expensive because of the subtle blend of neurotoxins it contained, harmless to her but positively dizzying to anyone near her who inhaled.

She watched in amusement as Mutt snorted, blinking rapidly as his eyes dilated. She took advantage of his confusion to nuzzle closer, touching the very tip of her tongue to the soft skin under the young werewolf's ear.

"How come every time we meet, you're naked?" she whispered.

"Stunningly good luck on your behalf; stunningly bad luck on mine," grunted Mutt, struggling to focus on the three Cyans who were standing in front of him. He picked the least blurry figure and scowled at it, wracking his brain for a suitable dumb vampire joke. For the first time in his life he couldn't think of one.

He must be more concussed than he thought.

Cyan chuckled. She ran her tongue over Mutt's jugular, watched goosebumps break out down his neck as she closed the movement with a light kiss beneath his jaw. She buried her other hand in the young werewolf's thick hair, using it as a handle to tilt his head back as her other hand crept lower.

She'd seen weaker men forget their reason with less provocation. Mutt remained unmoved, turning his head away with a sharp growl as she gently kissed his neck before moving down in a series of soft nips that drew an involuntary grunt of pleasure from his throat.

"Tell me," she murmured. "What's this secret of yours? Why should one such as yourself… choose to ally himself with his sworn enemies… a group of misguided civilians and con artists who have killed more of your own kind over the years… than the vamps and the cops combined?" She lifted her head and gazed up at him. Her violet eyes glowed in the dim light, drawing him in hypnotically. "What possible reason could you and your wolves have had to protect Karrel for all these years?"

Mutt swallowed thickly, trying to hide how turned on he was becoming despite his bone-deep hatred of the vampiress. He was thankful of the darkness of the room and he backed up a little, putting some slack in his chains, trying to put some space between himself and her. "Maybe I'm gay," he said with a careless shrug. "Perhaps I was just trying to get into his pants."

"Even after he and his men slaughtered your entire family?"

Mutt's face went completely blank. His body didn't move, his expression didn't change, but Cyan felt a pulse of menace come from him that was so strong that she involuntarily backed off a pace.

She smiled uncertainly, trying to cover her momentary lapse of control. "So it's true, then," she said in wonder.

"Take your presumptions and your high horse and get the hell out of this room," said Mutt. His voice was so low that Cyan had to strain to hear it.

"Gladly." The vampiress smiled devilishly, her confidence swiftly returning. She straightened her white lambskin jacket in a businesslike fashion, tossing her long dark hair back over her shoulders. "But first I'll make you a deal. You tell me why everyone wanted Karrel dead, and I'll release you."

"Why do you care, you hog-humping bitch?" Mutt's voice was still dangerously quiet. He leaned forward until the chains that held him to the wall were taut, his eyes burning with a dark fury. "You got what you wanted. I'm sure the fifty bucks they paid you for butchering my best buddy was more than worth it."

"It wasn't about the money, precious. You know that," said Cyan, grinning impishly. "And by the way, it was sixty bucks. That's how much they paid me and the boys to kill Karrel."

She knew Mutt would leap at her, ripping his veins open on the barbed cuffs, but to his credit he merely clenched his jaw, regarding her from an inch away with a look of utter hatred. She felt the animal heat coming from his body in waves and leaned in closer, basking in the warmth. Vampires were cold-blooded, and they took as much enjoyment from human warmth as they did nourishment from their blood.

"Just so you know," she murmured, trying to provoke him further. "I took more pleasure in sending that son of a bitch straight to Hell than I've had with any man, before or since. Let's just say I was returning a favor he once did for me."

She brushed aside her silken dark hair, revealing the metal plate embedded in her skull. She tapped it with a long-nailed finger. "But that was before I knew."

"Knew what?"

Mischief glinted in Cyan's eyes as she stepped forward and brazenly slid her arms around Mutt. She brushed her cheek up against his, purring under her breath. She felt a lightning bolt of tension go through the werewolf and his entire body went rigid, but still he made no move to attack her. Adrenaline sizzled through her and she felt her bioblades stir, but she clenched her fists, willing them to stay down.

She wasn't ready to kill him.

Yet.

"That's just it," she said, burying her nose in his neck, pushing her luck as far as it would go. She could smell the blood pounding sweetly just beneath the surface of his skin; she lazily licked a line down the artery thumping in his throat. When she lifted her head again her eyes were unfocussed, a drowning blue suffusing the rich violet of her irises. "I know nothing. I killed Karrel because I was told to. I did it for the money, but no one ever gave me a reason. Whatever personal issues I had with him were a bonus, nothing more."

This produced no reaction, so she went on. "Then I find out he's Numero Uno on everyone's hit list, and that the original death warrant came not from his enemies, but from one of his own men."

Cyan tilted back her head, gazing up into Mutt's golden-green eyes.

"Can you imagine how curious I was? The vampires wanted him dead. The werewolves wanted him dead. Even his own men turned against him in the end, terrified of what he knew." She touched the tip of her pointed tongue to her teeth, gazing at Mutt's lips through heavy-lidded eyes. "So tell me this, cutie-pie. Why would the Hunters order the very public and extremely messy execution one of their own kind, unless he knew something terrible about them? Or more specifically... unless they knew something terrible about you?"

Mutt eyed Cyan for a long moment, then laughed.

"You know what?" he said. "You're wrong. What you said before—I *do* know you. I've met you before, in a hundred different bars, on a dozen different streets. You're the girl the guys talk about after their tenth pint in their local strip joint. The one they dream about on their wedding nights and wake up in a cold sweat, thanking God they married their little Jenny. You're the one the women glare at when you gatecrash someone else's party and leave with someone else's man, while secretly wishing they had the body and the balls to wear a skirt that short. You're The One That Got Away, the one they write about on the wall. The woman every mother is afraid their daughter will turn into if they watch too much MTV and forget to wear clean underwear when they go to the library." Mutt doubled up, his snort of laughter turning into a groan of pain as his bruised ribs complained. "You think they're jealous of you, Cyan, that they fear you, even respect you. But you're wrong. They pity you, nothing more. And you know why?"

"I have every faith that you'll tell me," murmured Cyan, brushing her lips over Mutt's bare shoulder.

"Because you'll never get a man like me."

"Excuse me?"

"You heard me," said Mutt. "Screw Karrel. This isn't about him, is it? It's about you, and your stupid ego. You can't stand anyone getting the better of you, can you?"

"Not so sure I'm following you, babe."

"Karrel did, from what I heard. He shot you in the head and left you for dead. That's one hell of a break up. I'd be pissed at him too after that, if I were you."

"Think what you want. I'm over it. He's dead."

"That's what *you* think."

"Excuse me?"

"You heard me, bitch. I said the brother ain't dead. You want me to spell it out for you?"

Cyan licked her lips, tilting Mutt's unshaven chin up with a finger to look into his eyes.

"Nice try, werewolf."

"Want me to prove it?"

"Go right ahead."

Mutt regarded the vampiress for a long, hard moment, his face inches from hers. Then he swiftly dipped his head, crushing his lips to hers. Cyan tasted the blood in his mouth and quickly deepened the kiss with enthusiasm, her tongue darting greedily over Mutt's sharp teeth as she plundered the depths of his mouth, nipping gently at his tongue with her own fangs. Blood began to flow afresh and Cyan gave a little sigh of surprise and approval, catching Mutt by his slim hips and pulling him tightly against her, purring under her breath.

This was more like it, she thought, as Mutt's arms tightened around her. Men were so weak. No matter how much they protested, how much they paid lip service to outdated concepts like virtue and faithfulness and trust, they always gave in to her in the end. Cyan found herself relaxing as her mind wandered along with her hands, wondering idly if she should stay his inevitable execution for a couple of days, for her own entertainment if nothing else. She could finish her interrogation later.

When Mutt eventually broke the kiss with a gasp and a growl, she was actually disappointed. She licked her lips with enthusiasm, eyeing Mutt's mouth greedily. "That's your proof?" she said breathlessly. "I like it."

"That wasn't my proof," said Mutt grimly, holding up his wrists. Two lengths of broken chain dangled from each one. Hot blood spilled from the barbed manacles now embedded bone-deep in his forearms. "This is."

Cyan stared in surprise for a split second before her reflexes cut in. She lunged for the door, but wasn't quite quick enough. Mutt's hand closed on her upper arm and he yanked her backward, spinning her around and slamming his elbow up. Cyan blocked the move with own elbow. Her hand flew over her shoulder to grip the hilt of the sword she wore in a sheath on her back. She barely got it out of its holster before Mutt counterattacked, whirling the lengths of broken chain over her head like nunchucks. The twin chains wrapped around the deadly blade of her sword and he yanked down on them, wrenching the weapon out of her grasp. It flew across the room and embedded itself a good five inches into the crumbling brick of the wall, vibrating with low hum.

"As I was saying, you dozy cow," Mutt went on, closing in on her. "Karrel ain't dead because he taught me everything he knew when it comes to women. And every time I pull one over a dumb, disrespectful slut like you, it's like he's still alive, cheering me on. You think you can control men by proving that they're weak, but all you're proving is how little you understand us."

He stepped toward her, eyeing her throat.

"What would you know of respect, werewolf?" snapped Cyan, backing off. She flexed her fingers like a gunslinger, preparing to deploy her bio-blades.

"I know that respect is something you *earn*, Cyan, not something you can force on guys by chaining them naked to a wall and then crying 'aha!' when they get cold and dare to ask for a little warmth." Mutt tossed his head in derision. "You think that's strength? You're crazier than they say you are."

Mutt stopped a bare foot away from her, regarding her coldly. He reached out toward her and Cyan tensed, but to her surprise he merely wiped a fleck of blood off her lips with his thumb. "No wonder Karrel fell for you. He was always a sucker for hard luck cases. You killed the one good guy who ever really gave a shit about you, Cyan. Nice job. I hope you're happy."

Cyan shook her head, curling her lip as her eyes raked disdainfully over Mutt's bare figure. "No such thing as good guys," she spat. "That's why I'm like this."

"Like what, Cyan?"

Cyan scowled in anger. "Fuck you, werewolf. It's guys like *you* that make women like me the way we are. If you didn't treat us the way you do, we wouldn't have to be like this. *I* wouldn't have to be like this."

Mutt shook his head slowly, his eyes glinting with a dark amusement. "Newsflash for you, kitten," he drawled. "Guys like me... the thing you've got to realize about us is that when it comes to women, we *just don't care*. We really don't. You might look like Martha Stewart on a bad hair day, but if we half close our eyes and kind of tilt our heads, you could be Halle Berry in a sexy wig. And if we drink enough, we might actually believe it."

"If you think that—"

"Show's over, darling. It's pointless trying to play us, because we've been doing it longer than you, and we do it far better. You run around with your airs and graces, trying to outstare the sun, and sooner or later it will burn you up. You'll never be happy, and you'll never find what you're really looking for."

"Which is?" murmured Cyan, her eyes narrowing to slits.

"A man who loves you enough to kill you. That is what you're looking for, isn't it?" Mutt's eyes glinted with an unholy mirth. "Because last I heard, Harlequin was washing his hair."

The humor slowly drained out of Cyan's face. "You're forgetting one thing," she said.

"Which is...?"

Cyan stabbed a finger at Mutt's steel collar. "You're still wearing *that.*"

In a move too fast for Mutt to follow Cyan snapped out her boot, catching Mutt a resounding blow on his injured left kneecap. As he folded in pain she pulled him back tightly against her own body, pinning his blood-slicked arms to his chest. She squeezed down hard, tightening her grip around him like a boa constrictor. She could snap every rib in his body should she choose to, but for the sake of her finances, she needed him to keep on breathing for a little while longer.

From the look on his face, Mutt knew it too.

Her voice regained some of its strength as Mutt bucked furiously in her arms. "Tell me everything you know about Karrel, including the home address of his cursed girlfriend Kayla. You'll walk out of here with what's left of your life, and maybe one or two of your ribs. Refuse to speak, and..."

The vampiress reached inside her jacket with her free hand and pulled out a slender remote control unit. The green button glowed in the semi-darkness as she traced it down Mutt's chest, watching the werewolf's eyes fasten on it and narrow dangerously, his body going still in her arms. Her mouth grew dry as her fangs unconsciously lengthened, ready to defend herself if need be.

"Or," she continued sweetly, "you can go up to that Ring every night, all night, and stay there until you've killed every human we have in stock. We have enough innocents to keep you well fed for at least another couple of months. Then, when you've killed them all, we'll release you. I'm sure your Hunter friends will take care of the rest."

The bravado slowly drained from his eyes.

Cyan smiled cruelly, stroking Mutt's brow.

"Your call," she said.

CHAPTER TWENTY-SEVEN

KAYLA CREPT THROUGH the musty basement of the police station, moving soundlessly as she scanned the area. Everything around her looked normal. Nothing seemed out of the ordinary.

It was hard for her to believe that there was a werewolf fighting ring down here somewhere, but that was L.A. for you. You never knew what you might find, if you dared to look.

Kayla slipped from shadow to shadow, her eyes searching the gloom for any clue as to where the Ring might be. Her small, blue LED flashed into all the doorways she passed. She still couldn't believe that she'd made it this far without being caught. She was a super sleuth, out here doing a mission all on her own, with nobody to nag her or tell her what she should or shouldn't be doing.

As she passed through a low brick doorway, her foot slipped on a slick patch of oil. Her foot flew out from under her and she caught herself awkwardly on a metal shelving unit, cutting her palm on the edge. She hung there for a moment, frozen, heart hammering as she listened for any sound that might indicate she had been followed.

The basement was silent. In the corner came a small scritching sound, probably a rat going about its business.

Relaxing, Kayla carefully righted herself. She glanced down, shining her blue flashlight at the floor to see what she had slipped in. The substance on the ground looked black in the beam of her light, but something about the way the light glinted off it made Kayla frown, peering closer.

If she hadn't known better, she would have sworn that the stuff on the floor looked like blood.

Footsteps sounded, ringing hollowly on the gantry.

Kayla darted behind some giant packing crates and ducked out of sight. A door slammed upstairs, and then silence descended again.

Kayla peered around the edge of the shelving unit to check that all was clear, then switched on her flashlight and started moving quickly toward the door at the far end.

A low, rattling growl came from the darkness.

She carefully turned around, holding her flashlight up in front of her like a shield.

"Oh, for fuck's sake," she muttered under her breath.

The blonde werewolf chained to the iron stairwell lifted its head and sniffed sharply at the air, pawing the stained concrete with a white forepaw, rumbling low in its throat. It growled again, backed up a step, and shook its huge head, its long muzzle flattening back into its face with a nauseating series of crunches and clicks. Upstairs, a door banged open. Footsteps came out onto the gantry once more and paused directly overhead.

There was a whisper of metal on metal.

Kayla's hand dropped down to her Hunters' belt, reaching for her hooked throwing knife. She had little confidence that she could use it to ward off the beast should it attack, but the chains that held it would at least buy her some time to get the hell out of there.

But if it started making a noise and drawing attention to her...

"Kayla?" hissed the werewolf.

"Shhhh!" Kayla put her fingers to her lips. Her brain caught up with what the creature had just said and she frowned.

"Did you just say my name?"

"Shhhhh!" The werewolf tilted its head and followed Kayla's gaze up to the gantry. It licked its lips and shook its head again, its face and shoulders becoming semi-human. "He's got a gun! Oh... *Jeeze Louise!*"

With a gasp it semi-collapsed against the bars of its cage, panting hard as its lupine body shrank, twisted, and became more human-shaped. Something seemed to stick halfway and the werewolf yelped, catching itself on a forepaw, semi-transformed.

Kayla moved cautiously around the struggling animal, her knife held at the ready.

"My name," she snapped, raising the knife. "You know who I am. Talk."

"Course I... know you. *Darn it* that hurts*!*"

Kayla's knife dipped a little. "Did you just say 'Darn it?'" she said dubiously. "What are you, from Kentucky or something?"

"Yeah. What's wrong with... Kentucky?"

"People there say 'Darn it!' instead of swearing. And they say 'Dash!' and 'Blast!' and 'Jeeze Louise!'"

"And your point is?"

"My point is," Kayla glanced behind her and took a deep breath. "Hearing a two hundred pound flesh-eating werewolf swear like my grandmother is deeply, deeply disturbing. Next thing I know you're going to be telling me to wear my thermal underwear and to not go outside with wet hair in case I catch my death of cold."

"I could, you know, savage you a bit or something," said the werewolf, sitting down mid-change. "If that would make you feel better. Live up to the stereotype."

"Okay, hearing you say 'stereotype' is even weirder. Do I know you?"

"You don't remember?"

"Refresh my memory," growled Kayla.

"At the club. Last month. We both got stood up, so we picked up those two guys. We were dancing. And then I..."

"...ate one of them. I remember." Kayla's voice hardened and her grip tightened on the knife. "Mia. I thought I knew your voice."

Mia pushed herself up and gave her blonde mane a defiant shake. "Like you wouldn't have done the same. They got what they deserved. Those guys were idiots!"

"That's no excuse for eating them!"

"I only ate one of them! To teach him a lesson! And don't even get me started on that other guy."

"Oh, Jesus." Kayla closed her eyes and pressed a hand to her forehead. "Mia. Listen to me. I'm in big trouble here. I've got to find that other guy. His name was Mutt. It's very important that I talk to him."

"Why?" Mia's eyebrows shot up and her furred snout crinkled. "Oh my God! Did he get you pregnant?"

"No!" Kayla clapped her hand over Mia's mouth. She could have sworn she heard a muffled noise coming from behind them, but when she turned around there was nobody there. "I mean, no. No way! We didn't even…"

"Oh yeah, right." The werewolf gave a disturbingly human grin, exposing enormous curved teeth. "I saw the way you two were looking at each other. I could actually hear the air sizzle."

"There was no sizzling… *shit!*"

Kayla spun around and dropped low as a door overhead banged open. Footsteps headed for the stairs. Kayla backed into a shadow. She put a finger to her lips.

Mia rose to her feet—half human, half wolf—a tall and muscular shape in the dark basement light. She peered up at the staircase, silhouetted against the faint yellow glow coming from the open door upstairs. Voices. Mia's lips drew back in a snarl as the short, suited figure of Ned Crawley slowly descended the stairs, his gun trained on Mia.

"Looks like it's time for your meds, girl," said Ned.

Mia's only response was a growl. Her hooked hind claws clicked on the tiled floor as she backed up a step, every hair on her body bristling. Ned raised his dart gun. Mia stared unflinchingly into the barrel.

"That's a really, really bad idea," she said quietly.

"Oh yeah? And why would that be?"

"Because," said Mia primly. "There's a big old vampire standing right behind you with a gun. And he looks *pissed*."

Ned had turned halfway around before Kayla cracked him over the head with a rusted metal pipe. He stared at her in utter confusion and fury and she hit him again.

"Ow!"

Ned's arm shot up and he grabbed the pipe. "What the hell are you doing?" he yelled.

"Trying to knock you out."

"Well, don't! It hurts!"

"Sorry."

Kayla held up her hands and backed away. Ned tore the piece of piping from her and hurled it to the ground, almost impaling Mia through the head. He had his dart gun halfway up before Kayla barrelled into him with a shout, sending him flying backward and bouncing the pair of them off an exposed concrete pillar. Kayla grabbed Ned's gun and tried to twist it out of his hand. Ned elbowed her hard in the ribs and shoved her away, sending her reeling into Mia.

"Lunchtime!" yelled Ned.

He raised his dart gun and fired into Mia's thigh.

Mia gave a loud yip. She sagged, clutching at her thigh, instantly changing back into a full-form werewolf. Her legs buckled as her leg-joints flipped backward, sending her sprawling. She crashed to her knees, snarling furiously.

Ned directed a piggy-eyed glare at Mia. "You wanna be next in the Ring, bitch? I suggest you keep your mouth shut before you get yourself into some real trouble."

Mia gave a growl as Ned fired another dart. She collapsed, thick fur sprouting out of her shoulder blades and her back in a blonde wave.

"And that goes for you too!" snapped Ned. "You two little whores, running around conspiring with each other. You're lucky I don't shoot the both of you."

"What does that stuff do to a human?" asked Kayla, eyeing the gun.

"Want to find out?"

"Not particularly."

Ned cocked back the slider on the gun. "Start talking. Why are you here?"

"It's a secret." Kayla gave a wry grin, feeling her confidence swiftly returning. This guy was an ass, but he had no strength in him. She had felt that when she had knocked him down. He was all macho bullshit and bluster in a five foot five accountant's body.

She looked him up and down, slowly, making sure her gaze lingered on his lips, then on his puny biceps, then lower. She saw the flash of hesitation in his eyes and almost laughed out loud. He was no different from the rich idiots who tried to pick her up at the bar. Plus he had a gun in his hand, which she knew straightaway dropped a guy's IQ by at least twenty points.

She locked eyes with him, biting her lip as she moved closer. She saw his Adam's apple bob as she closed in on him, and risked a glance down at Mia. She was fighting to get up, gritting her teeth and glaring daggers at the back of Ned's head. Kayla smiled to herself.

This was going to be too easy.

"Tell me," she began, eyeing Ned's aggressively-polished badge. "How long does it take to get into the force these days?"

"That wasn't the question!" spat Ned, but Kayla's practiced eye saw him straighten almost imperceptibly and thrust out his chest. She had him.

"Does it involve, you know, lots of working out? Pumping iron and so on?" Kayla moved closer, running her eyes seductively down the detective's body.

Ned suddenly jerked, his eyes flying wide open. His mouth opened in a soundless scream. Blood poured out of his mouth in a crimson flood. His body jerked again, then pitched over and hit the ground like a ton of bricks.

Shocked, Kayla looked down at the twitching body of the detective. The piece of rusted pipe was sticking out of his back. Mia had stabbed Ned right through the heart.

Mia flashed Kayla a lupine grin and sat back on her haunches, looking extremely pleased with herself. Kayla watched as the werewolf flexed her hands, just as they mutated back into claws. Mia gritted her teeth to halt the transformation, fighting the effects of the drug.

"Good timing," said Kayla, fighting the urge to throw up.

Mia nodded. "Always," she said around her mouthful of wolf-sized teeth.

Kayla cautiously circled around the fallen detective. Blood spread around him in a shallow pool. Kayla shook her head. "They say the way to a man's heart is through his stomach," she said, pulling a face.

Mia sniggered. "Sure. But if you go in through his back then he can't scream."

"Mia!"

"I'm a doctor. I know these things."

"Damn." Kayla edged around the detective and rooted around in his pockets, searching for keys. She jumped back with a little scream as his arm came up and took a swing at her.

"Automatic reflex," said Mia in a monotone. "His body's shutting down."

"I'm so pleased you know that," said Kayla in a faint voice. She stood up and shrugged. "No keys. How am I supposed to—oh."

Mia kicked off her chains and set to work on the final manacle, holding a sliver of bent metal between her teeth and twisting her head to dig it into the keyhole. Moments later, she was free.

"Been working on those cuffs all night," she said with satisfaction. "Honestly! Chaining me up like a common dog, that guy deserved—er, Kayla?"

Kayla watched Mia warily, backing around her with her hunting knife at the ready.

Mia stepped out of her restraints and padded toward Kayla, who jerked the knife up higher. Mia stopped a few feet from her and gave her a lopsided look.

"What's with the knife?"

"You're a werewolf!"

Mia looked down at herself. "So?"

"So, what if you eat me?"

"She'd probably get indigestion, for starters. All that slutty makeup you're wearing kinda sticks in the throat. And those pointy boots would give her terrible gas," said a voice from the packing crates behind them.

Kayla glanced sidelong at Mia. Wordlessly, the pair of them split up and moved to either side of the crate. Kayla eyed Mia, then pulled out her knife and nodded at her in unspoken communication. The big blonde werewolf reared up on her hind legs and gave the top crate a hard shove, knocking it over onto the floor and shattering it to kindling.

A dazed and bloodied Mutt spilled out.

Kayla gasped. Mutt had been beaten badly and left for dead in the crate; the very same ones used by the L.A.P.D. to transport bodies to the morgue. Most of the skin had been stripped from his forearms, leaving them raw and bleeding. A dull puncture wound in his side showed the point of a broken rib, half sticking through the skin. The ragged remains of his T-shirt hung from shoulders scored with dozens of knife wounds.

Mutt shook his head and blinked.

"You going to stab me with that thing, or make me a sandwich?" he asked, with a grin. "I'm starving."

CHAPTER TWENTY-EIGHT

MIA AND KAYLA half dragged Mutt through the darkened basement of the police station as they searched for an exit.

"You know, there's no need for you girls to carry me," slurred Mutt. "I'm fine."

"You're in shock," said Mia. "Try not to talk."

"Yes, please," muttered Kayla.

"Are you drunk?"

"Drugged."

"Jesus. What happened to you?"

"Many, many bad things. Harlequin... he was there. Tell ya about it... later."

"Shit." Kayla shifted her grip further up Mutt's blood-slicked bicep, trying not to touch the worst of his wounds. Already she could feel the sticky warmth of his blood seeping through her clothing. She wondered how long he had been in that box, and what had been done to him.

Oh, this wasn't good.

She felt Mutt catch his breath as she slid her other hand across the curve of his well-muscled back—to get a better grip, of course—and risked a glance across at Mia. The effects of the drug were starting to wear off, but she was still stuck in half-wolf form, which was causing her problems with running. Her knee and ankle joints were trying to flip directions to become human every few paces. Her fur covered her nakedness for now; Kayla wondered what would happen if the drug wore off completely. She'd be all alone miles from anywhere with a naked girl from Kentucky and a half-dead werewolf.

Another nice mess she'd gotten herself into.

Kayla glanced up at Mutt and shook her head, wondering why was everyone so dead set against using the Dark Arts back at the Hunter base. Those powers had helped her locate Mutt, after all, and now she had the key to finding out what really happened to Karrel. Mutt was the only one left alive who knew the truth. If he made it home alive.

As though reading her thoughts, Mutt groaned and began coughing violently, almost losing his footing. Kayla gave him a little shake.

"Keep quiet!"

"Can't help it." Mutt cleared his throat and gave her a bleary look. "Hurts."

"Serves you right, running off and getting kidnapped like that."

Mutt gave a snort of derision, then coughed again.

"You're an idiot, Kita."

"Kayla. Excuse me?"

"I said, you're an idiot. Points for the tracking job, but do you have any idea what's going on here?"

"We're rescuing you. So shut up and let us rescue you."

"Please, just leave me here. This is bad. Really, really bad. You have no fucking clue what the deal is here. Do you?"

Mutt suddenly gave a cry of pain. Mia stopped dead, causing Kayla to swing around and almost drop Mutt. Kayla shifted her grip and grabbed Mutt around the waist before he fell.

"What are you doing?" hissed Kayla.

Mia's lips pulled back in a silent snarl as she stared up at the ceiling, her hackles slowly rising. Mutt lifted his head and followed her gaze.

"Come on! There's nothing there, girl!" whispered Kayla. "I mean, Mia. Sorry."

Mia gave her a pained look.

"Let's just get out of here," said Kayla. "If we don't get back to base before sunrise..."

"He's here," said Mia, almost to herself.

"I know," replied Mutt in a toneless voice. "I saw him."

Kayla looked helplessly between the two werewolves. "And don't start that 'Brotherhood of the Wolf' shit. Just because I don't go furry once a month doesn't mean I don't know exactly what's going on here." She paused. "What exactly *is* going on here?" "You don't want to know," said Mutt.

"How 'bout you tell me now and keep all your limbs?"

"Because there's a bunch of cops coming down the stairs," said Mutt. Hobnailed boots clanged as a half-dozen cops rounded the corner and poured down the staircase.

"Take him," said Mia. "These guys are *mine*. It's about time I had a little fun."

Mia practically threw Mutt at Kayla. She dropped down on her haunches with a growl and shook her body, transforming quickly back into a full-form wolf. Mia gave a snort of wrath and lowered her head, taking off toward the cops at full speed. Kayla pulled Mutt back into an alcove as Mia hit the stairs, jumping over them four at a time, causing the oncoming cops to scatter like ninepins. A burst of semi-automatic fire lit up the basement as one of the cops fired at Mia. It stopped when she hit him at full speed and tossed her head like a bull, throwing him screaming over the railings. The man plummeted two stories and struck the ground beneath with a wet thud.

"This way!" Mutt said and grabbed Kayla by the hand, dragging her back the way they had come.

"No! We can't leave Mia!"

"Sure we can. She'll be fine."

"But—" Kayla stared back at the stairwell where Mia was bucking and jumping and kicking with gleeful relish, sinking her teeth into arms and legs and tossing cops over the edge one by one as they unloaded their pistols into her. She was a one-woman maelstrom of destruction. A fully-transformed werewolf could absorb dozens of bullets with no lasting ill effects due to their amazing healing abilities. But stuck in human form, like Mutt was, they were as vulnerable as the next person.

"Shit!"

Mutt pulled Kayla back. A volley of bullets whizzed past them and slammed into the concrete pillar just feet from them. "Oh yeah. Great plan, Wonder Woman," he muttered, shaking bits of plaster out of his hair. "Come down here and get yourself stuck in a basement between a cop-verses-werewolf firefight. Nice work, Kelly."

"Kayla!"

"Whatever. Listen, we've got to get our asses out of here. The fate of the world may depend on it."

Kayla snorted. "You're *such* a drama-queen!"

"Speak for yourself, baby."

Kayla grunted and shook her head. "Just shut the hell up and listen to me for once in your life. Get ready. When I tell you to run…"

"Gotcha."

The pair listened to the gory sounds of snarling and screaming and gunfire. The cops fell one by one, until there was only one pistol left firing.

Then that too ceased.

Cautiously, Kayla grabbed a piece of packing crate from the garbage-strewn floor and stuck it around the edge of the pillar. Nothing happened, so she dropped it and poked her head out.

Wounded and dying cops lay everywhere, weakly groaning and calling to each other in the blood-spattered gloom. At the top of the stairs the door gaped, spilling yellow light down into the basement. There was no sign of Mia.

Mutt poked his head out above hers, taking in the scene with a sigh. "I have to say, girlie. You've got great taste in friends. Who do you hang out with on the weekends, Jack the Ripper's daughter?"

"Be quiet and follow me," said Kayla. She turned to scan the maze of subterranean pathways, then set off toward the nearest doorway. It was barely visible in the dim glow of the light from above.

Mutt watched her go, half-slumped against the pillar.

Kayla stopped by the first doorway and tugged on the handle. It was locked. "You coming?"

"Baby, I ain't even breathing hard yet."

Kayla closed her eyes and banged her forehead against the door. "And now I remember why I didn't miss you."

"Of course you missed me." Mutt threw an alarmed look toward the stairwell as one of the wounded cops broke into a coughing fit. He pushed himself away from the pillar and limped after Kayla. "Girls always miss me."

"Yeah, keep telling yourself that," said Kayla, trying the second door without success. Mutt made his way down the row of locked doors opposite, trying each one in turn. "How the hell do we get out?"

"There's always the stairs."

"And walk right into whoever sent those cops down here. Great." Kayla yanked violently on her forth locked door, fighting the urge to panic. "I'm surprised this place isn't already crawling with fuzz."

"Don't worry. They're probably cordoning the place off as we speak." Mutt threw a wry glance at Kayla. "Unless your little blonde girlfriend already ate everyone in the station. That's quite an appetite she's got there. Stand back."

"Why?"

Kayla jumped back as Mutt's booted foot whistled past her face, shattering the doorknob into a dozen pieces of snapped metal. Mutt gave the door two more savage kicks. After his second kick the hinges flew off with a clatter.

Bolts rolled underfoot and Mutt extended a hand toward the doorway in mock-graciousness. "After you, m'lady."

"Thought you'd never ask," said Kayla, slipping through the door.

Mutt followed her and pulled the door shut the best he could, locking it in place at an angle. The hallway opened out into a disused service area filled with broken office furniture and discarded wiring.

A faint glow of light was visible overhead from the light-blue dawn sky.

Shouting voices echoed behind them. The pair quickly climbed the rusted fire escape set into the wall and emerged through a filthy service hatch at the rear of the building. The underground parking lot of the police station.

Kayla scrambled to her feet and darted for cover behind a pair of empty squad cars. Mutt swiftly followed suit, grumbling and wincing the whole way.

Kayla ducked down as a trio of cop cars barrelled down the ramps and screeched to a halt, sirens blazing. The doors were flung open and armed SWAT team members spilled out, guns drawn, charging toward the building. A window shattered and a screaming cop was thrown through it, landing in a crumpled heap in a bank of shrubbery. The sounds of shouting and snarling spilled out into the morning. One of the cops got on the radio and called for reinforcements.

Kayla waved Mutt to stay down. She could see the tantalizing shape of the black Hunter truck, parked just up the ramp in the above-ground lot. Unfortunately, to get there would mean walking out in the open. The underground parking structure was unlit and they were fairly well hidden, for now. There was no one else around. All the activity seemed to be centered upstairs, where Kayla was sure that Mia was creating enough of a distraction for them to slip away.

They had to get out, and fast. If she was missed at the Hunter base before the daily roll call, she would have much more serious things than the police to worry about.

Kayla glanced across at Mutt, slumped against the trunk of the smaller police car. He was bruised and bleeding, but he seemed otherwise okay. He lifted his head and poked his tongue out at her, then flicked a pointed glance back up the ramp at the police station.

"Sounds like your friend's working out a few of her issues in there."

"You're a fine one to talk."

Mutt simply smiled. He slipped around the side of the police car and helped Kayla up. Kayla felt the incredible strength in Mutt, despite his condition.

"You got a plan for getting out of here?" Mutt asked, as the pair of them gazed over the roof of the cop car. His eyes flicked appreciatively over Kayla; he reached out a dirty hand to smooth a flyaway strand of hair.

"Nope." Kayla batted Mutt's hand away and tucked her long chestnut hair behind her ears. "Looks like we're stuck for now. Any ideas?"

"Just this one."

Kayla yelped as Mutt shoved her hard against the cop car. As she opened her mouth to protest he crushed his lips to hers. His tongue darted between her teeth and Kayla immediately shoved him away, furious. Mutt knocked her hands away, pinning them beneath his arms. Kayla elbowed him hard in the ribs, unable to breathe as Mutt blocked her in with his body. He pushed himself up hard against her and kissed her again and again, harsh, demanding. Kayla growled low in her throat and kicked him in the shin. She ripped one of her hands free, grabbed a fistful of Mutt's unruly black locks, and yanked his head back.

She glared at him. "What the hell are you doing?" she burst out when she could breathe again.

"Nothing. You just imagined I did that," replied Mutt. He slowly licked his lips, and dropped his gaze to Kayla's mouth. His own lips parted in a soft, short pant. He raised his eyebrows, as though waiting for a response to a silent question. His grin widened as Kayla pulled her other hand free and stepped back, shaking her head.

"Are you *insane*?" she hissed. "We've got a roomful of dead cops back there, and an escaped werewolf on the loose. Someone could be along any minute to gun us down for even being here, and I—*Mutt!*"

"What?"

"Your hands. *Move* them!"

"But—"

"Now!"

"All right, fine!" Mutt stepped closer to Kayla, watching her in amusement as she brought up a hand in warning, ready to shove him away again. "Mutt."

"Yes, m'am?"

Kayla didn't move a muscle. She put on her best stern face and mouthed, "No."

Mutt didn't back down. "I don't like that word," he said, blinking up at her. "Remember?"

"Oh, I remember just fine." Kayla backed off, putting some space between them. "In fact, I remember lots of things about the last time we got together, and—Hey!"

With a speed born of many years of practice Kayla grabbed Mutt's hand as he reached out for her. She gripped his wrist, gazing into his eyes. "*Enough*," she insisted, shaking him gently. "We have to find a way out of here. *Now!*"

"You don't mean that."

"I do."

"I missed you."

"You couldn't even remember my name. And you're a werewolf, Mutt. I don't trust you an inch."

"Pity." With a snap of his wrist Mutt broke her grip on his arm. He grabbed Kayla by the scruff of the neck, pulling her in close. He met her open mouth with his again, kissing her insistently. Kayla drew back to kick him again and Mutt quickly angled his body to avoid the blow. He shoved her raised knee to the side and carried the move through into a hip throw that ended with Kayla pressed up against the side of the police cruiser again.

"So why did you come to rescue me, if you didn't miss me?" Mutt breathed into her neck.

"I need to talk to you." Kayla had to fight to keep her voice from shaking. "To find out why Karrel died." She could feel the reassuringly solid warmth of Mutt's body pressed up against hers. The familiar scent of him—dirty denim tinged with ancient cigarette smoke and just a hint of whisky—made her mind go places it definitely shouldn't be going at this particular moment. A police siren sounded on the next level and Kayla stiffened, torn between the overpowering urge to flee and the desperate need to talk to Mutt.

She needed to find some peace.

As she wrestled with herself, Mutt ran his lips up the back of her neck, tracing his thumbs along opposite side of Kayla's collarbone. "You know why he died," he whispered. "He was a Hunter. That's what happens to all Hunters in the end, I'm afraid."

Kayla pushed Mutt away, one palm flat on the bloodied mess of his chest. "What do you know about Hunters?" she snapped. "You're a were-wolf."

"I wasn't always like this."

"And what the Hell's that supposed to mean?"

Mutt glanced up at her, mischief flickering briefly in his eyes. He stepped back from her, then reached down and started to undo the buckle on his pants.

"Mutt!"

"Just wait."

Mutt pushed his belt buckle to the side and pulled the top of his pants down. Despite herself, Kayla's eyes lowered. She gasped. A pair of interlocked H symbols were tattooed on Mutt's hip, cleverly hidden inside one of the more ornate tribal tattoos that formed an interwoven band around his slim hips.

The initiation mark of the Hunters.

"You have *got* to be kidding me," she said.

CHAPTER TWENTY-NINE

KAYLA BACKED SLOWLY around the police car, staring at Mutt.

"I don't understand," she said.

"I told you that Karrel and I used to be best buds," said Mutt with a trace of smugness. The dark shape of a police cruiser was backing around toward the entrance of the station. "It's not my fault if you didn't believe me."

"You were a Hunter? *You?*"

"I was the best damn Hunter that squad ever had," said Mutt proudly. "I could kick Karrel's ass in a heartbeat."

"Bullshit. Tell me truth. How did you really get that thing?"

"Now's not the time to chat about it, kitty cat," said Mutt, buckling up his pants and throwing a quick glance over his shoulder. "We've got to make tracks. Just trust me on one thing: you really don't want to be hanging out with the Hunters. They're the bad guys, in case you haven't noticed. You need to get away from them, and fast. You're better off on your own."

"The Hunters?" Kayla shook her head. "They're the good guys, Mutt."

Mutt laughed, a tinge of bitterness in his voice. "Think what you want. You'll find out the truth sooner or later."

"And I suppose you know the truth."

"I do. Not telling."

"Why?"

"I don't want you getting yourself dead, too. Your ass is too cute to wind up as worm food." Mutt's green eyes creased in affection and he reached out to tap her on the nose. "Not that there weren't times in the last month when I didn't wish you dead."

"Likewise," said Kayla with feeling.

"So what next?"

"We get you back to base. We talk. You tell me what you know."

"Nuh-uh. You're not listening, girlie. The Hunters will skin me alive as soon as look at me. If I'm lucky. Those guys make the Predator look like Mother Teresa." He shivered, rubbing his bare arms.

"I have friends," hissed Kayla, ducking hurriedly down as a clatter of gunfire came from outside the garage. "They could help us."

"Friends who aren't Hunters?"

"Er…"

Mutt's hand snapped around Kayla's throat with a burst of speed, so fast that she was taken aback.

Mutt ripped the silver pentangle off her throat, breaking the hair-thin chain.

"Jesus fuckin' *Christ!*" he breathed, holding it up to the light. "Where did you get this?

"First up, *ow,*" said Kayla, rubbing her neck. "Second, why is everyone so fascinated with that damn necklace?"

"Because this damn necklace, my girl, could be the key to saving humanity."

"Oh." Kayla stared at the trinket. "Cool. What does it do?"

"It wards off Avenging Angels, of course."

"You're a whack job. Did I ever tell you that?"

"Several times." Mutt stuffed the necklace into his pocket.

"Hey! That's mine!"

"Mine now. I'll explain later. Suffice it to say, you're really lucky you met me, and really lucky that I know what the fuck is going on. In the wrong hands, that necklace could do a lot of damage. Could you pass me that rock?"

"This rock?"

"Sure."

Kayla reached down and picked up a fist-sized lump of plaster from the gutter. Mutt weighted it carefully in his hand, then turned and pitched it over Kayla's shoulder. There was a muffled "*Ooof!*" followed by a heavy thud.

Kayla turned to see an armed cop sprawled out on the concrete, just inside the door. She sighed. "Not that we're not already in enough trouble or anything."

Mutt was already moving. He hopped over the hood of the police cruiser and knelt down by the

fallen cop. He snatched the car keys from his outstretched hand with a cry of triumph, then began
stripping off the man's clothing.

Kayla watched in tired bemusement.

Mutt buttoned the cop's jacket across his bare
chest. He put the cop's pants on over his torn black
jeans. Already, Kayla could see the blood seeping
through. Mutt dangled a set of keys in front of
Kayla's face and gave a wolfish grin, then jerked his
head toward the squad car.

"You up for some fun?"

"Mutt. *No.*"

"Oh, come on. Live a little. It's the only way out
of this place. They're looking for a rampaging
werewolf. Who's gonna pay attention to yet another cop car?"

Kayla opened her mouth to reply, then ducked
down behind the cab as an agonised scream rang
out. The sound of crunching metal filled the air,
followed by several loud gunshots.

"Oh, for Christ's sake," she hissed. "What
now?"

"Ah. There's my girl. My other girl, I mean."

Mia came galloping down the parking ramp like
a stampeding bull, her tongue lolling, blonde hair
streaming out behind her. She spotted Mutt and
Kayla and braked to a halt. She trotted over to
them, head held high.

Kayla recoiled, her hand flying to her mouth. The
female werewolf had a large hole in her skull right
above her left eye, through which bleeding gray
brain tissue was clearly visible. The fur had been
completely torn away from her left flank, revealing
black skin shredded and pitted by gunfire. Ribs

gleamed white amid the ragged mess. Her blonde

gleamed white amid the ragged mess. Her blonde fur was drenched with blood, and two of her front teeth were missing. Her tail was on fire.

She pulled her lips back in a snaggle-toothed werewolf smile. Mutt circled gingerly around her, giving Kayla a look of dismay. He flinched back as Mia's semi-destroyed face began to twist and transform, ending up in a rough parody of her human visage.

"Don't suppose you've got the number of a good twenty-four hour vet?" she asked with a wince. "Or a fire extinguisher?"

GRIT CRUNCHED BENEATH the tires of the police car as Mutt guided the cruiser over the rough dirt track that led back to the Hunters base. He scratched fitfully at the itchy cotton of the cop uniform he was wearing, glancing for the hundredth time in the rear view mirror. "You sure we're not being followed?"

"I'm sure."

"This is a terrible idea," he muttered.

"Shut up," said Kayla, too tense to listen. "We're nearly there. This will all be over soon."

"Hmm. You're bringing two werewolves into your top secret underground Hunters Headquarters, and you expect the other Hunters to be pleased about this?"

"I'm not bringing you *in*," explained Kayla. "You guys will have to stay down in the basement till I've talked to people about you. When they find out that you know where Harlequin is, they'll welcome you with open arms. Trust me."

"Great. I'm going to die wearing a cop's uniform, with no clean underwear and a dead werewolf in the back of the car," said Mutt, sitting back in his seat. "Fantastic. My daddy would be so proud."

"I'm not dead," insisted Mia, from the backseat. "I'm just resting my eyes."

"Pity," sniffed Mutt. He changed gear and guided the cruiser around a fallen tree branch. "Don't worry. The day is young. There's still plenty of time for Kayla to get us both killed."

"Look," started Kayla. She put a hand on Mutt's arm. "Just so you know. That time with the burning building? I already said I was sorry. How many times do I have to—"

"Shhh!" Mutt gripped the wheel, staring through the windshield. "Did anyone else hear that?"

Kayla and Mia shook their heads.

"Just be quiet and drive," said Mia in a perfect imitation of Kayla's voice, winking at her in the mirror.

Kayla grinned back at her. She sat back in the passenger seat and let her eyes slide shut. She had done it. She had rescued Mutt, who not only knew what had happened to Karrel and where Harlequin was, he also seemed to know something about the Pentangle necklace. If it could stop the Avenging Angels, whatever the hell they were, then great.

Her first solo mission was a raging success.

Cool.

Kayla realized something was wrong when they pulled into the hidden driveway that ringed the Hunters' base. The base was underground with only one visible exit – a small concrete parking garage that from the outside looked derelict. The "garage" was the main entry and exit point for the various Hunter vehicles. As they approached it, heading toward the back hatch Kayla had originally come out of, they saw that the front of the garage was open. There was nobody visible inside and no Hunter vehicles in the vicinity. All the lights were off. There was no sign of the guards who usually patrolled the entrance. It was too quiet.

Something felt wrong.

"Pull over." Mutt cut the wheel to the side and rolled to a halt on the track ten yards from the entrance. "Something's up."

"What?" Mutt flipped down the sun visor and critically examined his bruised, bloodied face in the mirror. He touched his split lip and winced. "I don't hear anything."

"That's the point. Wait here."

Kayla glanced in the back seat at Mia, then opened the car door and got out. She circled around the darkened entrance to the base, keeping to the bushes in the dull morning light. There should have been at least two burly men with Dobermans and semi-automatic weapons running toward her by now for being so close to the base entrance, but the night was still.

An irrational sense of dread began to rise inside Kayla as she made her way around the back of the hidden complex, her boots crunching on the circular path that marked the outer limits of the base. By the time she reached her hidden trapdoor she was puffing, not from the exertion but because she felt like she suddenly had an iron band around her ribs. She couldn't breathe.

Kayla rounded the corner and stopped dead.

The back hatch to the base was open, flung wide on the soil. The long grass around the hatch that normally hid it from view was scuffed and torn, leaving the hatch in full sight of anyone passing. Kayla knew that whatever had opened the hatch didn't just stumble across it by accident.

Her breathing suddenly seemed loud to her ears, and her heart began to thump in her chest. She had left the hatch blocked open, sure, but she had hidden it well before leaving. It had been the dead of night and there had been nobody around to see her leave.

Except Marius. Of course. Marius had seen her leave, and knew she was planning to go out without authorization.

That little son of a bitch.

Kayla let out her breath in a flood of relief, then clamped her mini-flashlight between her teeth and started climbing down the rungs of the ladder inside the service hatch. The little shit must have followed her down to the basement, then fooled around with the service hatch to mess with her head. He was probably waiting for her down there right now, ready to jump out at her and give her shit for falling for his little ruse.

Kayla reached the bottom of the ladder and stared around in suspicion. "Marius!" she hissed.

No reply.

Kayla shook her head in disgust and marched across the cluttered, dusty basement to the elevator. She punched the button and stood there fuming. The elevator descended with a slow rusty groan of gears. After a long pause, the doors dinged open.

Kayla gasped, her hand flaying to her mouth. Marius lay on the floor of the elevator in about four pieces. The floor was swimming with blood.

Kayla jumped as a hand touched her on the shoulder. She gave a yell of fright and spun around.

"It's okay," said Mutt. "It's me." He peered down into the elevator, shaking his head. "Jesus. I leave you alone for one minute…"

Kayla couldn't take her eyes off the body. The guy she had been talking to just a few short hours ago had been turned into so much meat, bloodied chunks of flesh that glistened a wet, dark red in the frozen beam of her flashlight. Parts of him were still recognizable, others had been chewed to raw hunks of flesh.

"Who did this?" Kayla whispered.

Mutt shrugged. "Nobody here but us. Where does this thing go?"

"Up."

"We should go up, then. Whatever did this might still be down here. Any other way up that doesn't involve standing in brains?"

"No."

Mutt stepped primly over the body of Marius. He found a relatively blood-free spot in the elevator to stand in and quickly beckoned for her to join him. After a moment's hesitation, Kayla did so.

When the doors slid open again, they revealed a scene straight out of her worst nightmares. Kayla gasped, burying her head in Mutt's chest, her eyes squeezed shut.

She was too late.

Bits of people lay *everywhere*. The corridor looked like some kind of full-scale war had been fought in it. The plasterboard walls were riddled with gunfire, and the cheap nylon carpet was soaked in blood. The bodies of Hunter recruits lay here and there on the floor in silent, unmoving heaps, mercilessly lit by crackling fluorescent lights. Most of them were still in their sleeping clothes, others were semi-dressed and clutching revolvers or pistols. Doors were off their hinges, and here and there a light hung from the ceiling.

Kayla's blood ran cold.

Either something had gotten out... or something had got in.

This couldn't be happening!

Mutt stroked her hair. "Good to be home," he muttered. "Remind me why I don't come visit more often?"

Kayla shook her head mutely, too nauseated to speak. For the entire time she had known the Hunters she had been told over and over again that their operation was a fragile one, a last outpost against the forces of darkness that could be discovered and erased any minute. Ninette had told her and the other young recruits the same thing, hoping to drive it into their skulls and weed out those who weren't entirely committed to their cause.

But Kayla had dismissed it all as scaremongering, pure and simple. There had been over three hundred Hunters living and working in the underground base, including their fully armed security staff. They had alarm drills every week, a full electronic lockdown on the base in case of emergency or attack, and anyone who wasn't religiously careful about closing the doors to the vampire or werewolf pens was severely disciplined or thrown out. The idea that something could get past all that security and cause devastation on this level was unbelievable.

Kayla reached down and pulled the cop's gun out of Mutt's holster. She began walking forward, slowly, staring around her in horror.

Every room she passed had been ransacked. Beds were overturned in sleeping quarters; offices had been destroyed in an indiscriminate frenzy of bloody destruction.

Everywhere lay the bodies of the Hunters.

Kayla gritted her teeth, searching for any signs of life.

Ten minutes later, she found some.

Dana blinked up at her from her broken pen, panting in pain. The svelte young werewolf had been pinned to the ground with a bar from her own jail cell, impaled through the shoulder. She lay amid a heap of broken plaster and metal, still handcuffed, bleeding her life out into the rubble.

All the other werewolf pens were empty.

Kayla approached the wounded werewolf. She crouched down and levelled her gun at Dana's throat, touching the tip of the pistol to the tiny jeweled collar Dana wore.

"Speak," she said hoarsely. "Who did this?"

Dana groaned, pale from blood loss.

"Dana. Look at me. What the hell happened here?"

Dana's eyes slid open a crack. She scowled.

"Yeah, it's me again," snapped Kayla. "Tell me who did this."

Dana bared her teeth, her features momentarily blurring and becoming more wolf-like as she tried to transform. A heartbeat later she sagged, giving up. Kayla looked down and saw the tell-tale shape of a red dart sticking out of her thigh, too far down for her to reach and pull out with her handcuffs on. Dana had been drugged with the Hunters' own potion, preventing her from changing into a were-wolf to start healing her own wounds.

Somebody had wanted Dana to die.

Dana's eyes started to slide closed again. Kayla slapped her face gently. Dana's eyes fluttered open.

"You've got about ten minutes."

"'Til what?"

Dana smiled enigmatically. She delicately extend-ed a middle finger, then broke into a coughing fit.

"She's gone, Kay. Leave her. We should just get outta here."

Kayla looked up to see Mutt standing in the doorway. She shook her head firmly.

"She knows who did this!"

"I know who did this," said Mutt, avoiding eye contact. "Whoever got in through that damn hatch did this."

"We don't know that!" protested Kayla. "Look over there. Those werewolf pens—empty! One of them could have escaped and let the others out."

Dana began laughing. She choked to a halt and rolled her brilliant blue eyes up at Kayla.

"You're such a dumbass. You know that?"

"She knows that," said Mutt automatically. Kayla silenced him with a glare.

"You think it was a coincidence, you guys just happening to catch me and take me in?" Dana shook her head, mirth dancing in her pain-filled eyes. "Sorry sweet pea, you've been had. Harlem's pack didn't ditch me. They've been tracking me all along."

"Excuse me?"

Dana tapped her bare thigh with a bloodied finger. "Tracking beacon. Under the skin. I hear they're all the rage these days in Stupidville."

Kayla felt her pulse start to pound. She gritted her teeth and jabbed Dana with her gun. "You're so full of it. You don't have a homing beacon. We'd have found that on you in a heartbeat."

"Oh, they did. Cut it right out of me. It hurt." Dana jerked her head toward a nearby table. A small silver bowl sat in the middle with what looked like a bloodied silver coin in it. "But they were too late. Didn't even make it to the big red alarm button before *POW!* We hit you guys." A faint smile crossed her bruised and battered face. "Our task was made even easier because *somebody* left the back door of this place wide open for us. Well done, Kayla. I couldn't have planned it better myself."

"Shut up," said Kayla fiercely. She aimed her pistol between Dana's eyes. "You're lying."

Dana laughed. She lunged wildly for the pistol, sinking her teeth deeply into Kayla's wrist. She jerked up short with a howl as the movement jarred her impaled shoulder. Kayla dropped the pistol and ripped her wrist out of Dana's mouth, feeling the werewolf's teeth scrape bone before she released her.

She backed up two steps, clutching her wrist in shock.

"Sorry, princess," said Dana, licking her bloodied chops. "No guns allowed. If you shoot me, it would be bad."

"Why?"

Dana ignored her, breaking into another mad little peal of laughter. Her laughter abruptly choked off into a coughing fit as she nodded owlishly over at Mutt. "I'm impressed you found him. So glad you followed my advice."

"Kayla," said Mutt, his voice dangerously calm. "What's she talking about?"

"Nothing. She's delirious."

"Am not," muttered Dana, panting shallowly. "So here's the breaks, little girl. I'm going to give you a heads up, although Christ knows you don't deserve one. You guys have eight minutes to get out of here. In that time you're not allowed to shoot me, or you're both dead, instantly."

"Why?"

Dana fingered the jeweled collar around her neck, panting as more blood flowed up her throat. "See these little sparkly things? Not diamonds. Harlem was always too... cheap to buy me diamonds. These are crystals of silver fulminate, suspended... in plastic caps in water. Very explosive. Very volatile."

"Silver *what*?"

"High explosives, darling. You're a Hunter. You should know this shit. This collar gets removed or tampered with, the water gets let into the caps and... *BOOM*! Got enough... juice in this baby to take out a tower block. Harlem set this collar to blow in about..." Dana glanced down at the collar. "Seven and a half minutes." She rolled her eyes at Kayla in a ghastly mockery of camaraderie. "Men suck, you know. You can't trust 'em. Remind me to never date anyone *ever* again."

Mutt and Kayla stared at each other.

Blood flecked Dana's lips as she coughed again, a big, dazed smile lighting up her face. "The Hunters are dead. Finally! We killed them all. And all thanks to you, my dear."

Dana's head sagged back and she passed out, lolling back on the spike that impaled her.

Mutt tactfully cleared his throat. "Time to go, I think."

Kayla stared at the unconscious body of Dana and clutched her bleeding wrist. Already, it was starting to throb. In the ensuing silence, a faint beeping sound was audible. It was coming from Dana's collar.

Bombs. Why did there always have to be bombs?

"Kayla. Really. Time to go."

Kayla nodded dumbly, unable to tear her eyes from Dana. A second later she felt Mutt grab her shoulder. He took the gun from her unresisting hand and pulled her gently away. They fled through the darkened, semi-destroyed rooms of the Hunter base, heading back to the elevators as fast as they could. After tolerating the gristly ride back down they fled across the darkened basement, heading for that welcoming square patch of sky at the top of the service hatch.

"Why does shit always get blown up when I'm around you," Mutt grumbled, as he climbed the ladder, taking the rungs three at a time. "I swear. You're like Demolition Jane or something."

Kayla shook her head in a daze as she followed him, too numb to even speak. *The Hunters were dead, wiped out. And it was all her fault.*

"We'll have to look at your wrist when we get home. That bite could turn bad."

"I'll live," Kayla managed, still in shock.

They both spilled out of the service hatch and ran for their lives.

Before they reached the cruiser, Kayla stopped. "Wait. The Avenging Angels."

"Yes, yes, the angels. That's nice," said Mutt, patting her on the head. "Building's about to go boom, baby. Let's make tracks."

"No. I can't let her do this!"

"What?"

"We can't leave her in there. The Avenging Angels are coming. The Hunters are the only ones who know how to stop them."

"The Hunters are dead, Kayla!"

"I don't buy that." Kayla spun around in a panic. "We have to go get Dana, get her out of there before her collar blows! There could still be someone alive down there!"

"But we could get killed!"

Kayla looked at Mutt grimly. "If there's even one Hunter left alive in the place, it'll be worth it. I can't save the world on my own. I need help. Come on. Are you with me?"

"Very heroic," said a deep male voice. "And very dumb. Tell me, bro. Are all your chicks as crazy as this one?"

Kayla spun around in alarm as an armed man stepped out from behind a Hunter truck. He was almost seven feet tall and wore a biker's helmet over long, black hair. He was muscled to the point where he couldn't even put his arms down at his sides. He was clad in a Hunter uniform soaked in blood, and was currently pointing a modified sub-machine gun at Kayla's head.

The three of them stared at each other in tense silence.

Then the newcomer relaxed, dropping the nose of his gun. He stepped forward to give Mutt a high-five.

Kayla watched in bewilderment as the pair grabbed one another in a giant bear hug, the black-clad man lifting Mutt clean off the ground before releasing him and turning to face Kayla. He stuck his hand out to her.

"The name's Monster. I'll be your driver tonight."

"My driver?"

Monster pushed back his helmet, revealing a swarthy face and gold-capped teeth. He swept back his hand to reveal the driver's door was open on the Hunter truck. Mia was sitting up in the passenger seat, staring out at them expectantly.

"We gotta roll, kids. The base has been compromised."

"You're telling me," said Mutt. "We've just been down there. Place is a clusterfuck." He turned to touch Kayla on the shoulder. "This one just got bit by a werewolf, of all things. Mind if you'd take a look at her? Don't want her going all furry in the back seat and peeing on the leather."

"I hear you, brother." Monster heaved a deep sigh, looking Kayla over doubtfully. "Where'd she get bit?"

"I'll tell you later. There's a bomb about to go off."

"Oh, great. Where?"

"Here."

"When?"

Mutt shrugged. "Now-ish."

"Why didn't you say?"

"Just did. Let's scoot."

"I call shotgun."

"Fuck you. I'm not driving."

"You always drive."

"Yeah. In your dreams."

"Guys!" shouted Kayla. "I'll drive. Get the hell in the car. *NOW!*"

Mutt lifted an eyebrow, impressed. They jumped in the back as Kayla climbed behind the wheel and started the engine.

"So are you going to introduce us properly?" Monster asked Mutt as Kayla put the car in gear. She floored the gas and rocketed down the drive.

"That's Kayla," said Mutt. "She's a Hunter."

"I'm not," said Kayla, glancing sheepishly at Mutt. "They just fired me."

"Well, chickadee. Fired or not, it's just you and me now."

"Excuse me?"

"Everyone else is dead. Been going through the channels on the CB like crazy. Nobody's picking up. They got us good."

"Are you sure?"

"Positive."

Kayla stared at Monster. "So what do we do now?" she asked. "The Avenging Angels…"

"Screw the Avenging Angels. I've got a plan to deal with those little fuckers, but we'll need some more manpower. There's a safe house back at the werewolf base, which I suggest we use. I vote we head back there and lay low for the night. In the morning we'll plan our next move."

"The werewolf base?" Kayla stared at Monster in the rear view mirror, then shifted her gaze to Mutt. He winked at her. "I didn't know the werewolves had a base."

"You'd be surprised what the werewolves have," said Monster, clapping Mutt on the shoulder. As the Hunters' base exploded, throwing ten thousand tons of soil into the air, he leaned forward to whisper in Kayla's ear.

"They *are* the good guys, after all."

CHAPTER THIRTY

HIGH UP IN the air above the Los Angeles Downtown district, shadowy shapes flickered through the mirrored windows of one of the high rise buildings. Inside, Harlequin rose to his feet and gazed thoughtfully at the hydraulically sealed smoked-glass door at one end of the long board-room. He was dressed in his favorite ceremonial gear, a richly embroidered red Chinese battle gown with golden polished armor worn over the top.

He looked dignified, regal, a long-lost echo of the warrior vampire he had once been.

But there the illusion of control ended. His silver faceplate was strapped in place with a chain, effectively muzzling him and hiding his two-inch incisors from nervous eyes. Steel handcuffs encircled each wrist, and four iron restraints tethered him to a steel ring set into a nearby wall.

The master vampire snapped out of his trance and blinked, stretching his muscled arms and shaking out his long white hair. He turned his head to take in the assembled werewolves who were sitting around the table: the pack leaders, ambassadors, the muscle-bound guards at each exit. He turned his head to stare blankly at the clergy members and the frightened human sponsors who huddled in an uneasy clump by the door. Some of them were wearing bandages and resting on crutches.

Mitzi was dressed in sleek black cotton and chain-mail used commonly for dog wrangling. The blind werewolf sat perched on the edge of the boardroom table, dangling his cowboy boots over the edge, his trademark sword absent. He held a steel net gun in one hand and a Taser in the other.

He looked bored.

Harlequin nodded to the assembled humans, pointing a taloned finger. "You brought me take-out?" he asked Mitzi in a low voice, but not so low the humans couldn't hear it. "How thoughtful."

"Not for eating," replied Mitzi, unfazed. "They paid cash. Lots of it. They want to meet your new friend."

He nodded toward the locked door.

Every eye in the room swiveled to examine the smoked-glass door. On the other side, a dark shadow was moving. A scuffling sound filtered through, followed by a crash.

The assembled humans jumped at the sound, glancing nervously at one another.

"Ah. Cash." Harlequin gave a curt nod. "I like cash. They can live."

There was a commotion at the back of the group. Harlequin heard the sounds of a hushed argument, then a slight scuffle as one member was pushed forward.

Harlequin fixed the newcomer with a disparaging look. The guy was young and scrawny, with bleached white hair. He wore a blue ceremonial costume that appeared to be made from a half-dozen beach sarongs tied together, with golden crosses stitched all over it. A thin wire crown glittered on his head, matching the wire-rimmed glasses perched on his nose. He did not look happy to be there.

"Damn hippies," Mitzi muttered.

The man cleared his throat and blinked rapidly, utter terror shining in his pale eyes. He turned toward Harlequin and held out his hands like a high priest.

"Greetings, fellow believers. We are gathered here today to welcome to California a very special guest, one who has been spoken of in Prophecy for so long. He is the Chosen One, the direct descendant of an angel, the member of our beautiful new race who will finally end our wars and restore peace to humanity."

"Yeah. He'll bring peace by killing all the humans," sniggered Jackdoor. He looked up from the bag of Chinese food he was holding and wiped the grease off his lips. "Does anyone want my spring rolls? I'm stuffed."

"Death will be but the beginning, foul fiend," intoned the blue-suited man, who looked more and more terrified by the moment. "My name is Blue, and I am California's foremost expert on angels.

My friends, today marks the beginning of a wondrous new era, an era where all races, all creeds, all religions are eliminated in the face of the one true God, the one true Faith. For within us all lies the universal life force, the soul, the true spirit of humanity: our blood. Our blood is the one thing that unites us as humans. The same blood flows within the veins of the Egyptian peasant beneath the pyramids, the untamed pygmy in the jungles, the revered prince on his royal throne. It is within us all, and it shall be our salvation. By harnessing that blood, the spirit of the eternal, we will all become one—one race, one faith, one soul. We will need no other. There will be no more wars, no more killing. Mankind will be saved."

"Yeah, but will you have soy sauce? Gotta have soy sauce. I'd kill for a bottle right now," said Jackdoor, chewing noisily.

"Silence!" shouted Blue. Beads of sweat rolled down his brow. He swung around and stabbed a finger at the ratty-winged werewolf. "Get this monster out of here. This is blasphemy!"

The rest of the group hung back, blinking at him in terror.

"Fine," said the man, pompously cracking his knuckles. "I'll remove him."

Jackdoor burped loudly. He grinned at Blue, exposing teeth the size and shape of broken razor blades.

"Moving swiftly on," continued Blue, stepping back without missing a beat. "The grand unveiling, part two. No doubt some of you here today will have been taken in by the propaganda spread by our media in the last forty-eight hours. Some of you may have even been at the hospital where the body was incarcerated, witnessed the wonder of its miraculous resurrection."

"Resurrection?" piped up a woman with a bandaged head. She was dressed in rich clothing—possibly an ambassador's wife. Her fingers and wrists were encrusted with diamond jewelry, most of which bore some kind of angel insignia on them. "Poppycock. I'll believe it when I see it."

"And see it you will, my lady," soothed Blue. "For it is true: the body of an angel was indeed recovered from the streets of Los Angeles. What is false is the assumption that was spread in the city regarding the angel's true origin."

Blue glanced around the excited little group, waiting for a reaction.

The group parted and an attractive young woman in a light tan business suit stepped forward. She had short dark hair and was wearing a large hat that obscured half her face with a curtain of elaborately woven white gauze twined through with crystal flowers. She wore matching gauze gloves, and a look of almost apologetic beauty.

"So the angel isn't real?" she asked. "I've come a long way to see it."

"Who the hell are you?" Blue frowned at her, pulling out a list of names. "I don't remember seeing you at the last meeting."

"I was there. At the back." The woman smiled warmly, touching his arm with a reassuring hand. "You can call me Doll."

Blue jerked slightly at her touch and blinked rapidly in confusion. "Now, tell me about this angel," Doll went on. "It's a fake, right?"

"Oh, it's real all right," Blue assured her, stuffing the list back in his pocket with a shrug. "However, the body is not."

"I don't understand."

"It's real simple," said Blue. "An angel can choose to take human form, should it so wish, but it is not human. It can never be human, although many have tried. An angel is simply an essence, a being made of pure light, a soul made solid. They can temporarily take human form in order to visit Earth, but they cannot hold that shape for long. If they remain on Earth for too long, or if they become stressed or injured, their biomorphic field will instantly reassert itself. When that happens—*poof*! No more angel."

"So… if you stab one, it vanishes in a big cloud of fairy dust?"

"That is correct, yes. And it's angel dust, not fairy dust."

"And that's why we don't find their bodies?" asked Dolldubiously.

"Indeed."

"So how did we find this one?"

"Because the angel was a fool," rumbled Harlequin, standing up. The group hurriedly moved back as the master vampire walked toward the glass door, his restraints clinking with each movement. He laid a hand on the door's smoked, opaque surface. It lit up and began to glow with a dull blue light.

"Why was he a fool?" asked the woman, in a quiet voice.

"Tell me," said Harlequin without looking around. "Has anyone here ever been in love?"

There was a deathly silence, followed by an uneasy murmur. Whatever the group had been expecting from the master vampire, it certainly wasn't this.

After a long moment, a cautious hand went up.

Harlequin nodded toward the man, a pale-faced politician dressed in his Sunday best. "You," he said.

"Yes, sir?"

"Tell me. What do you do when you're in love?"

"You don't want to know. I mean, last year, there was this really great chocolate shop down my road, and my girl adores these chocolate caramel crèmes they sell. So one day I—"

"I'll *tell* you what you do when you're in love," interrupted Harlequin. "You do really stupid things. That's what you do."

His hand crept up to brush the silver mask he wore. "Really, truly stupid things."

"...so I sold my '57 Cadillac to buy her the world's biggest caramel crème egg," finished the politician. "She had seen it in the window every day when we walked past on our way to work."

"I moved five thousand miles and changed my name for this really beautiful girl I met on MySpace," interrupted another man in the group, folding his arms. "That change was shortly followed by my locks and my bank account, when she turned out to be a guy."

"You think that's something?" snorted a third man, getting into the swing of things. "I climbed a mountain in Canada to get my girlfriend this really rare flower she'd been going on about forever. Turns out she'd seen the flower in a movie, and the mountain was really in Switzerland. She married me anyway though."

Harlequin glared at the group to silence them. "You humans have no idea what you want, do you? You bicker amongst yourselves, shed blood over mere ideas, end lives because of what you believe. But the one thing we all believe in is love. Besides your blood, it is the one thing that unites you. And it has been the downfall of us all. Even an angel, a being made from light, is not immune. But in the end, we must all pay the price."

He turned around and stabbed a button inset into the wall. Giant plasma screen TVs flickered into life. They all showed the same image; a live feed from the basement of the building, a room containing just one person.

The crowd gasped.

Blue timorously spoke up. "Is that...?"

"The angel? Yes."

The angel was lying in a silver-plated room, on a slab of what looked like pure glass. It was naked and lying on its back, its wings folded beneath it, unmoving. Blue and white flames engulfed it, but its body was unburned, completely untouched by the fire that raged around it. "Is it dead?" asked the woman.

"No. It is in a kind of stasis. The fire cloak protects it from harm." Harlequin tapped the nearest screen. "But the body you see is not the angel. It is a shell, a revolutionary creation of my own design to aid in the transference of souls."

"Now you've lost me," said Blue.

"The body you see before you is that of a vampire. An immortal, like myself. It was engineered by a team of our greatest scientists, with the unique ability to be able to withstand one element: fire. We knew of the angel's coming by means of an ancient prophecy, and we were ready for it when it arrived."

"You knew the angel was coming?"

"Indeed. When the angel came to Earth it was tricked into accepting the body as a gift, an inhuman shell that could not be injured or killed, so enabling it to successfully complete its mission."

"So you trapped the soul of an angel in the body of a vampire. That's a new one." Blue shook his head in slow wonder. "How was it tricked?"

A ghost of a smile crossed Harlequin's face. "Because it loved. It came to Earth to save a woman, another like itself, trapped in the body of a mortal. It could not stand to see her suffer and so it came to save her. But its mission was unsuccessful. Now, the angel belongs to me."

Doll touched the image of the burning body on a screen. "That's evil," she breathed. "Release him!"

"No." Harlequin said the word without any great emotion. "The angel is mine. This fate was his choice. He did not fall, nor was he pushed. He chose to give his life willingly so that another could live. And so he must now pay the price."

"Which is?"

"He will be the salvation of mankind. A drop of his angelically-charmed blood was used to alter the DNA of a common vampire, so uniting the two species in a physical form. And our new race has some rather unique abilities when it comes to repro-duction."

Harlequin wheeled around, stabbing a finger at Mitzi. "You!"

"What?"

"Show them."

He tapped a steel-plated knuckle on the glass door.

"You think that's wise?" said Mitzi. "We talked about this. You know what happens."

"I did not become great by being wise," snapped Harlequin. "I became great by being foolish, and then killing anyone who did not make themselves accountable for my foolishness. The time for secrecy is long over."

Mitzi shrugged one shoulder fractionally. "Your call. *Boss*."

Mitzi typed a pass code into the digital lock. He stepped to the side as two pressure seals cracked open. Sulfuric gas hissed out into the room, along with a gust of white smoke and a shaft of blinding white light.

Then the light slowly faded.

"Holy shit," said Blue. "Is that really an angel?"

CHAPTER THIRTY-ONE

SLOWLY, BLUE STEPPED forward, not daring to blink in case the apparition in front of him vanished.

"It's an angel," he murmured. "A real, live angel. Oh my God."

He waved a hand in front of his face to clear away the smoke. He wished to God that he had brought a camera. Everyone would finally believe him, stop telling him he was crazy for believing.

Could you photograph an angel? Screw it. Finally, after all these years of believing, the miracle had happened.

She was here.

The angel was female. That was the first thing he noticed about her. She was standing coyly just inside the door, her hands clasped in front of her, gazing at him through the smoke. She had the most brilliant blue eyes he had ever seen. Her irises were

the color of rich, warm tropical seas, sparkling
with love and kindness. Her features were exquisite, with high, curving brows, a soft mouth. There
was a faint smile on her Cupid's bow lips. As the
smoke slowly dissipated, he could see that she was
wearing a simple gown spun out of gold thread
that fitted her willowy, perfect figure. Her wings
were magnificent, just as he had always imagined
they'd be: two finely arched clouds of the softest
feathers, folded demurely around her narrow
shoulders like a cape. The perfect feet poking out
from beneath her gown were tiny and bare, her finger and toenails the color of polished
mother-of-pearl. Her expression as she looked at
him was kind, benevolent, all-accepting, and utterly loving.

Blue felt the world fade away. The angel looked
exactly as he had always pictured her. She was the
most beautiful thing he had ever seen in his life.

Blue's heart pounded. He was in love.

Without a thought as to the others in the room,
Blue held out his hand to the angel. The angel's
smile widened.

Then Blue stopped walking. His breathing
stopped as well, and his body began to convulse.

He bent double, clutching his head as a sudden
and horrible seizure gripped his body. His glasses
flew off and smashed on the floor. Blood poured
from his nose. He collapsed, writhing soundlessly
on the polished mahogany floor.

The assembled company jumped and clutched at
one another as the angel coolly turned to face them
each in turn. They screamed and squirmed under
the angel's blue-eyed gaze, which was suddenly not

so soft and innocent. Within seconds, every human in the room had fallen to the ground, curling into fetal positions as they shrieked and clutched at their heads.

All save one.

Jackdoor was the first to move, snaking over to Doll's side and poking her rudely with a dirty fingernail.

"Sumpthin's wrong, boss. This one won't go."

Harlequin regarded Doll with a blank stare, trailing one finger down one of the chains that bound him to the wall. He tugged on it gently, as though testing its strength. "Move her closer. If there has been an error..."

Jackdoor grabbed Doll by the collar, ignoring her struggles, and threw her on the floor in front of the angel. The heavenly being inclined her head, her eyes seeming to glow brighter. There was a faint zapping noise and the angel shook her head, blinking. "Nope," said Jackdoor, with relish. "She's stuck. Hey bitch, spill. What's your story? Are you an Atheist or something?"

Doll stared up in horror, wrestling with the burning anger inside her at what had been done to the other angel.

The other angel. Her great love.

He had come to earth for her—to save her.

Now he was in Hell, burning for her.

She, the last angel on Earth.

God help her.

But she would be damned if she was going to tell a common vampire her secrets.

Doll's face twisted with revulsion at what she saw before her. She didn't know what the creature was, but she knew a thing or two about illusion. She guessed that she was the only one who saw the angel, the *thing*, for what it truly was. The others, she surmised, saw only what they wanted it to see.

Or what the angel wanted them to see.

Doll saw only the truth.

The angelic being tilted its head in arrogant confusion. It gave a chirrup and stalked closer.

Doll gazed at it in disgust. Stripped of its cloak of illusion, the angel-vampire hybrid was as tall as a human and roughly the same shape, but there the resemblance ended. The creature's skin was white as snow, glowing with an internal phosphorescence. Its huge, spider-like eyes were a luminous black that burned with tiny pinpricks of blue in their bottomless depths—the true blue of infinity. A real angel was simply a being-shaped portal to another dimension, a place that the humans called Heaven and others like Doll preferred not to name at all for fear of what might be called forth by the act of naming it. An angel had a personality, but it had no free will. It was guided from above by forces beyond its comprehension.

This thing was a monstrosity.

It was an angel's essence trapped in the body of a vampire, and it was furious about it. Its soul was divine, a carved sliver of eternity, a spark created from the universal and mysterious life force of the universe. But now it was cut off from its source of power and love and forced to become corporate, to possess and guide an unclean vampire body from which it knew it could never escape.

And from the look on its face, the angel hated it.

Doll cringed back as it opened its fearsome mouth and squalled at her like a baby, revealing the spinning black pit of chaos inside it that both powered and guided it. It reached up with a multi-joined back leg and scratched sharply at its own face, as though trying to free itself from the skin that imprisoned it. A gash opened up on its cheek, but instead of blood, white light spilled out of the creature's translucent skin. Then blue fire raced around the edges of the wound, sealing it shut. Every bone in its body was visible through its skin as if carved from pure light. Its nose was snubbed like that of a bat, its face flattened and childlike.

"Dear God," murmured Doll. "You're an ugly little bitch, aren't you?"

The angel responded instantly to her voice, hissing and spreading its membranous wings. The creature had no arms or hands, for—like a bird—its wings were joined directly to its powerful breastplate, and its 'arms' flipped backward at the elbow to become wings. Instead of feathers, the wings were coated in what looked like serrated white scales, angled down and shaped like miniature cones to create lift.

Doll spun around with a surprised yip as she was lifted clean off the floor. She gaped down at Harlequin as he dangled her from one hand, studying her from all angles.

"You'd better start talking," he said calmly, drawing his sword. "The angel. What do you see when you look at it?"

Blue suddenly stood up and crossed the floor to stand next to the angel creature, his movements zombie-like. His eyes flew open, two whirling black pools with a spark of blue at the bottom of them.

One by one, the other humans got up and joined him, standing in silent and scary rows. Their eyes were all the same. Their silence was terrifying.

Harlequin lowered Doll to the floor but did not release her. He slid his broadsword back into its sheath and gave Doll a hard shove, sending her spinning into the waiting arms of Mitzi.

"Watch her," he said.

Mitzi nodded. "The test was successful?" he asked.

"Indeed. All humans but one were converted."

"Excellent. I suggest we begin Phase Two of our plan."

Doll didn't like the sound of that at all. She twisted in Mitzi's grip, ripping an arm free and dealing the blind werewolf a swift uppercut to the chin. He growled at her and slammed her sideways, smacking her head on a brick pillar with blinding force.

Doll slumped down in his arms, semi-conscious.

Mitzi removed his dark glasses and polished a tiny speck of blood off the lenses. His eyes beneath were emotionless, his entire eyeball covered by protective black contacts that shone with a silver-green sheen in the light. He replaced the shades, then straightened his immaculate black jacket.

"Take her down to the labs," said Harlequin. "Have her tested. If any humans have any kind of immunity to the angelic conversion, we need to know about. We cannot afford to lose any time."

"Yes, sir."

Doll groaned weakly as Mitzi threw her over his shoulder. She gathered her strength and pushed herself up, her head thumping with concussion, her eyes seeking the familiar and comforting face of the other angel—the true angel—on the TV set.

The flames still burned around his naked body. He lay there motionless on the slab, eyes closed, unmoving.

"Baby," she whispered, gazing at the screen. "I'm so sorry."

A low rumbling sound filled the air. Doll tried to focus on what was going on. Harlequin had turned back to the werewolves and was holding out his arms. He launched into some kind of speech, but Doll's ears were ringing so badly she couldn't make out the words.

Harlequin's speech reached a crescendo and the second set of doors in the room opened, spilling a gust of smoke and refrigerated air into the room.

When the smoke cleared, Doll's heart stopped.

"Oh, sweet Jesus," she whispered.

Behind the double-doors was a cavernous room lit with a white light. It was a cross between a laboratory and a giant playpen, staffed by human-form werewolves dressed in identical black chainmail and wearing thick black goggles. Every wolf carried a Taser, which they used with disturbing frequency as they tended to their charges—smaller versions of the hideous angel-hybrid who stood before her. The baby angels glowed from within, each created from a fraction of the original angel's soul, each housed in the body of a young vampire.

Doll watched numbly as they yowled and flapped in their enclosures, fighting to get out and seek revenge on those who had done this to them.

Harlequin had created an army of angels, and they were all in his image. Humanity's days were numbered.

Mitzi paused en-route to the door. Doll glanced blearily up to see Harlequin beckoning him over, his golden-eyed gaze fixed on her. She struggled to remain conscious as the master vampire reached out for her and pulled off her hat, ripping the tape that held it in place. His eyes scanned her scarred face with interest, then he reached into his pocket, pulled something out, and held it up beside her.

Harlequin had an old photograph of her. It was crumpled and folded and stained with what looked like dried blood, but it was unmistakably her picture.

Doll frowned, coughing weakly. Why did Harlequin have a photograph of her? How? Only one person she knew of had a photo of her.

Unless…

Before Doll could complete the thought, the vampire's mouth curved into a cruel smile behind his slatted silver mask. He put the photograph away and reached out to gently stroke her hair. He whispered something to Mitzi. Then he patted her on the back and waved at Mitzi to take her away.

"See you later, my little angel," he called out, with a grin.

Doll slumped down in Mitzi's arms. She was busted. She needed a miracle to save her now.

Doll squeezed her eyes shut, thinking fast. There was only one person she could think of who could help her, and she hadn't seen him in a month. She had hired him to help her track down her love, the angel, at great personal expense and risk. Then he had vanished, just like all the others.

But she had faith in him. He wasn't like the others. He would come and find her, just as he had promised, and help her save humanity from the forces of darkness. It had been their plan all along.

"Karrel, you crazy fool," Doll whispered. "Where the hell are you?"

CHAPTER THIRTY-TWO

THERE WAS LIGHT in the room, only just.

Karrel stepped forward in the dim red candle-light, his hands stretched out in front of him like a sleepwalker, expecting any moment to trip over something that would leap up and bite his head off. As it was, he made it all the way to the mahogany desk before bumping into Skippy's leg.

"Watch it!" Karrel snapped.

Skippy slid his leg back with a hiss of claws on carpet, but didn't reply. The big creature was casting back and forth uneasily, opening and closing his mandibles like a woman fiddling with her knitting. He shook out his tattered wings and folded them down again carefully.

Karrel frowned. It was hard to read the moods of a ten foot tall anthropomorphic Death entity. If he hadn't known better, he would have said Skippy was nervous.

A quiet clink from behind the desk drew his attention.

Karrel felt a strange sense of dread roll over him. What he could see of the room in the dim light was dominated by the enormous desk, big as a dinner table and almost as tall as he was. It was inlaid with dozens of ornate silver drawers with carved white bone handles and covered in stacks of paperwork so high he could barely see over it.

A single candle burned in a wax-covered stand in the center, flickering with a red-blue flame. In the semi-darkness Karrel could make out a few of the letters on top of the pile written in red ink.

"...*regret to inform the defendant that the trial shall be adjourned until the month of May, 3007, when the prosecutor shall meet with the jury to begin proceedings on the recovery of the soul of Mr. Theo D. Kraven, fifth level, jurisdiction 9465 section ii of the Book of Chance, paragraph 616...*"

"*THE DEATH CREATURE SHALL LEAVE US.*"

Karrel jumped back. No one else was visible in the office. The voice that had spoken was male, forbidding, and utterly commanding. There was a darkly callous edge that suggested instant, messy death should its wishes not be complied with.

Karrel wished to God that he had his Hunter knife. "The 'creature' stays," he replied loudly to the room in general. "He's my friend."

The disapproving silence that followed drew all the shadows in the room into sharp focus, honing their blurred edges until every one seemed like a potential threat, poised to leap out and grab him by the throat.

"S'cuse me," said Skippy.

"Hmm?"

Skippy's tail flicked back and forth like an irritated cat. "I'm not your friend," he said. "I'm here to guide you through Hell."

"That's my definition of a friend," said Karrel. He settled down against the desk and waited. A shadow moved and his hand went automatically to his belt. He hated being weaponless. He cautiously peered over the top of the desk, but the executive's chair behind it was empty.

The disembodied voice rang out again, a touch of annoyance darkening its tone.

"STATE YOUR BUSINESS HERE, HUMAN."

Karrel shook his head, folding his arms. "Show yourself," he commanded, fighting to keep his voice level. "Only a coward hides in a dark room. I will only talk to you in person."

The darkness seemed to grow a little darker.

"THAT IS NOT POSSIBLE. I REPEAT—"

"Oh, give it a rest. I don't have time for this PR bullshit. Either come out and play, or point me in the direction of the nearest After Death Helpdesk. God knows I could use one right now."

The temperature in the room dropped sharply. "And put some freakin' lights on," he continued, talking loudly and brashly to keep up his nerve. "A man could have an accident in here." He glanced pointedly at the candle, then at the stack of dry paperwork.

"Er..."

Karrel glanced up sharply, his nerves jangling. "For Christ's sake! What now?"

Skippy paced, tossing his head up and down like a skittish horse. His black quill-like spines slowly rose, and he lifted a scythe-arm as if to ward off an invisible adversary.

"Skippy. What is it?" Karrel asked, and then winced. "We have *got* to do something about that name of yours."

"It's… there's been an error. It is not possible—" Skippy's head revolved creepily, exorcist-slow, as though tracking something. Then he gave a drawn-out hiss, baring teeth that would've put a killer shark to shame. He backed up into the room as far as he could, pressing up against the wall in the far corner.

A woman stood framed in the doorway. Her curly brown hair gleamed a muddy pink in the red candlelight.

"Excuse me," she said, holding up a clipboard. "Do you have an appointment, or shall I just throw you out now?"

"Do I need an appointment?" Karrel asked. "I'm dead. I was just talking to—"

"Everyone needs an appointment," the woman snapped testily. She folded her arms with the air of someone who dealt with this kind of crap on a daily basis. "Didn't you read the sign?"

"Sign?"

"Yeah, buddy. The sign on the door. It says 'No Pets.'" She jerked a well-manicured thumbnail at Skippy, as though he were a puppy who had just relieved himself in the corner rather than a ten-foot tall skeletal Death-beast. "Do you think the rules don't apply to you just because you're dead?"

"The rules never applied to me," replied Karrel. He was on safer ground here. Women he could deal with. This one was Latina, with curled, waist-length hair and a disapproving look on her pretty face. She didn't seem to be in any way supernatural.

Karrel held out his hand, all confidence and swagger. "Hi. I'm Karrel," he said. "That bundle of overstrung nerves over there is Skippy. We just need to talk to Lucifer for two minutes. Then we'll be on our way."

"I'm Julissa." She frowned. "Lucifer?" She didn't take his hand, and after a second Karrel dropped it, feeling foolish. "You've got the wrong office. This is Acquisitions."

"Acquisitions?"

Julissa nodded vigorously. "New souls and what-not. Lucifer doesn't deal with them directly. He doesn't like the paperwork." She directed a fresh glare at Skippy, who bared his teeth at her. "We have our middlemen take care of those."

Karrel turned around accusingly. "Skippy? Isn't that your job?"

There was a nervous clatter. Karrel and Julissa glanced up. The Death-entity was standing hunched up in the corner, his scythe-arms crossed protectively over his chest. He was still staring at the desk.

"Skippy," said Karrel sternly. "Then who were we just talking to?"

Skippy tried to sidle even further away from the desk, his eyeless face a mask of terror. "It is not possible," he hissed, his undead breath rattling in his throat. "It does not exist. But it is here. And yet it is not."

"What's he talking about?" asked Julissa.

"I dunno. Something's got him spooked."

"The angel," breathed Skippy, voice dripping with dread. "It has arrived."

"Angel? What angel?"

Skippy backed slowly around the woman, keeping the maximum possible amount of distance between them. He touched the tip of one of his scythes to the pile of paper, pressing down to spear the top sheet. He held it out silently to Karrel, who glanced at Julissa before taking the piece of paper.

His eyes scanned it and his mouth fell open. "Impossible!"

"Correct," said Skippy. "Yet it has happened."

The letter was handwritten on thick card stock and embossed with some kind of golden metallic seal. A rainbow of colors seemed to flow across its translucent surface, as though the paper was just the skin on a pool of water hiding the deeper, darker things that lay beneath it.

"*Fiet... Finito*," he read aloud. He bit his lip, trying to remember his high-school Latin. "Doesn't that mean...?"

"*THE LAST*," said the voice.

Karrel spun around.

A short, tubby man stood in front of the big desk. He hadn't come through the door, and he sure as hell hadn't been there a moment ago. The newcomer glowered up at them with the surly, sardonic expression of one who had been to Hell and back before breakfast and is now wondering what to do with his afternoon.

The man stuck out a plump white hand and tapped his ivory-handled cane impatiently on the floor. He wore a rumpled cream suit with food stains on the tie.

"Are you… Him?" Karrel asked cautiously.

"Depends on who you were expecting," replied the man snippily. Now that they could see him, the voice seemed a great deal less threatening.

"I have to say… I was expecting someone a little…"

"Taller," said the man, with a hint of a smile. "Go on. Say it. I will be offended, but I promise not to kill you or eat your spleen or anything like that." He looked at Karrel expectantly, waiting for a reaction. "Okay, fine. I'm not Lucifer. I'm his Personal Assistant, Ricky. But he's training me to do The Voice." Ricky grinned and dropped his voice about two octaves, making the panes of glass rattle in the darkened window. "*COOL, ISN'T IT?*"

"Lucifer has a P.A.?" Karrel asked. "No, wait, forget it. I don't care. I don't care about anything except how I can save my girl." He stabbed a finger at the room. "Can one of you help me, or should I go and look for Lucifer by myself?"

"I told you," said Julissa. "He's out of the office right now, dealing with this angel case. But I can take a message."

"I don't want to leave a message!" yelled Karrel. He wheeled around and waved a wild arm at Skippy, who was cowering in the corner. "Hey, Stinky. Let's split. We're wasting our time here. These people can't help us."

He threw the sheet of paper onto the floor in disgust and strode toward the door. "Angels," he scoffed. "You're all out of your skulls."

Karrel was halfway down the hall before he realized something was missing. He spun on a steel-capped heel and cupped his hands around his mouth. "*Skippy!*" he bawled. "Get your skinny undead ass out here!"

Finally, the Death-entity appeared. Karrel put a hand on his hip and glanced at an imaginary watch on his wrist. Skippy sidled slowly and reluctantly around the corner. He ducked his head to pass under the light fixture in the corridor. He stumbled as though hit by an invisible dodge ball, skewing sideways on all eight legs. He slammed into a wall. He shook his head, hooked a scythe-arm over the ornate hanging light for support, and then hauled himself upright, swaying drunkenly on his skeletal, claw-like legs.

"Oh, Christ on a bike." Karrel rubbed his eyes. "What now?"

"The angel," Skippy managed, wheezing loudly.

"Yeah, the angel. Little fluffy thing with wings. I'm sure it can sort itself out." Karrel held out his hand reassuringly. "Come on, man. Get over it. We've gotta go find Lucifer so we can save Kayla."

He paused, running a tongue over his teeth as he considered what he had just said. "I am having a *really* weird day."

Skippy stiffened, as though listening to a silent dog whistle. He snapped to attention, his eyeless, triangular head spinning around and locking in on Karrel. His mouth opened scarily wide, like a Venus flytrap unfolding and he hissed loudly at Karrel. Saliva dripped from thousands of needle-like teeth.

"Er, Skippy?"

Skippy came at him in a stiff gait, claws raised, jaws gaping.

Karrel backed off, holding up his hands.

"Hey, I'm sorry. Didn't mean to offend you."

"You're dead," snapped Skippy. "You will come with me now."

"Whoa, little buddy. We've just done this. Remember? You told me I belonged to Hell, and that I had to come with you. Then you said you'd cut me a deal. Right?"

Skippy made no reply, picking up speed as he lurched toward him. He raised both scythe-arms, ready to strike.

"Skippy?"

The Death-entity whipped up his head and snarled at Karrel, the sound seeming to come from everywhere at once. Two lights blinked on in the eyeless top half of his triangular face, burning twin pits of Hellfire. He opened his mouth to reveal a crackling inferno inside his head, tiny flames licking around his teeth. A gust of noxious black smoke belched out of his mouth; the stench of brimstone and ammonia filled the corridor.

Karrel coughed. The smoke grasped his lungs like an evil black hand trying to rip them up through his throat. His eyes watered violently and he staggered back down the corridor, waving the smoke away from his face.

"Skippy, c'mon!" he coughed. "We had a bargain!"

"You will come with me now."

"You already said that!"

"There's been an error."

"You said that too. Skippy, I'm warning you—"

Skippy lashed out with his long, skeletal tail, knocking Karrel off his feet and slamming him head-first into a nearby wall.

He slumped to the floor, unconscious.

Skippy stood over Karrel's limp body. Slowly, the deathly light faded from his eyes and was absorbed back into his head, leaving it smooth, featureless.

"An error," he whispered. "Oh, you have got to be shitting me."

With a distressed mewl he folded double and crashed to the ground. Lights flashed off and on inside the gleaming wet muscle and bone of his body.

Moments later, the exoskeleton that protected his torso cracked open along his back. *Something* shoved its way out of his body and stood up, stretching its muscular arms to the ceiling in relief.

It had horns, and a forked tail.

It stared down at Karrel. "*Well*, now," said Lucifer, with a grin. "What do we have here?"

EPILOGUE

IN HER ROOM deep in the depths of the were-wolves' base, Kayla lay uneasily in her bed, eyes twitching beneath her closed eyelids. Her breath came raggedly, sporadically, catching in her throat as she rolled this way and that, moaning in her sleep. The window was open, and the ceaseless ocean wind blew in, bringing with it wisps of fog, pollution-tinged and yellowed, drifting over the cracked windowsill and stirring her rumpled hair.

The door creaked open and a dark figure crept into the room. Stopping by the bed, it gazed down at Kayla for a long moment, silhouetted by the light from the window.

If he'd had a gun, he could have killed her.

Instead, he leaned over her for a kiss.

Kayla felt lips brush her forehead and blindly turned her face into the kiss. She yawned and gave a sleepy stretch, her eyes still closed. "Morning, sleepyhead." A voice murmured in her ear. "We've got a storm front moving in from the West. Waves are coming in close to six feet." The bed creaked as the figure sat down on it. "Me and the boys are heading out to catch a few. You cool with that?"

Kayla gave a good-natured groan of protest. She opened her eyes a crack and gazed up at Karrel, leaning over her in the blue light of dawn, his wet-suit half on. His tousled hair hung down over his eyes, and he had an adorably excited look on his sleep-rumpled face. Kayla rolled over and snuggled up against his legs, sleepily admiring the hard per-fection of his tanned, lightly freckled body, the gentle curve of his biceps, the narrowness of his hips and his strongly-muscled legs currently sheathed in the flexible rubber of his wetsuit.

He was the most beautiful man she had ever laid eyes on, and he was all hers.

She still couldn't believe that it was true.

Karrel reached down to muss her hair.

"Wanna come with?"

Kayla rolled over, feigning sleepiness, and swal-lowed back a yawn. "Do I have a choice?" she asked, knowing perfectly well what the answer would be.

"Nah. But points for trying." Karrel grinned down at her, then grabbed her blankets and ripped them off the bed. "Hey! Screw surfing! There's a naked lady in my bed!"

He fell onto her and tickled her, delighting in her shrieks.

Kayla twisted away from him and grabbed her pillow to bat him away, the dregs of her tiredness vanishing like mist. Giggling, she lunged to her knees and seized him around the waist, nearly losing her balance on the overstuffed mattress. She got him in a headlock, then pulled him down on top of her, grinning as he smothered her face in kisses.

"Okay, enough!" she protested. "I'm up!"

"Me too," laughed Karrel, waggling his eyebrows at her.

Kayla gave him a Look. "Uh-uh. No way. The wetsuit stays on. I just got all the sand out of the bed after last time."

"What's life without a little sand in it?"

"A life I don't have to get out of bed and vacuum."

"C'mon, kiddo! Live a little!"

"I'd rather sleep a little, thanks all the same."

"Even if I do this?" Karrel hopped down off the bed, tapped his foot a couple of times, and then started dancing. His movements were exaggeratedly clumsy and comical. Kayla sat up in bed and watched him, her lips twitching, as her big, tough boyfriend pirouetted across her sheepskin rug like an excitable three year-old. When he started doing The Robot she laughed out loud.

"Please stop dancing."

"Why?" Karrel asked, jiving around her nightstand, a look of mischief in his green eyes.

"Because you can't dance."

"I know. That's why I'm doing it."

Kayla giggled as he spun around her standing lamp like a strip pole. "I'll pay you to stop. Honestly. You look ridiculous. You dance like my grandma."

"Ah, but can your grandma go this?" Karrel gave a comical little shimmy, then did an impressive back flip on the spot in the center of her room. It would have been more impressive if he hadn't kicked over a shoe stand in the process. Shoes rained to the floor. Karrel seemed not in the least bit perturbed, striking a heroic pose amid the mess he'd just made. He grinned at her, like a dog waiting to be petted for doing a trick. "And there's that smile I love."

"It was either that or throwing rotten fruit," chuckled Kayla.

Karrel relaxed his pose, his hair hanging down over his face. "That's why we men do it, you know."

"Do what?"

"Everything. We just want to be smiled at by a pretty lady." He gave a little shrug. "Nothing else much matters."

Kayla smothered a giggle with her hand, then raised an eyebrow at Karrel as he slunk toward her, head lowered, his face alight with mischief.

"Karrel," Kayla said, a mock-warning tone in her voice.

"Kayla," replied Karrel, imitating her voice perfectly. He slowly climbed up onto the bed, moving as stealthily as a jungle animal, grinning all the while. Kayla rolled her eyes at him, then giggled again as Karrel pushed her down flat against the pillow. Licking his lips, he climbed on top of her, staring down into her eyes. Bracing his elbows either side of her neck, he settled the deliciously cool weight of his body on her and cupped her head with his hands and forearms. His thumbs stroked her forehead and he cradled her face, gazing down at her adoringly.

"You're still naked, you know," he informed her.

"And you're still wearing that nasty old wetsuit," replied Kayla with a grin, poking him in the stomach. A trickle of dried sand scattered down onto her bare belly. She brushed it off with a shake, reaching up to smooth flyaway strand of hair out of Karrel's eyes. "See? Now there's sand in the bed again. Remind me why I put up with you."

"Because you love me."

"That's your answer to everything."

"That's 'cause it's true."

And it was true. Kayla's smile relaxed into an expression of sleepy contentment as Karrel leaned over her, his eyes alight with pride and love. He kissed her eyelids then nuzzled his cheek against hers like a dog, sliding his hands under her and squeezing her body to his. Kayla drew in a happy breath, filled her lungs with warm air, and let it out again, sighing deeply with contentment. Everything in her life was perfect. With Karrel's arms around her, she felt safe and secure, as though nothing bad could ever touch her. She wished she could stay like this with him forever.

"Never leave me," she whispered.

There was no reply.

A moment later Karrel shifted, lifting his weight off her. Kayla shivered with a sudden and inexplicable feeling of emptiness. She opened her eyes a crack, curious, then opened them wider and looked around the room.

Karrel was gone.

Kayla propped herself up on her pillows, panicked. The bedroom door was ajar. A faint blue light spilled out from it. She walked toward the door, a light dusting of sand crunching beneath her bare feet.

The hallway outside was flooded with white sand, glittering blue in the pre-dawn light, although there was no visible light source in the hall.

Kayla frowned.

Carefully, she walked through the door and out onto the sand, blinking in confusion as she looked around her.

She was out on the beach, the dawn mist rolling off the sea and shrouding the sand. The familiar landscape of Venice Beach surrounded her, but the darkness of the distant mountains was somehow threatening. The lights of Santa Monica burned with a sickly red glow that crept up into the clouds, polluting them with their alien light. The lights of the ferris wheel on the pier looked out of place. The rolling waves before her were dotted with the tiny black shapes of surfers, which merged and blurred before her eyes, becoming things that she'd rather not see.

Kayla stepped haltingly onto the beach, fear growing within her as her bare feet touched the sand dunes. Every step she took away from the door, the greater the sense of fear became, until it was almost overwhelming. Every single thing around her was now somehow changed, somehow different, and not in a good way.

A wind kicked up and Kayla shivered, realizing that she was still naked.

Kayla relaxed. She was naked and out on the beach. That meant she was dreaming, of course. This was a dream, and when she woke up, everything would be all—

Reality hit her like a truck in the face.

Everything wasn't all right, was it?

Karrel. Karrel was dead. Kayla gasped and put both hands over her mouth, clamping down on the thought before it could spill out of her, into this land. She knew that by merely thinking it, it would become real. She may have already condemned herself, already lost him.

She remembered when she was little, when she dreamed of finding immense riches, wonderful lands, beautiful jewels, and flying dragons, all of which would vanish the moment she awoke. She remembered the terrible, crushing sense of loss as these treasures were snatched from her grasp by the simple act of waking.

She knew then that she would have to stay here, to find Karrel, or she may never see him again.

Karrel had just been here a minute ago, dammit! Why did she have to remember now? There were a million things that needed to be said, to be done.

She needed to see him, talk to him, touch him, hold him. She needed to tell him that she loved him, that she needed him, that she missed him. She wanted to tell him so many things she'd never had the time or the occasion to say. Nothing big or earth shattering. Just little things about her, about him. About her day. About her life and her dreams. About who she was, what she'd been. About who she wanted to be. The kind of small talk lovers have without even thinking, over breakfast, over dinner, during a snatched moment before work, or in passing on the stairs. Idle chit-chat with no meaning or purpose other than oiling the wheels of the relationship, keeping day-to-day life moving smoothly.

She'd always assumed that she'd have a lifetime to tell him these things.

But now he was gone, and she couldn't say any of those things to him, ever.

Kayla felt the weight of those unspoken words upon her chest like lead. With each step she took the wind increased, driving gritty, bitter sand into her face, whipping her long hair into tangles.

A storm was coming, Karrel had told her. Already she could feel the change in air pressure, the drop in temperature. She could feel the anger in the ocean as it began to heave, the wave height rising by the minute as the incoming swell moved closer to land.

Kayla walked onwards.

Darkness fell over the beach as the clouds moved to block out the light. Trash rolled over the sand like plastic tumbleweed. The sea boiled and thrashed, becoming a poisoned, stinking soup that reeked of decay. Rotted palm fronds fell around her like dead birds; black smog rolled in from the city, mingling with the ever-present sea mist. Then the clouds parted, just for a second.

A single beam of silver-gray light shone down to Earth, and she saw Karrel. He stood on an outcrop of rocks, looking out to sea. His back was turned to her and his wetsuit was zipped up as if he was readying himself to dive into the waves.

Something about him seamed wrong, but Kayla ignored the feeling, rushing toward him with a cry of joy. She wrapped her arms tightly around his waist, hugging him to her, overwhelmed by her feeling of relief.

"I thought I'd lost you," she whispered.

Karrel didn't reply. The landscape around her flashed and suddenly Karrel was wearing black armor, like the commandos she'd seen back at the Hunter base, his hair scraped back in an efficient ponytail.

The landscape flashed again and Karrel was back in his wetsuit, his loose hair flopping over his eyes.

"You already have," he replied. His voice was as soft and insubstantial as the sea breeze. "I'm sorry, Kayla."

"No. I don't accept that. I'll *never* accept that."

Kayla released her grip on his waist and shoved him away. Circling around him, she began determinedly stripping off Karrel's armor, piece by piece. It was his cursed involvement with the Hunters that had gotten him killed, dammit! If she'd done this long ago, then maybe he'd still be...

Don't think it!

Deliberately blanking her mind, Kayla gritted her teeth and unbuckled Karrel's vambraces and let them fall to the sand. His bulletproof flak jacket and tooled leather belt followed them, their calf-skin straps stiff and corroded with sea salt. As gray storm clouds piled up overhead, she pulled Karrel's black combat vest over his head, tears streaking her cheeks even as the rain began to fall in thick, heavy drops that stirred up the sand and soaked her bare skin.

Karrel just watched her, an expression of infinite sadness in his sea-green eyes.

Kayla ran her fingers over the smooth, cool skin of Karrel's exposed back, willing her hands not to tremble as above them the Heavens opened. She pressed her face into his shoulder, against the bunched muscles on either side of his spine. She breathed in the pure, unadulterated scent of him: sea salt and surf wax and just the faintest hint of lemon-and-lime from the cheap-ass drugstore shampoo he used. It was a scent she'd grown to know well over the time they'd been together. Now it flooded through her mind like a foaming breaker on the seashore.

Karrel trembled beneath her touch, and she turned him around to face her.

"Don't say it," Karrel whispered.

Kayla gazed up at Karrel hopelessly, the tears blurring her vision and mingling with the falling rainwater. She was afraid to blink in case he disappeared. Although he was standing right in front of her, it suddenly seemed as though a chasm had opened up between them, a void filled with a lifetime of pain and regret. Kayla wavered on the brink of it, unwilling to move in case Karrel simply vanished again.

But he didn't vanish. He stayed there, reassuringly solid.

He didn't move when Kayla stepped up to him, nor did he move when she kissed him. Kayla knew it was a dream, that he wasn't real. But if it was all an illusion, it was one she desperately wanted to last. She felt the heat of his hand on her cheek as they gazed longingly into each other's eyes. Karrel tilted her chin with his finger and kissed her, softly at first, then harder as their passion built.

Oh God, Kayla thought, *I can taste him.*

When her fingers went to his belt buckle he didn't push them away, and shortly his black jeans joined the rumpled pile of armor lying beneath him on the sand. He stepped out of them, completely and spectacularly naked in the silvery-gray storm light. Taking Kayla in his arms, he kissed her mouth, her cheeks, licking away the tears running silently down them.

They lay on the sand together, Karrel supporting his weight on his arms as he moved softly inside her, filling her aching emptiness the way only he could.

"I have to tell you some things," breathed Karrel. Kayla put a cool finger to his lips, biting back tears that even now were threatening to fall.

"Shhhh," she whispered. "Another time."

Kayla gazed into the eyes of the man she loved. She saw herself reflected in their liquid depths, framed between his soft black eyelashes. His face was alight with love for her, with sorrow, with anguished yearning that Kayla knew she could never ease. He had been stolen from her so rudely, so abruptly, with no warning or time for her to prepare. Karrel was truly gone, and all she had now was this moment, this brief interlude of warmth between the two dark looming walls of ice that were her past and her future without him. Their love was like a flash of light in the darkness of eternity, as short-lived and fragile as a human lifetime, meaningless and inconsequential but so all-consuming. For the short time he was here, he was her universe.

And that was all that mattered.

Thunderclouds amassed in gray legions, the rain-water flashing silver as it poured down in heavy droplets, stinging Kayla's eyes. It chilled her skin in aching contrast to the newly-awakened heat that flooded within her, rolling over inside her like a restless animal. Heat boiled out through her pores and drove the goosebumps from her skin. The sand beneath her was still warm from the heat of the day. Kayla dug her hands deeply into it, through the wet top layer into the pillow softness and warmth of the sand beneath, arching herself up against Karrel as he urged her softly onwards.

It wasn't enough. It could never be enough.

Impatiently, Kayla wrapped her arms around Karrel. She rolled the two of them over in one smooth movement. Karrel didn't protest. Kayla sat astride him for a long moment, her legs folded back around his waist, the wind whipping her long wet hair around her. She turned her tear-streaked face to the sky, breathing shallowly as the pain of loss roiled within her. Lightning flashed in the distance, pin-wheeling across the sky in creeping white claws of light, the electrified veins of the Heavens. Kayla's lips parted as she slowly bowed her head. Tears trickled down the side of her face, and a choking knot of grief grew inside her.

"Kayla."

She saw the hunger building within him as he devoured her beauty, his hands creeping across her flat belly with its taut covering of delicate muscle before slipping down to proudly cradle her hips.

Kayla leaned forward to plant a soft kiss on his forehead, trying to smile, to be brave. She felt his long eyelashes tickle her cheek. Then his hands tightened on her hips and he began to move beneath her again, moving cautiously, watching her face carefully as though seeking permission. He caught his breath and closed his eyes as Kayla began to move with him, her fingers digging into the sand beneath them to clutch at the soft skin of his back. Her hands gripped cool muscle as he thrust inside her, picking up the pace.

Thunder growled above them, resonating through the earth, moving up through Karrel and into her as they melted together, in open defiance of death and tragedy and anything else the universe cared to throw at them.

Kayla's eyes opened and she gazed up at the sky, moans falling from her lips as she rocked her hips in a lazy rhythm, surrounded on all sides by a thick curtain of stinging, splashing rain. Then the clouds above her briefly parted and the stars became visible. The world swung around her and dizziness swept through her and the universe shifted. Thunder ripped across the heavens, the sound of immense cosmic gears grinding, creaking with the strain as the worlds of the living and the dead collided. Light blossomed over the water as the moon emerged from behind that break in the clouds, waxing and waning, passing through days and weeks and seasons.

Kayla's body jerked as she felt a sudden stab of pain rip through her.

She looked down and gasped.

Karrel's hands were stretching, changing, even as they still gripped her hips. His fingernails changed color and grew longer and sharper, becoming impossibly curved ebony claws that immediately drew blood. He gave a low moan and clutched her to him, his face changing from soft ecstasy to agony in one soul-searing moment.

Kayla tried to push herself off him, to get away, but Karrel's hands were locked on her hips. His body bucked beneath her as a wave of pain crashed through him, his grip tightening, driving his newly-formed claws bone-deep into Kayla's skin. Kayla had the sickening sensation of the tips of his claws scraping against the bones in her pelvis. She shoved at him harder, trying to cry out, but she couldn't make a sound.

This is a dream, she told herself frantically. *I have to wake up.* But waking up would mean giving up Karrel. Kayla knew that as instinctively as she knew her own heartbeat.

She couldn't do it. She couldn't lose him again. Not so soon.

As she wavered, torn between two worlds, Karrel threw his head back and cried out beneath her, his body temperature rising exponentially as he started to change, sweat pouring from every inch of his skin. Silky black fur burst from his shoulders and ran down his back. Bones flexed inside his body like demons fighting within him. Veins popped out of his chest and neck, pumping blood to his growing and hardening muscles. His body jerked and he rolled over, still deep inside Kayla, slamming her into the sand and trapping her with his body.

"Kayla... please... I have... to tell you..."

Karrel broke off with a growl that resonated inside her very bones. He ducked his head and buried his face in her shoulder. Another spasm wracked him and he convulsively sunk his teeth into her shoulder, through the muscle of her neck. Kayla yelped as a poisoned heat spread through her, radiating out from the wound. She felt it steal treacherously through her bloodstream, altering vital things deep inside her.

With a yell she clutched Karrel's shoulders and heaved with all her might, pulling his teeth from her flesh, ignoring the blazing pain as her skin tore. Karrel's head came up and she saw that his eyes were on fire, blazing a startling multifaceted orange as beautiful as it was frightening. He stared at her, through her, his tangled hair plastered to his face by the pouring rain, the water running in rivulets through the blood that coated the lower half of his face.

Kayla gasped and doubled over as fire blazed in her belly. The poison inside her spread through her veins. Molten heat coursed through her body, blistering her flesh from the inside out and filling her with an immense power unlike anything she had ever felt before. She cried out silently, her neck arching as every muscle in her body contracted. Every bone, every joint was melting, then flash-fusing together in one overwhelming, mind-splitting burst of pain.

She threw her head back and screamed, clutching Karrel in agony as jagged fangs burst from her gums and drove down into her lips. Ivory claws erupted from her fingertips and she sank them into Karrel's back. Blood started to trickle down his flanks, turning the sand beneath them pink as the rain washed it away. White fur pushed its way through her skin like a legion of mice running over her naked body, their tiny claws prickling her.

A loud snarl came from above her. It did not sound friendly.

Panting, Kayla rolled her head around. Karrel's face was flexing and changing, his pupils contracted in fascination. He was still human—only just—but the way he was looking at her had nothing to do with love or lust or any human emotion she had ever seen.

He was looking at her like she was food.

Kayla fought to regain control of her suddenly-frozen muscles to break free from Karrel, but it was too late.

Karrel drew himself up and roared at her again in a hot blast of noise, his lips curling back from jagged canine teeth. Then his head flashed down with the force of a pile driver, his sabre-like canines punching into her chest.

Kayla's mouth opened in a soundless gasp of shock. His teeth tore into her chest with awesome strength, ripping sickeningly through skin and bone and blood and muscle as though they were no more than wet tissue paper, until they closed with a snap around her heart.

With a growl of triumph, Karrel ripped Kayla's heart from her chest.

As Kayla died, the last thing she saw with her fading vision was her own naked, bloodslicked limbs growing fur and buckling into unnatural lupine shapes.

Then everything drained away to black.

THE CLOCK STRUCK midnight as Kayla lurched upright in bed, panting, sweat running down her face. Her panicked gaze flew left, then right, her pulse beating wildly in her throat.

She was back in her bedroom at the werewolf base. The strange room loomed around her, dark, threatening, utterly alien.

Gasping, Kayla blinked the sweat from her eyes and tried to control her breathing. Her heart was pounding so hard that it felt like a living being in its own right, seeking to burst through her chest.

Again.

She licked her dry lips, tasting blood where she had bitten through them in her sleep. She rolled out of bed and staggered on shaky legs through to the bathroom. She turned on the light and went over to the washbasin to wash her mouth out.

Blinking Kayla straightened up and gazed at her blurry image in the mirror. As her reflection drifted into focus, she realized something was wrong.

Her hand flew to her face, touching the two tiny white fangs peeking out over her lower lip.

"Ah, crap," she said.

ABOUT THE AUTHOR

Natasha Rhodes is the British-born author of a
number of original novels and movie
novelizations, including the smash-hit movie
blockbuster *Blade: Trinity*, *Final Destination: The
Movie 1 and 2*, and *A Nightmare on Elm Street:
Perchance To Dream*. She lives in L.A. and works
at a rock club on Sunset Strip, although she is
currently thinking about taking up a less
dangerous profession, such as mud-wrestling bulls
or naked bee-keeping. You can write to her at
www.myspace.com/natasharhodes

Book One of the Chronicles of the Necromancer

"Attractive characters and an imaginative setting combine in an excellent, fast-moving quest novel."
— David Drake, author of the Lord of the Isles series

GAIL Z. MARTIN
THE SUMMONER
Book One of the
CHRONICLES OF THE NECROMANCER

ISBN: 978-1-84416-468-4

The world of Prince Martris Drayke is thrown into sudden chaos and disorder when his brother murders their father and seizes the throne. Cast out, Martris and a small band of trusted friends are forced to flee to a neighbouring kingdom to plot their retaliation. But if the living are arrayed against him, Martris must call on a different set of allies: the ranks of the dead...

www.solarisbooks.com

 SOLARIS FANTASY

Book Two of the Chronicles of the Necromancer

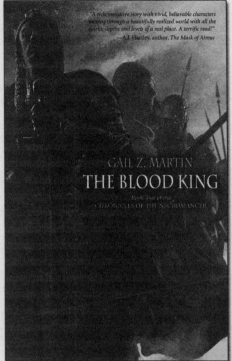

ISBN: 978-1-84416-531-5

Having narrowly escaped being murdered by his evil brother, Jared, Prince Martris Drayke must take control of his magical abilities to summon the dead, and gather an army big enough to claim back the throne of his dead father. But it isn't merely Jared that Tris must combat. The dark mage, Foor Arontala, has schemes to cause an inbalance in the currents of magic and raise the Obsidian King...

www.solarisbooks.com